The Devil's Own Luck

W.A. PATTERSON

CHAPTER 1

T he only sounds to be heard on this cold, bleak, early spring morning were the rhythmic tapping of hammer on metal from the blacksmith shop and the murmur of wind through the leafless branches overhead. A tall, white-haired woman absent-mindedly swept the road outside her cottage, as she'd done a thousand times before. She was thinking about Gortalocca and how it was dying, like so many other towns the length and breadth of Ireland. Times were hard and the population had suffered a dramatic decline in the last ten years. Evictions, emigration and famine had followed the great freeze of 1740, the Year of Slaughter, and had devastated the communities of mid-eighteenth century Ireland. Hers was just one more blighted village in its death throes.

Time had crept by in Gortalocca, the gradual changes barely noticed. Like the imperceptible greying of an old friend's hair, they were unremarkable from one day to the next. Where once the surrounding

Tipperary countryside had been dotted with the remains of ring-forts, the limestone from their walls was now gone, used to feed kilns which provided the manure needed to fertilise the exhausted soil. Mature trees and patches of woodland which once grew had been all but decimated, cut for firewood to fuel either the forges or the limestone kilns.

The once vibrant village had been mortally wounded when Hogan's spirit grocery closed down, wrenching the heart from the little community's breast. The sound of laughter and revelry which had spilled out on lively Saturday nights was now just the hollow echo of a distant past. Gortalocca was in imminent danger of losing its identity, of being reduced to a mere clachan, just a cluster of dwellings set on either side of an unexceptional rural road.

Roisin stopped sweeping for a moment and looked forlornly over at a sign which once proudly announced the village. Its post was rotting and the ragged board, with its peeling paint, lay on the ground, as faded as the community it once heralded. Her mind harkened back to the day her long-dead husband had put up the sign. Liam thought it would last forever, but then he'd thought he would last forever too. She cast a bitter glance over at the closed store, where a broken window seemed to wink at her, mockingly. She moved her gaze up to the wintry sky and closed her grey eyes. She was startled from her contemplations by a shout from the blacksmith's shop.

'D' ya think we'll get a bit of snow, Mam?'

It was Michael, her youngest. He was leaning against the door of the forge wiping his hands on his smithy's apron, his face covered in soot. Michael was forty-two years old now, his hair and beard still untouched by grey. The wrinkles which furrowed his brow were filled with ash from the forge and they traced the age on his face. Just then, Jamie Clancy joined him in the doorway. Roisin thought how alike they seemed, more like father and son than best friends and partners in the forge. Jamie looked every day of his fifty-eight years, his grizzled beard hanging down to his chest. He was by no means the fresh-faced boy Liam had taken in when Jamie's parents passed away, but he still maintained a childlike innocence. Roisin knew she would never truly be without Liam as long as she had the two men he'd raised. He had left a part of himself behind in them.

The old woman turned her face back up to the sky just as a few big flakes of wet, March snow began to fall. She pulled her shawl closer around her.

'Have you seen your brother?' she asked.

'I haven't seen him since he came around a few days ago, tapping me up for more money, the idle bugger.'

'You mind your tongue, Michael,' she snapped.

Jamie playfully put his soot-blackened forearm around his partner's neck in a mock chokehold and Michael stuck out his tongue as if he'd had his wind cut off.

'Will I t'rottle him, missus?' smiled the big man.

'Not 'til after he's brought a pile of turf over to the house!'

Jamie released his hold. 'Yer mam says ya can live anudder day.'

'Did Robbie say what he needed the money for?'

'Agh, sure you know yourself, Mam. Said he owed money to someone and had to pay up. That sod always owes money to somebody.'

Roisin's response was rhetorical. 'He collected the rents in October. He ought to have plenty.'

Jamie piped up. 'I offered to give him a shillin' fer

Liam's auld tools. Dem t'ings have been sittin' in d' carpenter's shop fer d' longest time, gatherin' rust and dust, but he told me to go to hell. Said dey was his. I don't t'ink he's even looked at 'em in years.'

'So did you give him anything, Michael?' Roisin pressed.

The blood went to Mikey's face and he felt his ears burn. 'I did not! Times are hard, Mam. Jamie and I have to work ourselves ragged just to make a penny. If he'd get off his lazy arse, instead of talking through it, he wouldn't have to rely on other people to keep him. He just comes over when he wants something and expects me to give him it, like he deserves it, like I owe it to him.'

Roisin knew this to be true but she offered a feeble argument just the same. 'Ah he's your brother, after all, son, and you know yourself how Robbie is.'

'I know how he is alright, Mam. He spends what little money he makes on the drink and the only reason he asks me for it is because he's already sucked you dry. He fecked things up so badly at the store that we had to close it. He spent what inheritance Uncle Robert left him and then he spent everything that was left to you. I'll be damned if he's going to ruin me too.'

Roisin flinched as her son's words stung her, more so because she knew them to be the unvarnished truth. Robbie had gone through the money he'd been left by their father's half-brother, Robert, like shite through a goose. She had been left destitute, her worst nightmare, and it was because she'd given in to her eldest son's whims and notions. She looked away and began her sweeping again. Mikey watched her for a moment or two, then joined Jamie back in the forge to get on with his work.

'Why didn't ya tell her d' whole truth, Mikey?' said Jamie, after a while.

Michael pulled a red hot piece of iron from the coals and put it on the anvil. 'I'd already said too much. I couldn't bring myself to tell her the rest.'

'What about Mr. Wall, d' solicitor? He said Robbie's debts was mountin' up and he can't afford to overlook 'em anymore. Said he's sent him a couple of letters, but yer brudder just keeps ignorin' 'em.'

Michael began to pound the hot iron with a vengeance.

'Easy, boyo,' said Clancy.

Mikey looked up, his expression sober. 'I don't know where all this is going to end, Jamie, but my guess is that the whole thing's going to hell in a shite bucket.'

He went back to thrashing the metal.

*

Robert Flynn sat in his cottage staring at the note in front of him. His wife, May, was preparing a meal of boiled potatoes and their two children argued noisily about the rightful ownership of a hoop and stick. He told himself the same lies that everyone who's made a mess of their lives tells themselves … If I only had a chance to do things over again, it would be different … If my brother wasn't such a cheap bastard, he could have helped me … If my mother hadn't been so slow in giving me money when I asked for it, this wouldn't have happened … All lawyers are thieves, it's the fault of that crook Wall.

He crumpled up the note and threw it into the fire, as if that would erase what it said, then he turned on the noisy children.

'Get the hell out o' here, the both of ye,' he yelled. 'Go outside and argue!'

May intervened. 'Jayzis, Robbie, it's snowin' fer God's sake. Da kids'll catch deir deaths.'

For one brief moment, a thought crossed Robert Flynn's mind that would shame hell. If one of the children were to die, or perhaps just become gravely ill, the sympathy he'd get would at least delay the inevitable. Sickened by his own thoughts, he turned on his wife.

'You can shuddup too, woman! I have important t'ings on me mind!'

She turned as if he'd slapped her face and went back to the business of preparing dinner.

*

When the work in the forge was done for the day, Jamie helped Michael to load a stack of turf onto a wheelbarrow and they headed towards Roisin's cottage with it.

'Jayzis, Mam, you burn enough turf for two houses!' exclaimed Michael, as they stacked the fuel beside her fireplace. Only then did the thought occur to him that he might be right, that his mother was probably sharing the turf with Robbie. He decided not to say anything because, if she was, then at least his nephew and niece would be warm. There was no reason for the children to suffer just because their father was a lazy good-for-nothing piece of shite.

'Agh, sure an auld woman like me feels the cold.'

Mikey lifted the lid of the pot on the fire. There was a single pitiful spud boiling inside it.

'Mammy, come over to the house with me and have

dinner with us and the kids. Morna has a lump of gammon cooking and if you don't come, I'll only eat too much.'

Roisin felt the saliva flow into her mouth. It had been weeks since she'd had a piece of meat.

'Thank you, macushla, but I'm trying to lose a bit o' weight. Look at me, I'm getting to be the size of a house.'

Michael knew his mother was lying, that she was just trying to save face.

'I have something I want to talk over with you, Mam.' It was Michael's turn to lie. 'I meant to say earlier but I forgot. C'mon, come over with me.'

'Well alright then. If it's that important to you, I'll come over for a while. I'd like to see the children anyway.'

There are certain formalities which are bred by poverty and the most important one is that you don't shove a person's pride down their throats. It won't fill their belly and, if it's all a person has left, then surely it's a sin to take it away. Michael knew this instinctively because he was Irish.

'Grand so. I'll walk you over, Mam. The kids'll be delighted.'

CHAPTER 2

T he wind intensified throughout the night and there were no signs of it abating when morning came. Although the snow flurries had ceased, they had been replaced by an icy rain which seemed to spit, scornfully. The wind freshened, propelling along the granite-coloured clouds and heralding a gale.

For three weeks, the two smithies had been busy forging hinges for a merchant from Cork and now they loaded the finished hardware into a barrel on the back of a wagon ... a quarter ton of wrought iron. In a few hours the deal would be done, the materials would be paid for and the two men would share almost four shillings profit between them. Michael breathed a sigh of relief. Money had been a scarce commodity in the township for quite some time and even the mounting storm couldn't dampen his spirits.

The wagon had frozen in place and no matter how much they coaxed the pony, the dray refused to budge. Both men dismounted and Mikey took the animal by the bridle, while Jamie leaned his shoulder into the wagon until it got started, then both jumped back up onto the seat.

'That's the ugliest, laziest, most foul-smelling beast I've ever had the misfortune to come across,' said Michael acidly.

'Dat's why I call him George,' grinned Jamie, 'in honour of d' English king. If ya want, I can unhitch him and you can pull d' wagon while he sits up here wit' me.'

It was only five miles to Nenagh but a freezing rain lashed at the two men and they pulled their capes tightly around themselves, shuffling closer together on the seat to conserve heat. It was slow going. On several occasions the wagon became stuck and the pony needed help to get it going again. Finally, they crossed the bridge spanning the Nenagh River at Ballyanny and turned onto the Borrisokane to Nenagh road, which would lead them into town. Someone was walking in the same direction, his head bent low and his back stooped, his brat pulled up around his face to protect him from the rain. Jamie slowed the cart. When he recognised the figure to be Michael's brother Robbie, he slapped the reins against the horse's back and sped him on again.

'That wasn't a very Christian act, Jamie Clancy,' said Mikey with more than a hint of amusement.

'D' walk'll do him good,' was all the big man had to say.

They carried on to the inn, on the outskirts of Nenagh, where their business was to be transacted. When they arrived, they were greeted by a short pudding-faced man. He was dressed in a shabby, unbuttoned waistcoat and a felt, Athlone hat which had seen the best of its days. He greeted Michael and Jamie with enthusiasm, perhaps even a tad too much of it for Michael's comfort. In his experience, a man who was about to hand over money had no cause for celebration, unless he had something up his sleeve other than his arm. The fat man took out his purse and counted out ten shillings onto the table.

Michael looked at the money, then at the merchant. 'The deal was for fourteen shillings,' he said. 'My partner and I have almost ten shillings in the iron alone.'

'Business is slow,' replied the dealer, 'and money's tight, as you well know. That's the best I can do. Ten shillings and not a farthing more, take it or leave it. Blacksmiths are a penny a dozen.'

Michael and Jamie exchanged glances. They owed nine shillings for the iron and, if they were to stay in business, the iron monger would have to be paid. Mikey saw Jamie's face flush crimson and he recognised the danger sign, so he swept the coins into his hand before the big man had a chance to lay the portly trader on the ground.

'C'mon Jamie, let's go. He has us over a barrel.' He bustled the furious man out the door and over to the wagon. 'He might have robbed us but that doesn't mean he gets the last word. C'mere, help me unload.'

The two men walked the heavy drum to the back of the cart and tipped it off onto the ground. The heavy cask disgorged its contents noisily onto the muddy road, attracting the attention of passers-by, and the merchant leapt through the door at the sound.

Michael looked up innocently. 'It slipped,' he said. 'Sorry about that.'

'You'll gather all that up immediately and put it back in the barrel,' spat the old trader.

'I will o'course,' smiled Mikey, '… if you pay me the four shillings you owe me.'

'I will in a pig's eye!' spluttered the fat man. 'Ye'll not get a penny more from me!' As he bent over to pick up one of the hinges, he let out an almighty fart.

Jamie elbowed Mikey. 'I t'ink d' auld toad just shite in his drawers.' The old merchant involuntarily felt the seat of his trousers with his hands and Jamie started to laugh. That made Michael laugh too, in spite of their loss.

'C'mon, Jamie,' he grinned. 'Let's go and get ourselves a beer. I think we've earned it.'

The two men walked the pony and wagon to McCarthy's bar, where their sombre mood soon returned.

'We're after floggin' our arses off fer t'ree weeks,' lamented the big man over a flagon of ale, 'and all we got to show fer it is a shillin'.'

'Ah sure it's a shilling more than we've seen in the last couple of months, Jamie.'

'If dis keeps up, I'm goin' to have to indenture meself to feed me family.'

'Don't be talking like that, man. That's like selling yourself into slavery.'

'If dat's what it takes, I'd rather be a slave dan see me wife starve.'

'Jayzis Clancy, you're a depressing yoke today! We'll manage somehow, we always do.'

'Well, ya'd better t'ink of a way quick, because dese is d' worst times I can remember.'

Michael was well aware that Clancy's mood was darkening so he changed the subject.

'Did you ever hear such a fart as the auld bastard dropped?'

Jamie's mood was not so easily improved. 'I don't care if he shite in his drawers. Dat auld bastard robbed us.'

Mikey knew it was going to be a long ride home.

The men nursed their flagons of beer, each lost in his own thoughts, until finally it was time to head home. Once on the road out of town, they again saw the figure of Robert, but this time he flagged them down excitedly.

'Dat's all we need,' said Jamie. 'Here was me t'inking d' day couldn't get any worse and now yer feckin' brudder wants a ride back wit' us.'

Jamie reined the pony to a halt and, without invitation, Robbie hauled himself up onto the already crowded seat.

'Lads, c'mere!' exclaimed Robert breathlessly. 'Yer man, Wall. He's only after tellin' me he's t'rowin' me outta me own house!'

'Throwing you out?' exclaimed his brother. 'Why? What did you do?'

'Me? I did nutt'n!'

'Yer as good as gone,' said Jamie, a smile creeping onto his face.

Robert looked at Jamie in surprise. The blacksmith seldom, if ever, addressed him.

'Ah sure he's just an auld fella. P'raps he'll forget.'

Jamie sneered. He'd hated Michael's brother ever since Robert had threatened him with eviction years ago, back in the days when Robbie had been a big noise around Gortalocca. Now it was Jamie's chance to even the score.

'Forget, me arse. Dat auld fella'll forget where he lives before he forgets a debt dat's owed him.'

Robert's eyes widened. 'He says he's goin' to send d' sheriff to me house t'morra … to formalise t'ings, if ya don't mind!'

'Well den, ya'd better get yer stuff packed, boyo,'

Jamie could barely contain his delight at Robert's predicament.

'Wait!' exclaimed Michael. 'You still haven't said what happened for him to threaten you with eviction.'

'Ah he'd sent one or two letters to me sayin' he'd bought up all debts on d' land in Gortalocca; said he'd foreclose on d' farms if I didn't go and talk to him, so I went to his office today. He had some people dere wit him and words were exchanged. I called him a t'ief and he got all flustered in front of his clients and and demanded I apologise. I wouldn't so he t'rew me out and told me to find meself and me family anudder place to live.'

'Dat means ya only have four days before he evicts ya,' snorted Jamie. 'Looks like you'll go before me.'

Robert looked at his brother's partner with disdain. 'I despise you, Jamie Clancy. I've always despised ya.' He turned back towards Michael. 'By d' way, Wall said he wants to see you about somet'in too.'

'Well why the feck didn't you tell me that when we were in Nenagh, you piss stain? Now I have to walk all the way back to find out what he wants. Agh, it'll only be bad news sure, it can wait 'til tomorrow.'

*

The next morning brought with it an icy pelting rain from the south, driven by a storm off the Irish coast. Sheriff Higgins rode up to the Flynn house and, after spending several minutes inside, he crossed the road to the forge where Michael and Jamie were cleaning up. He motioned for Michael to come with him and put his arm around the younger man's shoulder as he led him away for a private conversation.

'You know how I detest getting involved in evictions, Michael, but Robbie has brought this on himself. He's lucky auld man Wall didn't challenge him to a duel.'

'A duel?' exclaimed Michael, finding it hard to suppress a smile.

'Now listen, it's no laughing matter to impune a man's honour in front of witnesses. Wall was only doing his job. You know yourself that he doesn't impose evictions lightly. He's as lenient as your da was when it came to that kind of thing, God rest his soul.'

'What would it take to put things right?'

'Before that eejit of a brother of yours ran his mouth off, I would've said a shilling or two would keep him in the house, but now it'll take a miracle. Before, it was just a matter of business for Wall. Now, Robert has made it personal.'

'Do you think it'd help if Mam talked to Wall?'

The sheriff smiled wanly and put his hand on Mikey's shoulder.

'Michael, you know full well that your mother can be just as hot-tempered as her eldest son, maybe more so. You have the temperament of your father so if Wall wants to talk to you about something, go and see him yourself. Perhaps some middle ground can be reached between the two of you.'

'Alright so, I'll go later today.' Mike scuffed his foot on the ground and looked on as the rain obliterated the scratch mark his brogue had made on the hard packed road.

'You do that, son. Reasonable men can usually come up with a mutually agreeable arrangement. By the way, Mikey, I heard about that tight-fisted auld bastard from Cork skinning you on the work.'

14

Mikey looked up at the sheriff in surprise and the lawman responded with a smile.

'There's not much happens in my jurisdiction that I don't get to hear about, sooner or later. And here's a piece of information you might find useful when you get to see the old solicitor. It wasn't him who bought up all the debts. He's just representing a client.'

'What? Who?'

'I don't know and even if I did, I wouldn't be at liberty to divulge the information. I just thought you might like to know that the solicitor is just the fiddle. It's someone else who's plucking the strings.'

The sheriff shook the blacksmith's hand. 'If you have time after you've seen Wall, maybe you can stop by my office and we can share a dram together.'

Mikey's eyes narrowed. Higgins was behaving in a more familiar fashion than was his custom and was clearly just as curious about the unknown client as he was. He nodded his consent but had already decided he would be too busy to drop by Nenagh Castle after his visit to the solicitor. He returned the sheriff's handshake limply and the lawman instinctively knew he was going to have to get his information elsewhere.

Michael watched as Higgins laboriously mounted his horse and rode off, the wind roaring and tearing at his uniform. He looked skywards. The clouds flew past like a stampede of sheep. There was a howler of a storm getting up.

CHAPTER 3

M ichael made his way back to the forge, his head filled with more questions than he had answers for. He was glad to be back inside, the heat from the fire providing a welcome respite from the bitterly cold wind outside. Jamie was busy repairing a wheel for the Gleesons' wagon and Michael watched for a while in admiration. His partner was equally as adept working with wood as he was with iron.

'You're a Jack-of-all-trades, Jamie Clancy, there's no doubt about it.'

Jamie looked up from his work and replied in his usual modest fashion. 'Not at all. Yer da, now there was a master. I'll always be d' student.' He went back to his work.

Michael thought about his father. Liam Flynn had influenced everyone he'd ever come into contact with. He was supremely confident in his own abilities but, at the same time, was a modest and unassuming man. What Jamie had said reminded him of how his own father used to speak. Although the words had come out of Jamie's mouth, it was as if his da had said them himself. Michael felt a pang of guilt for having left his parents' house all those years ago on a fool's errand. He was painfully aware that he'd gone to the seminary out of spite. His father had high hopes for his younger son to become a yeoman, like himself, and Mikey had left the house in defiance of him. He hadn't even been there when his father died and that was a self-inflicted wound he knew would never heal as long as he lived.

'I have to go and see Mr. Wall this afternoon, Jamie.'

'Not a bother, we ain't got any work, anyway,' his partner replied, without looking up. 'When I'm finished wit' dis wheel, I'll call it a day meself. It's a fair auld bit o' weather brewin' up out dere. Will ya be takin' d' horse?'

'I won't, no. If I walk, it means I can stay in the lee of the hedgerows. If I ride, I'll get blown all the way back to Borrisokane.'

'I wonder what dat auld fella wants wit' ya anyhow. Ya never know, he might have some work fer us. Ya better get yer arse movin'. Mind yerself now.'

Michael left the blacksmith shop and, pulling his felt brat tightly around his shoulders, he went next door to tell Morna he was off into town. When he walked in, he gave her a kiss on the cheek and she studied his face.

'Don't look so worried, love,' she smiled. 'We'll manage, whatever auld Wall t'rows at us. Oy'll say a prayer he has some business fer us.'

Michael tried to force a smile but in his mind he'd convinced himself he was about to get his eviction papers, just as his brother had. His face grew dark and he took his wife's still beautiful face in his hands.

'Don't raise your hopes, macushla,' he said quietly. 'It's a man's duty to provide for his family but, no matter how much I want work, there just isn't any to be had. I'm at a loss to know how we'll manage, Morna, and I'm frightened for us.'

She could think of nothing to say that might relieve her husband's suffering. She'd never seen him so despondent, even in the worst of times.

'Ah g'way outta dat. Sure haven't we our health and aren't our kids d' finest? We've a roof over our heads and a few spuds on d' fire. We even have a few pennies in our pockets. Yer lettin' Jamie's melancholy get to ya. We'll manage. Haven't we always? Now g'wan, off to town wit' ya.'

Morna's optimism buoyed his spirits and he kissed her cheek, then her mouth, tenderly. Before he left, he looked to see what was cooking in the pot on the open fire. There were indeed a few spuds boiling away, but too few.

'You and the kids and Mam eat supper and I'll get something for meself in Nenagh. I don't know how long I'll be so ye go ahead and eat.'

'Yer a lyin' sod, Michael Hogan. If ya lose any more weight, you'll blow away. I know d' reason ya ain't been eatin's not to save food fer d' family. If ya t'ink starvin' yerself will make t'ings better fer me and d' kids, yer tellin' yerself a blasphemous lie. Where in God's name would we be without ya?'

Mikey should have known better than to try and deceive his wife of eighteen years. She knew him better than he knew himself. He smiled, gave her another peck on the cheek and headed out of the cottage. He trudged out of Gortalocca in the direction of Nenagh.

It was already midday and the wind had taken on gale-like proportions. As he leaned into it, its force ripped at his clothes and its cold seeped into his bones. There are two kinds of chill. One is merely the temperature of the air, the other is that icy grip of dread that creeps into a man's very soul. Michael shivered with both and thought again about his father. He'd always seemed to have things under control. He'd relied on his wits and the lessons life had taught him. Failing that, his father had hoped for the devil's own luck, which he'd seemed to have in spades. Whenever things had been at their worst for Liam Flynn, it was almost as if some divine hand of good fortune intervened. Michael thought about what Morna had said and wondered if she was right. Perhaps Jamie's sporadic depressions had influenced his thinking. After all, they did spend almost every day together and Jamie Clancy, for all his good traits, always managed to see darkness rather than light beyond the horizon. A sudden gust of wind almost knocked Michael off his feet. He lowered his head and pushed against the gale. The twigs in the hedgerows either side of him rattled like so many bones and winter leaves scurried across the frozen earth at his feet.

Finally he reached the market town although today it seemed almost abandoned. The weather had chased away the denizens from its normally bustling streets and they all huddled inside, by their fires. There were only a few stragglers left and a deputy and, if they'd had a better place to be, thought Mikey, they'd be there now. He hesitated a moment before entering the solicitor's office, then mustered up his courage, squared his shoulders, and walked in.

*

When Jamie finished work on the wagon wheel, he put the tools he'd been using back in their rightful places and loaded it into the back of his cart. He would take it to the Gleeson place and mount it on their dray. If he was lucky, he'd get a penny for his work. If not, as Gleeson was the local distiller, perhaps he'd get a jug of poteen instead. Paulie Gleeson was delighted to see Jamie and to get his cart repaired. Once the wheel had been successfully mounted, Paulie invited Jamie to sample the latest product from the Gleeson still. The two men sat and sipped and talked and a few minutes turned into an hour and an hour into two. The wind gusted incessantly outside with occasional bursts which howled and moaned and Jamie was in no great hurry to leave.

Back at the blacksmith's shop in Gortalocca, the forge fire breathed with each gust of wind and the coals glowed as the chimney became like the windpipe of some great invisible beast, huffing and snorting. One of the embers flew out and found its home in a pile of straw and kindling in the corner of the room. After smouldering for a while, it burst into life as a tiny flame. The infant fire grew, darting here and scampering there until, fed by the draught from the chimney, it greedily devoured the straw and combustibles. The flames snaked their way up the walls and lapped at the dry beams and thatch of the ceiling. On any other day, the thatch would have burned slowly, with the loose pieces of reed shrivelling first black, then turning to pale grey ash. It would be like setting fire to a closed book. But today, fed by the gale, the flames snarled and crackled until the entire interior was ablaze. The sparks refused to be confined and, once a hole had burned through the roof, they caught the breeze and swam downwind like a school of tiny fish, showering themselves on what had been Hogan's spirit grocery. Within minutes, the flames had eaten their way deep into the thatch, insatiable, hungrily devouring anything that would burn. Finally, the west wall of the daub and wattle forge collapsed under the onslaught and the main body of the inferno was liberated.

There are Four Horsemen of the Apocalypse … conquest, war, famine and death … and Ireland had suffered them all, more so than most. But there's a fifth horseman who, although not as familiar, can be just as devastating. Fire!

As Jamie sat chatting and laughing with Paulie, the oldest Gleeson boy, Peter, burst in through the door yelling that there was smoke coming from the direction of Gortlocca. The two men immediately snapped into sobriety. They both lived with fire every day and it was their ally, but its potential as an enemy was ever present and was a terror they all dreaded.

By the time they reached the village, both buildings were completely engulfed by fire and, instead of the flames leaping skywards, they were being swept along horizontally by the gale. Thankfully, the ferocious fire was being carried away from the cottages which housed the Clancy and Hogan families and Robbie Flynn stood by, dumbly watching as the blaze progressed downwind of his own cottage.

'Get some buckets!' he yelled.

'It's too late for that,' cried Gleeson.

Their raised voices soon reached Morna and her mother-in-law, who both burst from their cottages out onto the road. Roisin lifted her apron to her face and began to cry silently as she helplessly watched Hogan's being engulfed by fire. Her father had built that store so very many years before and, in her heart, she'd always believed that one day it would be open again for business as usual. For the old woman, this wasn't just a building on fire, it was her home burning and with it her dreams. Jamie looked on vacantly, his mouth open, thinking that if things had been difficult before, now they were desperate because their only chance of salvation was hopelessly ablaze.

*

'Sit down, won't you Michael,' said the old solicitor cordially, gesturing to a seat on the other side of his desk. 'Will you share a glass with me?'

Mikey nodded his head grimly. He watched in silence as the old man poured out the amber liquid and waited for him to deliver whatever bad news he was preparing him for.

Edward Wall placed the glass on the desk in front of Michael. 'I've been instructed by a client to make you a business offer,' he said.

Michael shifted his weight forwards in his chair and sipped at the whiskey. 'What client?'

'I'm afraid I'm not at liberty to reveal his identity at this point. What I can tell you is that I've spoken with his representative at length and, if you consent to speak with the man himself, you will receive five shillings, whether you accept his proposal or not.'

'Five shillings? Just for talking?'

The old man smiled and passed a small pouch across the desk. Michael reached out to take the bag but the solicitor held onto it. 'May I take that as your agreement?'

'Yes, sir, you may. When and to whom will I be speaking?' Mikey was trying to restrain his excitement at the thought of the contents of the purse.

'Tomorrow,' replied Wall. 'Transportation will be provided to take both you and James Clancy to Galway.' Michael tried to prevent his eyes from widening. 'The man with whom you will speak is a Mr. John Rackham. He is the captain of a vessel currently moored in Galway Bay.'

The old man studied Michael's face, trying to work out what he was thinking. His curiosity wasn't lost on the blacksmith and, for a moment Mikey wondered what he might be getting himself into. He decided that, whatever it was, both he and the village of Gortalocca were on the verge of extinction and there was nothing to lose, so he nodded his acceptance of the proposal. Wall released his hold on the purse containing the coins and Michael clutched it as if it was his very salvation.

'What about the evictions, sir?'

The old man chortled as if he'd been told a joke and a smile spread across his face.

'Never you mind about the evictions, Michael Hogan. Sometimes, just sometimes, things are not quite what they seem.'

With that, he held out his hand and Michael knew that any further questions would be met with answers just as enigmatic. He stood up, shook the old man's hand and headed for the door. Before he got to it, the old solicitor grumbled ominously.

'And you can tell that brother of yours he hasn't heard the last from me yet.'

Outside, the gale had abated a little and, on the blacksmith's way home, the wind was behind him. It began to spit rain again but, as he made the long walk back to Gortalocca, Michael was completely oblivious to the weather. There were just as many silver coins jingling in his pocket as there were worries whirling around in his head, cancelling each other out. Michael had already made up his mind. No matter what was proposed, he would accept it and he would convince Clancy to do the same. As he crested the last hill, he stopped in his tracks and his jaw slackened as he saw the devastation spread out before him. The two main structures which had defined the village of Gortalocca lay in ruins. He stood and he stared and he knew that if things had been difficult before, now they had become desperate … and desperate men have been known to do foolish things.

CHAPTER 4

M ichael broke into a run and, aided by the wind and the descending slope, it wasn't long before he arrived, breathless, to join the gathering crowd. He surveyed the damage. The forge was just a pile of smoking stones and only the shell remained of what had been the store. Jamie sat on the road with his face in his hands and the jug of poteen at his side, while Morna made a feeble attempt at consoling him. Roisin stood alone, away from the rest of the crowd, staring vacantly in shock at the still-smouldering rubble. Michael asked Gleeson what had happened and he told him in a whisper that he suspected Jamie had forgotten to close the damper on the chimney when he'd left the forge, allowing the wind to fan the embers into an inferno. He said it was a miracle no one had been killed or injured and that they should thank God the houses were upwind of the fire.

Michael walked over to where Jamie was sitting on the ground, reached down for the jug of whiskey beside him, and took a long pull from it. Jamie looked up at him.

'It's all my fault, Mikey. Look what I've done. I've destroyed d' village.'

'The village isn't destroyed, Jamie,' replied Michael,

'at least not yet. When things have cooled off, we'll get the kids and the women to retrieve the tools and we'll rebuild it.'

'Agh, you know yerself we ain't got no money to rebuild,' lamented Clancy, retrieving the jug from Michael and lifting it to his lips.

Mikey jingled the coins in the purse. 'We have money alright,' he said, 'and if you pull yourself together, we'll have more.' Michael wasn't even sure himself whether what he was saying was true, but he needed to drag Clancy out of his misery.

'Where did ya get money from?'

'I got it from Wall. It's an advance for a job you and me are going to do.'

Jamie eyed his partner suspiciously. 'What kind o' job?'

'Is it choosey you're getting in you old age, boyo?'

'God no. I'll do whatever it takes, Mikey. Dis is all my fault.'

'Ah stop with the self-pitying shite, Clancy, will ya. Take another belt outta that jug and give it here.'

Clancy took a long gulp and handed the jug to his partner. Michael took a long chug too, then poured the rest of the whiskey onto the ground.

'C'mon now, Jamie, get yourself cleaned up and have some supper. We have to take a trip in the morning and we might be away for a couple of days.'

'Where are we goin'?' slurred Clancy.

'Galway. There's a man there wants to talk to us.'

'Dat's a long way to go fer a talk. Will we walk dere?'

'As much as a good long walk would do you good, James Clancy, we have transportation.'

'Can't ya tell me what kinda work it is we'll be doin'? So far, yer story smacks of summt'n yer da would get himself mixed up in. He had a habit o' gettin' himself into hot water, always goin' off on some adventure or other.'

'I can't tell you because I don't know myself. Think of it exactly as that, Clancy, me and you are off on an adventure.'

Michael's face was crossed with the same curious smile Jamie had seen many a time on Liam's countenance and, although he didn't know it, his partner's words may have been the understatement of the decade. The two men were indeed about to embark on what was to become the adventure of their lives.

Michael told Morna and Roisin what had transpired in town that day and, although Roisin was convinced it was an act of divine providence which had saved them from eviction, she was more than skeptical about the circumstances involved. Her misgivings weren't alleviated when she heard about the mysterious stranger who had requested Michael's presence in Galway.

'Agh! Galway,' she snarled. 'That den of sin is full of pirates.'

'The man only wants to talk to me, Mam. Don't worry.'

'Don't worry, says he. That's exactly what your da, God rest his soul, said just before he got himself into a pickle barrel that almost cost him his life. But if you want to get yourself mixed up in some scoundrel's affairs, then you'll only have yourself to blame if it leads you into trouble and you needn't come running to me for help.'

If there had been any doubts in Mikey's mind up to now, his mother had just unwittingly eliminated them.

Whether it was defiance this time, pig-headedness or just pure Irish rebelliousness, he was going to Galway in the morning. By God, he thought, I'd rather get dead all at once than have Ireland slowly grind me to grist.

The next morning dawned fair, but there was a wind blowing which threatened a change in weather later in the day. When the coach pulled up, Clancy was already waiting outside. He gave a low whistle when he took in the immaculately dressed driver and the open wagon, the kind that squires would be happy to travel in. The horses were stamping their hooves and eager to leave by the time Michael appeared at his door. He gave Morna a hug and a kiss on the cheek and did the same to his teenage daughter, Siobhan. He held her at arm's length and thought how much like her mother she looked when he'd first met her. She had the same fiery red hair and full eyes which would someday capture a man's heart as her mother's had his. Siobhan's eyes were as bright a blue as bluebells, though, not the sea-green of her mother's. He threw a bag into the coach and, once he'd climbed in after it to join Jamie, the driver set off. Their adventure had begun.

Once on the road, Michael attempted on several occasions to coax the driver into conversation, trying to find out anything to add to the sparse facts they already had, but to no avail. When Jamie muttered something about pirates, the driver abruptly reined the horses to a halt and turned to them.

'Ye'd better not utter dat word in front of Captain Rackham, dat's if ye value yer necks!'

Both men were startled by the man's sudden outburst but once the floodgates had opened, there was plenty more to come.

'D' captain's da was hung as a pirate before his son was even born. I'll tell ye a wee story fer yer own good, but ye're to keep it under yer hats or he'll have me flogged. Captain Rackham's da was known as 'Calico Jack'. He plied his trade down Jamaica way but he's best known because of his mam, Anne Bonny. She'd been sentenced to be hanged alongside her husband but she got a reprieve because she was quick wit' child and d' English don't like hangin' pregnant women. Anne Bonny's da was William Cormac from Kinsale … used to be called Kingsale, down in County Cork. He was a solicitor and when he got Anne's mam, Mary Brennan, pregnant, dey had to run off, away from Ireland. Dey went to Charles Town in d' Carolinas. Anyway, d' auld man used his connections and somehow he got Anne out o' gaol before she had to dance a jig on d' end of a rope. She went back to Charles Town and now she's a respectable lady, married to a rich fella she is, name of Joe Burleigh. Captain Jack is d' child she had and he's fierce touchy about anyone using d' word pirate around him … so mark my words.' With that, the driver turned back and rode on.

This sudden and vast amount of information with all its names had come completely unexpectedly and the two partners just looked at each other, Jamie's mouth was agape.

'Jayzis,' he said. 'I don't want no pirate gettin' mad at me. You can do all d' talkin'.'

Michael agreed that this might indeed be for the best so he nodded. Even if this fellow is a pirate, he thought, at least he's a half-Irish one. He imagined it might be an appropriate profession for someone from Cork. The only man Mikey had ever met from there was Ned Flood and he was sure it wouldn't have taken much for him to become a 'sea rascal' ... except for the fact that he'd hated boats, of course.

It was late afternoon when they arrived at Loughrea and the driver stopped at what looked to be a very high-class inn. He leapt from the wagon and entered. In a couple of minutes, he had returned with the proprietor.

'Arrangements have been made, gentlemen,' said the driver. 'Enjoy yer evenin'. D' master's already taken care of d' bill so have yerselves a good time.'

Once the two men grabbed their bags and jumped down, the jarvey was quick to disappear with the carriage, leaving them standing outside the door. The owner ushered them in and showed them to a huge table which was covered with an immaculate white linen cloth and set with bone china and English silverware. Another man came and lit two candles set in silver holders on the table, then asked the yeomen if they would care for a drink. They both nodded silently. The weather outside had now taken a turn for the worst and the wind howled like a pack of wolves, but the fire in the hearth was warm and cheery. The waiter placed crystal glasses in front of them and poured a little sherry fino into each. Jamie sniffed at his, then pushed it away.

'D'ya not have summt'n fit fer an Irishman?' he asked. The waiter took on a pinched expression, gave a snort of derision and brought out a huge flagon of ale. He looked at Michael, suspiciously.

'Ah no,' said Mikey. 'This little drink will be grand for me. What is it?'

'It's sherry, sir, from Spain, top quality. Your host

has given us instructions to spare you no expense.'

A small bowl of water with dried rose petals floating in it was placed in front of each of the Irishmen.

Once he'd gone, Jamie hissed, 'What d' feck's dis?'

'How should I know?' Michael hissed back. 'It must be soup.'

Jamie picked his bowl up and drank some. 'Don't taste of nutt'n.'

'Drink it anyway. We don't want to be rude after yer man's gone to the trouble.'

The waiter came and took away the fingerbowls, finding it hard not to laugh out loud. He replaced them with bowls of soup made from turnips and carrots.

'Which one o' dese t'ings do I eat wit'?' asked Clancy, surveying the silverware arranged around his bowl.

Mikey shrugged. 'I don't know but I'll tell you what I do know. We should use whichever one gets the most into our gobs the fastest because I think this fella has mistaken us for someone else.'

Clancy gave up on the business of choosing an item of cutlery and, picking the bowl up by the rim, he gulped it down in one go. Michael picked up the largest spoon. The waiter returned and, when he saw Jamie, he coughed politely then discretely pointed to his own chin. Confused, Jamie leaned forward and peered at the man's face.

'Excuse me, sir, but you have soup dripping from your chin,' said the waiter.

'Ah, right,' said Jamie. 'T'anks. I must have a hole in me bottom lip.'

Jamie wiped his mouth with his sleeve. The servant picked up the linen napkin which was still folded on the table next to Jamie, and handed it to the blacksmith.

'Jayzis man,' Jamie said, looking at the crisply laundered napkin, 'I can't use dat, it's too clean! Yer wife'll kill ya if she finds out someone wiped his face on her nice clean rag.'

The waiter raised his eyes to the heavens. 'Dat's what it's for, ya daft eejit.'

So, thought Michael, for all his frills and tight britches, he's just an Irishman like us.

The waiter composed himself. 'We have roast beef and roasted pork for tonight's dinner,' he informed them, having resumed his affected accent.

'Good fer you,' said Clancy.

'No, sir, you misunderstand. I will be serving you either roast beef or pork for your meal tonight.'

'Ah dat's grand. I'll have both so.'

Michael kicked Clancy in the shins under the table. 'I'll have the beef,' he told the waiter.

'That's a good choice, sir.'

'I know,' said Michael.

The waiter ignored the remark. 'Would you like the beef rare?'

'Ah no, that's alright. The everyday stuff'll do me.'

Clancy put his hand in the air as if he was in school and addressed the waiter. 'I have a question,' he said, pointing at one of the items of cutlery. 'What's dis?'

The waiter's own accent returned at the same time that his patience left him. 'Ah fer feck's sake,' he said, throwing his hands in the air, 'don't ya know anyt'ing? It's a fork, man. It's fer holdin' down yer feckin' meat while ya saw t'rough it.' He walked away from what he considered to be the two bog-Irish peasants, shaking his head and Mikey heard him mumbling to himself.

'I don't get paid enough fer dis bollix…'

The two men ate and drank their fill, then ate and

drank some more until the innkeeper himself arrived and showed them to their room.

'Jayzis!' exclaimed Jamie. 'Will ya look at d' size o' dat bed. It's almost as big as me house!'

While the two blacksmiths stood looking around the room with open mouths, the proprietor announced that a bath had been drawn for them in a room next to the kitchen. He invited them to follow him down and, sure enough, two huge copper tubs awaited them, each filled to the brim with steaming water. The inn-keeper sprinkled a measure of sweet-smelling powder into each tub and Jamie asked him what it was.

'It's bath salts,' said the owner brusquely, and left the room. A mighty growl came from Jamie's stomach and he looked down at it as if it was interrupting the conversation.

'I t'ink I'm goin' to be sick, Mikey. Me belly ain't used to all dat rich man's food.'

'Well don't do it in here, Clancy, or I'll be seeing my own food again!'

Jamie bolted for the back door and, a few minutes later, he returned with a decidedly green pall to his complexion.

'I was wonderin' while I was out dere. Do dey have cannibals in Galway?'

Michael had already lowered himself into the tub and was letting the haze from the alcohol he'd consumed engulf him.

'You're a mad fecker, Clancy. What makes you ask a daft question like that?

'It makes sense. First dey stuff us full o' food, den dey put us in big copper pots full o' boilin' water. Dey even put salt in it!'

Michael ignored his partner, closed his eyes and

drifted gratefully into an intoxicated stupor, unaware that Jamie's observation wasn't too far off the mark. The two men were indeed being fattened up, but not for a kill, rather for a seduction.

CHAPTER 5

W hen Michael woke, sunlight was streaming into the room from an east facing window, illuminating Jamie who had a smile on his face and his arms and legs wrapped around a bolster pillow. Michael searched the room for a bucket to relieve himself in and, finding none, his eyes settled on a glazed, lidded clay pot in a corner of the room. He pondered for a brief moment before he made his decision. It was either go in that or out the window. When he lifted the lid, he realised Jamie must have been confronted with the same decision during the night. Jamie awoke to the sound and looked over at Michael.

'We'd better get outta dis place,' he slurred groggily, 'before d' landlord finds out we pissed in his soup pot. You'd t'ink he would o' left us a bucket, seein' as how we drank a bellyful o' beer last night.'

The two men dressed hurriedly and went downstairs to await the carriage which was to take them the rest of the way to Galway. The innkeeper was there to greet them with a hearty breakfast and a cup each of tea.

Jamie was the first to address him. 'Dat feather pilla's even softer dan me wife,' he grinned.

'It's eiderdown from up north,' declared the landlord proudly.

When he left the men to their meal, Jamie nudged Michael. 'Did ya hear dat eejit?' he said. 'Eiderdown from up north, says he. It's eider from down south or up north sure. What d' ya t'ink o' dat, Mikey?'

'I think we'd better stuff this breakfast down us and get out of here before he finds out we pissed in his soup pot.'

'What's dis?' asked Jamie, taking a sip of the tea. He screwed up his face. 'Ach! Tastes like washwater.'

'I don't know, just drink it.'

The weather had improved dramatically during the night and the wind had blown the clouds away. The air was fresh and the morning sun revealed a sparkling blue sky.

It was early afternoon by the time the coach sped into Galway town, slowing to a crawl when they came up against a throng of people bustling around. The streets were lined with warehouses and shops as well as the type of establishments which catered to the shipping industry … sail lofts, blacksmiths and ship's chandlers. The two Tipperary men had never seen such industry. There were wagons pulled by teams of horses and filled with bales, boxes and barrels of every size and description. Crates and other cargo were being unloaded from ships and stacked onto beasts to be carried to warehouses where customs men would levy taxes on them. Tradesmen, labourers and shoppers milled around and scurried about like ants, seemingly just as mindlessly. To the two blacksmiths from Gortalocca, the sights and sounds of this prosperous city were strange and almost overwhelming.

Finally, the carriage stopped beside a vessel which was compact and sleek with tall raked masts. Men were holystoning the wooden decks and a surprisingly young fellow in uniform appeared to be overseeing the entire operation. He would lean over and transmit his orders to a large black man who was leaning on a walking stick. He would then, in turn, shout the orders to the men who obeyed without question. Michael counted eleven men on their knees, scrubbing the deck until it was as bright as bone. A teenage boy stood nearby, silently observing. He was well-dressed but rail thin, as if he'd recently undergone a growth spurt and was waiting for his body to catch up.

The jarvey gestured for Michael and Jamie to alight the carriage and, as they did so, they caught the attention of the young fellow in charge. He immediately made his way to the gangway and, with the easy agility of a cat, leapt onto the dock. He looked the two yeomen up and down, his expression serious.

'Is one of you two gentlemen Michael Flynn or Hogan?'

'I am,' replied Michael.

'Which is it? Flynn or Hogan?'

Michael could tell by the tone of the man's voice that, despite his youthful appearance, he was accustomed to being in authority. The young ship's officer surveyed him, his sharp eyes taking in the measure of the man, and Michael involuntarily did the same. This brought a smile to the officer's face.

'Well, sir? What do I call you, Flynn or Hogan?'

'I answer to both.'

'Ah, as inscrutable as a Chinaman, but you still haven't answered my question.'

'I go by the name of Michael Hogan.'

'Well, Mr. Hogan, you've kept me in port for a week longer than I had intended, but it's just as well because, as fortune would have it, we were here in dock when a fierce storm struck a few days ago.' The captain's eyes flicked momentarily onto Jamie, then back at Michael. 'Anyway, you're here now. I'll tell Mr. Washington that he is to assume my duties while I entertain you.'

The captain walked over to the gangway and, for the first time, he raised his voice. 'Carry on, Mr. Washington. I shall be back in due course.'

The big black man gave a half-hearted salute of acknowledgement and the well-dressed teenager craned his neck to try and see the men ashore, then turned his attention back shipboard when the black fellow said something to him.

The officer returned to the two men and extended his hand to Jamie. 'By the process of elimination, you must be James Clancy, sir.'

'Most people call me Jamie.'

'I'm not most people, Mr. Clancy.' Once again, the amiable smile had been replaced by the air of a man in authority. 'I'm Captain Rackham of the Chesapeake Schooner, Prosperity. I will call you James or Mr. Clancy, either is more fitting for a grown man.' Jamie dropped his eyes to the ground, cowed by the man's surly manner, but it was instantly replaced with one of cordiality. 'Come gentlemen. Let us go to the Anchor Inn and have ourselves a drink to whet our appetites.'

The three men walked alongside each other, the captain instinctively turning to take a look at his ship. Michael was the first to speak.

'If you don't mind me saying, sir, you seem very young to be in command of your own ship.'

'Is that a statement or a question, Mr. Hogan?'

'It's an observation.'

'I'm thirty-two years of age, sir, and there is little I can do about my appearance. I have been at sea since I was eight years old, started as a cabin boy on the frigate Courser. I was promoted from midshipman to ensign when I was sixteen and, by God, I'd be lucky to have even made lieutenant now if I hadn't left His Majesty's Service.'

'I meant no offense, sir.'

'None taken, Mr. Hogan. There are only a few things I am sensitive about but my appearance is one of them. And please, call me Jack, except when we're aboard my ship. I will, if you'll forgive the familiarity, call you Michael.' He held open the door of the alehouse for the two yeomen to enter. 'After you, gentlemen.'

The three men sat in the cool darkness of the bar and a buxom young barmaid came over to them.

'Well hello, Captain,' she cooed, leaning over to expose more cleavage than Mikey and Jamie were comfortable with. 'See anything you'd like?'

'I can indeed, Kate,' said Rackham, pointing to a bottle on a shelf behind the bar containing a dark amber liquid. 'That bottle of Barbados rum will do us nicely.'

The girl pushed out her lower lip in a feigned pout and sashayed over to the bar. She returned with the bottle and three pewter tankards.

'Is there anything else I can do for you?' she purred suggestively. 'Anything at all?'

'There is something I would very much like, Kate,'

said Rackham, leaning closer to her. The girl inhaled so deeply that, for a moment, the Tipperary men were afraid she'd burst out of her blouse. 'I'd like some privacy. These two gentlemen and I have important business to discuss.'

The barmaid smiled sweetly, batted her eyelashes at the captain, drew her hand slowly along his arm, then walked purposefully back to the bar, her hips swaying.

Both blacksmiths had watched the performance goggle-eyed.

'Pay no attention to Kate, gentlemen,' the captain laughed. 'It's a game that she and I play. She throws herself at me and I duck out of the way. Now, let us have the first drink of what I hope will be many.' He raised his glass. 'To King George's health!' he exclaimed heartily, then added quietly, 'may he get a scrofulous canker on the end of his piss-pipe.'

That was a toast they all drank to.

The first bottle was drained and they were halfway through the second when Jamie spoke for the first time. 'Dat darky on yer ship. Is 'e a slave?'

'Firstly, Mr. Clancy, Abraham Washington isn't, as you say, a darky, he is a negro. Secondly, he isn't a slave, he is one of my business partners.'

The two yeomen couldn't have been more surprised if Rackham had announced that the pope was Protestant.

'Mr. Washington was a slave but, when he injured himself, he was no longer of use to his master and, no matter how much the bastard beat him, Abraham was no longer physically able to do the manual labour. My senior partner bought him from his owner because of his invaluable knowledge of tobacco growing. A few years later, Washington gained his freedom papers and my partner asked him if he'd be willing to embark on another venture. Right now, he's schooling Alexander on how to run a business. In a matter of a few years the boy will be a captain, perhaps the youngest captain there ever was, and Mr. Washington will have become the richest negro in all of America.'

There was a prolonged silence as the two Tipperary men tried to take in and comprehend all that they'd been told.

'Who's Alexander?' asked Michael.

'Alexander is my senior partner's son, a bright lad … perhaps somewhat of a landlubber by my measure, but then I've spent so much of my life at sea that I'm surprised I haven't turned into a fish. He's a quick-thinker, like his father, and a good-looking young lad. If he ever stops growing and starts to fill out, he'll break some hearts, I'm sure. His father wants him to learn the shipping business from the bottom up.' The captain studied the liquid in his glass against the light of a candle. 'Yes, he's a clever man, my partner.'

'Who is this partner of yours?'

Rackham smiled a foxy smile and suddenly appeared much older. 'You haven't agreed to the terms of your contract yet.' He placed a purse on the table in front of them. 'There are five shillings in there.'

Jamie's eyes widened. 'Jayzis!' he said, 'I'd sell me almighty soul fer five shillin's. I'd even give ya change.'

'I don't want your soul, Mr. Clancy. All I'm asking for is some of your time and your expertise. I have a wagon-load of empty hogsheads. If you agree, we'll hook a team of draughts up to it tomorrow and you will take them back to Gortalocca. After you drop them off, you will return to Galway and pick up a second load, then a third. That's it, that's all there is to it. Once you have all the empty barrels stowed away in your village, you will await further instructions. No laws will have been broken. My partner will be in touch with you when the time is right, which will be sooner rather than later, and then there will be more money involved for you, perhaps much more.'

Michael didn't wait for Jamie to digest the information. He held out his hand and answered for them both.

'Agreed.'

'Good!' said Rackham and, for the first time, a genuine smile crossed his face. 'Now, let's get some food in our bellies to soak up some of this rum, then we'll see if we can find some suitable entertainment for you fellows. Have either of you ever had corned beef? It's sailor's fare, very common in the colonies.'

'I'll eat anyt'ing dat don't eat me first,' said Jamie.

'That's the spirit, James,' laughed Rackham. What about you, Hogan? Are you ready to try beef from a barrel?'

Mikey wasn't convinced. 'I'd say yes to beer from a barrel anytime, but I don't know about beef.'

'Oh, come along now, where's your sense of adventure? It's not as if I'm asking you to eat worms. KATE!' he shouted. 'Bring us three plates of corned beef and cabbage!' He looked at Michael and laughed. 'Oh, and pick out the worms, would you? Mr. Hogan here has a delicate constitution. And we'll need a few flagons of ale, if you please.'

The amply rounded barmaid disappeared through a door at the back and, in no time, she reappeared carrying plates filled to capacity with the victuals. She stood with her hands on her hips, chuckling, as the two yeomen inspected the lump of fatty beef for worms.

'It'll never replace bacon,' said Mikey, swallowing a mouthful, 'but it's not bad.' Jamie nodded in agreement and tucked in to his food.

When they had scraped the last evidence of food from their plates, a piece of treacle cake drenched in rum was placed before each of them, a dollop of cream sitting on top.

After one bite, Jamie put down his spoon. 'I never tasted anyt'ing so good in all me life. I have to find out how to make dis so I can tell me wife.'

'Ah you won't find the ingredients here in Ireland, James. They're tropical spices. There's cinnamon and cloves from the Indies, molasses and allspice from Jamaica and Barbados rum.'

The two blacksmiths devoured their cake and, just when they thought the evening was over, Captain Rackham announced it was time for entertainment. Jamie and Michael looked at each other, then towards a smiling Kate.

'No, no, boys. Not that sort of entertainment. Have you ever seen rat-baiting?'

A crowd of men packed around a pit at the end of the wharf. Several of them had small terriers with names like Tiger, Badger and Shark and the others stood around shouting out wagers on each of the little dogs. The Tipperary men couldn't discern who was more excited, the mob or the dogs. One of the terriers was put into the arena, then a rat-catcher dumped half a dozen rodents into the pit, rats bigger than Mikey and Jamie had ever seen. In a matter of moments, the dog had grabbed the rats in turn and dispatched each with a shake of his head.

'Why don't dey just t'row d' rats into d' sea?' asked

Jamie. 'Or hit 'em wit' a shovel?'

'It's a sport, man!' replied the captain incredulously. 'Can't you feel the blood rise in you?'

'If d' rats all got together, I'll bet dey could've taken dat little dog.'

'You're right, of course, James,' laughed Rackham, 'but the rats are like the Irish. They can't get themselves organised.'

Michael felt the sting of the implied insult and he stepped back.

'Oh, don't take it personally, Michael, it's just an outsider's observation. One of these days, if the Irish ever join forces with each other instead of running around squabbling amongst themselves, they'll be able to take their country back.'

The evening passed quickly and it was soon time for the smiths to turn in. A room had been provided for them and they slept soundly, blissfully unaware of what events the following day would bring.

CHAPTER 6

T he next morning they were woken by a sharp rap at the door.

'Ugh,' moaned Jamie, 'me head feels like an egg dat's been cracked. Last night I t'ought I'd like to be a sailor. Dis mornin' I t'ink I'd radder be one o' dem rats. At least if I was dead, me noggin would stop poundin'.'

Michael had his own problems. His belly was turning over and over like a butter churn and his eyes were glued shut.

'Come on, you two, there's work to be done!' came the now familiar voice of the captain from the hallway. 'A nice hunk of fatty bacon and some runny eggs should settle your stomachs,' he added mirthfully.

Michael leaned over the chamber pot and retched and a laugh came from the other side of the door. 'The room's spinning, Clancy,' gasped Mikey. 'I'd have to wait 'til the next time the door came round to open it. You let him in.'

Jamie got up and staggered to the door as if he was walking in post holes. When he pulled the bolt back, the door swung open and the captain stood there grinning.

'Call yourselves Irishmen?' he laughed. 'You're a

pair of lightweights. You should be ashamed of yourselves.' He walked into the room and saw Mikey with his head hovering above the chamber bucket. 'You'll not be wanting a nice greasy breakfast then?' he said. Michael retched again and put his head back in the pot.

The two men threw cold water on their faces from a bowl on a wooden stand. While Jamie left the water on his face, Michael wiped his off with his sleeve.

'Are we ready now?' asked the captain. 'Before you leave this fair city, there are a couple of people I need you to meet and, judging by the looks of you, a walk in the fresh morning air will do you some good ... or kill you, one or the other.'

They followed the ship's officer downstairs and out onto the street. The glare of the low morning sun was almost painful and they squinted into it.

'First we need to go to the Customs Office. I'll introduce you to the man in charge there, a fellow by the name of MacCarty. He's a Scotsman but we don't hold that against him, he's just as greedy as the rest of us. Then I'll take you to the warehouse where the hogsheads are stored and we'll meet Mr. O'Toole. You'll be seeing him over the coming weeks.'

MacCarty was a middle-aged man with a paunch which stretched his buttoned uniform coat. His most distinguishing characteristics, besides the Scots burr in his voice, was his fiery red hair and a beard the same colour which came down to the middle of his chest. When the three men entered his office, he greeted Rackham cordially and shook his hand.

''Tis a braw day the day, Cap'n.' He cast a glance over at the two hungover smiths and grinned, '...at least it is fer some o' us.'

Jack Rackham made the introductions and, after exchanging a few pleasantries with the Scot, he handed him a purse which the redheaded man hefted as if gauging its weight.

'You'll be sailing soon then, Cap'n?'

'With the tide, Mac.'

'Godspeed, then, Jack, and mind yourself now. There's a thirty-two gun English frigate posted off Fastnet Rock and she has an escort accompanying her.'

'Is it a sloop?'

'Och no, she's an old brig, probably French-built.'

'That's good, it means we can sail closer to the wind than she can. If she gets too curious, we can outrun her. What flag should we sail under?'

'Put up Dutch colours. The last I heard, we weren't at war with them. The Froggies and the Austrians are going at it hell fer leather but, so far, the Sassanachs are sittin' this dance oot.'

'Thanks, Mac. I'll see you in a month or so, God willing.' The men shook hands like old friends and the Scot made a slight bow of acknowledgement to the Irishmen.

'Right, gents,' said Rackham, 'let's get you to the warehouse. You can pick up your cargo then I'll bid you adieu for a few weeks.'

Mr. O'Toole was a thin man with squinty, bloodshot eyes and a pallid complexion. He greeted the captain as cordially as had Mac, though he eyed the Irish strangers suspiciously.

'This is Mr. Hogan and Mr. Clancy, Tom. They're new partners in our endeavor and the boss says they're to be treated as you would treat himself.'

O'Toole relaxed. 'Ya have to watch out fer spies and informants, sir.'

'Good man, Tom, you're right. Can't be too careful. Now, what do you know about the pickets at Fastnet?'

'One o' dem's yer auld ship, sir, Courser.'

'But Courser was a twenty-eight gunner.'

'Not anymore, Cap'n. Ya know yerself how dem English is always tryin' to squeeze more firepower on board dose boats. But d' one ya really have to watch out fer is d' brig she's got wit' her. It ain't d' boat, mind, it's d' feckin' lieutenant in command of it. Willoughby's his name. He's a mad bastard.'

'What do you know about him?'

'He's on a fast track … got friends in d' Admiralty and he ain't afraid o' nutt'n'. He'll risk d' ship and all aboard 'er to get his mission done. Dat bugger's won enough prize money to make himself rich and he could have been promoted to a bigger ship long ago but he said no … likes d' chase too much.'

Jack Rackham lost himself in thought for a moment, then his face brightened. 'So then, he's a sportsman. Splendid! What better sport can there be than if you're willing to risk everything to win the prize?'

O'Toole shook his head. 'Don't forget, Jack, d' way to play d' game is to make as much money as fast as ya can, den get yerself out o' d' game while ya still have yer skin on.'

'Sometimes, O'Toole, you can be such an old woman. Life is a game inside a game. How do you know you're alive if you don't play them both?'

'Agh! Ya always make me jittery, Jack. I'm never sure I know what's in yer head.'

'Nobody knows what's in my head, Tommy O'Toole, that's why I'm good at what I do. Now, let's get down to the business at hand. Have you the hogsheads loaded on the wagon?'

'I have, sir, and I have a team o' draught horses waitin'.'

'Excellent. Get the team hitched and we'll send these gentlemen on their way.'

Within five minutes, the wagon was ready and waiting to leave. Jamie had stopped taking in anything at all after the conversation he'd heard in the Customs House but Michael was still busy trying to make sense of it all. They both shook hands with O'Toole who wished them 'safe home'. The captain, still in a jovial mood, told them he was happy to have made their acquaintance, shook their hands, then turned abruptly and headed back towards the dock where his ship lay waiting.

'He reminds me of someone,' said Mikey.

'He reminds me of yer Uncle Robert, wit' dem muddy, green-brown eyes dat seem to be lookin' right inside ya. I don't mind tellin' ya, Mikey, he scares d' shite outta me.'

'Maybe that's who I was thinking of, there's certainly something dark about him. He can change moods just like Uncle Robbie. One minute he's laughing and joking and the next he's watching you like he's trying to get inside your head.'

'Mikey, I'm not sure about any o' dis. I never broke d' law in me life and now here I am sharin' d' craic wit' a pirate.'

'Well, James, we ate his food, we drank his beer and we took his money so we're up to our ears in this now, whether we like it or not. We have no choice but to ride it out and see where it takes us.'

*

Two miles west of Gortalocca, in Johnstown, the big house was being made ready to receive its first occupants since old Mr. Johnson died twelve years before. His son, the heir to his estate, had no interest in vacating his comfortable residence on the outskirts of London. He knew that Irish farms were prosperous so, as long as he continued to receive the income they provided, Ireland was not his concern. He jumped at the opportunity to lease the manor house in Johnstown to an Irishman who seemingly had struck it rich in the Americas.

The dust sheets had been pulled from the furniture, the china carefully cleaned and the silverware polished until it gleamed. Windows were opened and the musty odour of disuse was aired out. The gardens, which had lain unkempt, were being tended and sheep were allowed to graze on the lawns. News that someone new was moving in soon got to Mick Sheridan. He had been in charge of the stables for as long as Johnson had been in residence at the house and now he'd been informed that his services were needed once again. Even though his head was now crowned with a thatch of white hair, Mick was still a formidable presence. In the intervening years, he had done fairly well for himself in the horse-trading business but now he was to be back at the stables where he'd spent the best years of his life. He only hoped the new master would be as good a one as old Johnson had been.

Mick took the bone-coloured walking stick which Roisin had lent him and he limped out to the pasture. There was an old horse there, equally as timeworn as himself, waiting, grazing and passing the hours. The horse walked up to him and nickered a greeting.

'Well now, Abel,' said Mick, 't'ings have bin lonely

fer ya since yer brother died. P'raps now ya'll have some company back up at d' big house instead o' spendin' yer days wit dis auld sod.' Mick ran his hand down the horse's neck, then cupped it over his nose. 'Ahhh, dere's no perfume as sweet as d' smell of a horse. C'mon, Abel, let's you and me go and find out what's wanted of us.'

Mick saddled the horse, slipped the bit into its grizzled muzzle and placed the cracked leather bridle over the animal's ears. He chuckled to himself.

'Bin a long time since eider of us was much use to anybody, eh fella? At least ya can save d' wear and tear on me legs while we get ourselves to Johnson's.' The old man let out an audible groan as he swung his leg up over the animal's back and into the stirrup and the ageing duo ambled slowly towards the Johnson mansion.

Mick walked the horse up the sweeping drive and, as they rounded the corner to the back of the house, he saw that the stable door was open. He dismounted slowly and, before he put all his prodigious weight on the ground, he shifted the walking stick over to his left hand. Holding the reins with his right, he limped to the door. Inside, there was a man in his early forties mucking out the stalls, forking the old straw and the ancient, petrified horse turds into a wheelbarrow. Mick watched silently. Finally the man became aware of Mick's presence. He straightened up and looked at him.

'Me name's Sheridan,' announced Mick, 'and I'm to be in charge here.'

The man smiled and shrugged his shoulders, then went back to cleaning out the stalls. Mick was pleased. He was a quiet man himself and he enjoyed the company of horses and other quiet men.

'I can see yer no stranger to d' fork, but I ain't seen ya round here before. Got a name?' The man looked up, flashed Mick a grin and went back to his work.

'Are ya an eejit, or dumb, or both?'

The fellow propped his pitchfork against the wall, set his feet apart, put his hands in his pockets and took a good long look at the old man. Finally he spoke.

'Oy ain't dumb and Oy ain't no eejit. When Oy have sumpt'n to say, Oy say it.' He was still grinning and it was starting to grate on Mick's nerves.

'What d' feck kind of accent is dat?'

'It ain't me wit' an accent, ya auld fart. You're d' one wit an accent.'

The man's perpetual grin was making Mick livid. 'Who are you callin' an auld fart, ya snotty-nosed young pup ya?'

'Oy'm callin' you an auld fart. What are ya goin' to do about it?'

Mick brandished his walking stick in the air. 'I ought to wrap dis stick around yer big head.'

'You'd better not try, ya monkey turd. If ya do, Oy'll shove it up yer arse.'

Mick threw the stick to the floor. The old horseman was slow to anger but this impertinent snip had managed to get him steaming in a matter of minutes.

'Try it and I'll fire yer shitty arse, ya gobshite.'

'Oy was t'inkin' d' same t'ing, ya feckin' auld goat. Oy should fire *your* shitty arse.'

'What did ya say?' Mick was taken aback 'Are ya sayin' you're in charge o' d' stables?'

The younger man could suppress his laughter no longer. 'Dat Oy am,' he laughed 'and d' house and d' grounds and everyt'ing else … Gortalocca too. Now, what d' ya t'ink o' dat?'

'But I t'ought it was an Englishman who bought all d' land,' said Mick, incredulously.

'Ah no, Mr. Sheridan, it's a hundert times worse. It's a feckin' Corkman!' He laughed so hard now that he had to hold his stomach.

While Mick tried to decipher what was going on, the younger man wiped his hands off on his trews and approached him with his hand held out.

'The name's Edmund Flood,' he grinned, 'but you can call me Ned.'

Mick took the man's hand and nearly shook it off his arm. 'Jayzis, Mary and Saint Joseph!' he cried. 'If it ain't d' Phantom Priest o' West Cork! Well, well, well. Funny, I t'ought you was bigger.'

'I'm big enough, ya auld sod and anyway, all dat was a long time ago. Oy'm a successful business man now, but Oy'd appreciate it if ya keep dat part of it under yer hat fer a few days. Oy want to do a bit of explorin' … gather a bit of information, like, and Oy can't do dat if folks are tryin' to kiss me arse.'

'Well, well, well.' Mick said again and now it was his turn to grin. 'Let's you and me have a little drink together, Mr. Flood. I got a jug o' d' good stuff at home.'

'Oy've got an even better idea, Mr. Sheridan. Will we go up to d' big house and pretend we're t'ieves, stealin' d' Lord o' d' Manor's whiskey?'

Ned picked up Mick's walking stick and handed it back to him. Mick slapped him on the back and the two men walked up to the big house together to make themselves at home.

CHAPTER 7

The ashes had cooled on Gortalocca's charred ruins enough for the Hogans and the Clancys to rummage around amongst the rubble, retrieving anything that might be of use. The smell of smoke still hung thick in the air and clung to their clothes. Roisin went through the wreckage of the store, stooping and bending here and there to pick up and inspect items which had once been of value. Sometimes she'd put them in the pocket of her apron, other times she'd finger something that had once meant something to her then throw it back on the ground. The initial shock had worn off and been replaced by a sense of numbness. It was the same feeling she'd had when her husband, Liam, died almost twenty years before. She worked alone, not wanting anyone to see the tears which occasionally welled up in her eyes. From time to time, she wiped her face with the back of a soot-covered hand. In her heart, she knew that this was the final nail in Gortalocca's coffin.

Morna was with Jamie's wife, Kate. They were rooting through the remains of the forge, retrieving the tools and trappings of the blacksmith's shop and placing them in a barrel. Morna's sixteen year-old daughter, Siobhan, was helping her younger brother, Liam, to clean and sort the various items rescued from the debris. If the tools could be salvaged, then there was a slight possibility that, out of the ashes, some degree of redemption could be reaped.

Robbie was delighted that he could lay the entire blame for the fire firmly at the feet of Jamie and he never missed an opportunity to do just that. Now he watched while the others toiled amidst the destruction, combing through the wreckage. Having worn out his welcome at the forge ruins, he made his way over to where his mother stood, in the midst of the four walls which had once been Hogan's.

'Ain't much left to d' village anymore, Mam. D' land had already gone and so's Hogan's now. I was t'inkin', p'raps I'll sell up and move somewhere else.'

Roisin could scarcely believe what she'd just heard. 'What did you say?'

'I was t'inkin' about selling d' cottage and headin' up to Connaught.'

'You'll do no such thing, Robert Flynn! Your father and Jamie built that house with their bare hands and you'll sell it to some stranger over my dead body. Anyway, you don't even own it anymore.'

'Agh, don't talk to me about Jamie!' he spat. 'Wasn't it him dat burned d' feckin' village sure and isn't it because of him dat dere's nutt'n left here anymore? And as far as not ownin' d' house, only d' family knows dat.'

'Even if you found someone daft enough to buy it, how much do you think you'd get for a cottage with no land?' she snarled, any sadness she'd felt having been replaced by anger. 'And how do you think you'll make a living in Connaught? Up there, you won't be able to sponge money off me or your brother. You'll starve, and your family along with you.'

'I might get four or five shillin's fer d' house and, wit' d' eight I still have from d' rents, I could open a spirit grocery like Hogan's. I've plenty of experience.'

'Wait! What did you say? You still have eight shillings left from the rents?'

'I do,' he said, with a hint of defiance, squaring his shoulders.

'Well you can hand that straight over to me, ya sod! We'll need every farthing we can get to rebuild.'

'I will not, it's mine! I'll be needin' it to start up a new business when we get where we're goin'.'

'Jayzis, Robert, you ran this one into the ground! What makes you think things will be any different somewhere else?'

'Because dat was Hogan's,' he said, 'and my business will be Flynn's.' The hint of defiance had been exchanged for one of hostility. 'Dat store was never mine. I always had you looking over me shoulder.'

Roisin felt her throat tighten as if she were going to cry. 'I did everything to keep that place going. I put every penny I had into it.'

'It wasn't just about d' money, Mam. Everyt'ing was always about Mikey. You always put him above me.'

Her son's words stung her to the core. She had always gone out of her way to favour Robert because Liam's favourite had been Michael.

'Agh, there's no talking to you sure. Do whatever you want, Robert, but you'll leave young Peg with me. She's too young to be dragged all over Ireland while you chase your daft dreams.'

Robert only had to think for a moment. If he left his

nine year-old daughter here, that would keep a bridge open between him and the rest of the family. If things didn't turn out as he hoped, he could always use the girl as an excuse to return.

'Alright so, Mam, but only until I get things going mind.'

He turned and, before Roisin could say another word, he walked back to his cottage, went in and slammed the door behind him. And so it was done. In less time than the fire had taken to consume the heart of her village, the fabric of her family had been torn asunder. Roisin held her soot-blackened apron up to her face as if wiping away the grime but, in truth, it was a vain effort to hide her tears from the rest of her family, who had borne witness to the confrontation.

*

'It'll take us a couple of days to get to Portumna, Clancy, and another one to Gortalocca,' said Michael.

'I still don't like it, Mikey. I have a bad feelin' about d' whole business.'

'Agh, you always look on the dark side of life, Jamie Clancy. Don't be such a little girl.'

'It's me nature, and I ain't never bin a girl, and it's bin a long time since I was little.'

'We're not doing anything wrong sure, we're just delivering a wagon load of barrels. What's wrong with that?'

'Did ya get a whiff inside one o' dem t'ings?'

'I did. Smells like they had rum in them at one time.'

'And what do ya t'ink happened to d' rum?'

'Well my guess is it got turned into piss by a bunch of Irishmen.'

'Maybe by pirates. Dat Rackham fella didn't tell us much.'

'He told us enough to know that I didn't want to hear any more. The less we know, the better. Now let's talk about something else, Clancy. I was alright 'til I started talking to you.'

'I reckon he was talkin' about runnin' a blockade.'

'And here was me thinking you weren't paying attention.'

'Oh I heard everyt'ing alright. He talked about it like it's a sport or sumpthin'.'

'Jayzis! I just remembered who he acted like, and it's not Uncle Robert.'

'Who?'

'Remember that deputy? The one who went down to Cork with Uncle Robert?'

'I do o' course. Ed was it?'

'It was Ned, Ned Flood!'

'Dat's it, Ned Flood, d' terror o' West Cork … and him such a mild lookin' fella too.'

'Tell that to the Prussians who were hunting him.'

'I'll never know how he got d' better of all dem soldiers.'

'They thought they were chasing a rabbit but it turned out to be a wolf and, by the time they realised they were the prey, it was too late.'

'He must o' had a streak of evil runnin' t'rough him.'

'Not at all, he was just a Corkman sure, having a bit of fun and playing a game of hounds and hares.'

'Went to America, didn't he? Wonder what happened him over dere.'

'The way Ned Flood pushed his luck, he was probably scalped by those red Indians, or hung by the English!'

*

Ned sat with his dirty bare feet up on old Mr. Johnson's desk, sipping whiskey and gazing upwards as the smoke from his Cuban cigar curled over his head.

'Not a bad auld life, is it Mick Sheridan? Want some more o' dat roast beef?'

'Ah I won't, sir, t'anks. I'm stuffed.'

'A cigar den?' Ned opened the carved ivory case and held it out to the old horseman.

'T'ank ya no, sir. I never got a taste fer it meself.'

Ned snapped the lid back down on the box and put it aside. 'Well it's a good t'ing ya still like a drink. Udderwise you'd be no fun at all.'

'So tell me, what's brought ya back here? I hope ya ain't come to collect any auld debts because dere ain't no money round here.'

'Ah no, Mick, nutt'n like dat. Oy'm here t' pay one back.' Ned watched again as the smoke from his cigar wafted gently towards the ceiling.

'Well, I hope yer payin' it back to someone round here. We could do wit' it.'

Ned smiled and abruptly changed the subject.

'Oy'll be needin' horses, Mick. Not shite ones mind, good strong ones, enough of 'em to plow a hundert acres. And Oy'll need some carriage horses, two of 'em. If ya can, find me a matched team o' greys, dat's me preference. Dey're a bit more flashy dan brown ones.' He winked.

'Jayzis Christ, sir! Dat's goin' to cost ya a fortune!'

'Not a bother,' replied Ned, accidently blowing a puff of smoke towards the old man, who responded with a choked cough. 'Sorry 'bout dat Mick.'

'How quick do ya want d' fields plowed? A decent

plowman can do about six acres a week if he rests his animals.'

'Good enough. Now, how fast can ya get twenty teams to Gortalocca?'

'Twen….? Holy Mary! Now dat's really goin' to cost some money! It's about tuppence a day fer a plowman and team.'

'Tell 'em Oy'll pay four.' Ned blew a smoke ring and watched it rise as its circumference grew, then disappear.

'Fou….? Jayzis, Mary an' Saint Joseph! Fer dat kind o' money, dey'll walk away from deir own fields to plow yours!'

'Grand. Dat's d' kind of ent'usiasm Oy'm after.'

'Did ya hear how Hogan's burned down d' udder day and d' blacksmith shop along wit' it?'

'Oy did, and Oy know a village widdout a pub and a smitty ain't much of a village. We'll rebuild.'

'I heard dem streets in Americay is paved wit' gold. D' way you're talkin' about t'rowin' money around, yer either d' richest man I ever met or d' biggest bullshitter I ever met.'

'Or maybe a bit o' both,' grinned Ned. He reached into a drawer of the desk and pulled out a heavy strongbox. He took a key that he wore around his neck and opened the box, exposing its contents. Mick almost wet himself. It was full to the brim with gold coins.

'Just a bit o' dat gold Oy swept off d' streets in d' New World.'

Mick took a gulp of his whiskey. 'When d' ya want me to get started, sir?'

'It'll keep 'til t'morra. Tonight we'll just sit and enjoy ourselves.'

'Don't mind if I do,' said Mick.

Ned re-lit his cigar from the flames in the open fireplace and poured his guest another glass of whiskey.

*

The two blacksmiths arrived back at the inn where they'd spent the night two days before. The innkeeper stood outside, smoking his pipe and awaiting their arrival.

'Oh shite!' exclaimed Jamie. 'He's waitin' fer us. Will we keep goin'?'

'He looks happy enough,' replied Michael. 'Maybe he didn't find the bowl we pissed in.'

The proprietor was indeed cordial and welcomed the two Irishmen warmly. 'I'm delighted to see you two gentlemen again.'

Jamie couldn't contain his guilt. 'We're sorry, sir,' he blurted out. 'We're very sorry we pissed in yer soup bowl.'

The man looked confused. 'What soup bowl?'

'D' one in d' bedroom. It's just dat dere was no bucket, and...'

'Oh. OH! That was a chamber pot. Yer supposed to pee in it. Anyway, fer d' four shillin's a night Capt'n Rackham's payin' me, ye can piss in me wife's ear if ya want.'

'Ah now, dat's good o' ya,' said Jamie innocently, 'but I don't t'ink I'll be doin' dat.' The innkeeper gave him a dirty look. 'Did ya see dat, Mikey? He's still angry wit' me. It must because I wiped me mouth on d' clean linen.'

'Pull yer wagon round the back and unhitch the team,' said the owner. 'The stable boy will take care of the animals.' He glared at Jamie again. 'When yer done, come in. I have supper waitin' fer ye.'

'See?' said Jamie. 'I knew he was still angry.'

'Shut the feck up, Clancy. Don't say another word until after we've eaten or we'll be sharing dinner with the horses.'

CHAPTER 8

As Captain Rackham walked back to the wharf, a new plan had begun to formulate in his mind. His ship was carrying ten tons of untaxed tobacco from Maryland. He made another stop at the Customs Office and MacCarty was genuinely surprised to see the young officer again so soon.

'Is there a problem, Captain?'

'No problem, Mac, just a minor complication.'

'How can I help?'

'I want to offload half my cargo. Do you have enough room here in the custom's warehouse to store it for me?'

'I have the room, sir, but I think it would be wiser if you left it with O'Toole. I'd have a hard time explaining it away if the Crown sent an inspector, and I'm getting a bit too old to be sent off to Jamaica to work in the cane fields.'

'Alright, Mac, no problem. Then I'd like you to stamp the papers to say the cargo has been inspected. That way everything will at least look legitimate and, if needs be, we'll pay the tariff on the load we're carrying.'

'Will ye be offloading the four-pounder stern-chaser too?'

'We will indeed. We need to look as innocuous as possible.'

There was a moment's silence and MacCarty knew that the officer's mind was working overtime. 'I can almost hear those cogs turning inside your head, Captain. Would you care to share your thoughts with me?'

'God no,' said Rackham, then his face broke into a grin and he left the office. He returned to his ship and called Mr. Washington aside for a private conversation.

'We just became legitimate, Abraham, at least on paper. Have the men offload half the cargo and get rid of the canon for this trip. Our official mission just changed.'

The black man studied his captain's face and knew that something was afoot. 'What's the mission now, Captain?'

'We're delivering Master Alexander Flood, along with his personal servant, to England to pursue an education.'

'What will Ned think about the whole load not getting to France? Won't he be angry?'

'He'd have a lot more to be angry about if the ship got boarded and the whole load got confiscated and the ship along with it. Get Alexander in here, will you? I need to tell him his new role in this.'

The youth appeared before the captain immediately, a tall, thin lad with long, light-brown hair and blue eyes. He stood half a head above the captain but weighed at least twenty pounds less.

'Alexander, my boy, from now on you're a passenger on this ship.'

'But, sir, I'm the second officer.'

Rackham grinned. 'You just got a promotion. Until I get you to Waterford you're a snotty, upper-class rich man's son on his way to attend Oxford or Cambridge or some other dung-heap of an English university. I don't want you on deck, relaying orders from Mr. Washington to the crew, until this little adventure is over, understand? Now I want you to help Washington in getting the crew to unload some of our cargo and the gun.'

'I doubt snotty rich men's sons do that sort of thing, Captain.'

'No back chat, Mr. Flood, you're as sarcastic as your father. Now get to it!'

'Yes, sir! Sorry, sir!' the boy grinned and saluted the officer with his middle finger.

'You're such a knob.' Captain Rackham returned the grin. 'Get out of here.'

*

Ned was dressed in a clean leine and trews when he came down to breakfast. Mick was already stuffing himself with the sausages and eggs that had been placed before him by a maid.

'Good man yerself, Mick. Eat away, you've a long day ahead o' ya.'

Mick swallowed a mouthful of food and washed it down with a gulp of beer. 'Good mornin', sir, I'm almost finished.'

'No hurry at all, work away, eat yer fill. Oy've a few t'ings to do and den Oy t'ink Oy'll take meself off to Gortalocca.'

Mick had piled a heap of food onto his eating knife and now he held it in mid-air, halfway to his mouth.

'It's a shame Michael and Jamie ain't back, dey'd be delighted to see ya.'

'Ah Oy'll be runnin' into dem two soon enough.'

'Ya have a fine ridin' horse in d' stables, I see. D' villagers will be impressed when ya ride into Gortalocca on dat beauty.'

'Ah no, Oy'm not making any grand entrances. Oy'll walk dere.'

Enough had been said. Mick tucked into the remainder of his breakfast and thought about what he had to do.

*

Michael and Jamie had already been on the road a good few hours.

'D' ya t'ink we'll be home by tonight, Mikey?'

'There's a good chance. The load's light and the horses are strong. If we get to Portumna by late afternoon, we might as well push on to Gortalocca. I'd like to get this trip over with and then we can rest the horses for a day and get ourselves back to Galway for Captain Rackham's second load.'

'He makes me nervous.'

'Agh sure everyone and everything makes you nervous, Clancy.'

'Dat's true, but I have a bad feelin' in me gut.'

'That's because you're not used to your belly being full and you're not used to a few extra shillings weighing down your pockets. I've told you, we don't know anything and we don't want to know.'

'One o' dem hogsheads still has a lid on it. Rackham said dey'd all be empty. Ain't ya curious to know what's in it?'

'Five shillings is in it, Clancy, that's all I want to know.'

'I was just t'inkin' out loud.'

'Think quietly instead and let me think about our five shillings.'

'Where'll we put d' barrels when we get home?'

'We'll store them in the old church. No one's used that place in years.'

'If we put 'em in dere, dat brother o' yours might go nosin' around.'

'Jayzis, man, I'll take care of it. I'll get Mam to handle him. Now why don't you shut yer gob and take a nap?'

*

Aboard the British brig, Albatross, Lieutenant Willoughby was pacing the deck, his hands behind his back. He was beginning to wonder whether he should have accepted the offer of a transfer to a bigger ship. This brig was uncomfortably small and the accommodations spartan. His ship's picket duty, to intercept smugglers, had been slow during the winter months and he was bored. He looked up and took a gauge of the weather. There had been a fierce storm a few days before and they'd had to put out to sea to avoid the shoals around Ireland's south coast. Now both his ship and the frigate, Courser, were back on post and repairing the damage caused by the tempest.

He looked out to Fastnet Rock and thought it looked like an obelisk carved by the hand of God himself. The ground swell crashed around its base and he watched as the seas broke on the shoals, before throwing themselves futilely on the jagged edges of

Clear Island, off the coast of Cork. He pulled his greatcoat tightly around him. He would much rather be in the Caribbean or the Med this time of year but, with England at peace for once, the pickings would be sparse there too. The name of the game was hunting and the profit made any discomfort bearable. The brig was fast, much faster than most commercial vessels, and soon it would be the season for smugglers. The winter storms were all but over and the sport would soon begin.

Willoughby was still only in his early thirties, his hair dark and wavy and his brown eyes keen. His family's naval ties reached back to the time of Drake, Willoughby himself having been on ships since his youth, coming into his own when he'd been put on the deck of the French-built Albatross. He was adept at hiding his ship and then, when the time was right, swooping like a falcon. It was as if he could read the mind of his prey and he knew exactly where to place his ship to its best advantage. He never missed his target and took the utmost pride in that fact.

He was looking out seaward and watching as the frigate came smartly about, several miles distant. It's a great pity, he thought, that once a man is put in charge of a rated vessel, he often becomes too careful. Now if he'd been in command of Courser, he would blockade the channel that passed between Fastnet and Clear Island, freeing up the Albatross to do what she did best.

'Bosun!' he snapped to the man in a striped shirt who stood beside him. 'Pipe the men for gunnery!'

*

THE DEVIL'S OWN LUCK

It wasn't yet noon when Ned arrived in Gortalocca and the women and children were still scouring the rubble for anything of value. When Roisin saw the stranger she straightened herself up and wiped her arm across her brow. She waited until he spoke first.

'It looks like ye suffered a fierce disaster here, missus.'

The old woman eyed him up and down. 'That's very observant,' she said sarcastically, 'for a foreigner.'

'Ah, dere ain't much gets past me,' he said with a grin.

'You can wipe that shite-eating grin off your face. There's nothing funny about any of this.'

'It depends on where yer standin', missus.'

'Well I suggest you go and stand somewhere else, ya gobshite. Are you a fool or what?' Roisin bent over and continued to kick through the charred remnants.

'Foolish is as foolish does, Roisin Flynn.'

At the sound of her name, the old woman straightened herself up again and locked her gaze on the stranger's.

'Do I know you?'

'Well, not in d' Biblical sense, no, but if ya mean did ya ever meet me, ya did.'

Roisin peered closer at the stranger and suddenly her face lit up with recognition. 'NED FLOOD!' she cried, and everyone stood up and looked over. 'Well, may the Saints preserve us! God love ya! I think about you and May all the time. I thought those red savages in the colonies must have killed ya!' She threw back her head and laughed. 'Only you would be so bold, Biblical is it?'

The grin had vanished from Ned's face. 'May's wit'

d' angels now,' he said reverently, looking skywards, 'God rest 'er soul.'

'Ah no, Ned, I'm so very sorry to hear that.'

Morna had heard too and she bent her head and brought her apron up to her face. Morna and May had been childhood friends back in their little West Cork village.

'Ah sure sometimes t'ings don't work out like ya expect. She's bin gone ten years dis summer.'

Roisin picked her way out through the debris of the ruined forge and threw her arms around the Corkman.

'Biblical indeed, ya reprobate? I'm delighted to see you, Ned, and Michael will be too. He's away just now.'

'Oy'm lookin' forward to seein' him. Now, are ya goin' to introduce me to dis mob or not?'

Roisin let go of Ned and went through the introductions.

'Do ya remember Mikey's wife, Morna?'

Ned held out his hand but Morna brushed it aside and gave him a hug. He caught her by the shoulders and held her at arms' length 'I do o' course,' he said, 'and she's just as be-ootiful as ever.'

'And you're just as full of blarney,' laughed Roisin. 'This is Kate, she's Jamie's wife. I think you met her too.'

'Oy did,' said Ned, smiling at Kate. 'You weren't much more dan a garl back den and here y'are a gorgeous woman now.'

Roisin rolled her eyes. 'Still laying it on thick I see, Flood.'

'Ye'll have to make allowances fer me,' protested Ned. 'It's bin a long time since Oy was in d' presence o' real Oirish women such as yerselves.'

Roisin flapped her hands at him and carried on.

'This one's Siobhan, she's Mikey's daughter.'

Ned put one hand in front of his chest and the other behind him and bowed at the waist, as if he'd been introduced to a princess.

'Well now, you're d' spittin' image o' yer mam when she was a girl. How old are ya, lass?'

Siobhan was overwhelmed by the stranger's presence. 'Sixteen,' she mumbled.

'Sixteen years an' never bin kissed, eh? Oy've a boy a bit older dan ya. P'raps we should get d' two of ye togedder.' Siobhan's face flushed crimson.

'Ah, not her,' said Roisin. 'This wan says she's having nothing to do with any poor Irishman, reckons she has bigger fish to fry.'

'Is dat right? Well fair play t' ya, girl. Now, who's dis handsome young fella?'

'I'm Liam Flynn, sir,' said Liam, excitedly. 'Is it true you fought d' whole English Army single-handed down in Cork?'

'Ah no lad,' Ned chucked. 'Just part of it.'

'Da told us d' story. It was like somet'in you'd read in a book.'

'Dat's d' t'ing wit stories, young fella, dey all get better in d' tellin'.'

'What brings ya back to Oirland, Ned?' ventured Morna.

'Ye might o' heard about a rich Oirishman from Amerrycuh stayin' up at d' big house in Johnstown. Well dat's where Oy'm stayin'.'

'Are you indentured to him?' asked Roisin.

'Oy suppose ya could say dat.'

'Things must've taken a bad turn over in America, so?'

'Let's just say t'ings didn't turn out d' way Oy expected.'

'Ah sure things over here didn't turn out the way we expected either.'

'Tomorra's anudder day, missus.' With that, Ned bid them all a good day and walked off, whistling a tune.

Roisin smiled and waved after him. 'Yer man's as crazy as a shithouse rat,' she declared, once he was out of earshot.

'We should've asked 'im about d' fella who's rentin' Johnson's auld place,' said Morna.

'It's probably the same shite-for-brains who's bought up all the land here. Well, he might be rich but, if he's hired Ned Flood, he must be some kind of lunatic.'

'I wonder if he has a son,' cooed Siobhan.

'Don't start getting any of your high and mighty ideas, missy,' Roisin replied to the rhetorical question. 'Even if he has, those kind are out of reach of the likes of us.'

CHAPTER 9

The ship's anchor was hauled into a longboat and rowed out almost a quarter of a mile. Once it had been put in position at the bottom of Galway Bay, the men leaned their backs into the capstan and began to pull the ship away from the dock, slowly but surely reeling themselves out into open water. The breeze was freshening from the south-west and, when they had kedged the ship almost over the anchor, they hoisted the sails and set the canvas which greedily filled with wind. The ship cruised over the anchor under her own power and the men winched it up and secured it.

'What course, Cap'n?' asked the man at the wheel.

'Due west. We'll take her out of the bay by way of the North Sound.' The captain watched as the sails were trimmed to get the most lift out of the wind. 'I'm going below. Let me know when the Arans are in sight.'

Alexander lingered for a while on deck, watching as the sails billowed and the ship took flight. The strain of the taught sails could be felt with each gust and, after a second's hesitation, the schooner would leap forward.

He felt so exhilarated that it was hard for the boy to contain himself.

'We must be doing nine knots,' he thought out loud. The seaman at the wheel thought he was being addressed so he answered.

'I'd say we're doing nearer eleven, sir.'

Alexander nodded in acknowledgement. He thought this must be as close to flying as a man could get. He looked up at the full sails and listened to the thrum of the wind through the rigging like an enormous bass fiddle and the whole scene aroused him. Once again he thought out loud.

'I wonder if being with a woman feels anything like this.'

The short, leather-faced man at the wheel laughed. 'It can, sir, and a hundred times better if you're in love.'

Alexander looked at him. 'Have you ever been in love, Jonesey?'

'I have o' course,' the bosun chuckled, 'every time I've been ashore.'

'Have you ever been joined with a woman?'

'I have,' he cackled, 'hundreds of times.'

'No, you fish-head. I mean have you ever actually been married?'

The bosun became serious. 'I was married to a girl in Charles Town but, agh, the cholera got her soon after.'

'I'm sorry. Would you ever marry again?'

'I would not! Ah, I don't know, maybe I would. It's a grand thing to feel you belong to someone and they belong to you. But it hurt fierce bad when she died. No, I don't think I'd do it again.'

'Thanks, Jonesey.'

'Not a bother, sir. Now why don't you get yerself

off down below and have a game of chess with the captain. Don't worry, I'll give you both a shout when the Arans come into sight.'

*

It was long after dark by the time Jamie and Mike neared Gortalocca. They met Mick Sheridan riding his horse to Johnstown.

'Where are you off to dis time o' night, Mick?' asked Jamie.

'D' new master up at d' house sent me out to do a bit o' business fer him.' Mick could have done without meeting these two, having promised Ned that he'd keep his mouth shut.

'What's he like?' asked Michael.

'Ah, he seems a good-humoured sort.'

'What's his name?'

'He sent me t' get some men and some horses. Says he wants to start work on plowin' d' fields.'

'Does he indeed? What's his name?' repeated Michael.

'He does, I t'ink he has some big plans. Sorry, I have to get goin' now. Safe home, lads.' With that he rode off, thinking the conversation had gone well and that he'd managed not to spill any beans.

'You learn something new every day,' said Michael with a hint of sarcasm.

'What did ya learn, Mikey?'

'I learned that talking to Mick Sheridan is nearly as useless as talking to you.'

Ten minutes later, they pulled up the team of horses in Gortalocca. Even though it was late, Roisin came rushing out of the Hogan cottage along with Morna and the two children.

'Michael, I'm so glad you're back. I have some news for you.'

Michael was exhausted. 'I hope it's good news, Mam,' he said, climbing down from the cart. 'You can tell me while I unhitch the team.'

'Robert's selling the old house and moving away.'

Mike turned from the draughts and looked his mother straight in the face. 'Well that *is* good news. Maybe now I'll get a neighbour who won't burn my turf.' He turned back and began to unharness the horses.

'And Ned Flood's back.'

'WHAT THE F...!'

'Mind your tongue, Michael, the children ...'

'I don't believe it! I was only talking to Jamie about him the other day.'

'Well he's back.'

'What's he doing here?'

'It's my guess he fell on hard times back in the colonies. He's working up at Johnstown for some rich Irish fella who's moved into the big house.'

'What's the new fella's name?'

'Emmm….. now you mention it, I don't know. I'm not sure if I asked him but, if I did, I don't remember him saying.'

'You're about as helpful as Mick.'

'What's that about Mick?'

'We're after meeting him on the road. He's working for the new fella too.'

Jamie was looking around him at the rubble which had once been the heart and soul of Gortalocca. 'If dis fella's hirin', Mikey, p'rhaps we can find work wit' him too.'

'It's worth a try, Clancy. We have to rest the horses

tomorrow anyway. After we've unloaded the hogsheads in the morning, we'll go up to the big house and pay him a visit ... if only to find out what his feckin' name is ...'

*

The schooner Prosperity passed between the most northerly of the Arans, Rock Island and Golam Head, just as the last rays of sun tinted the western sky orange. Now, with the open Atlantic ahead and the protected waters of Galway Bay astern, the ship climbed and dropped with the oncoming ocean swell.

'What course, Cap'n?' enquired the helmsman.

'Due west for another hour, then south to Loop Head. Wake me if there's any change in the wind. We should be there around dawn tomorrow. Carry on.' He turned to Alexander now. 'If the wind backs a bit, like I expect it to, we'll make good time down to the Blaskets, then we'll carry on to the Skelligs. In four days, I should be putting you ashore at Waterford. You can get a coach from there to your father. Come down to the wardroom, Alexander, I need to talk to you.'

'Aye aye, sir.'

'Well now, aren't you getting salty, Master Flood,' smiled the officer, and he led the way.

The dark wood-panelled room was dimly lit with candlelight. It was barely five feet high and the men had to bend over to avoid cracking their skulls against the bulkhead.

'Close the door, lad. This is for your ears only.'

Alexander did as he was instructed and Rackham motioned him to a chair.

'We're carrying half a load, Alex. To maximise

profits, after I drop you off in Ireland, we're by-passing the English coast and going straight to Cherbourg.'

'I don't know why you didn't just leave me in Galway. It would have been closer and I could have travelled to Father with those other two men.'

'No. Your father left it with me to teach you as much about the shipping business as I can in the time we have so, until you need to go, the ship is where you'll be.'

'Why Cherbourg, sir?'

'It's like this, Alexander. For us, war is good business and right now the French and the Austrians are all over each other. If I dropped the tobacco in England, we'd be lucky to get eight pounds a hogshead. Then the English would apply a tariff and an admiralty tax and we'd be lucky to clear four pounds. Then the English shippers would send the load to France and get more than twice that amount. Even in times of war, Alex, the rich need their vices. If I take the tobacco direct to France, we bypass English Customs and we sell directly to the Frogs. Better yet, I might trade the hogsheads for French brandy and then we can sell it for almost twenty pounds in Britain. Even with half a load, we can make as much and maybe more.'

'What about the warships at Fastnet, and the ones in the Channel?

Captain Jack Rackham smiled a wolf's smile. 'Ah, that's the spice in the recipe, lad. The profits are the meat of it, but danger provides the spice.'

*

Aboard the brig Albatross, repairs to the rigging and spars were underway but it was taking far too much time for Willoughby's liking.

'How much longer?' he asked his second-in-command.

'The master of sail says it'll be at least two weeks if we do the repairs at sea, sir. If we put in at Baltimore, he says he can have it done in a week. That's Baltimore in Cork, sir.'

The brig's commander was growing impatient. 'I know where Baltimore is, you moron.' It was still a little early for the smuggling season so he made a split-second decision. 'Have the ship ready. We sail for Baltimore immediately.'

Willoughby had decided it was better to take a week out now than to wait until the ships had already begun to arrive from Jamaica and the colonies. In another month or so, business would start to get brisk and he wanted the vessel in Bristol condition for when the chase began.

*

Michael and Jamie unloaded the wagon and began the two-mile walk up to Johnstown.

'I wonder who dis new fella is,' said Jamie.

'I don't care if he's Cromwell as long as he's got work for us.'

'Do ya t'ink he will?'

'That old place hasn't been lived in for years so it's bound to need work doing on it.'

'I'd scrub and paint fer a penny.'

'Ah, he might even have something more permanent for us, you never know.'

'Dat'd be grand. We wouldn't have to worry about starvin' den.'

'Don't forget our obligation to Captain Rackham, Jamie. Even if yer man does have something for us, we wouldn't be able to start right away. He's bound to prefer someone who's available now.'

'Ah now yer makin' me depressed again.'

'Wait. I suppose you could get started and me and Liam could go and fetch the hogsheads from Galway. After that, we could both get to work and Liam could help us.'

'What about d' forge?'

'Ah feck the forge. If we get a job that pays money, we won't have to worry about it. Anyway, we're getting ahead of ourselves. He might have nothing at all for us.'

The two men turned up the drive and began the long walk up to the big house. Almost immediately, they ran into Mick Sheridan coming the other way.

'Is the master about, Mick?' asked Mikey.

'Lads, c'mere, dere's someone I want ye to meet.' He led them back to the barn where Ned was busy wiping down the big riding horse. 'Ned, look what just blew in.'

Ned dropped the cloth and rushed over to the two men. There was an outburst of handshaking and back-slapping and even one or two slightly awkward man hugs.

'Well, well, aren't you a sight for sore eyes, Ned Flood, you reprobate!' grinned Michael, whereupon the three men went through the greeting ritual again.

'Oy was in Gortalocca yesterday,' said Ned. 'Oy heard you two was busy.'

'It's the first real work we've had in a long time, Ned,' Michael told him.

'Well how are ye fixed fer a bit more real work?'

'If it pays money, Ned, we're interested. That's why we're here, to talk to the new master. Is he around?'

'He's ... emmm ... he's busy just now, talkin' to some men.'

'So when do you think we can see him?'

'Emmm ... dat's a hard one. D' master's a busy man sure, but Oy'll put in a good word fer ye.' Ned turned to Jamie. 'Oy see you're as talkative as ever, Jamie Clancy.'

Jamie spoke for the first time. 'I'm better at workin' dan I am at talkin'.'

'Fair play t' ya, James. Most people talk too much anyway.'

'This new master, Ned,' said Michael, 'what's his name?'

'Ah now, d' master's a private sort o' fella, Mikey. Oy'm not sure he'd be happy to have his name bandied about.'

'Jayzis,' exclaimed Mikey. 'What's all the secrecy about this fella's name? We can keep a secret, can't we Jamie?' Jamie nodded.

'Do ye promise not to tell anyone, not even yer wives when ye're ticklin' 'em in bed? And Mikey, do ya promise not to tell yer mam, even if she t'reatens to pull yer ears off?'

'Ah for the love of God,' sighed Michael. 'We promise, Ned, you have our words on it.' Jamie nodded enthusiastically.

'Alright so. D' property belongs to Michael Flynn.'

Mikey stepped back in surprise. 'That's the name I was born with, before I took Grandad's name, Mam's da!'

'I know,' grinned Ned, 'it's quite a coincidence, ain't it Mikey?'

'Do you think he's kin?'

'Ah ya never know now, boyo, stranger t'ings have happened.'

Michael and Jamie said they had to get back to Gortalocca and they bid Ned and Mick good day. As they left, Ned smiled when he heard Jamie mumble to Mikey, 'If Ned was in charge, sure we'd all be in tall corn.'

Mick looked at Ned suspiciously. 'Yer a lyin' toe rag, Ned Flood.'

Ned feigned offence. 'Don't know what ya mean, Oy'm sure. What lie am Oy supposed to have told?'

Mick thought for a moment. 'I can't t'ink of one offhand,' he said, 'but ya didn't tell d' truth, dat's fer sure. What in God's name was all dat about Michael Flynn?'

'It's a lot easier, Mick Sheridan, to dance wit' d' trut' dan an outright lie. If you'd care to check d' records, you'll find d' land was purchased by one Mr. Michael Flynn.'

'But dere ain't any Michael Flynn sure,' objected Mick, puzzled, 'only Michael Hogan.'

'Well dat's where yer wrong, boyo,' said Ned, with a wry grin. 'He might only exist on paper, but he exists just d' same.'

'I knew a fella, once,' said Mick. 'He used to dance round d' truth too. I t'ought he was d' best at it, but you put him to shame.'

'Sounds like he was my kind o' fella.'

'I'm sure he was. His name was Liam Flynn, Mikey's da.'

CHAPTER 10

'We'll be leavin' tomorrow, Mam.'

'As soon as that, Robbie?'

'I don't t'ink I asked enough fer dat cottage, you know. Mick agreed d' askin' price o' four shillin's without even haggling.'

'Did he indeed? I knew Mick had done alright for himself in the horse trading business but I'd got no idea he had that sort of cash.'

'He just pulled out his purse and paid me d' money, if you don't mind. Said he wanted d' house as soon as possible. Told me dere was good business to be had up in Donegal and dat I ought to get meself up dere.'

'Ah it's a long way to Donegal, son.'

'I know, and once yer in Donegal, it's a long a way to Tipperary. I got d' feelin' he wanted me as far away from here as possible.' Robbie grinned. 'Hey Mam, maybe Mick's got eyes fer ya. He seemed fierce anxious to get his hands on d' cottage.'

'You mind your tongue, Robert Flynn, I'm still your mother. Ah, it'll be grand to have Mick for a neighbour. I never really thought you'd leave, I hoped it was just another one of your bright ideas.'

'I have no choice, now, Mam, d' house is sold.'

'You'll be leaving young Peg with me so?'

'I will. I thought she'd be heartbroken about us leavin' without her but she took it well. In fact she's bin helpin' us pack our stuff.'

'Ah sure who knows what goes through a young girl's mind, Robbie.'

'I feel like everyone's waitin' in line to kick me in d' arse to leave. I don't care. I outgrew dis place a long time ago.'

'Well I for one am sorry to see you go, Robbie, but you have to follow your dream.'

'I doubt Mikey an' dat shite-fer-brains Clancy will be sorry to see d' back o' me. By d' way, what in God's name are dey doin' wit' all dem barrels?'

'Not a clue, son.'

*

'I am pleased to report dat you are now d' proud owner of d' Flynn cottage, Ned,' said Mick.

'Grand. When's Mikey's brother leavin'?'

'Say's he'll be gone by tomorra.'

'And when will d' fields be plowed?'

'As soon as he's gone. What d' ya want me t' do wit d' cottage anway.'

'Give it to Michael's mam.'

'Roisin? She won't take it sure.'

Mick saw the enigmatic smile he'd begun to grow accustomed to. 'Yes she will,' replied Ned.

'You're wrong, I'm tellin' ya.'

'You let me worry about dat, Mick. Now, what about Hogan's? Can it be rebuilt or do we have t' tear it down?'

'D' walls are still good, but d' whole inside is gone. It'll need a new roof too.'

'How long will it take?'

'If Mikey and Jamie get to work on it, and if dey can get d' wood, I'd say a month.'

'Michael and Clancy ain't available. Anyway, a month's too long. I want d' bar and shop up and runnin' in two weeks. A village ain't a village without a spirit grocery.'

'But dere ain't no village, sir,' lamented the white-haired man said sadly. 'Gortalocca's dead. It went up in smoke a few days ago.'

'Get away out o' dat, Mick Sheridan. Sure aren't we only just getting started? Now, do ya t'ink ya can get Roisin and Morna to pay me a visit?'

'Are ya plannin' on tellin' 'em who ya are?'

'Not yet, Mick,' grinned Ned. 'Oy'm havin' far too much of a good time playin' Santy Claus.'

*

A fresh wind had begun to blow from the northwest as Captain Rackham stood on the deck. He had a sextant in his hand and he took a shot of the sun.

'Time?' he asked Alexander, who stood holding a big silver watch.

'Nine forty-four and thirty-seven seconds, sir.'

'It's time for us to do our mathematics, Alexander. Come below with me. We'll do some trigonometry and calculate where we are.'

'Yes, sir.'

'Mr. Washington, check the cargo. With the seas increasing, I don't want one of those hogsheads getting loose. It would be bad enough to get sunk by a cannon ball or a reef. I don't want to get holed from the inside out.'

The black fellow knuckled his forehead and smiled. 'I've heard tobacco can be hazardous, sir.'

The captain nodded. 'See to it,' he said, 'and meet me in the wardroom later. We'll have tea and discuss our plans.'

Alexander was already engrossed when Rackham arrived below deck. He was checking the sextant reading and the time and working out the calculations. He looked up at the captain excitedly.

'I think I have it, sir.'

'Do you think you have it or do you know you have it?'

'I have it, sir.'

'That's better. Now you look it up in the declination book while I check your calculations.'

The boy toiled at the tables and finally announced. 'We're about nine miles west-north-west of Tearaght Island, sir.'

'About? Alexander!'

'Sorry, sir, it's eight point seven miles.'

'A third of a mile can get you killed, lad, and wreck the ship into the bargain.'

'Sorry, sir,' the boy repeated.

'I don't want you to be sorry, I want you to be accurate. Sailing is an imprecise art and there's no room for avoidable error.'

The boy hung his head. He should have known better than to give Jack Rackham a position that the captain would view as dead reckoning.

'There's no harm done this time but don't do it again.'

There was a knock at the door and Abraham Washington entered.

'The cargo is secure, sir. You wanted to talk to me.'

'I did, come in. We'll be past the Skelligs in a few hours, then Dursey Head in a couple more. I was thinking that, with this fair wind, we could make a direct run to France. But first I need to know where Willoughby's brig is.'

'Then you're taking us to France!' exclaimed Alexander, his face lighting up.

'Not you I'm afraid, Alex, nor Mr. Washington. I'll put you both ashore near Castletownbere or we'll hail a fishing boat to take you to Bantry. You can get a coach to Limerick, then another one on to Tipperary.' The young man looked crestfallen. 'It could get hairy,' said Rackham, 'if we find ourselves caught between Courser and Willoughby.'

Washington frowned. He knew that since his captain hadn't named the brig but rather its captain, it was personal. He also knew that when two big dogs live in the same house, sooner or later they're going to tangle with each other.

'Transferring passengers at sea could be dangerous, sir,' ventured the black man.

'We'll pull into Bantry Bay, the water's protected there.' He smiled and clapped his hand on Alexander's shoulder. 'We have to make sure this young man here has something to tell his grandchildren.'

The captain had already made up his mind so there was no further discussion about the merits or debits of his plan. Aboard ship, the captain's word was as solemn as God's own.

*

Robert and his wife left for Nenagh first thing the next morning. He gave his mother a kiss on the cheek and told her that one day he'd come back a rich man and then everyone could kiss his arse. It wasn't how Roisin had anticipated her son's departure, but Robbie was Robbie. Young Peg watched as her family left and, instead of shedding tears, she smiled, took Roisin by the hand and walked back inside the cottage without even a farewell glance.

Mick showed up an hour later leading a parade of horses and ploughmen and he had soon set them to work, tilling the fields. Shortly afterwards, four men from Borrisokane showed up and began to survey the ruins of Hogan's. They began to pick their way around the charred stones, discussing the damage.

Roisin saw them and marched over. 'If ye're thieves or looters, ye're too late. We've already picked through and there's nothing left of value so get your arses out of here before I really lose my temper.'

Mick had just been making his way over. 'Hold yer horses, missus,' he called. 'Dese lads are here to rebuild d' place.'

'Oh well, in that case they're not thieves at all … they're feckin' madmen.'

'Not as mad as ya t'ink, Roisin. Dey're gettin' ten shillin's fer it and dey're goin' to make it bigger.'

'Says who?'

'Says d' new owner. Dat reminds me, he wants you and Morna to go and visit him up at d' big house.'

'Has he lost the use of his own legs? You can go and tell Mr. Bigshoes that if he wants to see us, he knows where he can find us.'

Mick knew only too well, from past experience, that Roisin was working herself up into a royal state and he wanted no part of it.

'I'll relay d' message, m'um.'

'You'll relay nothing, ya sheep head! Never mind. I'll get Morna and we'll go down there ourselves. Can ya believe the bollocks on that cow flop, asking a frail old lady like meself to walk all that distance, just to pass time the time of day with a mad Corkman and his eejit of a boss?'

Mick wished he could witness the imminent confrontation up at the big house but he was too busy overseeing the workmen.

'Morna, get your shawl!' yelled Roisin. 'We're off to pay Mr. Flood and Mr. Bigshot a little visit.'

In less than an hour, Roisin was pounding on the door of the Johnson house, first with her open palm and then with her fist. A maid answered but, before she could say a word, Roisin had pushed past her into the entrance.

'You can tell Ned Flood and Mr. Highbritches that Mrs. Roisin Flynn has come … as summoned!'

'Mr. Flood's out riding, madam, and there's no Mr. … Highbridges, was it? … in residence here.'

'Well you'd better go and find someone, deary, before I start breaking things.'

'Please madam, stay calm,' said the maid. 'Have a seat, won't you.' She motioned to a large settee inside the receiving room. 'May I get you something?'

'You may! You may get me a big stick because I'm going to start smashing things around here soon.

'I meant can I get you something to cool your temper?' said the maid, 'a bucket of water, perhaps?' With that, the girl picked up her skirt and sprinted out of the room, leaving the two women sitting on the settee, Roisin fuming. She ran to the stables where Ned was involved in a one-sided conversation with a horse.

'Mr. Flood! Mr Flood! There's a mad woman in the

house. I really think you ought to come. Her face has gone purple and I'm afraid she'll burst a blood vessel.'

Ned patted the horse's neck and smiled. 'Ah yes, Oy was expectin' Roisin.'

'You might want to bring a pitchfork or at least something to defend yourself with, sir. The woman's in a fierce state!'

'D' ya t'ink Oy'll get by wit' me charms, Nelly?'

'You'll need all of them, sir, I think that woman's a banshee.'

A couple of minutes later, Ned entered the room where Roisin and Moira sat and, on seeing him, Roisin stood up and clenched her fists at her side.

'Calm down, woman,' he laughed. 'If we get into a fist fight, Oy t'ink Oy can take ya.'

'Are you threatening me, ya turd?'

Ned held up his hands in surrender. 'I wouldn't dare,' he said. 'Now, what seems t' be d' problem, missus?'

'Hogan's is the problem, my store. There are men down there and they're nosing around. They're talking about rebuilding it.'

'Well Oy t'ought dat would make ya happy.'

'How can I be happy when someone else is rebuilding what belonged to me. I should've been consulted. My permission should've been asked.'

'D' boss don't need to ask nobody's permission.'

Roisin's face began to flush again. 'You listen to me,' she fumed, 'my da built that business up from nothing and I was born and raised in that place.'

'What if Oy was t' tell ya dat place is still yours?'

'I'd say you were a bigger gobshite than I thought.'

'Maybe you're right but it don't alter d' facts. D' new boss wants Gortalocca to come back to life an' he says it can't do dat widdout Hogan's.'

'Is his name Hogan?'

'No, it's Flynn.'

'I know it is, Mikey told me. So you tell me, how the feck can it be Hogan's if a Flynn owns it?'

'Oy didn't t'ink Mikey would be able to keep dat secret. Dat's why d' boss wanted ya to come here yerself. He wants ya to run it fer 'im.'

'I'm not working for somebody else in my own place!'

'Oy t'ink you need a drink, missus,' said Ned, heading for the oak sideboard. 'Oy know Oy do. Let me get us one an' den Oy'll explain d' proposition.'

Ned poured some whiskey from a crystal decanter into a small glass. He held the little glass up, looked at it and shook his head. He picked up a large tumbler, poured the contents of the small glass into it, then filled it to the brim and handed it to Roisin.

'Dere now, missus, dat'll settle yer nerves.'

Ned held out the whiskey decanter to Morna who shook her head, then he poured himself a large glassful before sitting opposite the two women on a matching settee.

'Now den, a village needs a bar and a grocery and dose t'ings need somebody to run 'em. I was talkin' to d' boss out dere in d' barn a while ago. He's rich and he could just as easily build a new one but he knows Hogan's was d' heart o' Gortalocca fer a long time and d' life and soul o' d' community around here. Make no mistake, he ain't doin' dis fer you. He's a businessman, after all. He reckons if he can bring d' village back to life, den it's good fer business.'

'What's the catch, Ned Flood?'

'No catch. After d' bills is paid every month, you give him a quarter o' d' profits, dat's all.'

'That place hasn't made a profit in years.'

'It will, Roisin, you wait and see.'

'When will I meet this new business partner of mine?'

'Ya might of seen 'im already, without knowin' it. He don't look like a rich fella … dresses just like any udder Oirishman. Ya know what dey say, ya can't take d' bog out o' d' Oirish, no matter how much money dey have.'

'Well what does he look like?'

'Ah he's ordinary enough, 'bout dis tall.' Ned held his hand high over his head and dropped it slowly down until it came to his own height, then dropped it to his side. 'Will ya have anudder glass o' whiskey?'

'I won't. We're going now. You can tell your boss that Mrs. Hogan agrees to his proposition, in principle mind.'

'I will, and if you don't want anudder drink, Oy know Oy do.'

Morna and Roisin left Ned draining the decanter and began the walk back to Gortalocca.

'I t'ought ya was goin' to kill him to start wit',' said Morna.

'I thought about it Morna, but how would you go about killing Ned Flood. Six Prussians tried it once and they're all pushing up shamrocks in West Cork. All we can do now is put our trust in him and our new benefactor, the mysterious Mr. Flynn.'

CHAPTER 11

Gortalocca was a veritable hive of activity. Even in its halcyon days the village had never seen such a mass of humanity, building and working the fields. Twenty teams of horses tilled the soil which had once been mostly pasture, while ten men worked on rebuilding Hogan's, expanding it so that it could comfortably seat twenty, perhaps even thirty people in the main room. Piles of burnt timber were removed and stacked at the back so the men could work unhindered.

Ned rode up on a flashy chestnut charger to survey the progress and Mick walked over to greet him.

'I see ya have yer skinny ridin' britches on, sir. Ya look a proper English gentleman.'

'It'll take more dan skinny britches to make an Englishman out o' me, ya cheeky turd.'

Mick smiled. 'Work's comin' on well, sir. Dey t'ink Hogan's will be ready to open in a week and d' fields should be ready to plant in a few days.'

'When do ya t'ink d' last danger o' frost will be, Mick'

''Bout two weeks I'd say, sir, mid-April or thereabouts.'

'Dat'll be just about right. Me udder partner, he's an expert when it comes to growin' d' crop. He should be here in a week or so.'

'What will we grow, sir? Wheat? Barley?'

'Neither.'

'What so?'

Ned changed the subject. 'We'll be needin' about fifty hands to tend d' crop. Two acres is about all one man can handle.'

'Dat's no problem, sir, dere's a lot o' men out o' work around here. We should be able to get fifty men fer, say, tuppence a month each.'

'In my experience, Mick, ya only get what ya pay for. Oy want d' best. Get d' word out Oy'm payin' t'reepence. Oy don't want drunks or lazy bastards or fighters, and I don't even care whether dey're men or women. Women are more reliable. We could leave d' men tendin' deir own fields and hire deir wives.'

'Dat might not go down too well, sir, beggin' yer pardon, if d' women take home more dan d' men.'

'Oy don't give a tinker's shite,' said Ned, mildly irritated. 'If money is tight, den dey ought to be t'ankful fer it, no matter how it comes.'

'If you say so, sir.'

'I do,' replied Ned and his easy-going humour returned. 'Now, d' ya know where Morna is? Oy need to talk to 'er.'

Mick had spent the entire conversation gently stroking the neck of Ned's horse. 'Dunno, at home p'raps,' he said absent-mindedly, his focus still on the horse. 'He's a grand beast, sir. Does he have a name?'

'He does, o' course,' replied Ned with a wry grin. 'Mick Sheridan, meet Mr. Michael Flynn.'

*

'Dursey Head off the port bow!' came the shout from a topman on Prosperity. At the announcement, Captain Jack Rackham appeared on deck, followed closely by Alexander, then Mr. Washington. It was spitting a fine rain, what the Irish would call it a soft day, but there was nothing soft about it. In this cold air and fresh breeze, the mist would soak a man through in minutes.

'Watch out for the shoals!' Rackham yelled back.

'Aye aye, sir!' came the reply from above the deck.

'We're off the Beara, gentlemen! Now we have to find a fishing boat and see if we can get some information, and we have to get you two ashore. Don't look so gloomy, Alexander, your journey's not over yet.'

'The best part of it is,' replied the young man.

'Steer north-by-east when Bear Island comes into sight, Bosun,' the captain told the man at the helm, who knuckled his forehead.

'Aye, sir.'

Jack handed the brass telescope to Alexander. 'Keep an eye out for a fishing boat, lad. If you spot one, give a shout.' The boy went forward to the bow and began to scan the calm waters in Bantry Bay. 'He's sulking,' said the captain to no one in particular.

'He's afraid he's going to miss the action, Jack,' said the black man.

'If that lad ever saw any action, Abraham, he wouldn't know whether to shit or go bald.'

Abraham chuckled. Considering the risks Jack Rackham took, the entire crew should be hairless and have full britches by now.

'Aye, sir,' he said, simply.

An hour later, Alexander returned and handed the scope back to the captain.

'Fishing boat four points off the port bow, sir.'

'How far?'

'A little over a mile, sir. She's small, looks like a curragh.'

Jack went to the bow to see for himself. 'Take her leeward of the boat, Bosun. Be careful not to run her over.'

'Aye aye, sir.'

The helmsman drew the ship up close, then headed it into the wind to allow the sails to luff. The vessel drew itself to a grudging halt and hovered within sixty feet of the fishing craft.

'Ahoy, there. Have you seen the British brig Albatross?' The men on the boat looked at each other as if a foreign language had been spoken to them. It had, the men only spoke Irish. One of them shouted something and the captain looked around him.

'Does anyone here speak this damn gobble-de-gook?' he yelled.

'I do, sir,' the topman shouted.

'Thank the Lord for that, Flanagan. Now's your chance to earn an extra ration of grog.'

'Should Oy come down an' talk?'

'Not unless you need the exercise, you bog-Irish. You can talk from up there. Ask them if they've seen the Albatross.

Flanagan conversed with the fishermen in the small boat for what seemed an age.

'Well? Have they seen her or not?' asked Rackham, impatiently.

'We didn't get dat far yet, sir. Seamus was jus' tellin' me about 'is sister.'

'Seamus, is it? Well unless Seamus' bloody sister is aboard the Albatross, we're not interested.'

'Aye, sir.' Once again, Flanagan engaged the fishermen in conversation and Rackham heard the word 'Albatross' thrown around. 'Cap'n, dey say she got caught up in d' gale last week.'

'The Albatross or Seamus' sister?' said Rackham sarcastically.

'The Albatross, sir. She got her riggin' badly damaged and she's in Baltimore harbour gettin' it repaired. Seamus wants t' know do ya want any mackerel?'

'Thank him and tell him no to the mackerel. Good man, Flanagan, you'll have an extra ration of rum tonight. Bring her about, Bosun. Let her fall off the wind. The heading is south-west. Let's get out of Bantry and head out to sea for now.'

'Am I coming to France with you, Captain?' Alexander asked hopefully.

'No you're not, but the plan just changed again. Leave me alone for a few minutes, I have to think this one out.' The young lad and the burly black man turned to walk away. 'Not you, Mr. Washington, you stay here, I need to bounce an idea off your skull.'

Alexander left and went below deck to sulk.

'I thought you already had a plan, sir?' said Abraham, as soon as the boy was out of earshot.

'I have.'

'Would you care to share it, since me and the boy seem to be part of it?'

'We're going to Baltimore.'

'Jesus Christ, Jack! The lion's in a cage, you have a clear shot to France, and what do you do? You decide you have to get in the cage with it!'

'Oh come now, Abe,' said Rackham with a glint in his eye. 'I just want to see what the vessel we're up against is like.'

97

'No you don't! You just want to get a measure of Willoughby. You don't give a damn about the Albatross, you just want to go eyeball-to-eyeball with that Englishman.'

'Ships don't fight ships, as well you know. It's the men who run them that go up against each other.'

'This is no game, Jack, the stakes are high here.'

'Everything's a game, Mr. Washington. Ned understands that and so do you.'

'We both know Ned's as mad as a March hare and I don't know why you're including me in your observations.'

'Because, you old hypocrite, you're still here even though you have more than enough money stashed away to live the rest of your life in tedious comfort.'

'The reason I'm still here is because Ned gave me my freedom and a lot more besides. I owe him a debt I can never repay and I have an obligation to see that you two don't get yourselves killed.'

'Well thank you for that, it's good to know. With you looking out for us, we have nothing to worry about. I wonder how Ned's getting on.'

'If I know Ned, he's probably got those poor Irishmen scratching their heads by now, or their arses, or both.'

*

'For the love of God, Jamie, are you going to be fidgeting all the way to Galway? Sit still.'

'I can't sit still. Me arse is itchy.'

'Then pull your britches down and scratch it, man.'

'Would ya ever have a look an' see if I have a boil or sumpthin.'

'I will not! I have a hard enough time looking at your face, never mind your arse. Can't you just go to sleep and leave me alone?'

'I'm glad dis is our last trip t' Galway. I'll be happy t' get home an' sleep in me own house, even if dat auld innkeeper does cook better dan me wife.'

'Maybe Ned has some job or other lined up for us. Jayzis Clancy! Will ya stop that feckin' scatchin'!'

*

Ned rode back to Johnstown, feeling pleased at how well his plans were going. He'd managed to get everything underway without revealing his identity or even having to lie in order to cover up his little conspiracy. He'd spoken to Morna and enlisted her services in cooking for those who worked the fields, having made sure an oven big enough to bake bread was built at Hogan's. He issued instructions that every person to put in a day's labour was to get a bowl of soup and a loaf of bread. Who said you can't buy loyalty, he thought.

When Michael and Jamie arrived back, Ned would put them to work building the drying house, probably on the hill where the faerie ring stood. The air would circulate better if the drying barn was on higher ground. Even a bountiful harvest would be wasted if the crop spoiled. Let's see now, a hundred acres and another two acres of hemp for twine. He calculated that he'd need a drying house about eighty feet long, twelve feet tall, and about fifteen feet wide. The Irish climate was unpredictable so he would have a fire pit down the middle of it. That way, there wouldn't be a day wasted if the weather became inclement. He imagined it to be a super-sized oast house, like the ones used for drying hops.

Ned began making calculations in his head. Five months wages for fifty people, that would come to about ten pounds. It would cost a few pounds more to get the land ready for sowing and probably another two pounds to put the village in order. Even with a short growing season, he should get almost one hogshead per acre. If he delivered his produce to England, he should get eight pounds for each, but if he was to bring them to France, it would be twice that. He counted on his fingers. That was a lot of money by anyone's standards. He smiled to himself. Whoever thought that doing a good deed would turn out to be so profitable?

'C'mon, Mr. Flynn, let's go home, fella. By next autumn, you'll be d' richest horse in d' world.' The horse snorted and nodded his head as if he understood. 'And don't worry, boy, dey don't hang horses … dey shoot 'em.'

CHAPTER 12

C aptain Jack Rackham stood on the bow of his ship scanning the horizon with his scope. He snapped it shut. The frigate Courser was patrolling between Fastnet Rock and Clear Island and, in the absence of the brig, its captain had moved his ship inshore. The wily old fox has us cut off from the open sea, he thought.

'Take an east-north-east heading, Jones,' he told the bosun. 'We'll take the pass between Sherkin Island and Cooslahan Point.' Rackham knew that if Captain Harford was still in command of Courser, he would be too cautious to risk the rocks offshore. That meant Rackham could take his ship north into Baltimore harbour and anchor there safely.

'I'll take the wheel,' he told Jones. 'You go and tell Master Alexander and Mr. Washington that I'll see them below for a briefing.'

The bosun knuckled his forehead and bowed back momentarily. 'They're waiting in the wardroom, sir.'

'Good. Take the helm, Bosun.'

Before Jones could respond, the captain had disappeared below deck. He paced the floor, his back bent to avoid the overhead, while he issued his instructions to Washington and the boy.

'Gentlemen, we shall be taking part in a little play-acting when we get ashore to Baltimore. Mr. Washington, you are to become this young gentleman's manservant.' The big man nodded and awaited further instructions. 'It's only a role you're playing but it's better if you don't speak unless it's absolutely vital. All you have to do is behave like an obedient negro. Alexander, you are to be the stuck-up rich brat from the colonies. You're travelling to England to finish your education.'

'Just so I'm clear, sir,' said Abraham, 'what exactly is an obedient negro meant to behave like?'

Jack sniggered 'You take orders and you say 'yes sir' to everything that's asked of you.'

'I do that already.'

'Good, then you have nothing to worry about. Now Alexander, your part may be a little more difficult. The most important thing is that you're not to give anything away to whoever we run into, especially if it's Willoughby. I've heard he's a very clever fellow and he'll be looking for whatever information he can get. Make believe that you're looking down your nose at him, that you're not impressed by the uniform and if he asks you a question, answer only with yes, no, or you don't know.'

'What if he asks me a question I can't answer with any of those options?'

'Then you must use your brain, lad, talk your way around it. You've heard your father do it often enough and don't forget, always remain aloof. No matter how friendly or cordial this fellow acts, he's an adversary … not an enemy, mind you …. just an opponent. I shall introduce you as Alexander Flynn, the son of a rich planter from…. oh I don't know, Savannah. Yes, that's it, I'll say you're from Savannah, in the Georgia colony. That way, if he does make any enquiries, he'll be looking for a phantom. Do you understand what you have to do, Alexander?'

'I understand your instructions, sir, but I can't say I understand the reasoning behind them.'

'Good!' Jack smiled. 'That's good. If a reasonable man can't decipher the reasoning, then unless Willoughby's a madman, he won't be able to either. Now, I'm going to fill my belly with biscuits.' The boy looked puzzled. 'And no, Alex, I won't tell you why.'

Alexander looked questioningly at Mr. Washington.

'I'd say the captain's getting ready for some serious drinking and he's going to use the ship's biscuits to sop up the alcohol in his gut.'

Jack winked at him and laughed.

*

Roisin stood looking about her, scratching her head. What she saw was almost inconceivable and it overwhelmed her. Just a week ago this village was all but dead and now it was as if it had been resurrected. The new addition to Hogan's was already in place and the roof was in the process of being re-thatched. The new fireplace was enormous compared to the one on which she'd cooked all those meals for all the hungry patrons who'd come into the bar for a pint and a bite to eat.

Mick was engaged in animated conversation with the builders. Hogan's had been a small thatched cottage like all the others in the village when Roisin's parents first arrived in Gortalocca. Whenever her father had needed more space, he would just build bits on in a haphazard fashion. This time it was being built as a dedicated spirit grocery with separate doors for the bar and the shop. The more Roisin looked at it, the more she realised it was going to be too much for her to handle by herself if ever it was to become busy again.

Morna walked over and stood beside her mother-in-law. 'Oy can't believe me eyes, Mam. I never seen so many people in d' village.'

Roisin nodded, neither had she. 'You're going to have to help me run the place, Morna.'

'Oy can't, Mam. Ned asked me t' cook fer d' people workin' in d' fields. He says dere'll be nigh on fifty people and dey all have t' have bread and soup.'

'I'll ask Kate Clancy so. She'll be glad of a penny a week.'

'You can't, she's helpin' me, Mam, and Ned says he'll pay us a shillin' a week each. I can get Siobhan t' help ya in d' bar and Peg can clean up a bit.'

'I won't have my granddaughters working in a bar.'

'Peg's no younger than you were when you started helpin' yer da in the shop and Siobhan's sixteen years old sure. It's about time she knew somet'in o' d' world. P'raps she'll even meet a nice boy.'

'She won't find nice boys in any bar.'

'Wasn't it in that very bar you met Mikey's da, Mam?'

Roisin assumed an indignant expression and stalked off without another word. She didn't like it when someone bested her in an argument and, to her, every discussion had the makings of an argument. She made her way over to where Mick had just finished talking with the builders.

'I suppose you've been telling those strangers how Hogan's should be, ya bold mug. Did it ever occur to you that I might like to put my two penneth worth in, being as how I'm going to be running the show?'

Mick wasn't sure why Roisin was in such bad humour but he thought he'd try to pacify her with some news. He was about to make his first and worst mistake of the day.

'D' Flynn cottage is still empty, Roisin.'

'Sure don't you think I know that already? When are you moving in?'

'I ain't.'

'Why not? You paid four shillings for it.'

'I did not.'

The colour had begun to rise in Roisin's face. 'Are you saying my son's a liar?'

Mick took a step back. 'No, well yes, everybody knows Robbie's a lazy, lyin' bag o' dung but it wasn't me who paid fer it. I don't have dat kinda money.' He grimaced and unintentionally looked down at the hole he'd just dug for himself.

'Jayzis! You're as big a gobshite as Ned Flood.'

'Dat's exactly it! It was Ned. Ned gave me d' money to pay Robbie on behalf of Mr. Flynn. Mr. Flynn bought d' cottage, but den he changed his mind, said 'e didn't need it anymore.'

Roisin narrowed her eyes. 'You mean Mr. Flynn took four shillings and threw it away, just like that?'

'He didn't t'row d' money away, I just explained. He bought d' cottage wit' it, den he t'rew d' cottage away.'

'You can't throw a house away, ya eejit. Look, there it stands'.

Mick felt himself sinking deeper into the hole. 'Mr. Flynn told Ned to give d' house to you. I told Ned you wouldn't have it. Says I, I know Roisin Flynn and she won't …..'

'Roisin Flynn won't WHAT?'

'… won't take Mr. Flynn up on 'is offer.'

'Hold yer horses, now let me get this right. Someone offers me a house for nothing and you take it upon yourself to decline on my behalf because *you* presume to know what *I'm* thinking?'

'Dat's about d' top an' bottom of it.' Mick was in imminent danger of disappearing down the hole now, never to be seen again.

'You're a feckin' eejit, Mick Sheridan! Now you get your arse down to Johnstown this minute and you tell Mr. Flynn that Mrs. Flynn accepts his offer of the cottage and thanks him kindly for it. Then tomorrow morning, first thing, you get that arse back here and you help me move my stuff. Have you got that?'

'Yes, m'um,'

'Feckin' eejit.'

*

Ned was in the barn feeding the horse when Mick arrived.

'In 'ere, Mick,' he called. 'Oy'm more comfortable in 'ere wit' d' horse dan Oy am in dat big house. Now, what news d' ya have fer me?'

'Everyt'ing's grand sure. Roisin's movin' back into d' Flynn cottage.'

'Didn't Oy tell ya she'd snap up d' offer ?'

'I didn't t'ink fer a minute she would, but ya never know what folks is gonna do, especially women, and especially anyone from dat Flynn family.'

'Oy'll bet ya didn't come out o' dat little encounter without a bruise or two. Ah well, come Judgement Day, Mick, d' Big Fella'll take it all into account.'

'She said I was to t'ank Mr. Flynn.' Mick put his hand on the horse's neck and the beast turned around to look at him, still chomping. Mick stared him straight in the face. 'T'anks a million, Mr. Flynn.'

The horse buried his face back in the feed bucket.

*

It was almost dark when Rackham and his two fellow conspirators climbed into the jollyboat to row across the harbour and into Baltimore.

'Very well, everyone has their instructions. Now if I'm not back by nine o'clock tomorrow morning, it means the jig is up. Jones, don't bother to haul the anchor, just slip the cable and get the ship out of here. Head for the Isle of Man and unload the merchandise. Don't bother going to France. Have you got that?' Rackham's fingers drummed on the leather-bound case in his lap.

The bosun nodded. 'Aye aye, sir. You don't want us to come looking for you?'

'I do not. I can take care of myself. I'll leave the ship in your hands and she is your highest priority.'

The next ten minutes was spent in silence, except for the rattle of the rowlocks and the water stirring as the oars dipped and lifted, and the sound of Jack's fingers tapping rhythmically on the box on his knees.

When the boat bumped into the dock, the three men clambered up and Jack whispered softly. 'See you in the morning, Jonesey.'

The captain looked around to see where he'd be most likely to find Willoughby. He spotted an inn which overlooked the bay and, from there, Willoughby would be able to observe his ship at anchor.

'Come on, boys. Let's see if our friend is receiving visitors.'

Willoughby was indeed inside. He was sitting at a corner table where he could watch the door, his back against the wall. It wasn't lost on Rackham. When Jack and the others sat at a table in the opposite corner, Willoughby nodded to them but made no further acknowledgement.

'Well that wasn't a great success,' whispered Alexander.

'Be patient,' the captain told the boy. 'Ignore him. If he has any ego at all, this will be killing him.'

It wasn't long before Willoughby stood up and straightened out his uniform.

'The fish is nibbling,' whispered Jack under his breath.

The Navy officer remained standing for a moment more, then strolled casually over to the table, feigning disinterest.

'Got him!' said Jack softly.

'Good day to you, gentlemen,' said Willoughby, ignoring Mr. Washington. 'Allow me to introduce myself. I am Captain Willoughby of his Majesty's Navy. Who do I have the pleasure of addressing?'

Rackham stood up and shook hands with him. 'I'm very pleased to make your acquaintance, sir. I'm Captain Rackham of the schooner Prosperity, from Charles Town.'

'Rackham, eh? Wasn't there a pirate called Rackham? The scab was hanged in Jamaica if I recall correctly.'

The Naval officer hadn't wasted any time in making a shot across their bows.

'Before my time, sir,' said Rackham.

'Indeed,' said Willoughby. 'I heard he sailed with a whore named Anne Bonny.' A broadside had been fired with no discernible effects.

Jack shrugged. 'Ah women,' he smiled, 'who knows what secrets their hearts hold?'

'And who may I ask is this?' Willoughby's gaze unnerved the boy and he shot up out of his seat to recite his line.

'I'm Alexander Fluh... Flynn, from Savanah in the Geo... Georgia colony, and this is my manservant. I... I'm going to England to finish my education.'

'Well let us hope they can do something about that stammer, my boy.' Alex blushed, he knew he'd botched the only line he had.

'May I have the pleasure of sitting with you gentlemen?' Willoughby glared at Abraham until he vacated his seat, then he took out a linen handkerchief and wiped the chair before he sat down. 'Really, my boy,' he said, eyeing the walking stick in Washington's hand. 'Surely you could have acquired a manservant who isn't a cripple.' Abraham gritted his teeth.

'I'd say he's somewhat more useful than your own, sir,' said Alexander haughtily, motioning to a marine sergeant who had passed out at Willoughby's table.

Willoughby followed the boy's gaze. 'Yes, well, good help is hard to find these days. Now, may I buy you two gentlemen a beverage?'

Alex looked at Rackham, who nodded, and Willoughby got straight down to business.

'Are you carrying any cargo other than your two passengers, Captain?'

'I am, sir, yes. I have ten hogsheads of tobacco from Maryland.'

'And I take it the documents for it are in order?'

'They are indeed. I see the Courser is accompanying your ship on blockade, sir. I served aboard her once as a midshipman and an ensign. Is Captain Harford still in command?'

'Yes he is and he's still every bit as stiff as I'm sure you remember him to be. He follows procedure so rigidly that I'm surprised you learned anything from him. He's known around the fleet as Hardfart.'

'What ship were you on when you served your time as a midshipman, Captain Willoughby?'

'I was on HMS Comet.'

'Were you really?' laughed Jack. 'We called her HMS Vomit, the slowest second rate in the fleet!'

Like two heavyweight fighters, each contestant was trying to discover the other's weaknesses.

'I'll wager your fellow midshipmen called you Rackie, am I right?' said Willoughby watching for some change in Jack's demeanor.

'Me? No, they called me Rocky … as in rocks and shoals. You were Willie, no doubt.' Willoughby felt a crimson flush creeping up from his neck so he feigned a cough and held the handkerchief to his face, then remembered he'd wiped the seat with it before he sat down and dropped the square of linen to the ground. Blood had been drawn.

'That was a long time ago,' he grumbled.

'Of course. Now if you'll excuse us, sir, I have to get my passengers bunked down for the night and find them a coach to Macroom in the morning. Perhaps when I return later, you and I could share a game of chess.'

Willoughby rose, gave a slight nod of assent and returned to his own table.

Jack organised a room for Alexander and Abraham then arranged passage for them to Macroom, where they would hire a coach to take them to their destination. Washington was more than a little perturbed at the Englishman's behaviour.

'Forget it, Abe. He was just fumbling around in the dark, searching for a weak spot.'

'I thought he'd found one when he made the remark about Anne Bonny. I'd never let a man get away with calling my mother a whore.'

'The truth often offends, my friend. When my mother was young she did have somewhat of a ... let's call it a reputation. Now you two get some sleep, the innkeeper will wake you in the morning. Under no circumstances must you go downstairs until the coach is here. If Willoughby sees you, he'll resume his informal interrogation and he's not to be under-estimated.'

The captain left his two charges in their room and returned to the bar. Willoughby joined him at his table and Jack set up the chessboard, making a deliberate show of taking the ivory and ebony chess pieces from their leather case and placing them on the board.

'You can tell a lot about a man by the way he plays the game,' said Willoughby, growing impatient.

'You can, indeed, Captain,' Jack agreed with a smile.

Several hours and two games later, both of which Jack lost, the two captains called it an evening. Jack considered it a success. He had learned everything he needed to know about Willoughby. The captain of the Albatross was delighted he'd won both games, oblivious of the fact that he'd just divulged far too much about himself by the manner in which he'd played. Those two seemingly innocent games had played an important part in a much larger, much more serious contest that was play out later.

CHAPTER 13

'Good mornin', Mr. Sheridan. Is it headin' to Gortalocca y' are to help d' widow Flynn move into her cottage?'

Mick was busy stuffing his mouth with bacon and mustering up the courage to face Roisin again.

'Dat woman has her temper on a hair-trigger, Ned. Maybe ya ought to come wit' me. Ya seem to have d' knack of tampin' down a fire before it gets out o' control.'

'Oy will o' course, Mick, Oy wanted to check d' work anyway. Oy need t' have a word wit Mikey and Clancy about somet'in too. Have ya put word out we're lookin' fer hands fer d' plantin'?'

'I have, sir. I'll have no bother gettin' fifty good people. Can I ask again, what is it we're plantin'?'

'Ya can ask, Mick, but I won't be givin' ya a straight answer, not 'til after Oy've talked to Mikey and Jamie anyhow. Now let me get some breakfast inside me, den we'll go into Gortalocca together.'

Michael and Clancy were up at the old church,

unloading the last of the barrels from the wagon, when Ned and Mick arrived. Roisin, Morna and Siobhan were already carrying various items over to the Flynn cottage and young Peg was busy inside, putting things away.

'Mick, you help d' ladies, I need t' talk t' Mikey.'

Ned made his way towards the church. Clancy saw him coming and spoke to Michael in a low voice.

'Now remember, Mikey, we must have work. We'll take anyt'ing he offers, agreed?'

Michael nodded. 'Don't worry, Clancy, Ned said he'd talk to Mr. Flynn. I'm sure he'll have something for us.'

'And how are yous two doin' dis fine mornin'?' Ned said cheerily. Just then, it began to rain.

'Grand thanks, Ned,' said Mikey. 'Did you manage to find work for us?'

Ned laughed. 'Dat's what Oy like, a fella who gets right t' d' point.'

'Well, do you have a job?'

'Oy do, in fact Oy have a big job fer ye. Ya might even have t' hire a few extra hands t' get it done. Come and take a walk wit' me, boyo. Oy'll explain.'

Michael left Clancy to finish the unloading and caught up with Ned, who was walking in the direction of Knigh.

'D' ya know what a hops oast is, Michael?'

'I do o' course, it's a building for drying hops. Is it hops we'll be growing?'

'Not exactly, Mikey, but we're goin' t' need a dryin' house. Can you and Jamie build it?'

'You just tell us where and how big and, if we can get the materials, we'll build it.'

'Oy want it over dere.'

Mikey followed the direction Ned was pointing in and found himself looking straight at the copse of trees which topped the faerie ring.

'You can't build there, man, that's the caher. Those places are haunted by spirits and if you violate one, it'll bring bad luck.' Michael coughed. 'At least that's what some people believe.'

'How's yer luck bin lately, Mikey?'

'I was only saying....'

'If you won't do it, Michael, Oy'll only have t' find someone who will.'

'But you don't understand.'

'No, it's you who don't understand.' Ned was becoming irked. 'Don't you talk t' me about violatin' sacred ground when here y'are after stashin' rum barrels in a church. Now you listen t' me, Michael Hogan. A long time ago, you was a priest, den ya fell in love an' den ya wasn't a priest anymore. Once Oy dressed like a Franciscan and Oy went around killin' soldiers, just so you and yer wife could escape. Me and you are goin' to burn in hell, my friend, one way or anudder. We might as well save d' village before we go. What d' ya say?'

Michael knew that everything Ned said was true and he felt the guilt of his own past weigh heavily as it came back to haunt him. He tried to rationalise things in his head.

'Well, I suppose faerie forts are only from the pagan days anyway. They don't really have anything to do with Christianity.'

'Dat's right, and don't worry about yer family's graves, we'll put a fence around 'em. Dey won't be disturbed.'

'You'll have to get someone else to help me clear

the land up there though. Jamie won't have anything to do with it.'

'Jamie's welcome t' keep his superstitions and starve if he wants to, dat's his choice. But unless Oy'm mistaken, if you say it's alright, den he'll go along wit' it.'

'You're a mystery, Ned Flood,' said Michael, and that familiar grin, the one which mocked the universe, spread across Ned's face.

'C'mon, Mikey, let's you an' me go an' help yer mam move back home.'

*

Jack Rackham returned to his ship in an ebullient mood.

'Let's get this ship out into open water, Jonesey. Raise her sails and haul anchor, it's time for us to go and make some money.'

'Aye aye, sir,' said Jones. 'The men were getting tired of hurling insults at the English brig anyway.'

'When we're out of the harbour, you and I will have a little conference below. Don't forget, you're second-in-command now, ya Cornish pasty.'

Half an hour later, Jones was below deck with his captain.

'We can't see Courser, sir. I have men looking out for her on the bow but so far there's no sight of her.'

'She's probably out west of Clear Island hoping to pounce on some poor Frenchie who wanders too close. England's at war with France … again.'

'Should we fly a Dutch flag, sir?'

'No. We'll stay under English colours until we get near France. We won't be able to use Calais or

Cherbourg. Every time France and England go at it, the Frogs end up with their fleets bottled up there. We'll go to Douarnenez. The Pouldavid estuary's too shallow to hide a French warship of any size so the Admiralty will probably ignore it, for a while at least. I'll plot a new course, Jones, I'll see you back up on deck.'

'There she is, sir!' The frigate was below the western horizon with just the mastheads visible. As the captain had predicted, she had been lurking just west of Clear Island.

'If we can see her then she can see us. No matter. Let's go to France and drink some wine, Jonesey. The heading is due east … next landfall, Tristan Island.'

'Did you know that island was named after a fella from my territory, sir?'

'I didn't know that. How did a Cornishman ever get an island in France named after him?'

'The Frogs have songs about it. An Irish princess called Iseult got rescued by a Cornish Knight, name of Tristan. There's tales of love potions and the like.'

'My guess is it was the cognac, Jonesey. Every time I drink that stuff I fall in love.'

'You might be right, sir, me too. It's not 'til I sober up I realise it's the brandy I'm in love with, not the woman.'

*

Captain Willoughby was up early and eating breakfast in the bar. He had determined from the manner in which Rackham had played chess the night before that he was a defensive player. Even when an opportunity had presented itself, or a trap had been laid, Rackham had been slow to react. This fellow had clearly been schooled in the art and science of tactics by Captain Harford. He was cautious, slow and measured. Willoughby's own strategy, on the other hand, was to attack and attack again, always keeping the opponent on his heels. He snorted in derision. Rackham had no doubt acquired his post through family connections and not by his own merit. It was obvious to Willoughby that Rackham had neither the brains nor the stomach to be a captain, much less a smuggler. Even so, there was something about the man that bothered him, something he couldn't quite put his finger on but made him uneasy. Of course Rackham could just be pretending to be a dullard but, if that was the case, he certainly didn't have the makings of a challenging adversary. Perhaps the nervous boy could provide more information when he came down for breakfast.

'Are we eating before we leave, Mr. Washington?'

'No, Alexander, we're not. If the captain's right, and he usually is, Captain Willoughby will be downstairs waiting for us. He told us to stay in our room until the coachman knocked.'

Willoughby checked his watch. He wanted to see the boy and his slave leave but he was also anxious to check on his ship. At a few minutes past nine, a coach pulled up outside and the jarvey entered. He asked the innkeeper which room his passengers were in then headed up the stairs. Willoughby rose from his chair and waited. Soon his prey would appear and he would be ready for the ambush.

The driver came back, followed closely by Alexander and Jeremy, and Willoughby stepped between the black man and the boy. In naval terms, he had broken the line.

'Ah, Master Fluh Flynn,' he said, mocking the boy's awkward faux pas from the previous evening. 'I was hoping you would join me for breakfast before you left.' Washington edged out from behind the blockade and stood close to Alex.

'I'm sorry, sir,' Alexander muttered, 'but we don't have time.'

'Oh surely you could spare a few moments.'

Abraham put his hand firmly on the young man's shoulder. 'We must be leaving, sir, your father will be waiting.'

Willoughby wasn't about to be thwarted by the impudence of a slave.

'Take your hands off of him, you black bastard,' he spat. 'Someone should teach you some manners!' He reached for the cutlass which hung at his side. Washington remained silent but gripped the handle of his walking stick until his knuckles grew pale. If Willoughby made even the slightest move to draw his blade, he would decorate the walls with his blood.

'He's no bastard,' blurted Alexander. 'I knew his mother and his father.'

The captain's eyes narrowed. He'd noticed the night before how defensive the boy became whenever he perceived any slight against the dark fellow.

'Ah yes,' said Willoughby, his eyes glinting. 'I've heard how a person can get attached to one of those. I imagine it must be the same as having a pet mongrel although, since I've never owned a dog or a slave, that's only conjecture on my part.'

Alexander's face flushed red and Abraham knew that Willoughby had found the weakness he was looking for. If he didn't get the boy out of there soon, he was likely to say something the Englishman could use against them. He rapped his walking stick against the boy's leg and it knocked Alexander back into the moment.

'It has been a pleasure to meet you, Captain Willoughby,' Alexander had resumed his composure, 'but I really must be going. My father is expecting me.'

Willoughby gave a slight bow and stood aside to let them pass but he kept on watching and listening as they left the premises.

'Did I do alright, sir?' whispered Alex, but not quietly enough for the naval officer not to hear. As the coach pulled away, Willoughby walked outside and watched as it disappeared down the road. Once again his eyes narrowed. There was more to this and he meant to find out what it was.

*

Roisin's belongings were neatly packed away in her old cottage and the big mirror which Liam had made for her so long ago was rehung in its rightful place above the fire. Michael lit a turf fire to chase away the early April chill and the men walked outside just as the builders were finishing their work for the day.

'C'mon, lads, let's go over to Hogan's and see how far d' men've got.' Ned walked over and began to inspect the building but Michael, Jamie and Mick stayed together in a knot.

'What's going on, Mick?' asked Michael.

'De're rebuildin' d' store sure.'

'You know, Mick, I can never tell whether you're just acting stupid or whether you actually are stupid.'

'What d' ya mean?' asked Mick, with a slight air of indignation.

'I meant what's the story with Ned and this Mr. Flynn and everything else that's been going on around here? First Jamie and I are paid silly money just to go to Galway and bring some barrels back, then Ned shows up with his boss and turns the place on its head.'

'Ah sure dat's an easy one to answer. Weren't we all ready t' bury Gortaocca, like so many udder Irish villages, just a couple o' weeks ago? Now look, d' place is busier dan it ever was. Don't ya see? It was all a test. God tested our strength and we stayed. We passed His test.'

'Or maybe God wanted us to leave and we defied Him. Did that ever occur to you?'

'Ah no, I don't believe dat fer a minute, Mikey. We needed help and God sent Ned to straighten t'ings out. Dere's yer proof, over dere, dere's Ned.'

'Did you ever think that maybe it's the devil who sent him?'

'I did not, and don't be talkin' like dat.'

'The Bible tells us that when Jesus went out into the desert for forty days, the devil showed up with food and offered Him the world.'

'Agh sure Michael Hogan, you don't have d' faith and anyway, d' divil never built Jesus a bar, did 'e now?'

CHAPTER 14

Michael broached the subject of the faerie ring with Jamie and, as he had predicted, the blacksmith wanted no part of it. The parishes of Killodiernan and Monsea had once been dotted with ring forts known as dun, liss or rath and many of the old people believed they were the dwelling places of faeries or wraiths. As times got worse and resources grew scarce, lime kilns were built next to them, their trees cut for down fuel and their stone harvested like a crop. Even so, there were still those who believed it to be sacrilegious, or at least unlucky for anyone who dared to desecrate one of them.

'But it's just some auld trees and a few stones, Clancy, nothing more.'

'I don't like it, Mikey. You don't mess wit' dose places. I've heard about people walkin' in dere and never comin' out again. I'll have nutt'n to do wit' it.'

'C'mon Jamie, come with me and I'll show you. I'll walk in one side and if I don't come out the other, then we'll both know you're right.'

'Well as long as it's not me what's got t' do it, you

work away. If ya come out d' udder side, den maybe I'll t'ink about it.'

'Right so. Let's go and get a stretch of the auld legs.'

Mike took the lead and Jamie followed. When they came to the edge of the wooded area, Clancy stopped.

'Dis is as far as I go,' he announced.

Where once still stood the scattered remnants of Ireland's ancient woodlands, only scrubby thickets of shrubs grew now, good for nothing other than hedge-bute, temporary fences, and plough-bute which was timber good enough for repairing ploughs. All the mature trees in the parish had gone, except for this little grove and a few on the big estates owned by the landlords.

Michael took a tentative step forward, then another. Clancy half expected him to disappear right there in front of his eyes but he watched as Mikey ventured further into the grove. The thick canopy of trees overhead made it hard to see but Michael could just make out the forest floor, carpeted with undergrowth and woodland debris ... leaves, half-rotted twigs and branches which had fallen over time. Occasionally a pile of stones, some stacked, others scattered on the ground, suggested that this place had harboured men at one time or another. As Mikey picked his way through, he was all of a sudden startled by the rustle of some small creature unseen in the undergrowth.

'Get a hold of yourself, man!' he scolded himself out loud. 'It'll just be a rabbit or a dormouse.'

He stopped when he estimated he'd reached the centre of the circle and took in his surroundings. It was peaceful, the shadowy silence interrupted only by the sound of the wind through the still-leafless branches of early spring. The blacksmith lost himself for a moment in the quiet stillness of this place and imagined an Ireland covered by forests, the trunks of old ash and oak trees forming columns, the envy of any cathedral builder. He was abruptly snapped out of his reverie by the sound of twigs cracking rhythmically, like foot falls, and his imagination momentarily ran away with him. His heart was beating so wildly that he thought it would leap out of his mouth. Perhaps Jamie had been right. Perhaps he really had violated some unspoken law and nature was about to wreak vengeance on him, face-to-face!

It was Jamie. Whether compelled by curiosity or loyalty, Clancy hadn't been able to wait outside.

'Jayzis, man, you scared the shite out of me! I thought you were an evil spirit or something.'

'Why? Have ya seen any?' asked Jamie, his eyes darting around anxiously.

'Of course I haven't. There's nothing and nobody here, Jamie, except me and you and some auld trees.'

'It still gives me d' screamin' habdabs, Mikey.'

'Don't let your imagination get the better of you, Clancy. We've cut down a thousand trees to feed the forge and there's enough wood in here to build three barns. Think about that.'

Jamie looked around him, this time at the trees. 'It'll take months to turn dese trees into wood we can use.'

'I'd already thought of that. If we cut down the trees, we can trade them at Ballyartella sawmill for sawn planks. That way we can start building sooner.'

Jamie eyed a moss-covered pile of stacked stones suspiciously. 'What d' ya t'ink o' dem, Mikey? D' ya t'ink somebody lived here once?'

'Who knows? Once, probably, but whoever it was left a long time ago.'

The wind picked up without warning and rattled the bare branches all around them.

Jamie shuddered. 'I t'ink somebody just walked over me grave.'

'Let's get out of here. It's going to start raining again and I have to get to Johnstown. I'm determined to talk to the mysterious Mr. Flynn if I have to wait all night.'

'If it's all d' same t' you, Mikey, I'm goin' home to spend some time wit' me wife.'

'It's all the same to me Clancy and if I had half a brain, I'd do the same.'

*

'Come in out o' d' rain, Michael. Oy have a story t' tell ya an' it might take a while. Here, have a seat by d' fire an' warm yerself. Oy've got somet'n dat'll warm ya from d' inside out.'

Mikey sank into a comfortable armchair near the fire and Ned poured him a whiskey, then went to sit beside Mick who was already seated on a couch facing Michael.

'Now,' said Ned, 'where do Oy begin?'

The blacksmith sipped at his whiskey. 'The beginning seems as good a place as any,' he said redundantly.

'Right so. Well, after we buried yer Uncle Robbie, an' don't forget Oy'm talkin' nearly twenty years ago now, me and Mary had a purseful o' money he left me and a dream of going to Mary Land in Americay, t' strike it rich. You know dat much, right?' Michael nodded. 'Well, we went from here to Queenstown and we booked passage on a ship dat was droppin' off a load o' tobaccy before goin' back to Mary Land wit' a cargo from England. Anyway, as it turned out, it didn't go straight to Baltimore, it stopped in New York first. Oy was watchin' while dey unloaded all d' stuff and I'd never seen so many riches. Most o' d' men doin' d' work was Scots Irish who'd fell on hard times and had to sell demselves in indenture t' feed deir families. Dey'd break deir backs fer seven years before dey'd get deir freedom, and den dey was cut loose. Most o' dem was broke and widdout jobs so most o' dem had to sell demselves back to d' bosses fer anudder seven years. Dey wus nutt'n but white slaves, Mikey, and it scared d' shite outta Mary to see d' poor craters. It didn't scare me though. It made me t'ink somebody must be makin' a lot o' money off d' sweat o' dem poor fellas.

'When me and Mary gets t' Baltimore, Oy heard an Oirishman talkin' one day. Dat fella had been in d' colonies fer more dan twenty years and he had a piece o' land. See, when he got dere, dey was givin' land away, so people would settle dere. Dis fella had two hundert acres dat d' gov'ner had given 'im and all he wanted t' do was get back to Sligo to 'is wife. So Oy gave 'im ten pounds sterlin' fer d' whole kit and kaboodle, widdout even seein' it. Yer man signed d' deeds over to me and all of a sudden, Oy'm d' owner of a feckin' big farm and a log house.

'Well you know how Oy was back in dose days, Michael. I was full o' piss and vinegar and Oy t'ought to meself, how hard can dis farmin' business be? Oy'd never known a farmer who was a genius. Oy supposed ya just turned over a piece o' land, t'rew some seeds in and it grew all by itself, so dat's what Oy did. We ended up havin' to buy our food dat year. Oy could see all dese big farmers around me makin' money hand over fist so Oy knew Oy was doin' somet'n wrong. Well, d' next year came and dere I was one day, hoein' d' ground, when dis black feller limps up, usin' a branch to help him walk. He sits 'imself down on a tree stump and 'e watches me. Next day, dere 'e is again, in d' same spot, and he watches me all day. Well, Oy'm gettin' fed up wit' dis so Oy walks over to yer man and Oy asks 'im what 'is name is and why he ain't workin' d' fields like everyone else. He says 'is name's Washington, bein' as how dat's d' name of d' fella who owns him. Den he asks me if Oy've got somet'n fer 'im to eat because he ain't eaten nutt'n but roots and seeds he picked up in d' woods. Well, Oy know what it's like to be hungry so Oy takes 'im home and Mary makes 'im some porridge. Yer man wolfs it down but I knew he was still hungry and too polite to ask fer more. I told Mary to give 'im anudder bowl and dat, my friend, was d' second smartest t'ing Oy ever done.'

Michael shifted his weight forwards on the chair because, once again, Ned had another tale that wasn't making any sense. His host poured him another glass of whiskey but didn't pour himself one this time.

'Will ya have somet'n to eat, Mikey? Ya will sure.'

'No, I'm grand thanks Ned. Just get on with the story.'

'Right so. Anyway, dis black fella, Abraham Washington's 'is name, he'd hurt his back so he wasn't any use to his owner and yer man just t'rows him out to starve. Well, maybe he wasn't any use to his owner but dat fella knew everyt'ing dere was to know about growin' tobaccy and Oy knew nutt'n. So Oy goes t' see his owner and Oy asks 'im if Oy can buy dis fella's papers. O' course yer man's delighted, t'inks he's sellin' me a lame horse so Oy bought Abraham Washington fer five pounds. Oy told him if he'd teach me how t' grow tobaccy, Oy'd give 'im his freedom and dat, my friend, was d' smartest t'ing Oy ever done. Sure dat year Oy made sixteen pounds and Oy signed Abraham Washington back over to himself. O' course he had no place to go so 'e stayed on wit' me. I told 'im he could be me partner and I'd give him a share of d' profits.'

'So your partner was a darky?' exclaimed Michael.

Ned grinned. 'Me partner still is a darky, as ya put it … d' last time Oy looked anyway, and he's a rich man too. Now let me get on wit' d' tale. So Abraham's no fool and he knows d' best way fer him to make money is fer me to make money, so he comes up wit' a plan. D' plantations were startin' to move away from indentured men and gettin' slaves to do d' jobs instead, so dere was all kinds of Oirish lookin' fer work. Most of 'em had worked tobaccy fields and dey knew d' job inside out. So d' next year, instead o' t'ree acres, we planted forty. Dose fellas were better at it dan Oy was and we turned a profit of nearly a hundert pounds. D' year after dat, we had all two hundert acres in crop and we made nearly six hundert pounds.'

Michael whistled when he heard the amount.

'D' t'ird year, we rested half d' fields, because tobaccy sucks d' life out o' d' land, and we planted half in clover and put twenty cows to graze on it. We planted d' udder half and still made four hundert pounds. By dat time, me son Alexander was born. Poor Mary had a hard time givin' birth and it took 'er a long time to recover. D' boy was grand because we had d' help of a wet nurse, who just happened to be Abraham's wife. He'd bought her freedom from d' farm where she worked.

'Now, as Oy told ya, Mr. Washington ain't no fool. He invents anudder idea … says we should plant tobaccy on d' mounds and plant clover in d' furrows. He says, dat way, we can keep all d' fields goin' at d' same time without spoilin' d' soil. So we did dat fer two years and made more dan a t'ousand pounds profit both years. Den, o' course, d' feckin' King raised d' tariffs and dat cut our profit by nearly half. Between d' shippers and d' Crown, dey bled us dry. We held production each year but d' profits were shrinkin'.'

Ned's expression became sombre and he turned his head towards the flames of the fire licking around the turf.

'Poor Mary died givin' birth to our second child and d' baby died along wit' her. Me whole world fell in on me.' He paused for a moment. 'Oy had money and Oy had me son but none o' dat made up fer d' loss. Oy decided Oy'd try and drink d' world dry and dat went on fer a bit until finally, one day, Oy looked at me son and t'ought, Oy ain't gonna do to him what me da did to me, so Oy stopped drinkin', just like dat. Around dat time, one o' d' local planters wanted to expand his operation. He made me an offer fer me farm dat Oy couldn't turn down so dere Oy was, at t'irty-t'ree years auld, a rich widower wit' a young son and nutt'n to do.

'Oy moved to Baltimore and Oy bought a big house. Ah sure Oy enjoyed d' life fer a while alright but society people had no use fer me, me bein' Oirish and all, so Oy went back to d' drink. One night in a bar, Oy ran into a young navy Lieutenant who was fed up like me and we got talkin'. One t'ing led to anudder and we agreed to meet again d' next night to talk business. Oy'm gettin' hungry, Mikey. Will we have some dinner? Oy can tell ya d' rest' o' d' story after.'

'Will we meet Mr. Flynn after too?' Michael asked. A smile began to spread across Ned's face and Michael's eyes narrowed. 'There is a Mr. Flynn … isn't there?'

Ned laughed. 'Oh dere's a Mr. Flynn alright,' he said, 'and after Oy've finished me story, Oy t'ink it's high time yous two met.'

CHAPTER 15

'We have company, sir.'

'I'll meet you up on deck, Jonesey. What is she?'

'Can't tell, sir, just a masthead above the horizon.'

The bottom rim of the rising sun had already cleared the open sea and it wasn't yet eight o'clock. The captain appeared on deck, buttoning his coat against the early morning chill.

'Where?'

His second-in-command pointed to a white dot gleaming in the distance. Rackham extended his telescope and watched for a few moments.

'Change course. Take us due south and let's see what she does.'

Jack went below. The cook brought him a mug of tea and he had just finished it when Jones appeared again.

'She's tracking us, sir. She's mirroring our course but still closing.'

'Very well. Reverse our course and take us north,

just to be certain. I'm going below to shave and get something to eat.'

Jones reappeared just as Jack had finished shaving and he was noticeably nervous.

'She's tailing us, Cap'n. It's a sloop, Bermuda rigged, about eight miles away.'

'She's faster than us and she'll point into the wind better. Get me the ship's carpenter.'

Damn bad luck, he thought. He'd never run into a patrol boat here before. The ship's carpenter appeared before him in short order and knuckled his forehead.

'Aye, sir.'

'I have a task for you, John. I want you to make a wooden canon as quickly as you can. It doesn't need to be perfect, just cobble something together fast, the size and shape of a six… no, make that a nine-pounder.' He grinned to himself as he imagined it.

'But sir, you can't shoot a wooden canon. The Irish tried it during the war. It blew up in their faces and killed the gun crew.'

'I know that John but if someone pointed a gun at your head, you wouldn't ask if it was loaded, now would you? Just do it.'

The captain went out on deck and checked the position of the pursuing craft.

'What do you think, Jonesey? About seven miles, would you say? Put us back on our heading to France and then run up French colours.'

'She'll be on us by noon, sir.'

The sloop was closing to around five miles when the hastily-made makeshift cannon was carried on deck by three men.

'Set it up in the bow, men. We're going to put on a little show for our guests.'

132

When the sloop closed to within four miles, the captain yelled, 'Bring her about, men! We're going to war!'

The ship reversed its course smartly and the sails filled, putting it on a heading straight for the hunter, the wooden nine-pounder bow chaser looking convincingly menacing from a distance. The sloop's commander responded by turning beam on and loosed two shots from her little two-pounders. The cannonballs plopped into the ocean over a mile short and the sloop continued her turn, trying to get some distance between her and the schooner. She continued to sail away until her mast disappeared over the horizon.

'How did you know she'd break off, Cap'n?' asked Jones.

'It was the wisest thing for her captain to do. He was outmanned, out gunned and taken by surprise. If you're getting chased by a dog and you keep running, he'll nip at your heels. If you turn and run after him, he'll think you're more ferocious than he is and he'll back off.'

'What would you have done if he'd called your bluff, sir?'

'I'd have surrendered, Jonesey. As captain, it would have been the wisest thing to do.'

*

The three men had finished their dinner and were sitting around the fire. Ned smoked a Cuban cigar, Michael puffed on his pipe and Mick coughed whenever their smoke found its way up his nostrils.

'Now,' said Ned, 'where was Oy? Ah yes, Oy'd just met Jack Rackham.'

Mike leaned forward in the chair, his elbows resting on his knees so that he could hear every word the Corkman said.

'Jack Rackham was bitter young man. He'd been passed up fer promotion by d' Admiralty, just because a few auld fellas still remembered his da was Calico Jack, d' pirate, and his mam was Anne Bonny. Oy told 'im, Oy says dere's all kinds of pirates and some of 'em are even in d' House o' Lords. He told me he calls it d' House of Forty T'ieves and o' course he's right, what wit' d' taxes and tariffs dey raise. Anyway, one t'ing led to anudder again and Oy told him Oy'd like to buy a ship. He says it ain't as easy as dat and he tells me ships cost a lot o' money. Oy had money but, just like growin' tobaccy, Oy didn't have d' knowledge. He tells me his grandfadder owns a shippin' company down in Charles Town, in d' Carolinas, but dat his sister Suzanne runs d' show because d' auld fella's past it. Next t'ing ya know … me, Abe Washington and Jack Rackham are on a coach headin' fer Charles Town.'

'Nothing you do happens at any normal pace, does it, Ned,' said Michael, shaking his head. 'You get an idea and, no matter how hair-brained the scheme is, you throw yourself right in. Lucky for you it seems to have a habit of working out.'

'Ah well let me finish d' story Mikey because it worked out even better dan ya t'ink. While we was on d' long ride, to pass some time, Oy told 'em about what happened down in West Cork, when Oy had a bit o' fun wit' dem soldiers. Abraham had never heard d' whole tale and Jack sat like a child listenin' to me adventure story. When Oy was finished, Jack shakes me hand 'til Oy t'ought me arm would come off me shoulder and he keeps sayin', "It's d' game, my friend, d' game, ya played d' game and ya won!'" Dat's d' first time Oy realised, it wasn't killin' dem poor Prussians Oy'd enjoyed, it was d' game.

'So we gets to Charles Town and Jack is still kissin' me arse like Oy was d' bare knuckles champion o' d' world. When we arrived at an office near d' docks, dere's a little fella wit' white fuzz on 'is head and spectacles on 'is nose and he's sittin' at a desk like he owns d' place. Jack walks right past 'im and goes t'rough a door to d' back, where dere's a woman sittin' at anudder desk. He whispers sumt'n to her and she stands up. She's short, and a bit on d' fat side, but not a bad looker mind. Anyway, it turns out she's Jack's sister, Suzanne. She runs d' business but people t'ink a woman ain't got a mind fer such t'ings so d' little fella out front is just fer show.

'Jack tells her about our plan and she seems interested but she keeps on lookin' me up and down like Oy was a prize bull at an auction. Den he tells her about what happened me in West Cork and, as she listens to 'im, she starts lookin' at me like Oy was Finn McCool himself. Well, Oy was gettin' embarassed but Oy don't mind tellin' ya, d' longer she looked at me, d' better-lookin' she got. Finally, when Jack was finished, Suzanne invites me home fer dinner. Oy was hungry and it seemed like a good idea so Oy says, says Oy, Oy will o' course. D' rest of us went and we got ourselves lodgin's and Oy got meself all dressed up, just like a proper Englishman.

'Anyway, Oy gets to dis grand-lookin' house about seven o'clock and a negro opens d' door. He invites me in like Oy was King George himself. Dere's a lady, about fifty years auld I'd say, already sittin' at d' head o' d' table and dressed up like a queen, wit' a fancy frock and sparkly jewels hangin' off her. She looks at me like someb'dy just dumped a cartload o' dung in her dinin' room and she don't say a t'ing ... just leaves me standin' dere, like a fence post. Den, t'hank God, Suzanne comes in, only dis time she's all dressed up too and she must have had a corset on because she looked grand, even if she couldn't breathe. She introduces her mam as Anne, and d' auld lady's still eyeballin' me. As soon as Oy opens me mouth, yer wan says, "Yer Oirish, so?". Oy tells her not only am Oy Oirish, Oy'm from Cork, d' best part of Oirland. Oy t'ink Oy saw d' hint of a smile on yer woman's face but she might have just had wind, I couldn't be sure.

'Suzanne invites me to take a seat at d' opposite end of d' table, so as me and d' auld lady can get a measure of each udder, den she tells her mam d' story Jack told her. Well, Oy had t' keep interruptin' because d' tale kept growin' in d' tellin' and she was makin' me sound more like Cu Chulain wit' every word. D' auld woman looked from Suzanne back to me a few times and Oy reckoned she t'ought d' whole t'ing was bullshite. When Suzy finished, Anne looks at me and she says, "Oy t'ought dat story about a phantom priest from Cork was a fairytale. At least," says she, "Oy t'ought you'd be bigger."

'We all ate ourselves a feast of a dinner and, when we'd finished, Anne told me some stories of her own. Dey was all about pirates and buccaneers. Wit' her all dressed up like a lady, she didn't look like no pirate to me but den Oy'd never seen a pirate before. Oy t'ink she was testin' me to see if Oy'd be shocked but, after what Oy've seen in my life, nutt'n she had to say bothered me an iota. Well I must have got d' auld girl's approval because she stands up, she looks at Suzanne

136

and she says, "Marry 'im.", just like dat. Den she got up and left. Dat's how our courtship began.

'Me and Suzanne spent d' rest o' d' evenin' alone and she explained a few t'ings about d' shippin' business. She said me and Jack had to shop around fer a proper ship and she talked a lot about stuff Oy didn't understand at d' time, but Oy pretended Oy did o' course. Ya know Mikey, dere's a funny t'ing about love and marriage. Too many people fall in love first and den, when dey're married, dey find out dey don't like each udder. Wit' me and Suzy, it was d' udder way around. We fell in like wit' each udder first.

'Now, it's gettin' late Michael and dere's still a lot left t' tell, but we'll conduct a bit o' business now and Oy'll tell ya d' rest anudder time.'

'Right so, Ned, but I would like to hear how the story ends.'

'Ah sure d' story won't end 'til dey pat me on d' face wit' a shovel. Business first now. Mick's bin overseein' d' work in d' village but it's time he started doin' what Oy hired 'im for. Michael, Oy want you to take over in Gortalocca. Any day now, Mr. Washington and Alexander will be here and den we'll start d' plantin'.'

'What crop are we growing?'

'Tobaccy, Mikey, Oirish tobaccy.

'So what's all the secrecy about?'

'Don't ya know it's against d' law, boyo? It's bin illegal t' grow tobaccy in Oirland fer fifty years or more.'

'Why?'

'Ach, don't ask me. Oy suspect it's because dey don't want d' small landholders here t' get deir hands on anyt'ing like big money. Or maybe dey're just protectin' d' big planters out in d' colonies, who

137

knows? Eider way, it's against d' law.'

'What happens if we get caught?'

'Don't worry, Mikey, dat won't be a problem.'

'Why not?'

'Because if we do get caught, d' only one who'll get d' blame is Mr. Flynn.'

'Your boss? So you'd sell him out?'

'He ain't me boss, he's me partner.'

'So you'd betray your partner?'

Ned smiled. 'Oy t'ink it's about time ya met Mr. Michael Flynn. He's been waitin' patiently out in d' barn. C'mon, let's introduce ye to each udder.'

CHAPTER 16

Michael sat at home in his cottage the next morning, his elbows on the table and his hands holding his head up. He'd woken up with a headache, not having slept at all well, and his poor brain was full to capacity. Just when he'd begun to process the news that a company had been set up in a horse's name, and that it didn't matter as long as no one knew it was a horse, he discovered that Ned owned a bank in Charles Town, that the horse had a bank account there and another one in London. If it's illegal to grow tobacco in Ireland, thought Michael, how in God's name can it be legal for a horse to have a bank account in London? Ned had told him that, as long as the taxes were paid, nobody gave a shite. He'd said the plan was foolproof. Michael wondered if Ned knew how clever fools could be.

'You got in late last night, Mikey, and ya never said a word about how ya got on up at d' big house.'

'I know, I'm sorry Morna. I had a headache and a lot to think about.'

'How's yer headache now?'

'Ah it's grand.' This was a true statement, the headache was indeed thriving. His poor head felt like it was going to explode at any moment.

Roisin bustled in, her face eager with anticipation. 'So,' she said, 'did ya meet Mr. Flynn?'

'I did.'

'And is he Irish?'

'Oh, there's no doubt about that.'

'Well? C'mon, Michael, tell us all about him.'

'What do you want to know?'

'Where's he from, for a start?'

'I didn't ask, but he's not from far away, I don't think.'

'Ah sure you'd know by his accent. That means he's not from Cork at least, thank God. How tall is he?'

'He's definitely taller than the average man.'

'... and ... well, what sort of build does he have to him?'

'Emmm ... I'd say he has a muscular build.'

'Michael Hogan, talking to you is like talking to Ned Flood.'

'I hope so.'

Roisin was getting frustrated with the lack of forthcoming information. 'Tell us what he looks like. What kind of a face does he have? What colour's his hair? What colour are his eyes?'

Michael rolled his eyes upwards in his head as if the answers were written on the inside. 'Well ... he has quite a long face ... but a kind look about him.'

'Ah God love him,' said Roisin, approvingly. 'That's the kindness of the Irish in him. The long face means he must be Anglo-Irish, some of them English look like woodpeckers. Go on.'

'Well let's see. His hair is a reddish-brown colour, he

has soft brown eyes and his lips are rubbery.'

'Ah, more Irish than English so. The English have such thin lips. We Irish have good mouths ... rotten teeth, but good mouths. How old is he would you say?'

'I don't know, Mam. I didn't look in his mou…, I mean I didn't ask. I'd say he's definitely in his prime though.'

'And tell us,' said Roisin, winking at Morna, 'is he handsome?'

Michael had just about used up all the answers on the inside of his head and he was afraid he'd give something away if he stayed much longer.

'He's handsome alright. Listen, Mam, I have to go. Jamie and I are cutting down trees this morning.'

'I heard about that Michael. No good will come of it, you mark my words.'

'Jayzis, Mam, it's just an auld pagan place. Anyone would think we were about to cut the legs off the Pope's throne.'

Michael left the cottage. His mother had found a subject for an argument and Roisin's world was full of them.

'Remember what I told you, Michael,' she shouted after him. 'No good will come of it!'

Jamie and Liam were already at the faerie ring when Mikey approached and Liam was watching Clancy as he finished putting an edge on one of the axes.

'A dull axe is a dangerous tool,' he told the boy. 'If ya hit a hard spot, d' axe might glance off and hit ya in d' shins and make a cripple outta ya.' The boy nodded soberly and Jamie continued with the lesson. 'Now, d' trees is close togedder so we'll need to plan which ones we should fell first.'

A soft breeze had already started to blow and the onset of an April drizzle began just as Michael joined them.

'I think we'll start with that ash, Jamie,' he said, pointing to a tree at the edge of the grove. We can hook Ned's team of draughts to the trunk and drag it out into the open, then Liam can start trimming the branches off it while we cut another.'

'Dere must be at least forty o' dem in here,' said Jamie. 'It's goin' t' take us a week or more t' cut 'em all down, an' den we gotta dig out d' stumps.'

'Well we'd better get to work so, Clancy. They won't cut themselves down.'

Liam cleared the twigs and branches from around the base of the tree so the men would have a clear place to work. The wind was blowing harder now and the rain had begun to pelt down. The trunk on the ash they had selected was a little over a foot in diameter. The seed it sprouted from had probably been carried here by a bird, or a fortuitous gust of wind, a hundred years before. Liam stepped clear and the two blacksmiths positioned themselves on opposite sides of the tree. They would alternate swings in a well-practiced choreography, cutting a notch into the same side of the trunk, a little more than halfway through. Mikey struck the first blow then waited for Jamie's swing.

Jamie hesitated for a moment. 'I'm tellin' ya, I really don't like dis, Michael.' Then he swung into almost the same place his partner had.

'It's just another feckin' tree, man,' Michael declared in response to his partner's protest. He swung his axe at a slightly lower angle and the first chip flew off the trunk effortlessly as the blade sliced the wood. The two men soon had their rhythm established and, within five minutes, the notch was cut and the tree was mortally wounded. The wind had begun to blow in gusts now. They moved to the opposite side of the trunk and began to cut another notch slightly above the first, so the two would intersect and form a hinge. After a few minutes the tree began to make an ominous cracking sound, then it went silent. The men stepped back and waited … and waited.

'You get out of the way, Jamie, take Liam with you. I think a couple more swings should do it.'

When he was sure that his partner and son were out of danger, Mikey swung the axe into the hinge. An errant blast of wind caught the leafless branches overhead and the trunk began to turn.

'Get out, Da!' cried Liam to his father. His warning wasn't necessary because Michael had immediately dropped the axe. First he back-peddled, then he side-stepped and then he broke into a crouched run. He'd only managed a couple of steps when he tripped over a tree root and fell on his face. There was no time for him to get up so he just closed his eyes and put his arms over his head. He heard a crack, followed by a groan, as the trunk split. After that, he wasn't sure if it was a thump he heard or whether he'd just felt it as the whole floor of the forest shook.

'Da! Are you alright Da?'

'I'm alright, Liam, I'm alright. What in God's name happened Jamie?'

'I'll tell ya what happened,' exclaimed Jamie. 'D' tree tried t' kill ya, dat's what happened!'

Michael stood up and brushed the forest debris off his clothes. His heart was beating as if it would burst out of his chest, but he wasn't going to let on to Jamie.

'Don't be such an eejit, Clancy,' he said, seemingly

unconcerned. 'Trees can't think anything or do anything on their own.'

'Well I seen it wit' me own eyes and I'm tellin' ya, when you was runnin' away, it was tryin' to catch ya!'

Michael finished brushing off his clothes and made his way to the tree stump. He needed to come up with a plausible explanation before Jamie got on his knees and began saying the rosary.

'Look at this, Clancy. The grain in the wood is kinked. There's a twist in it and, with the wind the way it is, the tree just took the easiest way to fall.'

Jamie wouldn't look. 'You said trees don't t'ink. If d' tree chose d' easiest way to fall, it must have bin t'inkin'.'

Michael decided that reasoning with Jamie was as fruitless as a dog chasing its own tail so he addressed his son.

'C'mere, Liam. Come and look.' The boy ran to see what his father wanted to show him. 'See the way the split ran up the trunk? It has a bit of a spiral in it. The tree had all those stresses inside the wood and when we made the cut, a hundred years of tension released all of a sudden, like cutting the string on a fiddle bow. Do you understand?'

'Where do the stresses come from?'

'Nobody knows for sure, lad, a combination of the wind and the rain and the sun probably. Or maybe it's like the beggar we saw that time in Nenagh with the club foot. Maybe they're just born that way.'

'Mam said she believed that man was cursed.'

'You're mam is from Cork, son, they believe a lot of strange things down there.'

'Ya mean God didn't do it?'

'He did not ... well, he might ... oh, I don't know.'

'Didn't they teach you that shite in priest school?'

'Maybe I was sleeping during that lesson, or maybe I didn't stay long enough to get all the answers to all the questions … and anyway, young man, don't be using 'shite' and 'priest' in the same sentence.'

'Sorry, Da. What'll we do now?'

'We'll get the team of horses, drag that tree out in the open and we'll clean the branches off it.'

'We won't cut any more trees today, so?' asked Clancy.

'It's too dangerous, Jamie. The wind's gusty and shifty, it's unpredictable. We'll clean off this log and we'll find something else to do.'

Jamie breathed a sigh of relief. No matter what perfectly rational explanation Michael had come up with for what had just happened, he had his own equally perfect irrational one.

'I'll hitch d' horses so,' he said.

Clancy began to make his way back to the pasture where the draught horses were kept but he'd only walked a short distance when he heard what sounded like a coach coming into the village from the direction of Nenagh. It came into full view travelling pell mell, slowed slightly as it went through the busy village, then continued on out at full speed.

'Did ya see dat, Mikey?' shouted Jamie. 'Dat's d' first coach I've seen on dis road in months.'

'Did you see who was in it?' Mikey yelled back.

'I didn't. D' windows was closed because o' d' rain.'

Michael thought it must be the mysterious Mr. Washington and Ned's son, Alexander. He was to find out soon enough.

*

'Lower the fores'il and the main, boys. We'll use the stays'il and the jib to manoeuvre ourselves behind Tristan Island. Nobody will see us from seaw'rd so we can get down to business.'

'Cap'n, the water's shallow at low tide. Do ya think maybe we ought to row an anchor out from the stern so we don't swing too much if the wind changes?'

'Good idea, Jonesey. Make it so.'

'Aye aye, sir.'

'Don't haul the jollyboat up when you're done, I need it. I want to pay the mayor a visit and get us out of here as soon as possible.'

'Aye, sir.'

Within the hour, Prosperity was anchored both bow and stern on the landward side of Tristan Island. Before he left, the captain told Jonesey to break out guns from the armoury and keep watch for anything suspicious. No one was to be allowed on board in his absence. Then the captain and four seamen rowed the boat to shore and the men stayed on the boat until the captain came back. A little over an hour later, he returned in a distinctly foul mood. As the men rowed him back to the ship, their captain was silent.

'Alright, Jonesey, here's the story,' he said, once he was back on board. 'The mayor says they don't have enough brandy or money at the moment. He suggested that we offload the cargo anyway and I suggested that he fornicate with himself. He said it'll take two days to get what we want and I told him he's got one day and that we'll sail to another town tomorrow afternoon on the tide if he doesn't come up with the goods. I don't trust that bastard. We'll post an armed guard all night to make sure he doesn't try an echaquier.'

'I'll make sure two men are armed and posted all

night, sir, but beggin' yer pardon, what's a 'hey jack queer'?'

'Echaquier, Jonesey. It means to relieve a rich man of his goods and maybe stick him in the belly with a knife for good measure. It's a term French highwaymen use.'

'Do you think he'll try something, sir?'

'I don't know but I'd rather be safe than sorry. Have the men keep an eye on the anchor cables. If I was going to meddle with a ship in shallow harbour, I'd cut the cables and let it drift ashore, then loot the cargo at my leisure.'

'Aye aye, sir. I'll post two extra men on deck at all times and give them three-hour shifts.'

'Good man. Now you get yourself something to eat and make sure the crew is fed. Tell the men they'll have to forego their grog tonight but that we'll give them each a triple ration when all this is over and we're safe back out at sea.'

'I'm sure they'll be pleased with that arrangement, sir.'

The captain knuckled his forehead. This trip had the makings of a nightmare. First the sloop of war and now a French mayor who Jack suspected to be more than a little crooked.

CHAPTER 17

T ed slapped Alexander heartily on the back. 'It's grand t' see ya, son. Jayzis, if ya keep on growin', you'll soon be able to eat peas off d' top of me head!' He extended his hand to Mr. Washington. 'Is he a good student, Abe?'

Abraham smiled. 'He's a good student alright. Jack says that, in a couple of years, he'll be able to run his own ship.'

'Fair play t' ya so, lad. Rather you dan me, Oy hate d' water.'

'I think Alexander is more than a little disappointed that he couldn't go to France with Jack. England's at war with them again, you know.'

'Agh, when ain't dey at war wit' someb'dy sure. Ah well, it's good fer business Oy suppose. D' English won't be sellin' tobaccy to d' Frenchies as long as dey're at war and dat means it's up to us t' keep dem snail-munchers supplied wit' leaves dey can stuff up deir noses. D' prices will be up and, if we get t'ings growin' well here, we can get it over dere in days instead o' months. So tell me, Alexander, what do ya t'ink of Oirland so far?'

'Well Da, there certainly looks to be some good farmland here but the country seems so … behind the times.'

'What d' ya mean, behind d' times?'

'It's the people, Da. They all live in such tiny worlds and they don't seem to know there's anything at all outside Ireland.'

'Dere ain't nutt'n outside Oirland, not fer dem, son. It's just d' same back home. Not everyone's d' same as you. You've lived all yer life in Charles Town, wit' ships comin' and goin' from every part o' d' world. But how much o' d' world do ya t'ink d' poor sods livin' back in d' hills see? When Oy was your age, Oy t'ought d' whole world began and ended in West Cork.'

Alexander rolled his eyes. 'We went through West Cork, Da, and I wouldn't give you a shilling for the whole place. It beggars belief that anyone could possibly wrestle a living off that land.'

'Well dey manage it, boyo.' Ned felt himself becoming defensive and a little hot under the collar. 'Maybe d' Oirish have a better imagination dan you.'

'I'm not arguing with you, Da. You asked me what I thought and I told you.'

'Ah sure maybe it'll grow on ya after a while, once you've seen its charm.'

'I promise to keep an open mind. Right now, I need to go and wash some of this Irish charm off myself.'

Alexander excused himself, leaving Ned and Abraham together.

'Young men are contrary individuals, Ned, especially when it comes to their fathers. When Alexander is away from you, all he does is talk about how wonderful his father is. When you're together, he feels the need to rebel against you. The easiest way to get him to say he likes something is for you to say you hate it. It's like the ships. He respects and admires Jack Rackham but he doesn't want to walk in his footsteps and be a ship's captain. He'd rather forge his own way in the world and go home every night to his own bed.'

'But Oy t'ought Alex loved ships just as much as you do.'

'I don't know what gave you the idea that I like being aboard a ship. I hate being away at sea, I've always hated it. I just knew that you disliked it more. You sent me out the first time because you didn't entirely trust Jack, even if he is your brother-in-law, and after that it was just assumed that I'd go out every time. I do it out of loyalty to you and so, you should know, does your son.'

'Jayzis, Abe, Oy'm sorry.'

'Don't be sorry, Ned. It's alright. Jonesey is second-in-command and he deserves it. All I do is relay orders from the captain anyway. Jones has been at sea for thirty years and he knows everything there is to know about ships. If you ever decide to expand the operation and get another ship, I'd put him in command of it if I were you. He might not be as daring or as flashy as Jack, but he's a good and steady hand.'

'Ah sure Jonesey's a grand fella altogether, Oy've always t'ought so. I see now dat Oy've never given him d' credit he deserves. Come to dat, Oy've never given you d' credit you deserve either.'

'Listen to me, Ned Flood. You took a poor, starving nigger and you turned him into a rich and prosperous man. Some things just don't need saying. Our next job is to raise a crop and help get some Irishmen out of hot water. Don't you worry about young Alexander, he'll turn out fine. He has a good heart, like his father. Now, let's you and me have a drink and a smoke.'

*

'What did I tell you, Michael Hogan? I said something would happen!'

'Ah Jayzis, Mam! Something's always happening, that's what somethings do.'

'Don't try and be a smartarse with me, ya spud. You're not too old for me to box your ears.'

'Whatever you heard, Mam, it probably wasn't what happened. It's sure to have been exaggerated.'

'How can you exaggerate being crushed by a tree?'

'Mam, if I'd got crushed by a tree I'd be dead, but here I am standing in front of you, alive and well. The only one to ever have managed that was Jesus himself.'

'You shut your wicked mouth! I won't listen to any more of your blasphemy.' Roisin put her hands over her ears.

'Good. Now I can say whatever I want, thank Jayzis.'

'I heard that!'

'I don't know why you're mad at me. I'm the one who almost got myself feckin' killed this morning by a haunted tree.'

'There, I knew it was true. You almost got killed and the tree was haunted, you've admitted it. And let me predict something else. That was just a little tree. When you get to the middle of that faerie ring, you'll be up against those ancient trees and they won't be outsmarted.'

'Trust me, Mam. I'm can outsmart a tree, even an

151

ancient one. Anyway, who told you what happened?'

'I heard Liam talking to Siobhan. When I asked him about it, his lips got tighter than an Englishman's pucker strings so I went and asked Clancy's wife. She told me what happened and she said Jamie's scared shiteless of that place.'

'Agh, sure you know as well as I do that Jamie's scared shiteless of his own shadow, Mam.'

'Did it ever occur to you that maybe he's brighter than you give him credit for?' With that, Roisin turned on her heels and walked away, her back as straight as a poker.

Who knows, thought Michael, maybe he is. He decided they'd attack the trees again tomorrow and, if there were any more accidents, then perhaps it would be better to burn the grove down.

*

'Can you hear it, sir?' said the seaman.

The captain tilted his head and, sure enough, he could hear the sound of men on shore, a hundred or more yards away in the darkness. They were speaking French in low voices and that, together with the soft clatter of a boat being prepared, sounded distinctly ominous.

'Wake all the men quietly. Issue them with weapons, I want cutlasses and boarding axes in all hands. There's to be no talking. Break out what muskets we have and reload them with fresh charges. Lower the boat, put four men with guns aboard and wait for my instructions.'

'Aye aye, sir.'

Jack listened past the normal night sounds of the

harbour, waves lapping against the hull and rigging tapping against masts. He could hear the sound of a boarding party ashore and he knew they were making preparations for a raid. The bastards were going to try and sneak aboard and steal the cargo, probably even the ship itself. Well, Mr. Froggy Mayor, he thought, you'll get more than you bargained for.

The men assembled silently on deck and the arms were distributed to them. The captain called his crew to him and he whispered as they huddled around him.

'Listen carefully, men. I reckon they'll send out two longboats with about ten men on each, so we'll be outnumbered two to one. They're relying on surprise so we're going to oblige them. One of the boats will try to cut the anchor cable and the other will try and get on board. Jonesey, you take three men with you and two of the muskets. Your job is to guard the anchor. They'll probably only have blades. Just stay in the darkness and wait. Muffle the oars with rags and don't make any noise. When they approach, take the cover off the lantern and shoot one of the guns in their direction. These turds are probably not used to being shot at. Alright, Jonesey, go.'

Without a word, the second-in-command knuckled his forehead, picked out three men and went aft to lower the boat.

'The rest of you, I want every lantern on the ship lit and covered so the Frenchies think we're sleeping the grog off. I'll man the swivel gun. When we hear Jonesey's shot, we uncover the lanterns. Light this place up like it's Charles Town on a Friday night and let out a volley. I'd rather there be no bloodshed so don't shoot directly into their boat. I'll cut loose with the swivel gun, then we'll make a racket like a horde of pirates.

Scream like you're blood-thirsty rogues. I doubt these villagers have much stomach for a battle. Let's invite ourselves to their little party.'

As it always is, the waiting was the hardest part. The captain could feel himself sweating, even in the cold April night, and he knew he wasn't the only one. Each member of the crew was just as nervous. They all knew that if the French had firearms, or if they sent out more than two boats, then this could turn ugly. The captain reminded himself that it was easier to defend than it was to attack, like in chess, except the stakes were higher in this game.

It was long after midnight when a splash from a careless French oarsman alerted the crew that a boat was approaching from the stern. The men gathered and the swivel gun was moved from midships to the rail at the rear of the ship.

'They're going to try and board before they cut the anchor, men. We'd better begin the festivities without Jonesey.'

Each crew member had every one of his muscles tensed and some of the more experienced gritted their teeth for the explosion that was to come. Rackham calmly primed the swivel gun and cocked the hammer.

'NOW!' he roared.

The lanterns were all uncovered, bathing the sea aft of Prosperity with an unnatural light. Jack pulled the lanyard on the little gun and the night erupted with an almighty flash and a boom, momentarily blinding the men with the muzzle blast. A volley of musket fire rippled from the crew into the darkness, followed by blood-curdling screams from the men. Jack felt the hairs on his neck stand on end.

The Frenchmen had been as tense as the ship's crew

and, when the mayhem began, they completely lost any cohesiveness. Oars backed haphazardly, churning up the water around the longboat as it turned clumsily abeam of the schooner.

'Quick!' shouted Rackham. 'Help me get another charge into the swivel gun!'

'We haven't got any more shot for it, sir!' came a voice from the crew.

'Doesn't matter! Ram another charge down the barrel. We'll send them off with a bang!'

After the second shot was fired, a voice rose above the others in the French longboat.

'Aie pitié, mon Capitaine! Have pity!'

As the French boarding party scuttled back to shore, Jack remembered that Jones was somewhere out in the watery darkness.

'Get yourselves fore'ard, men, Jonesey might need some help!'

The crew clambered to the bow of the ship and the anchor cable. Jack could hear shouts and see a lantern. There was the clatter of wood against wood but no musket fire. He strained his eyes in vain to see what was happening but the muzzle flash from the swivel gun had rendered him night-blind.

'Can anybody see what's happening?'

'They're in an altercation with another boat, sir, but they're fighting with oars!'

'Shoot in their direction, not too close or you might hit our men!'

A stuttering volley shattered the night and a few seconds later a musket shot came out of the darkness. For a few seconds there was silence, except for the sound of a boat being rowed hastily back towards the shore.

Rackham cupped his hands around his mouth 'Are you alright, Jonesey?' he shouted.

'I think so, Captain, but we have a man down.'

'Who is it?'

'It's Coffey, sir. He ain't dead but one of the Frenchies gave him a good crack around the head with an oar.'

Within a few minutes the men from the jollyboat were back on board Prosperity. Coffey had his shirt off and was holding it against his forehead.

'What happened, Jones?'

'We were rowing around out there in the dark when all hell let loose up here on deck. While we were busy watching that, we almost crashed into a longboat with six Frenchmen in it. I uncovered the lantern, like you said, and next thing you know we're all swinging oars at each other. The only Frog who had a weapon was the fella in front and that was a hatchet to cut the anchor rope with. I pointed the gun at him and he dropped the hatchet into the water and dived in after it. When his head popped up, Coffey tried to bash him with an oar but one of the others got Coffey first.'

'Why didn't you shoot, man?'

'I tried sir but, with all that splashing, the priming got wet. While the others were swinging oars, I was busy ducking them and finally I managed to get some dry powder in the pan. Just then you shot at us and everybody ducked. I fired the gun and that finally got rid of them.'

'Are you alright, Coffey?' the captain asked the young seaman.

'I'll live, Cap'n. I'll just have another dent in me head to match the others.'

'Alright. Get the carpenter to patch you up.'

'Aye aye, sir.'

The young man turned to go below deck and the captain called after him. 'Did you get the Frog in the water, Coffey?'

'No sir. I poked him a couple of times with the oar and just when I was lining him up to crack his skull, the other Frenchie got me first.' Coffey hesitated before he went below deck. 'It sounds mad, sir, I know. I was scared to death when it was all goin' on but now, when I look back on it, I think I almost enjoyed it.'

'It's what keeps us playing the game, sailor,' smiled Jack.

CHAPTER 18

'Me and Alex are off t' Gortalocca, Abraham, it's probably best if you stay here fer now. Dose people ain't never seen a man o' your colour. We'll make d' proper introductions when we get ready t' plant. Alexander, you're comin' wit' me and mind now, leave yer English ways behind ya. Dese are Oirish people and dey don't trust nobody who looks or sounds or even smells anyt'ing like a landlord. I got some clothes fer ya. Put 'em on and ya'll fit right in. Ya can talk, but keep it short and remember, we all work fer Mr. Flynn.'

'I'd rather stay here with Mr. Washington, Da, I saw as much of Ireland in the last few days as I care to.'

'Agh! Dere ya go again sure, actin' like yer shite don't stink. Now listen t' me, boyo, yer mother was Oirish and yer father's Orish and ya can put on all d' airs and graces and fancy clothes ya want, but yer still an Oirishman and ya always will be.'

'I am not! I'm American, not Irish.'

'Cut dat out right now, ya young gobshite. Yer my son and yer whatever Oy say ya are. Anyways, dere ain't no such t'ing as an American … unless yer one o' dem red heathens.'

'Whatever you say, Da.'

'And don't go all sulky. Just put on yer grown-up britches and behave yerself.'

'Are we going by coach?'

'Ah fer feck's sake! Dis stay in Oirland will do you d' world o' good, fella. It might even scrape some o' dat gentry shite off ya and replace it wit' some good auld Oirish dung.'

An hour later, father and son entered Hogan's where Roisin and Morna were cleaning up and stocking shelves.

'T'ings are lookin' grand, ladies. When do ye suppose we'll be ready fer business?'

'Well we have the groceries,' replied Roisin, 'and the beer, and we're just waiting for Gleeson to deliver some poteen now, but we could open today if we had to.'

'Dere's no hurry, tomorra's grand, and Oy t'ink we should have a few festivities to celebrate d' re-openin' of Hogan's.'

'No one round here has money for that sort of thing.'

'Dat's no problem, missus. D' party's on Mr. Flynn.'

'Will we meet him so?'

'Ah ya never can tell wit' Mr. Flynn. Mick's better able t' predict what dat fella'll do.'

Roisin motioned towards where Alexander stood. 'And who is this handsome young man?'

'Dis is Alexander Flood, me pride and me joy.'

'Da!' said Alex, blushing floridly.

159

Roisin walked over to the boy and gave him a hug that nearly engulfed him.

'Ah God love ya. I haven't seen a man blush like that since my own dear Liam passed.' If there had been a hole he could fit into, Alexander would cheerfully have jumped in and pulled the cover over himself. 'I'm Roisin and this is Morna and if there's any doubt about who really runs this village, you just ask your father.'

'It's true, Alex. She ain't d' mayor or d' sheriff. Dis woman standin' before ya is d' queen o' Gortalocca.'

Before Alexander could process the information, Siobhan came in from the back room carrying a jug of whiskey from Gleeson's and the young man's jaw dropped at the sight of her. Siobhan stopped in midstride, frozen, the jug still in her hand. Love at first sight is something that's often spoken about and, even more frequently, written about. In reality, it's as rare as a unicorn.

'Say hello to Alexander,' said Roisin. She might as well have been speaking in tongues because the girl hadn't comprehended what she'd said. Instead she glanced briefly at her grandmother, then back at the tall young man with the blue eyes.

'Well? Where are your manners, girl? Aren't you going to introduce yourself?'

Siobhan glanced at Roisin again, then back at Alexander. Morna took the jug gently from the girl's hand before she dropped it.

'Lost yer tongue, lad?' said Ned. 'Say hello to d' girl.'

To Alexander, his father's voice sounded like someone talking to him from under the sea. He was swimming in this girl's pale blue eyes and he had no desire to get out of the water. Finally, Ned put his hand on the lad's shoulder and shook it gently. Alexander was startled and flinched slightly at his father's touch. He had forgotten there was anyone else in the room.

'I'm ... Alexander Flood. Right, Da?'

Siobhan covered her face with her apron, spun on her heels and ran out of the room the way she'd come in.

'I'm sorry, Alexander,' said Morna, bewildered at her daughter's behaviour. 'Oy don't know what's come over d' girl. Oy'll see if Oy can fetch 'er back fer a proper introduction.'

The girl's mother followed Siobhan while Alexander stood gazing at the doorway.

'What just happened?' asked Roisin.

'Not a clue, missus. Oy never seen anyt'ing like dat before. Oy heard o' people gettin' struck dumb but dat's d' first time Oy ever saw two people get struck daft.'

Morna was in the back room with her daughter and Siobhan was wiping tears from her eyes.

'What in God's name's d' matter wit' ya, child?'

'He's too skinny!' choked the young woman.

'Who's too skinny? D' ya mean Ned's son? Too skinny fer what?'

'He's too skinny fer me!'

'Oh, I see,' said Morna, the penny having dropped. 'Dere's nutt'n wrong wit skinny young men, love. Most lads dat age who are anyt'ing udder dan skinny get to look like pork chops when dey have a few years on 'em.'

'And he's poor,' said Soibhan, still blubbering.

'Well his da works fer a rich man, and he seems t' have a good deal of influence.'

'It's not d' same t'ing, Mam, you know it's not.'

'C'mon now, macushla. Let's me and you just go

back in and see what happens.'

Siobhan stood up defiantly and smoothed out her clothes and her hair. 'Are me eyes red, Mam?'

'Not at all sure,' Morna lied.

'Alright so. I'm goin' out dere and I'm goin' to tell 'im he's too skinny and too poor.'

Morna inhaled deeply, then sighed. 'Alright, pet.'

Siobhan straightened herself to all of her five feet two inches and strode back into the room. She walked straight up to the handsome young man and was promptly struck mute again. She opened her mouth a few times but couldn't remember what she'd rehearsed in her head.

'What's the matter with your eyes?' he asked innocently. Siobhan glared accusingly at her mother, picked up her skirts and ran back out through the door to the storeroom.

'Your son has a way with words, doesn't he?' said Roisin sarcastically.

'He's bin on a ship fer four years. He's not used to bein' around women.'

'Is that right? I never would have guessed.'

Alexander was totally oblivious that he was the subject of the conversation. He just stood gazing at the doorway, hoping that the beautiful young woman with the pale blue eyes and the red hair would come back through it.

'C'mon, Alex, let's go and find Michael. Maybe we'll find yer tongue too.'

'It's raining, Da. Can't I just stay here?'

'Alexander, do ya see dat lady over dere wit' her arms folded across her chest? Well, if Oy leave ya here, she might just have ya fer supper.'

'I'd like to stay for supper.'

'You'd be d' main course, son, now c'mon.'

Ned half dragged the boy from the store and they went in search of Mikey. They found him with Jamie and Liam, still attacking the perimeter of the faerie ring.

'Yer makin' good progress dere, lads,' called Ned, pushing Alexander in front of him. 'Dis is Alexander, me son.'

Michael shifted the axe to his left hand and offered his right to the young fellow. Alexander gave it a half-hearted shake, then gazed around the faerie ring.

'Why wasn't this land cleared before now?' he asked.

'Legend says it's bad luck to disturb these places,' replied Michael.

'It ain't no legend,' protested Jamie. 'You ask the McTierneys. Deir auld man t'ought dey was a waste o' ground so he cleared one years ago, down near Knigh Cross. Dat very same year, his wife had a daughter born wit' milky eyes. Dat poor lass can only see light and dark.'

'She's still the best lace-maker for miles around,' ventured Mikey.

'It's a well-known fact sure,' said Ned. 'When God takes away one o' d' senses, he makes d' udder senses keener.'

'That's true enough,' agreed Mikey. 'That girl could hear a mouse squeak from a hundred yards, and she remembers everything that anyone's ever said to her. She can even tell you what weather's on its way hours before it comes, says she can smell it.'

'Dat's little comfort fer bein' as good as blind,' replied Jamie. 'What about her brother Billy? Dat young feller was d' best farmer anybody ever knew. After auld Will died o' fever, dat lad took over d' farm and he got more out o' dat land dan anybody else round here. And what happened him? He fell off a roof and broke both his legs. Now he's a cripple, scoots around wit' his stumps tied to a plank!'

'He's still the best farmer around here,' claimed Michael. 'He can get more out of those two acres than some can get out of four, plus he's the best feckin' fiddle player I ever heard.'

Ned took the opportunity to change the subject. 'Ah grand, we need a fiddler! We're havin' a get-together at Hogan's tomorra evenin' fer all dem who'll be farmin' fer us. We'll have a little meetin' first and Oy'll explain some rules. After dat, everyone can drink deir fill, and if Billy McTierney wants to make a few pennies fer himself, he can play some tunes fer us.'

'Billy would be glad of the money alright,' said Michael, 'but there's a lot won't go near him because of the family curse.'

'Agh pishogue! Anybody who believes dat auld bullshite shouldn't be workin' fer Mr. Flynn! God help me, Oy'll drag dis feckin' village kickin' and screamin' into d' eighteenth century if it kills me!'

'You might want to start with Clancy, Ned.' Michael laughed.

Ned turned and looked at Jamie who had been listening intently. 'Mister Clancy,' he said, a mischievous grin spreading over his face, 'Oy've a job fer ya.' He reached into his purse, pulled out three pennies and put them into the blacksmith's hand. 'Oy want ya to go and give two pennies to Billy McTierney and keep one fer yerself. Tell Billy d' festivities start at sunset tomorra.'

Jamie looked at the coins in his hand then back at Ned. 'So I get a penny just fer walkin' to McTierney's and givin' Billy a message?'

'Dat's right.'

'Well when d' ya want me t' go? I still have work here sure.'

'I want ya t' go now, James. No time like d' present.'

Jamie put down his axe and set off, making a purposeful beeline towards Knigh Cross.

Ned winked at Michael. 'Well Mikey,' he said, 'he don't seem too bothered about any auld curse now, does he?'

*

'Sir, there's a boat approaching from shore,' announced Jonesey, 'and they're carrying a white flag.'

'Very well, Mr. Jones. I'll put on a clean uniform and see you up on deck.'

'Aye, Cap'n. Do you think they're surrendering?'

Jack smiled. 'I doubt it,' he said. 'I'd say Mr. Mayor has come for a bit of a parlez. Get the men armed again and have them put on their fierce faces. We'll give His Honour a bit of a show of force.'

Within minutes, Jack was up on deck basking in the early morning French sun, his countenance grave. 'There's only the mayor and two oarsman in the boat,' he said. 'Train the swivel gun on them when they approach.'

'It's not loaded, sir.'

The boat was within ten yards of them now and the mayor addressed Jack first. 'Pardonez moi, mon Capitaine. There was a grave misunderstanding last night. The men were merely here to help you unload the cargo.' He spoke in thickly-accented English. 'Permission to come aboard?'

Jack nodded. He still hadn't spoken and he held his

hand on the grip of his cutlass for effect. The thin Frenchman was manhandled up on deck like a sack of spuds, then he and Jack began to speak in French.

After a few minutes the captain excused himself and went to speak to his crew. 'He thinks we're pirates,' he said in a low voice. 'and he knows that pirates elect their captains. When I told him I had to speak to you men, that's what he thinks we're doing, electing a captain. He did say something that bothers me though. When I invited him to inspect our cargo he declined. He said we could "trust each other". The only time a man says that is just before he slips a knife between your ribs.'

'We might have another problem, Cap'n,' said Jonesey. 'They've moved a little two-pounder onto the dock along with the barrels.'

'Shit! I hate negotiating down the barrel of a gun.'

'It could be a bluff, sir, like the one we pulled on the sloop.'

'Maybe, maybe not. I can't take the risk. I'm going back to talk with that ferret.'

The captain went back to the mayor. Their discussion suddenly became animated and Rackham pulled the cutlass from his belt and held it to the man's throat.

'We've come to an agreement,' he shouted back to Jonesey. 'Rig a block and tackle to the fore boom and load a hogshead of tobacco into their longboat.'

'He's under a white flag, sir.'

Jack ignored the comment. 'When they get the tobacco ashore, they'll send the boat back out with a barrel of brandy on it. We'll do that until the last of the cargo is gone, then we'll send them their mayor back. In the meantime, tie the worm to the mainmast. This might take a couple of hours.'

'But sir, the conventions …'

'We're pirates, Jonesey,' the captain shrugged. 'We make up our own rules.'

CHAPTER 19

Gortalocca was heaving. Hogan's was full to capacity and the throng spilled out onto the road. Over a hundred had turned out, the offer of free drink too much for the locals to resist, thought Roisin cynically.

Along with the beer, Mr. Washington was also one of the main attractions and even he was amused when people asked if they could touch his skin. If there was a main event, he was it. A hundred questions were asked of him and he showed infinite patience, trying to answer each one in turn. People asked about darkest Africa and, even though he'd never set foot on the continent, he regaled them with tales of ferocious animals and curious customs. The only request he denied was that of Gleeson, the local brewer and distiller, who asked if he could have a look at his arse to see if was the same colour as the rest of him.

Once the crowd's curiosity had been satiated, Ned called a brief meeting of those who were to be working the fields.

'Now then,' he announced, 'Oy only have t'ree rules, but if any of yous violate any one of 'em, yer finished

… and Oy won't have ya back. Me first rule is Oy want all of ye here and workin' by half an hour after sunrise. If yer sick, Oy want to know what's wrong wit' ya, Oy won't tolerate sluggards. Me second rule is dere'll be no fightin', not under any conditions. You'll leave yer feuds and yer grudges at home. Dat brings me to me t'ird rule. Oy won't tolerate d' drinkin' of hard liquor during d' week. Ye can drink beer, but ye'll save d' hard stuff fer Saturday nights, and den Oy'll buy d' first round. Any questions?'

'I have a cough,' came a voice from the crowd. 'Are ya sayin' I can't have a nip to sooth me poor auld t'roat?'

'Are ya too sick to work?'

'No, sir.'

'Den save yer coughin' fer Saturday night. Anyt'ing else?'

'What are we growin', sir?'

'Dat's a good question. We're growin' … emm … Indian cabbage. Yes, we're growin' Indian cabbage, den we're sendin' it to China. D' Chinamen feed it t' d' worms dat make d' silk.' Ned was thinking fast, not well, but fast. He knew the locals would work out what they were growing in due time but now was not that time.

A murmur went through the crowd and a female voice spoke up. 'What's silk?'

'It's a type of cloth, a bit like linen, only finer.'

'We got worms here, sir. Can't we teach ours t' make silk?'

'Not at all, woman, dem's Oirish worms. Chinese worms is much cleverer.'

Before any more questions could be asked, Ned declared the proceedings to be over and called for the festivities to begin. Billy McTierney began to play a reel on the fiddle and beer was poured into a hundred cups. Ned made his way over to the fiddler so he could hear him better. He bent down and spoke in his ear.

'Mr. McTierney, ya play a grand fiddle but dere's a hundred or more people here and dey can't all hear d' music.'

Billy was more used to being shunned than he was being the center of attention. 'Would ya ever get me up onto a table, Mr. Flood, sir? Dey'll be able to hear me better dere.'

A table was dragged out of Hogan's and placed in front of the door, so people could dance outside on the road. Ned yelled at a couple of men who he knew weren't afraid of the curse being contagious and they stepped forward to do his bidding.

'Jayzis, Billy! Yer as heavy as a bag o' boulders.'

Billy grinned. 'I've bin haulin' me arse around on me arms fer ten years, lads. I have plenty of muscle, from d' waist up at least.'

With the fiddler safely in position on a table top, the music recommenced and the crowd joined in the revelry. After a few sets, Billy's mother and his blind sister Lizzy arrived. Alexander got up from his seat and offered it to the girl and Mr. Washington followed suit, giving his chair up to the widow McTierney. A large youth appeared out of nowhere and stood over Lizzy.

'Dere ain't no room fer witches here!' he spat. The music stopped and the only sound was whispering from amongst the crowd. Alexander stepped in front of the young man.

'There are no such thing as witches. You, sir, are an ignoramus.'

'Is dat right, stickman? Yous all heard 'im! He called

me a pig anus!' With that, the youth shoved Alexander to the ground and laughed.

Ned came to his son's defense. 'Why don't ya try me on fer size, pig-anus?'

'Don't do it, Casey!' came a shout from the crowd. 'He's the phantom priest from Cork!'

Casey's eyes widened. 'Go 'way out o' dat! Sure I t'ought you'd be taller.'

'Oy'm tall enough to take on d' likes of you.'

By this time, Billy had managed to fling himself down off the tabletop and was rapidly knuckling his way across the floor to the scene of the action. Casey turned his attention away from Ned towards the disabled man and laughed.

'And what are you goin' t' do, stumpy?'

'I'm goin' to have yer nuts fer playt'ings, ya gobshite!'

Just as Casey raised a leg as if he was about to kick Billy's teeth down his throat, Ned stepped in again.

'I said no fightin'! Jayzis, dere's only t'ree rules!' A sinister smile then crossed Ned's face as if a devil had just possessed him. 'But dis is an exception. Affairs of honour will be judged by me.' There was about to be a second main event.

'Will ya say sorry to d' lady, pig-anus?'

'I will not!' said Casey. 'She must be a witch to make lace as good as she does without bein' able to see.'

'Do you want to fight Casey, Billy?'

'I'd love ta sure, but d' only fella strong enough t' hold me up is Mick Sheridan.' Mick stepped out of the crowd.

'Oy've got a better idea,' said Ned. 'Somebody get a couple o' pieces o' rope and we'll tie Mr. Casey's legs so he's about d' same height as Billy here. Now each fighter needs a second to give 'im instructions. Mick, will you stand fer pig-anus?' Mick nodded. 'Den clear a spot on d' floor,' announced Ned. 'We shouldn't need much room … just enough fer pig-anus to fall on.'

Casey limbered up his muscles and began shadowboxing. Mick leaned over and whispered in his ear.

'If you beat Billy McTierney, I will personally tear off both yer legs and shove 'em where ya sit.' Casey looked at Mick, who nodded and smiled a dangerous smile. Casey remembered the tale of how Mick had lifted up a pony just to win a bet. It was a local legend.

The two combatants were positioned on the floor about three feet apart. Billy stared into the eyes of Casey, whose attention was divided between his opponent and Mick Sheridan. He knew that, even in his old age, Mick was the more formidable of the two. His mouth was a thin slit, his lips tight, and the fighter could see the muscles in his jaw as he gritted his teeth.

'Begin!'

Casey moved his head from side to side and threw a weak left hand. Billy absorbed the tap and watched. Casey threw another lazy left but Billy caught him by the wrist and popped him a return left on the jaw. Casey's ears made a buzzing sound from the blow but he wrenched his wrist free and threw a hard left, right combination. Billy spat blood and threw a nasty right which broke Casey's nose and knocked him off his knees and onto the floor. Mick picked him up.

'Remember what I told you,' he whispered.

Casey looked into Mick's eyes, wiped the blood streaming from his nose on his sleeve and decided that, to save himself from getting beaten to a pulp, it was time to feck foolish pride and take a dive. He didn't have to think about it too long because, as he turned away from Mick, he looked straight into an oncoming right hand which knocked him sprawling. He held up his hands in surrender.

'Alright, alright!' he yelled. 'I was wrong! Yer sister ain't a witch.'

'Don't apologise to McTierney,' said Mick, 'apologise to his sister.'

Casey's legs were unbound and he stood up, stumbling at first, then moved around to get his circulation going again. He made his way over to where Lizzy sat and made his apology to her.

'How are yer hands, Billy?' asked Ned. 'Can ya still play?'

Billy opened and closed his fists a few times. 'I can o' course,' he grinned. 'Get me back up on d' table.'

Casey spoke quietly to Mick. 'Did I do alright, Mr. Sheridan?'

Mick gave him an amicable swat on the back of the head. Mick's hands were the size of shovels and the friendly swipe made Casey's ears ring again.

'Ya did d' right t'ing, lad. I'll talk to Ned and make sure ya still have work.'

*

'That's the last of the hogsheads, sir. The mayor wants to talk to you.'

'Very well, Jonesey, let's see what the blaggard has to say.'

Jack made his way over to where the skinny man was still tied to the mast. The mayor began to speak rapidly in French, the captain replying only when necessary, then Jack pulled a pistol out of his belt and the little man began to pray.

'Are ya going to shoot him, Cap'n?'

'Of course not, I'm just putting the fear of Christ into him. I need to talk to the fellow in the longboat.'

The captain then strode over to the rail and spoke at length to the man who'd been left in charge of the French longboat.

'It would seem we have somewhat of a stalemate, Mr. Jones. The fellow in the boat says that if we don't turn the mayor over to him, he won't send us the last barrel of brandy. When I told him we'd hold the mayor hostage until we got the last barrel, he said in that case we can keep the mayor and he'll keep the liquor. I think we need a new plan.'

The captain returned to the Frenchman trussed up against the mast and told him what transpired between the ship and the longboat. The mayor began to scream and curse at the crew of the boat.

'I think we just witnessed a coup d'etat, Jonesey. Cut the stern anchor cable.'

'Sir, the ship will swing into the wind.'

'Raise the mains'il and let her luff. Get the men up front on the capstan and winch us up to the anchor. As soon as the anchor starts to slip, trim the mains'il and we'll get ourselves out of the harbour on the north side of Tristan Island. We might be able to get on the lee side of it before they can get off more than one or two shots with their pop gun.'

'The water's shallow there, Cap'n.'

'We're not drawing more than five feet, Jonesey, we have a light load. It'll be even lighter when I toss the little bastard overboard.'

'What about the two-pounder, sir.'

'It seems to me that the fellow in the longboat is in

charge and it'll take at least ten minutes for him to get back to shore. Now let's make haste.'

The men raised the main and it flapped uselessly. They all put their backs into the capstan and inched the boat forwards into the wind. The ship swung on the remaining anchor cable. Jack lent a hand on the winch.

'Put your backs into it, men! We're abeam of the shore gun and at this range, even a Frenchman can hit us.' Jack took a moment to look towards the shore. The longboat was close enough to the quay now and the man in it was already shouting instructions to the canon crew.

Smoke and flame erupted from the barrel of the little shore battery. A second later the sound reached them and there was a splash a hundred or so feet short of the mark. The crew took a second to look up from their work and cheered.

'They couldn't hit the wall if they were in a closet,' came a voice from the capstan.

'Stay with it, men!' yelled the captain. 'He was trying to bounce one off the water to hole us at the water line. Somebody over there knows what they're doing.'

The men had resumed their efforts at a more frenetic pace when a second shot rang out. This time the water splashed about fifty feet away and the ball bounced off the surface of the bay and whined overhead.

'The bastard's skipping stones!' exclaimed Jonesey. 'He can't sink us with that little gun but if he holes us, and we take on water, the ship'll draw too much to clear the bay.'

'I'll be your eyes,' said the captain suddenly becoming calm. 'Don't look, just do your jobs. I'll tell you what's happening and we'll get ourselves out of this bloody mess.'

The anchor began to slip and several of the men ran to trim the main without the order being given. The canvas grew taught and the ship began to creep slowly up towards the anchor, making the job of the men on the winch easier and faster. A third shot came from the shore and this time, after a geyser of water erupted, there came a second whapping noise as the ball struck the main sail, halfway down.

'Raise the fores'l! They're getting the range!'

The two sails now began to push the ship forward. It was slow at first but when the speed began to increase, Jonesey yelled to the captain. 'The helm's responding, sir. We have enough speed for steerage.'

'Port helm, Mr. Jones. Let's see if we can get the island between them and us before they get off another shot.'

'It'll be close, sir. We have the tide running against us.'

Just before the ship reached safety, the last shot boomed out. The French gunner had abandoned hope of piercing the hull with a skipping shot so this time he'd gone right for the heart or, in this case, the arse end of the ship. There came the sound of splintering wood aft and Jack leaned over the rail to assess the damage. There was a two and a half inch hole in the hull, about three feet above the waterline.

'Get Mr. Reardon to inspect the damage, Jonesey.'

The ship's carpenter hadn't needed to wait for the order, he was already on his way. A minute later he was back on deck, juggling the still hot two-pound shot from one hand to another.

'Ya have a new window in yer quarters, Cap'n,' he said. 'The ball was laying in yer rack, right where yer head should be.'

'What about the damage, Reardon?'

'I can have it patched in a couple of hours, sir.'

'See to it, then. I'll stay on deck until we get clear of France.'

'What about the mayor, sir?' asked the second-in-command.

'Cut him loose and toss him over the side.'

'What if he can't swim? We ain't pirates.'

'Toss the wooden canon over with him. They're both useless.'

CHAPTER 20

'Liam can't work today, Mikey.'

Michael knew by the tone of Morna's voice that she was concerned.

'Why? What's wrong with him?'

'He got a splinter in his t'umb d' udder day and he never told anyone. It's all festered today and 'is hand is all swole up.'

Infections in the eighteenth century were not a matter to be treated lightly and even the smallest could become life-threatening in a matter of hours.

'Let me see. C'mere to me, son.'

'Ah I'm grand, Da, it only hurts a bit,' said Liam bravely.

'I said c'mere, let me look at it.' Michael examined his son's hand. It was indeed considerably swollen and the colour was somewhere between purple and pink. The boy's fingers looked like sausages.

'Did you get the splinter out?'

'I tried but all I did was push it in deeper, so I soaked it.'

'When did it happen?'

'The day before yesterday.'

Michael squeezed his son's thumb gently and yellow pus, along with watery fluid, flowed from the tiny puncture. He squeezed a little harder and the boy winced in pain.

'We'll have to cut the splinter out, lad, or this is going to get worse.'

Morna's concern had turned to worry. 'P'raps if we soak it again, Mikey…'

'I think it's too late for that, love, but we can try. There might be enough corruption in there to push the splinter out if we soak it. I'm going to ask Jamie to find Mick Sheridan. The old man's experience of treating horses with this sort of thing might come in useful.'

Morna began to heat water in a pot over the fire while Michael went next door to speak with Clancy. It seems that Mick had already arrived in Gortalocca, along with Alexander and Mr. Washington, and they were out inspecting the fields.

'I've had a t'ousand splinters in me life, Mikey,' said Jamie confidently. 'Let me have a look at d' lad. I'm sure it ain't as bad as ya t'ink.'

Michael reluctantly agreed to let Clancy take a look but as, they were returning to Mikey's cottage, they ran into Mick Sheridan and his two companions. Michael hastily told Mick about Liam's splinter.

'Will you look at it for me, Mick? I'm no expert but it doesn't look good to me.'

'Ah sure it's probably not as bad as ya t'ink,' said the big fellow, sharing Jamie's casual approach to the matter.

When Mick entered the cottage, he found the boy sitting with his hand in a bowl of salty water.

'I'm grand, Mr. Sheridan,' he protested, when he saw Mick. 'It's all a big fuss over nutt'n.'

'Whisht, boy, I'll be d' judge o' dat. C'mere, let me see.'

Liam tentatively offered his hand to Mick who examined it, turning it over several times, then put it back in the bowl. He looked at Michael and his light-hearted expression had been replaced with a solemn one.

'Let's you and me step outside and have a word,' he said, trying his best to be nonchalant. Mick was not a good actor.

Once they were outside, the big man spoke quietly. 'I don't like it Mikey,' he said. 'Dat's as bad as I've seen in a long time. Dem red streaks goin' up d' boy's arm, dat mean d' blood's poisoned.'

'Blood poisoning? That can't be right sure, he's not shivering.'

'Ah he will, Mikey, and after dat he'll go to sleep. And if d' worst happens, he might not wake up.'

'What in God's name are you saying, Mick?'

'Just prepare yerself for what might be t' come.'

Michael squeezed his eyes tight, trying to stop the tears before they started, then coughed in an attempt to clear his rapidly tightening throat.

'Is there nothing you can do, Mick?' he croaked.

'I've treated quite a few horses wit' d' same t'ing in me time and I'd say it's about half.'

'What do you mean, half?'

'Half make it and d' udder half don't. Eider d' fever gets 'em or dey die o' lockjaw a couple o' weeks later.'

Michael's mind was spinning and he uttered the unthinkable. 'Will we save him if we cut off his arm?'

'Don't ask me to do dat, Mikey. I never did anyt'ing

like dat to a person before and dat boy is like me own family.'

Both men's faces were grim as they walked back inside the cottage. The boy's colour had turned from pale to flushed and he was shivering. Morna had wrapped him in blankets but they didn't seem to be warming him. Abraham had Liam's hand in his and was turning it one way and then another.

'It's time we did something to help this boy,' he said abruptly, 'instead of standing around like a bunch of sheep.' The onlookers were startled by his sudden air of authority. 'Woman, get some water on the fire and put clean rags in it. Somebody get me some whiskey.'

'This is no time to be drinking,' protested the boy's father.

'Well, I might have one to steady my nerves but the whiskey's for the young man here. This is going to be painful for him. We'll feed it to him until he passes out and then we'll get to work.'

His tone changed when he addressed the feverish boy. 'Your name's Liam, is that right, son?' he said, tenderly.

'Yes, sir,' said Liam weakly.

'You can call me Abraham. Now listen to me carefully, I'll tell you what's going to happen. First you're going to drink some whiskey. It won't taste very nice but you can just sip it until it starts to make you feel drowsy.'

'Yes, sir … Abraham.'

'Then I'm going to cut out that old splinter. Now I don't want you looking while I'm doing it so just keep your head turned away. Do you understand?'

'Will it hurt, Abraham?'

'Yes boy, I'm afraid it will hurt more than anything

you've felt before. Are you afraid?'

'No, sir,' he lied. 'I'm not a baby.'

Washington was well aware that, even through his fever, this boy was trying to offer him consolation.

'That's right Liam, you're not a baby. You're as much a man as anyone in this room. We all have to be brave, isn't that right?'

'Yes, sir.'

Years of being second-in-command aboard a ship hadn't been wasted on Washington. 'Leave the boy's mother with him,' he instructed. 'She can feed him sips of the whiskey until it's time. Alexander, you and Michael come with me.' They followed the black man outside. 'Alex, you're used to taking orders without question. You'll be my assistant.'

Alex knuckled his forehead. 'Aye aye, sir.'

A flicker of a smile crossed Abraham's face. 'We're not aboard ship today. Today we're surgeons.'

'Yes, sir.'

He turned to Michael now. 'I need some tools. Get me a long, thin nail to probe the wound with.'

Mikey turned to go and Washington stopped him. 'Wait. That's not all. I need a knife, a short one, and sharpen it like a razor … and I need a saw, a small one, the sort a cabinet-maker uses.'

Michael could taste the bile as it rose up into his throat. A saw could mean only one thing and it was the second most unfathomable thought he could conceive. Abraham saw the panic in his face and replied to the question that hung in the air.

'I won't take the arm unless the meat inside is rotten. Now go.'

Michael raced away before anyone could see his tears. At best, his beloved son would be a cripple after this. A thought flitted across his mind. Had violating the faerie ring got something to do with this? He immediately shook off the superstition, as indeed his own father had done all those years ago. Ireland had enough problems, after all. To be yoked to the myths and fantasies of the old days was just one more the Irish didn't need.

'Liam can you hear me?' There was no response to Washington's question. The boy breathed heavily and rhythmically, the alcohol having rendered him unconscious. 'Move him outside. The light's not good enough for me to see in here.'

Mick Sheridan scooped up the young man in his arms as if he was a baby and limped outside with him.

'Somebody get me a table,' instructed Abraham. 'Get me two, so we can lay him down. Be quick, in case the whiskey makes him throw up. Alexander, you take off your belt and wrap it around his arm twice, just above the elbow.' Alex obeyed the order without hesitation. 'Take the boy's parents away. I don't want anyone fainting around me.' As soon as Liam and Morna were gone, he glared directly at Roisin. 'You too!' he snapped.

Roisin wasn't used to being ordered about. She was the one who delivered the orders.

'Don't you know who I am?' she said, haughtily. 'I'm the boy's grandmother.'

'I don't care if you're the Virgin Mary, you're standing in my light. Now get yourself away!'

Roisin walked off, muttering to herself. When this was over, she would give that mud man a piece of her mind.

Abraham spoke to Alexander in a voice low enough for the bystanders not to hear.

'I've never done this before,' he said, 'and I've only seen it done a couple of times. Dip the nail into the whiskey. I have to probe inside the lad's hand and it'll help.'

Alexander did as he was instructed and the black man poked the nail into the wound, pushing it down the tract made by the splinter. Blood and pus flowed out profusely and the odour was the sickeningly sweet smell of rot. He pushed it deeper until the nail wouldn't go any further. He sighed with exasperation.

'Agh! The damn wood's in the fleshy part of his thumb, I can't feel it.' He hesitated for a moment, then said, 'Dip the knife in the whiskey and hand it to me. I'm going to open this up a little so I can push it in further.' Alexander handed him the blade and, again, he hesitated. 'Now the blood will spurt when I cut, but it'll stop quicker if you keep your belt tight around his arm.' Washington pulled the nail taut against the skin from the inside so he could follow its margins, then he cut a slit in the skin on top of it, about two inches long. Blood gushed out like a geyser at first but it soon subsided. Alexander wiped the pool of blood away without being asked and Abraham pushed the nail in deeper.

After about an inch, and a minute which seemed like an hour, the probe couldn't advance any further. 'I've got something,' said Washington, 'but I'm not sure if it's the wood or if it's something that's supposed to be there.' He left the nail in place and wiped the sweat off his brow with his sleeve. Even in the cold spring air, the tension had caused him to perspire profusely. 'I need to make the cut longer so I can see what's in there.'

He opened the slit another inch until he reached the

point of the nail. The wound welled up with blood, diluted by a thin yellowish liquid, and he dabbed it clean, spreading the margins of the incision with his fingers. Just before it filled again, he caught a glimpse of something black, deep inside.

'Get me a needle, quick!' he shouted to no one in particular.

In a matter of moments, Roisin appeared with a needle and handed it to him. She looked over his shoulder at the wound and felt her head spin. She turned and hurried away.

'Hang on to that belt, Alex,' said Abraham, 'and when I tell you to blot the blood, do it!' Alexander fought the urge to say, 'Aye, sir.'

'Now!'

Alex dabbed at the wound and Washington tried to spear the wood with the needle. 'Damn it, I missed! Do it again!' This time, he managed to prick the splinter, but it slipped away from the needle. 'I've moved it out a little. One more time!' The third time was the charm and the piece of wood lay in the open cut. Abraham reached in with his fingers, pulled it out and held it aloft in triumph.

'Got the bastard!'

The sliver of wood was no more than three quarters of an inch long and a quarter inch at its widest. The oak was black and covered with a slimy coating.

'Have we finished?' asked Alexander, his shirt stuck to his body with sweat.

'Not yet. I want to open up where the wood rested. I need to make sure the poison's out.'

He reintroduced the nail into where the sliver of wood had rested and he made a final cut. Blood spewed into the wound as if a spigot had been opened.

'Damn,' he said, 'I must have cut something.' He turned to Jamie. 'Get me another nail,' he barked, 'and heat it red-hot.'

It took a few minutes but it wasn't long before Jamie returned holding a small spike of metal in a pair of tongs.

'I couldn't get it red-hot on d' turf fire,' he panted. 'It's only blue-hot.'

'It'll have to do. Go and get another one in case I need it.'

Jamie handed the tongs to Washington and the surrogate surgeon applied the hot nail to where he thought the blood was emanating from. The base of the wound sizzled with the heat and the blood slowed momentarily, then began to flow again.

Liam had begun to rouse from his stupor and Abraham leaned close to the boy's ear. 'Easy now, lad. You're going to feel some pain and smell some stink, but just stay with me and we'll soon be done.' Liam groaned quietly.

'I need a poultice!' shouted Abraham. 'Somebody get some bread and salt and knead it into a ball and put it into one of the hot rags from the pot.'

'Are ya goin' to sew him up?' asked Jamie.

'Not yet, we have to let the corruption drain. We'll apply a bread poultice and see how it goes.'

Alexander moved closer to Washington and, because he knew Liam was regaining consciousness, he whispered in the black man's ear.

'Will he make it, sir?'

Liam heard him and, in his drunken haze, he replied, 'I will o' course make it, I'm feckin' Irish! Did ya have to cut off me arm, Mr. Abraham, sir?

Washington shook his head. 'Don't worry, son, you

still have both your arms, but mind it's not over yet. The next few days will tell. You're a brave lad, Liam, as brave as any man I've met.'

Abraham asked for a clean bucket of water. His hands were covered in as much blood as if he'd just slaughtered a pig. He took off his blood-spattered shirt and wiped his face with it, then went to find his patient's distraught parents.

'Did you cut off his arm?' asked Roisin, still smarting from the black man's dismissal.

He ignored her and spoke gently to Morna and Michael. 'I managed to get the wood out but the blood poison's still in there. The next few days will be touch and go. If the corruption spreads, I will have to take the arm off and, even then, I'm not certain the boy will live.'

'Is there anything you are certain of, I wonder?' asked Roisin bitterly.

Abraham glared at her and spoke slowly. 'Yes there is, as a matter of fact. I'm certain that you're accustomed to getting your own way. Well so am I, but this time it isn't up to either one of us. It's down to the mercy of the Lord Almighty and that boy's will to live.'

Roisin had rarely been challenged before and this was the first time she'd had anyone look her straight in the eye who she felt she wasn't able to bully, intimidate or overwhelm.

'Well!' she declared indignantly, 'I don't know what to say, I'm sure.'

'Why don't you start with "thank you"?'

Roisin ignored him. 'I'm going to see my grandson,' she said and strode out.

'I apologise for my mother,' said Michael, with resignation. 'She's used to being in charge and she can be, well …'

'Formidable?' offered Abraham, managing a wan smile. 'Oh don't worry, I've dealt with women fiercer than your mother. Ned's mother-in-law now, Anne Bonny … that old sea hag is, well, to call her formidable would be an understatement.'

CHAPTER 21

'Cap'n, would you come up on deck? I think we might have another problem.'

'Good God, Jonesey, what the devil is it now?'

'There must be thirty sails on the horizon.'

'I'll meet you up there.'

The captain thought this trip had already suffered misfortune enough for three. He hurriedly threw on his greatcoat and was soon standing at the bow with his bosun, letting his eyes get used to the predawn light. Jones offered him the telescope. He took it and began to scan. When he'd seen enough, he snapped the scope shut and handed it back.

'What do you think, sir?'

'It's a British fleet. They're heading south, probably to Gibraltar. They must be on their way to reinforce the fleet already stationed in the Med, to help them blockade the French ports down there.'

'Shall we head north and sail around them, sir?'

'No, they've already seen us. That would raise suspicion.'

'What do you make of the squadron, sir?'

'I'd say there are at least eight small scout vessels way out in front and, on the flanks, about ten frigates, supply vessels and a couple of ships of the line following in the rear.'

'What are your orders, sir?'

'Stay on the same heading, but hoist a British flag.'

'That'll put us on course to break their line, between the frigates and those big bastards.'

'I hope so,' smiled Jack.

'Aye aye, sir.'

By Jones' tone, Jack could tell his bosun had doubts about sailing through the middle of an English fleet. The captain was already formulating a plan however and, if it worked, they would not only cross the battle formation but might even get the chance to exact a modicum of revenge on the French village that had been so hostile the previous day.

'Fetch me the carpenter, I'll see him below.'

A few minutes later, the carpenter knocked on the captain's door. 'Come in, Reardon. I have a job for you and you don't have much time to get it done.'

'Aye, sir?'

'We need to change the name on the stern of the ship, just in case the sloop we ran into a few days ago made a report.'

'Aye, sir. I have a barrel full of 'em. What nationality do you want?'

'Make it English, and make it inoffensive. We want to appear as innocent as possible.'

'I have a 'Camille'.'

'Hmmm, Camille's too French. Change the 'e' to an 'a' … Camilla … that sounds more sophisticated.'

'Camilla? What sort of name is that?'

'Just get the new name on the stern, Reardon. Go

on, man, as quick as you can!'

'Yes sir, sorry sir. O' course I wouldn't know sophisticated if it bit me on the arse.'

Jack suddenly longed for the company of Alexander and Washington. At least he would get some intelligent conversation from them.

*

No one left Liam's side the whole long night. When dawn broke and he was still breathing, Abraham was surprised. Twice during the night the fever had caused fits and the boy would let out a 'whoop' as he inhaled, then his muscles would contract into a knot. His arms would fold up tight against his chest and his legs would fold underneath him. His head would tip back at an unnatural angle, followed by tremors. The second time it happened, it was almost two minutes before he began to breathe rhythmically again. The black man thought he'd died and he wondered if these Irish people would seek retribution from him, as he was the one in charge.

Michael was ready to make a deal with the devil at this point. 'If you cut off his arm, can you save him?' he asked Washington with a husky voice.

'It's too late for that now. Maybe if we'd done it yesterday it might have stopped the poison spreading, maybe not. Isn't there a doctor locally, or at least someone who knows how to use herbs? It's the fever that will take him if we can't stop it.'

Roisin interrupted. 'You're African. Don't you have some secret spell or some potion you can give him?'

Abraham knew Roisin was still annoyed with him from the previous day's set-to and he didn't have the heart to argue with her.

'Mrs. Flynn, I'm sorry I was abrupt with you yesterday but my mind was on the task at hand … and no, I don't have any knowledge from the jungle. I was born in Virginia.'

'I still have d' herbs auld Moira left behind,' blurted Mick Sheridan. 'I was savin' 'em in case she ever came back, but I don't know how to use 'em.'

'Go and get them, Mick,' pleaded Mikey. 'Maybe Mam can remember how to use some of them.'

The black man spoke again. 'If anyone has a weak stomach, they'd better leave now,' he said. 'This dressing has to be changed and the smell is going to be God-awful.'

No one left the room. If anything, they hovered closer as Jeremy began to unravel the bulky bandage from around Liam's hand. The initial stench was overpowering and became even more putrid when the poultice underneath it was removed to expose the wound. Morna turned away and covered her face and Roisin wrapped her arms around her daughter-in-law. It wasn't the smell that was distressing Morna, it was the knowledge that her baby, her beautiful son, lay rotting from the inside.

'Help me take him outside,' said Washington. 'He's burning up with fever.'

'We'll do no such thing,' said Roisin. 'We need to keep him inside and cover him with more blankets. We need to sweat the fever out of him.'

'If you want to cover him up, madam, you might just as well use a shroud and save yourself time later,' replied the black man.

The old woman cast him a withering glance. If things got worse, at least she'd have the satisfaction of laying the blame firmly at the feet of this former slave.

'He's MY grandson,' she spat.

'The bad air in here will kill the boy, Michael,' argued Washington. 'He needs to be cooled down.' He turned to Roisin. 'You asked if I had any magic from Africa. Well I don't, but I do have a pagan secret.'

Roisin hesitated. She remembered old Moira, the wise woman, who kept the secrets of the Druids and dispensed her knowledge and her healing in the village long ago.

'Ah sure do what you have to,' she sniffed, dismissively.

'I can't lift the boy myself, I have a weak back. Alexander, you and Michael take the boy outside. You women, get me some warm water and rags.'

Alexander folded Liam's arms over his chest and he and Michael gently carried the boy outside, where they laid him on a blanket.

'Alexander, swab the boy down with water,' instructed Washingon. 'If he shivers, pay no heed, just keep trying to cool him off. I want to examine the wound in the light.'

A thin film of grey slime covered the inside of the boy's hand. Jeremy took a piece of rag, rinsed it in the warm water, and tried to clean the wound. A blue-bottle fly sensed the putrefaction and hovered overhead, awaiting the chance to lay its eggs. Michael waved it away.

'Leave it, sir,' ordered the black man. 'Maggots will clean rotting flesh better than any surgeon could.'

'If that's your pagan secret,' snarled Roisin, 'I don't think much of it.'

Abraham ignored her and addressed Morna. 'Talk to the boy,' he said. 'Tell him you're here with him and that you love him.' He turned to Roisin. 'You make another poultice. When Mick gets back with the herbs, we'll see what he has. You can mix the herbs in with the bread and salt … and leave the flies alone.'

Roisin snorted and stalked off, her back as straight as a poker.

'Sorry,' said Michael, 'it's just that she's used to having the last word.'

'Don't apologise,' replied Abraham. 'She's like a captain who's lost command of his ship, that's all. She'll get over it.'

Michael shrugged, 'I doubt it,' he said. 'Whatever the outcome of this is, she's got it in for you.'

'I can live with that,' replied Abraham, 'as long as your boy lives.'

*

Two seamen had removed the name of the ship from the stern and were balancing in bosuns' chairs, dangling precariously over the stern, as another seaman handed the new placard down to them. The line of ships was now only seven miles away and the hulls were plain to see.

'It looks like we'll have company anytime now, sir,' said Jones.

Jack Rackham looked through his scope, then slammed it shut in annoyance.

'Shit! It looks like the same sloop from the other day, and she's coming over to give us the eyeball. Let's not be too professional with the handling of the ship. If we look as if we're bungling it, they'll perceive us as less of a threat.'

'Aye, sir. Should we let the sails luff a little, Cap'n?'

'No, don't overdo it, Jonesey. Just let the canvas

ease a little so that we spill some air.'

An hour later the sloop was within a quarter mile, amidships with Prosperity.

'He's giving us the once-over, Jonesey. Hold your course until he signals us.'

'It looks like he's going to sail right past us, Cap'n.'

'He won't do that. He'll come around our stern and check the name.'

In no time, the agile sloop was abeam on the starboard side and, with the advantage of the weather gauge, had closed to within hailing distance.

'She has the tampons off the guns, sir, and she has them run out. Now she's signalling for us to heave to, Cap'n.'

'Then do as she orders, Jonesey. She has the upper hand now.'

Prosperity allowed all the wind to spill from her sails and the ship slowed, her only movement sideways from the wind. The sloop mimicked her actions.

'Ahoy! Camilla!' came a young voice through a speaker horn. 'This is His Majesty's sloop, Whippet. Who do I have the pleasure of addressing.'

'Captain John Rackham, sir, out of Charles Town, late out of Galway.'

'I'm Lieutenant Sally. What is your business in these waters?'

'We were chased by a schooner, sir, a privateer, almost to the French coast two days ago.'

There was a moment of silence as the Lieutenant digested the information. 'You're travelling light,' he said.

'We are, sir. We had to jettison our cargo to keep from losing the ship.'

'What were you carrying?'

'We had ten hogsheads of tobacco, sir. We were bringing it from Galway to Southampton.'

'That's a very small cargo, Captain,' said the English officer suspiciously.

'Our principle assignment was to deliver the owner's son to Ireland. We picked up the cargo just to make a small profit from the mission.'

'From a little smuggling, perhaps.'

'Certainly not, sir. I have the official paperwork here. It's stamped by the Customs House in Galway.'

The lieutenant was disappointed to discover that his hopes of confiscating the vessel as a prize had been dashed. 'Very well, Captain. When and where did you last see the privateer?'

'We dumped the last hogshead a couple of miles off the Pouldavid estuary early yesterday morning. When the schooner stopped to retrieve it, we made our escape.'

'I'd say it was an equally matched pursuit,' said the officer, still suspicious. 'She looked very much like your own vessel.'

'All these Baltimore schooners look alike, sir. The damn Americans have no imagination.'

'That's true enough. How was the ship armed?'

'I only saw the nine-pounder bow chaser, sir. I was too busy trying to get away.'

'Very well, Captain Rackham. Follow me and I will escort you to the Admiral's flagship. He can decide what to do with the information.'

Captain Sally held Rackham in total disdain. Those cowardly colonials were only good for one thing when confronted and that was to run. He'd conveniently forgotten how he himself had turned tail from the schooner several days earlier.

It was a long hour's sailing before they reached the main fleet. The old two-decker second rate had run a pair of its thirty-two pounders out to cover the approach of Whippet and Prosperity. One shot from those heavy guns would reduce the schooner to flotsam. The Lieutenant in command of the sloop was busily raising signal flags at the large vessel, communicating the information he'd received from Rackham. The flagship, in turn, was signalling the frigate sailing ahead of it.

The two smaller ships crossed the line, the sloop and the schooner dipping their flags in salute. The young naval officer thanked Jack for the information by way of the speaking horn.

'Godspeed, Captain Rackham, and watch your back. The admiral is sending us and the light frigate to blockade Douarnenez. If we find your tobacco, we'll have a smoke in your honour. If we find the schooner, I'll buy you a flagon of rum when we next meet.'

When he was out of earshot, Jack exhaled loudly. 'Thank God the admiral was in a hurry to get to Gibraltar, Jonesey,' he said. 'If they'd come aboard to investigate, they'd have found the bloody brandy. They would have confiscated the ship for sure and I'd have been thrown in a dungeon.'

'I'd have been thrown in the next cell,' said Jones.

'You're wrong, Mr. Jones. They'd have hung you. I have family connections.'

CHAPTER 22

A few hours later, on the two-decker flagship Gallant, the ship's captain appeared on deck with a large book.

'Admiral, sir, I've been through the records and I can't find a schooner from Charles Town registered with the name 'Camilla'.

The ageing officer put the back of his hand to his mouth and coughed. Then he looked off to the west, clasped his hands behind his back, and began to rock back and forth.

'We've already dispatched a frigate and the Whippet to chase the French privateer, Captain. I can't afford to waste any more ships chasing an unarmed smuggler. We have a mission in Gibraltar. What was that captain's name again?'

'Rackham, sir.'

The admiral thought for a moment. 'Rackham, eh? There was a Calico Jack Rackham once, a pirate in the Indies. He got his neck stretched in Jamaica, as I recall.'

'If he changed the name of his ship, sir, we don't know who he might be.'

'The bold bastard, he sailed right through a British

THE DEVIL'S OWN LUCK

line. Ha! I admire his nerve. Record it in the ship's log as "unknown schooner".' The admiral had no intention of besmirching his own record in the admiralty office by making it known he'd been outsmarted by a colonial brigand.

'Should I log the captain's name, sir?'

'You should not, Captain! That scoundrel will get his comeuppance eventually if he carries on pushing his luck.'

The captain left the quarterdeck, still smarting from the admonition. The admiral looked westward and smiled to himself. Yes, you're a cheeky bastard alright, Rackham, he thought, but it's rogues like you who make this game entertaining.

*

'Alexander, you're to stay here with Liam and keep him cool. There's work I have to get done for your father and I've already been off the job for a day. Those fields have to be hoed and the seeds planted and there's nothing else I can do to help the boy at the moment. You are my eyes and ears. If there's any change at all, you're to let me know, understand?'

'Aye aye, sir.' Alexander knuckled his forehead in salute, just as he had done a thousand times when given orders aboard ship.

As soon as the black man had gone, Siobhan approached and stood with her mother at Liam's head. Morna looked at the girl forlornly. 'Stay here with your brother, macushla. Your grandmother and I need to get food ready for the workers.'

That left only Michael and Jamie with the three youngsters and they weren't there long. Michael took a long last look at his prostrate son and set his jaw.

'Come on, Jamie,' he said. 'You and I are going to burn that feckin' caher to the ground.'

Clancy hesitated for a moment as a hundred doubts went through his mind. 'Hasn't messin' wit' dat place done enough harm already, Mikey?'

'You can stay here and twiddle your thumbs if you like, Clancy. I'm going to make sure that place is razed to the ground and, if there are any spirits or demons in there, they'd better start looking for a new home.'

Michael stalked off, followed reluctantly by his partner, and Siobhan and Alex stayed behind to minister to the suffering boy.

'I saw ya,' she said to him. 'You saluted Mr. Washington. Are you a sailor so?'

Alexander stopped rubbing Liam down with the wet rag and straightened himself.

'No, miss, I'm not a sailor,' he said, somewhat haughtily. 'I'm a ship's officer.'

'Well pardon me, yer majesty, I'm sure,' she replied indignantly. 'I hadn't meant to insult ya.'

Alex realised he'd just stepped on his own tongue and he quickly tried to rectify the situation.

'Oh no, you didn't. I didn't mean to…. I mean….'

Alexander was back on his heels and the girl saw her chance. 'You're cruel,' she said. 'First ya tell me dere's somethin' wrong wit' me eyes and now you're actin' all superior, just because you've seen more of d' world dan me.'

The young man had been hit with a left-right combination without the girl having lifted a finger.

'On the contrary,' he said hesitantly. 'I think your eyes are … beautiful.'

'Do ya really t'ink so?' replied Siobhan coquettishly.

Alexander felt himself blush from his toes up. 'I.… er.… yes, I do.'

Women have instincts which have always remained a complete mystery to men and which they develop at an early age. Siobhan instinctively knew that, if she didn't want to frighten Alexander away, she was going to have to tone down her manner and play to his ego.

'So have ya seen much of d' world?'

The young fellow was like a fly caught in a spider's web. 'I've seen all the colonies in America,' he boasted, 'and I've been to Cuba … Jamaica too.'

The spider was getting ready to tie up the fly. 'Dat's unbelievable! A ship's officer and a world traveller already. How old are ya?'

Alexander straightened himself to his full height. 'I'll be seventeen in July.'

'I'm sixteen.'

'Really? You look older. I thought you were at least nineteen.' The fly had turned the tables on the spider.

'You did?' she said, twirling a strand of her red hair around her fingers.

'I just said so, didn't I?' Alexander was as thick as a box of hammers when it came to the opposite sex, with all its intricacies and intrigues. Years spent aboard ship in a man's world had rendered him ignorant in the art of flirtation.

'Give me that rag,' she said stonily. 'I'll cool Liam off for a while.'

She reached for the cloth he'd had been rubbing Liam down with but he wouldn't let go of it.

'Mr. Washington said it was my job. I'm under orders.'

'Will ya let go of dat!'

'No, get your own.'

'Gimme it or I swear I'll box yer ears fer ya!'

Liam stirred and muttered something in a weak voice. The tug of war ceased immediately and both young people leaned closer to him.

'What's dat, macushla?' implored Siobhan. 'What are ya tryin' to say, Liam dear?'

Liam's eyes flickered and he struggled to open them. 'I said shut d' feck up.'

Siobhan and Alex looked at each other in astonishment, then Siobhan ran to get her mother, leaving the young man tending her brother. Liam spoke again. His voice was barely audible and Alex leaned closer.

'I'm ill,' rasped Liam, 'not deaf.'

'What do you mean?'

'I heard everyt'ing … just too weak to open me eyes or talk. I'm tired… goin' t' sleep now.'

'Can you just stay awake long enough to speak to your mam and grandma? They've been beside themselves with worry.'

'I'll try … so tired.'

As soon as Morna and Roisin arrived, Alexander ran to get Mr. Washington. Furrows were being hoed in the fields and the work was progressing nicely, so Abraham took time off to go and see if the crisis had passed. When he arrived, Morna was stroking Liam's head and Roisin held his left hand. Both women looked elated and even Roisin felt a little more hospitable towards the black man.

'It's not over yet,' he warned them. 'The poison is still in the wound with all the rotten flesh. We'll cover the boy's hand with a damp cloth and leave the maggots to do their job over the next few days.'

'I still don't like it,' said Roisin.

'I know you don't and I'm sorry but we might even have to do it again, once they've eaten their fill and formed shells. There's a lot of dead meat in there and it needs to come out or we'll be back where we started.'

Liam pulled Roisin towards him and spoke weakly to her. She nodded her head, placed his hand back on his chest and hurried away. When she came back, she had a bowl of broth and a hunk of buttered bread and gammon. She handed it to the black man.

'Liam said I was to feed the doctor,' she said tersely. 'Siobhan, take Ned's lad back to Hogan's and make sure he gets a decent meal inside him. Morna and I will get a few spoons of broth inside our patient.'

Abraham tucked into the food. He'd not eaten a thing since the whole incident had begun, the day before. Roisin watched as he ate.

'I think we might have got off on the wrong foot,' she said. 'I'm not saying I was wrong, mind. You're still the colour of a donkey but perhaps you're not as big an ass as I thought you were.'

'Damned with faint praise,' retorted Abraham, between mouthfuls.

'We'll call a truce so. Maybe, when Liam is up and around, we can resume hostilities.'

Abraham hauled himself up and bowed slightly. 'I shall look forward to it, madam,' he replied. Something caught his attention out the corner of his eye and he looked in the direction of the faerie ring. When he uttered a murmur of surprise, everyone else followed his gaze. The whole copse was burning furiously.

'Looks like Mikey decided to take it out on d' poor trees,' said Morna.

'Well I, for one, will be happy when every bit of that cursed ground is scorched,' replied Roisin.

Siobhan had ushered Alexander to a table in the bar and was dishing out ham and spuds onto a plate.

'Mam said ya need fattenin' up.'

'Mr. Washington says I'm thin because I put on a growth spurt.'

'Yer already as tall as Jamie Clancy sure ... ya probably only weigh half as much dough.' Alexander was shovelling the food into his mouth. 'Slow down, you'll choke yerself.'

'I haven't had a bite to eat since yesterday morning.'

The small talk was over as far as the girl was concerned.

'So do ship's officers make lots of money?'

'I don't know. They must do, I suppose. They all live in big houses.'

'And d' ya have a girl waitin' fer ya back in Amerrycuh?'

Alexander swallowed another bolus of food, oblivious of the reason for Siobhan's interest. 'No. I've been on a ship for four years or more.'

'What do ya t'ink of Ireland so far?'

The young man remembered his father's words from a few days before. 'It has its charm,' he said, and spooned more food into his mouth.

'How did ya get to be officer on a ship at your age?'

'It's easy when your father owns the ship.'

There was a long pause as she narrowed her eyes and digested the little scrap of information which the blockhead had blurted out. Alexander was still too obsessed with what was on the plate in front of him to realise that the cat had just escaped from the bag.

'I t'ought Ned Flood was yer da.'

Siobhan had thrown a banana peel on the ground and Alexander had slipped on it.

'Er … yes … that is correct. My father is Ned Flood.'

'Well ya just said yer father owns a ship.'

'Er … yes … I did say that, didn't I. What I meant to say is that my father runs things for Mr. …' he couldn't for the life of him remember what the damn horse's name was.

'Mr. Flynn?' she offered.

'Yes. Yes, that's it…Mr. Flynn.'

'Yer lyin' t' me, Alexander Flood, I just ain't worked out yet what yer lyin' about. C'mere, let me get ya some more food.'

'No!' he protested. 'I mean no thank you, I'm full, and I have to get back and take care of your brother.'

'Well alright so,' she said. 'You go, but you and me ain't finished talkin' yet. By d' way, you was very brave stickin' up fer Lizzy d' udder night, even if ya did get knocked on yer arse.'

Alexander hung down his head. Fisticuffs was not his forte and, if he'd had time to think about what he was doing a couple of nights ago, he probably would have stayed on the sidelines and let his father do the fighting.

'Oh I just did what I thought was right.'

'Well I t'ought it was very noble of ya.'

'You did?' he said, smiling and pulling himself up to his full height.

'I just said so, didn't I?'

*

'I think we've given them the slip this time, Mr. Jones. Set a course for Bournemouth. We'll drop the cargo off and see what the market brings us.'

'Are we going into Poole, sir?'

'No, not this time, Jonesey. There have been enough close shaves on this voyage already and I don't want to get bottled up in that harbour. I'll go ashore and get some oystermen to carry the brandy to the docks. The customs officers there have been friendly ever since the locals drove off those rogues from Kent.'

'I heard the Hawkhurst gang laid siege to the place. Is it right what they say, that the townspeople drove them off?'

'They did indeed,' smiled Jack. 'Those fellows from the New Forest don't want outsiders poaching on their turf.'

'You'd think there was enough coast for everybody to bring the goods in. Those arses from Kent just got greedy.'

'Well, that's not our concern,' said Rackham. 'We just want to drop our cargo, collect our money and leave the fighting to them.'

'We're a barrel short, sir.'

'At least we still have Prosperity and what we don't make on this trip, we'll make on another. If Ned gets those Irishmen into full production, we can make the run there and back in a few days.'

'I'll steer west, Cap'n, until you give me a proper course.'

'There's some weather moving in, Jonesey. Have the men shorten sail while I go below and get a course charted.'

'Aye aye, sir.'

CHAPTER 23

L iam's fever subsided dramatically outside in the cool air and he was moved back into the cottage. Michael and Clancy waited until the fire was well established, then headed to Hogan's to get themselves a bite to eat.

'We've done it now, Mikey,' lamented Clancy. 'If d' spirits in dat faerie ring was angry before, dey'll be furious by now. Sure God only knows what'll happen.'

'Old wives' tales and superstitions, Jamie. I told you, it was just a pile of auld stones and trees and nothing more. In a couple of days, when it's cooled down, we'll go back with the horses and start clearing the stumps.'

'Roisin said Liam was awake earlier but she says he's still weak, that he just wants to sleep.'

'She told me too.'

What Michael didn't say was that Roisin had also given him an earful about violating 'holy ground', warning him that they could expect nothing but trouble from now on.

'When we've finish eatin', we'll call back in on d' lad.'

Liam was sleeping peacefully when the two men arrived at the cottage. Siobhan sat watching over her brother. When her father walked in, she turned her attention away from her sleeping sibling and addressed her father.

'Dat fella, Alexander, he's a quare one.'

'What makes you say that?' asked her father.

'Told me he was a ship's officer, if ya don't mind. I told Mam and she said he was just tryin' to impress me. Mam says dat's what young fellas do.'

'Well don't be too hasty in doubting him. After all, the first time I saw him, he was standing on the deck of a ship with Mr. Washington.'

Siobhan was silent for a few moments. 'He said somet'n about his father bein' d' owner of d' ship, and den he couldn't remember Mr. Flynn's name.'

'Ah sure, you Hogan women have that effect on men.'

'Only when d' men are lyin'.' Siobhan eyed her father. 'And I have a feelin' you're not exactly tellin' d' truth yerself right now, Da.'

'Ya mustn't talk to yer da like dat, girl.' Jamie put his hand on Liam's chest and felt his breathing. 'He's a lot better now d' fever's down a bit.'

'Mr. Washington said we're to keep an eye on 'im,' said Siobhan, 'and if d' fever starts up again, we're to cool 'im down.'

'Right so,' said Michael. 'We'll be back in a couple of hours, love. Jamie and I have to go down to Ballyartella.'

'Ya needn't bother, Da. D' miller says he'll have nutt'n t' do wit' ya. He says yer cursed and so is d' whole family.'

'Where did you hear that?'

'Mick heard it from Gleeson ... 'e heard it from somebody else.'

'Is that right? Well now, I'll take a walk down there anyway. We've been doing business for years with auld man Connors.'

Clancy looked at Michael as if he was looking at a dead man.

'Ya see, Mikey? An' dis is just d' start of it.'

If Jamie had been aware of what was happening with Jack Rackham, he would have known that the jinx was already several days old.

*

'Ten pounds a barrel?' exclaimed Jack. 'Are you mad? You can get twice that for the brandy!'

The customs officer leant back in his chair and clasped his hands behind his neck. 'You're right, I can. But you can't, now take it or leave it, that's the price.'

'What's the price of tobacco?'

'That's down too. You'll be lucky to get six pounds a hogshead.'

'How's a man supposed to make an honest living at those prices?'

The officer shrugged. 'It's the cost of doing business. We've had loads stolen and, what with the Crown tightening the thumbscrews, well, the risks have increased.'

Jack had been delivering barrels of every size and description for more years than he cared to remember but this was the first time he'd ever found himself well and truly over one. He had loaded the brandy onto fishing boats, offshore, and they had rowed them into the harbour at Poole. The containers had then been floated through the sewers to a basement under the Customs Office. Only at that point, when the labour had already been done and it was time to collect, had the agent delivered the blow.

'You're nothing but a thief!' spat Jack.

'And you're a smuggler. Report me to the authorities, why don't you?

The port of Poole, like many of the towns in coastal England, derived most of its income from the importation of contraband. Tariffs and taxes had made the risk more than worthwhile. The officer in charge of the Customs House made an official salary but, with each shipment received, his purse grew heavier and the town grew more prosperous.

'Very well. I'll take the ten.'

'That's a very wise move, Captain. Had you tried to remove the goods, I would have been forced to arrest you.'

Jack was on thin ice and he could hear it cracking under his feet. If he pushed too hard, he might find himself in gaol, with no payment for the brandy. The thinly veiled threat had been enough. Jack counted the money. This bastard would not be above shortchanging him. At least the Frenchman had used a gun to cheat him and Jack had had the satisfaction of throwing the gobshite over the side.

Jones was waiting at the dock with a few oarsman to row the captain back to Prosperity which, if the current state of affairs persisted, could quite aptly be renamed 'Destitution'.

'How much did we make, sir?'

Jack handed him the pouch and Jonesey weighed it in his hand.

'Jesus, sir, it feels like you only got half what we'd thought!'

'We sail in the morning, Mr. Jones. We'll head up

the west coast of England to find another market.'

'I still know people in Cornwall, Cap'n. They might at least be able to set us in the right direction.'

'Good man. I'm considering using Waterford to load the ship instead of Galway.'

'We still have those ten hogsheads of tobacco in Galway, sir.'

'I'm aware of that, Jones. I'm hoping Ned can get those two Irish bumpkins to bring them to Waterford.'

*

'We'll move Liam up to d' big house,' said Ned. 'He'll be a lot more comfortable up dere.'

'You will in a pig's eye!' snapped Roisin. 'He needs his family around him now.'

'You have d' bar to run, and Morna's busy cookin' fer d' workers.'

Roisin knew Ned was right. 'Alright so,' she said, 'but Siobhan will go with her brother. I only need her help in the bar on Saturday nights.'

'Tell d' girl to pack her t'ings. Oy'll get a carriage down here to pick up her and d' boy dis afternoon.'

Roisin had been trying to find a weak spot in Ned's reasoning and found only a minor one.

'You keep a close eye on that son of yours. There's something going on between him and our Siobhan. I can sense it and I don't like it.'

'Oh, Oy'll be doin' dat alright. Sure I've hopes of Alexander gettin' himself hooked up wit' one o' dem rich farmer's daughters.'

'Is that right?' said Roisin, all of a sudden indignant. 'So you don't think my granddaughter is good enough for your precious son?'

'Jayzis woman! Has every feckin' conversation wit' you got to be an argument? Oy said Oy'd keep an eye on 'em and Oy will.'

Michael returned from the saw mill, where he'd found himself to be less than welcome. The old miller had been decidedly hostile towards him, telling Mikey that he'd sell him the wood he needed to build the drying barn but on one condition, that he would only deal with Jamie. The miller hadn't blamed Clancy for the destruction of the faerie ring, believing he'd been under the evil influence of Michael.

When Mikey got back, he found Roisin tying scraps of cloth to the rag tree which grew beside the holy well. That tree, at least, had remained intact. Michael watched his mother for a while. His father had always dismissed the tradition as nonsense but had accepted Roisin's belief in it.

Siobhan was preparing for the trip to Johnstown. A few hours before, it had seemed like Liam was on the road to recovery but the fever had returned and now he was once again dipping in and out of delirium. His face was burning red and the sweat was pouring from him like it had on that first night. Mr. Washington was summoned and he immediately interrupted his work to return to the boy's bedside.

'You'd better get his mother and father,' he told the girl.

Abraham knew that the sudden turn in Liam's condition didn't bode at all well for the young man. The fleeting improvement he'd experienced earlier had been merely a fey, a flash of well-being, the likes of which sometimes occur just before a person sinks into the final throes of extremis.

He met Michael and Morna at the door. 'There's

nothing I can do,' he told them. 'He needs you now.'

Roisin had been following close behind them and, when she saw Abraham, she glared at him accusingly.

'Liam was getting better,' she spat, her voice full of venom, 'then you let the flies at him. You killed my grandson and I'll never forgive you, you bastard.'

Abraham bore the rebuke and lowered his head. 'I did the best I could for him, m'um. I swear on my immortal soul that I did my best for the boy.'

Roisin spat on the floor in front of him. 'Your immortal soul, is it?' she snarled. 'Your kind don't have a soul.'

*

Mick Sheridan was back in the barn at Johnstown and he was fingering a shred of paper which he'd seen hanging on the stall where the horse was kept. When he'd approached it, the paper had flown off the stall and landed at his feet as though blown there by a gust of wind, even though there wasn't a breeze to be felt. A sudden shudder went through his body. Someone's walkin' on me grave, he thought. The big man stooped down, picked up the paper and peered at what had been scrawled on it in charcoal. He read the words out loud.

'I am waiting for you.'

He turned the scrap of paper over a few times in his hand, then looked around in the gloom of the barn. He crumpled the note up in his fist and turned to the horse.

'Learned how t' write now, have ya?' he said mirthfully, but glanced around the barn again. He straightened out the paper, read the words once more,

213

then threw the note to the floor and began to saddle up the big horse.

'I might be goin' mad in me auld age, big fella, but I have a funny feelin' there's somewhere we need to be.'

*

Morna held Liam's bandaged hand and sobbed quietly; her heart was breaking. Her only son was breathing spasmodically, his breath gurgling in his chest, and with each of his hesitant breaths her heart stopped, fearing it would be his last. Michael was holding the boy's other hand and trying to will his own life into the lad.

'This is my fault,' he croaked, trying to be strong in front of the women.

Roisin closed her eyes tightly and prayed harder than she'd ever done before, while Siobhan gently wiped the sweat from Liam's brow. There's something terrible about a death watch. It's a time when mortality and impotence collide, a time of inconsolable grief as you watch the life force drain from the person you love, knowing that the end is inevitable. Their boy was strong and, for him, the process of dying could be a long one. They all prayed he wouldn't suffer.

*

Mick mounted the horse, dug his spurs into the beast's flanks and ducked as they passed under the barn door. Once out in the open, the horse gathered momentum and they galloped down the carriageway leading from Johnson House. When they came to the main road, Mick wheeled the horse right and they

214

headed towards Gortalocca at breakneck speed.

Ned heard the commotion and looked out the window. 'What in God's name's got into dat daft auld sod?' he said. 'And dat's my horse he's ridin'!'

'Something must have happened in the village,' ventured Alexander. 'I'll saddle up Mick's horse and see if there's anything I can do to help.' Without pausing for a second, Alexander bolted from the room and headed for the barn.

The old man had a five minute head start by the time Alexander had the hobby saddled and the young man calculated that Mick would be halfway to Gortalocca by now. Mick was indeed halfway there but instead of heading directly to the village, he reined the horse to a halt and turned the animal off the road onto an ancient path. When the scrub became too dense to ride any further he dismounted, tied the horse to a bush and continued on foot. The path was all but obliterated by undergrowth but Mick knew the way. He slowed to a stop and hesitated for a moment, thinking that his brain must have become addled, then carried on through the dense thicket, compelled by something he couldn't explain. The path was darkened by overhanging branches as Mick trudged onwards, pushing twigs out of his way and ducking those too big to move.

Finally, he came to an opening where once had stood a tiny mud cottage. He looked around him. He knew that this was where he was supposed to be but he didn't know why. A frail voice startled him.

'Bout time too,' it said. 'It's a good t'ing ya never married, Mick Sheridan. You'd be late fer yer own weddin'.'

There followed a soft cackle of laughter and the big

man wheeled around to where the ruins of the old cottage still stood. When he saw the tiny ancient woman, his jaw dropped and he tried to speak but the words caught in his throat.

She smiled a toothless grin. 'Don't be afraid,' she rasped, 'I ain't no ghost. Come over here and let me feel yer face. I've bin blind these last thirty years.'

'Moira? Jayzis, is that you, Moira? It can't be! Wh…where've ya been? It's bin….'

'Quiet, boyo, I'm here for Liam.'

'But … but Liam's bin dead twenty years sure.'

'The other Liam, ya simpleton, d' young lad. C'mere, I said. I need ya to help me. I can't get around too well on me own so you'll have to carry me. Hurry up, ya big ox! We haven't much time.'

CHAPTER 24

'The big money is in slaves of course, Captain Rackham.'

Jack was sharing a jug of ale with a Cornish businessman. 'The colonies need workers,' said the finely-dressed man, quaffing his beer, 'and it's been discovered that blacks are more productive than indentured labourers.'

'Who discovered that?'

'The plantations in America are getting bigger and they're able to produce more with slave labour. They've already had as many as they can get from Jamaica and the islands so they've begun to import more from West Africa. The Arab traders make alliances with the local kings, then they raid the villages for prisoners. The number of slaves they ship is only limited by the transport available.'

'So the price of tobacco is down because they can produce more?'

'That's right, it's simply a question of supply. Right now we're swimming in tobacco so the prices are down, especially since some of the farmers in the Midlands are growing it now too. Domestic production isn't subject to the shipping and Admiralty fees, you see.'

'Give me a price.'

'The best I can do is eight pounds per hogshead and, by next year, I expect it to be down to six. You really should think about getting yourself involved in the slave trade.'

'Forget the slave trade, it's not practical. My ship isn't big enough to carry more than twenty, thirty at the most.'

'If your ship was properly kitted out, you could carry up to a hundred if you packed them in like salted kippers.'

'I'll stick to tobacco and alcohol,' responded Jack indignantly. 'I have a certain.... moral objection to the concept of slavery.'

'My intention wasn't to upset your sensitivities I'm sure, Mr. Rackham. I was merely suggesting a solution to your dilemma.'

Jack Rackham possessed many qualities which contributed toward his prowess as a smuggler. He was daring, intelligent, cunning and able to make split-second decisions, but his most abiding quality was his total lack of scruples.

'What's the going rate for a slave delivered here to Newquay?'

'In the region of fifty pounds, sir.'

Jack gave a low whistle. 'And what does it cost to buy a slave in Niger?'

'The last I heard, a fit male could be had for fifteen pounds. Of course you could always buy one in Morocco or Algeria for around twenty and that would save you about six days of travel each way. Perhaps you and I could form a mutually-beneficial partnership of sorts.'

Jack snapped himself back into the moment.

'I have two other partners I have to consult first, sir, and they're in Ireland. I should be able to get back to you in two to three weeks, God willing.'

God wasn't playing much of a part in what was going on inside Jack Rackham's head right now. It was the jingle of a full purse that shaped his thoughts. He drained his glass of claret and headed back to the harbour where his ship was anchored.

*

Alexander reigned the hobby to a halt when he saw Mr. Washington walking back to Johnstown with his head hung low.

'What's happened?' he called.

Washington looked up, startled from his thoughts by the sound of the hoof beats. 'The boy is dying. They're going to blame me.'

Alex didn't answer, but spurred the old horse into a gallop.

'Jayzis, Mick, don't drop me or dese auld bones will crack like a clay pot.'

'I'm not goin' to drop ya, auld woman. It's just me knees ain't what dey used to be. We'll be back to where d' horse is in a few minutes and den we can ride d' rest of d' way to Gortalocca.'

'D' years ain't done much fer yer memory, Mick Sheridan. Did ya forget I never ride on animals? God gave me two legs o' me own, sure why would I?'

'But dem two legs He gave ya ain't much good anymore, auld mother. D' horse'll get us dere quicker.'

'Everyt'ing has to be fast in today's mad world,' said

the old hag wistfully. 'Speed and money, dat's all anybody cares about dese days.'

When they arrived at where the horse was tethered, Mick untied it and slapped it on the rump, knowing it would find its own way back to the barn. The unfettered animal didn't gallop away as Mick had expected but instead turned and sniffed at the old crone.

'Get yerself off home, friend,' said the old woman, and the horse took off for its stable.

'I see ya still talk t' d' animals, Moira.'

'I get more sense from 'em. Now hurry yer arse, Mick Sheridan, we haven't much time.'

'I'm goin' as quick as I can, auld woman, I'm not a horse.'

'No, yer an ass, now shut up and get a move on.'

Alexander leapt down from the old hobby and, without bothering to tether it, ran into the cottage. A small group of people were huddled around the prostrate figure of young Liam, who lay in front of the fire. Alexander instinctively knew that the end was not yet here, but that it was in sight. He stood behind Siobhan and put his hand on her shoulder.

'I just can't believe dis is happenin',' she said tearfully. 'Just last week we was fightin' and squabblin' like we always do, and now I have t' say goodbye t' me little brother ... and I never told 'im I love 'im.'

Alexander's heart ached for her and he searched for something to say. 'He knew... he knows that you loved... that you love him.'

There are times when, no matter how eloquent a person is, there just aren't any right words. Silence settled like a shroud on the room for what seemed an eternity. The only sounds were the crackle of the turf fire and Liam's laboured breathing, which came in gasps now.

Everyone stood up, startled by the door being kicked open, and Mick crashed in, a grey bundle in his arms.

'Mick Sheridan!' shouted Roisin. 'Have you no respect?'

A soft cackle came from the bundle.

'What in God's name do you have in there?' asked Michael.

'Put me down, Mick' rasped the bundle, 'near d' boy.'

Roisin blessed herself and clasped her hands together on her chest. 'Holy Mary, Mother o' God, it's Moira. How did…?'

'Whisht, woman, don't anyone make a sound.'

Moira ran her bony fingers across Liam's face and smiled. 'Ah sure you're d' image of yer grandad, lad, yer namesake.' Her thin fingers traced themselves down to the bandage on his right hand and she slipped it off, exposing the wound and exploring it gently. 'Maggots. Good. Dem little beauties'll clean it up.' She leaned closer to Liam's face and tilted her head so she could hear him breathing. 'Dat auld poison's got into his lungs and 'e can't breathe. Roll 'im over onto 'is side. It'll be easier fer him to get some air.'

Liam was rolled over and, almost immediately, his breathing became more regular, although still dangerously shallow.

'Hand me me bag.' Six hands simultaneously reached for the sack. 'Just one of ye!' she scolded. Mick handed the bag to her. 'Do ya have any spuds on d' boil?' asked the ancient one. Morna reached for the pot which was hanging over the stove and answered her.

'You'll have t' speak up, pet, I'm as blind as an earthworm.'

'I have some po-tatoes in the pot here,' annunciated Morna.

'Good. Take one out an' bring it here to cool fer a bit. Dat's grand. Now take d' rest out and bring d' pot over wit' d' hot water in it.'

Moira rummaged through her bag, pulled out a few small sacks and poured some of the contents of each into the pot.

'Somebody get me a blanket. I'm goin' to put d' boys head over d' hot water and d' blanket over his head.'

Siobhan handed her a blanket and the old woman took it, holding onto the girl's hand for a moment. 'You'll do very well fer yerself, my dear,' she said softly. 'You can rely on it.' Siobhan pulled her hand away as if she'd been scalded by the hot water and the old crone turned her attention back to her patient.

'Dis'll make d' boy cough but dat's good. He has to get rid o' d' pus in his lungs.'

'What are ya goin' t' do wit d' spud?' asked Mick, totally absorbed by the goings on.

'I'm goin' t' eat it, ya eejit. I almost starved t' death waitin' fer you t' come t' me.'

Roisin couldn't keep quiet any longer.

'We all thought you were dead, Moira. You've been gone this last five and twenty years.'

'Five years, five and twenty years, it's all d' same t' me.'

'But where were you?'

'Wherever I was needed.'

'Why did you leave?'

'Ah me work here was done, and I'd left Liam in charge so I knew d' village was in good hands.'

'Liam's been dead eighteen years. Why didn't you come back?'

'I t'ought d' village would be safe wit' yer man over dere.' She cast a scowl in the general direction of Mikey, who lowered his head.

'So why now?'

'You should know dat, Roisin Hogan. Sure wasn't it yerself who tied a bit 'o cloth t' d' rag tree?'

'I've done that a hundred times.'

'Ah but dis time it was different. Dose udder times ya prayed wit' yer head … dis time ya prayed wit' yer heart and dat makes all d' difference.'

'Well I don't know what you're annoyed with me for,' protested Michael. 'All I was did was try to save the town, just like Da did.'

Moira turned to where the voice had come from. 'Dat's how ya started off, but den ya t'ought ya could make money by forgettin' about d' auld ways. Well, d' auld ones haven't forgotten about you, Michael Hogan. What you did wasn't d' way yer father would've done t'ings. He always respected people's beliefs, even if he didn't believe 'em 'imself. And as fer savin' d' town, sure didn't ya nearly lose it altogether?'

Before Michael could respond, Liam began to cough … a heavy, wet, raspy cough.

'Mick!' snapped Moira. 'Slap d' lad on d' back, not too hard mind.'

'I can do it myself,' objected Mikey.

'Haven't you done enough already? Now get out o' me sight.' The old blind woman chortled at her own joke.

Michael stood outside in the fresh air and inhaled

deeply. Moira looked much as she'd done twenty-five years before. He hadn't been much younger than his son when he knew her and she'd seemed so old to him. Then he remembered that anyone over twenty-five had seemed old to him back then.

'I want ye all out o' dis room now,' ordered the hag, 'except fer Roisin and Mick.' The room emptied quickly and, once they were alone, Moira began. 'After d' auld priest died, I stayed on fer a while to watch t'ings. Once I'd satisfied meself that Liam could manage, I got an urge t' go. I reckoned that if I told anyone me plans. dey'd try and stop me, or at least try and talk me out of it.

'I was up in a village in Mayo and a few weeks ago, a fella and 'is wife came t'rough who I knew to be Robbie. Robert always was a loose talker and he had some money so o' course he was drinkin' and talkin'. I t'ought dat's how he'd grow up and he did. Anyways, I heard him talkin' about how his da had died years before and it made me so sad to hear it. I t'ought of Liam like a son. Robbie blabbed on about how Mikey had taken over and how t'ings had changed in Gortalocca. Now I'm old enough to know dat t'ings change and at first it didn't bother me, but after a while d' same urge I'd had to go wanderin' made me want to come back and see fer meself, maybe put a few flowers on Liam's grave and hang somet'in on d' auld rag tree. Dat's where I first met Liam, did ye know dat?'

'Liam and Jamie searched for you for a long time after you disappeared,' said Roisin.

'Ah I know sure, and it broke me heart, but I couldn't tell Liam I was leavin'. He would've tried to get me to stay. He wouldn't have understood, ya see.'

'How old are ya, Moira?' asked Mick

The old hag cast him a withering glance, then cackled her familiar laugh. 'Don't ya know you should never ask a girl how old she is? I won't tell ya, but I'll tell ya dis. I can remember Cromwell ravagin' Ireland, and dat was near ninety years ago.'

'But ya don't look any older dan ya did twenty-five years ago.'

'Neither does Knigh Castle, down de road,' Moira cackled, 'but if ya look closer, you'll see dere's a few more cracks and a few more stones fallen off it. Slap Liam on d' back again, will ya Mick.'

Mick did as he was ordered and Liam began choking and spitting out a thick yellow exudate.

'Good lad,' urged Moira. 'Get dat shite out o' yer lungs.' Liam's breathing was becoming a little less raspy now. 'Whoever administered t' d' boy's hand saved it wit' dat poultice and d' maggots. I could smell d' bread in d' wound. Dem maggots'll clean it, not a bother. In a couple o' days, I'll be able to sew it up.'

Roisin looked down at the floor. She felt ashamed that, in her grief, she had placed the blame on Abraham Washington. Even if it wasn't in her to apologise, she would try to make it up to him in her own way.

'How did ya get all d' way down here?' asked Mick.

'A farmer took me to Galway. He owed me a favour fer takin' care of his wife when she got d' fever after havin' a baby. A tinker took me to Portumna. Now, dere was a man who still believes in d' auld ways. From dere, a friend of his took me to Borrisokane and den I only had to walk a little way and another farmer on 'is way to Nenagh took me all d' way t' me auld cottage. D' world is full o' kind people. I might tell ya more later, Roisin. Now would ya ever send Michael back in here t' me? I have a bone t' pick wit' him.'

By now Ned had arrived on his horse, which had
returned safely to his stall in the barn. He stood holding
the reins and was deep in conversation with Michael
when Roisin came out and told Mikey that Moira
wanted to talk to him. Ned handed the reins to
Alexander, who was standing next to Siobhan, and
followed Michael inside.

'Close the door!' scolded Moira. 'Were ye born in a
barn?' Ned slammed the door shut, startling the blind
woman. 'Agh! A Corkman! None of ye have manners.'
Ned stared at the blind woman in disbelief, then looked
at Michael.

'How did she…?'

Moira smiled and her laughter lines piled in on top
of the wrinkles already etched into her weathered face.

'Maybe I'm a witch,' she said, 'and maybe I ain't.'
The blood drained from Ned's face. 'Or maybe it could
be d' smell o' dat perfume yer wearin'. Ya smell like
gentry instead of a Corkman. I heard dat big horse o'
yours gallop back up to yer house.'

'And how did ya know Oy'm a Corkman?'

'Ah, it's no big secret. Mick told me about ya when
we was on our way to Gortalocca. So, you're d'
phantom priest from Cork, are ya? I t'ought you'd be
bigger sure.'

'Oy get dat a lot,' replied Ned.

'I'll talk t' you later. Now get yerself away while I
talk t' Mikey here … and don't slam d' door. Mick, you
can leave now too. Me and dis fella have a good few
t'ings t' talk about.'

CHAPTER 25

'Cap'n, we've got a sail to the west. We should cross her in an hour or so.'

'What is she, Jonesey?'

'Looks like the brig we saw in Baltimore, but she's still too far away to know for certain.'

'I'll meet you up on deck, Mr. Jones.'

The captain extended the sections on the brass telescope and stared at the ship on the horizon.

'Hold your course, Mr. Jones. It's too far from Fastnet to be the same one.'

On the deck of the Albatross, Willoughby was staring through a scope at Prosperity.

'Helmsman, steer a course to intercept that schooner.'

From the conformation of the ship, the English officer had already surmised it was Rackham returning to Ireland. He thought he was sailing a little north for the passage at Fastnet. Perhaps he intended to call at one of the ports on Ireland's east coast. A sudden spring squall momentarily obscured the view. I wonder if you're carrying a bit of contraband, Jack Rackham, he thought. If you are, this could be a profitable meeting for me.

During times of war, vessels could be impounded by the Admiralty for the slightest infraction. The ship and its cargo would be sold and the proceeds divided up between the captain and crew of whichever vessel captured it. The crew of the captured ship would most likely be impressed into the Royal Navy and the officers fined and incarcerated for the violation.

Within the hour, the two ships were abreast of each other. Rackham had eased the sails and let the wind spill out of them, keeping just enough speed to allow the helm to respond. Willoughby's crew expertly pulled the brig alongside, keeping the weather advantage, and the Englishman spoke through a speaking horn.

'We meet again, Captain Rackham,' he said cordially. 'I hope that your trip was profitable.'

Rackham didn't wait for the speaking horn to be brought him. He cupped his hands around his mouth.

'Hardly, sir,' he shouted. 'We had a run-in with a privateer and had to jettison our cargo.'

'That's unfortunate, Captain. I'm sure the owners will be most disappointed.'

'Oh there will be the devil to pay, Mr. Willoughby.'

'Ah yes, the devil. He always takes his cut first. What cargo are you carrying?'

'We're as empty as a pauper's purse, sir. You are welcome to inspect us if you wish.'

'No thank you, Captain, I'd rather not get wet. Where are you bound?'

'Tramore, sir. What are you doing in the Irish Sea yourself?'

'Ah, pampering to the whims and vagaries of those who sail desks, Jack. What say I accompany you to port? I can do a thorough inspection there and perhaps we can share an ale or two?'

'Aye aye, Captain. I'll shorten sail so you can keep up.'

Willoughby winced at the sting of the last remark. Rackham knew he could outrun the old brig and he was rubbing salt into the wound.

'No need for that, Captain, we'll be in a few hours behind you. That will give you time to tidy up your ship for inspection.'

Willoughby was on to him and Jack knew it.

*

'C'mere to me, Michael, let me touch yer face.' Moira ran her fingers across Mikey's features, 'D' picture of yer auld man, it's like havin' him here next t' me.'

'I wish he was here. Something tells me things would be different then.' Michael looked down sadly at his gravely ill son.

'Let me tell ya somet'in about yer da, Mikey. Liam was different to most people. He never stopped learnin', not as long as I knew him, and he was brighter than most. He had a kind o' wisdom where he could see a problem, get to its root and den fix it, in his own way. He might not always have done d' right t'ing, but he always did what he did fer d' right reasons.'

'I'd do anything to save the village, Moira.'

'I know you would, Mikey, and sure why wouldn't ya. After all, if it wasn't fer yer da, dere wouldn't be a village here in d' first place.'

'I never really thought about it that way.'

'When Liam Flynn first showed up, more dan forty years ago, Gortalocca was on its knees. D' Church was just about holding it together t'anks to auld Father Grogan and his common sense, but he was gettin' old and d' laws changed and took away whatever power d' Church had. All d' land around here was about to be confiscated, den yer da shows up, and he brought hope to d' village.'

'It was a good thing for Gortalocca that he came when he did.'

'He never got any t'anks fer it, mind. God knows he almost got himself killed. D' very people he was tryin' to help turned on him and almost beat him to death.'

'He never talked about that much.'

Moira smiled wanly. 'He wouldn't, it wasn't his way. He knew when he made plans wit' auld Father Grogan dat he'd be resented, but he never bore a grudge towards dem rapparees.'

'Didn't the leader get himself hanged? Sean... something, wasn't it?'

'Sean Reilly. Ah yes, a bad seed if ever dere was one, but d' hangin' wasn't down to yer da. Liam's half-brother, Robert D'Arcy, he wasn't as understandin', and o' course he was High Sheriff. He made a fearsome reputation d' day he kicked Reilly off d' gibbet in front of a crowd down at Nenagh Gaol. Paulie Gleeson's older brother got himself killed by d' posse dat night too.'

'I didn't know that.'

'Dere's a lot ya don't know, Michael. People forget, or dey choose not to remember. I don't forget nutt'n and dat's d' reason I'm here. Will ya walk me over to yer da's grave?'

'I haven't been there in a long time.'

Moira gazed sightlessly into Michael's face and he fidgeted uncomfortably in his chair.

'Is dere somet'in ya need to tell me, boy?'

'I burned the faerie fort.'

'Did ya have to do it?'

'No. Ned told me to clear the land but I set the fire out of spite.'

'I see,' said the blind old crone. 'Did ya t'ink it had somet'in to do wit' what happened to young Liam?'

'I don't know, Moira, maybe. I just wasn't thinking straight.'

'Do ya t'ink mabe ya did it because ya felt guilty? It sounds like somet'in dat hot-tempered mother o' yours would've done. If d' boy had got a splinter workin' on yer house, would you have burnt yer house down?'

'I suppose not.'

'And you of all people. You trained to be a priest. Did dey not tell ya anyt'ing about so-called curses in priest school?'

'Not that I remember.'

'Well I'll tell ya meself so. Dere's a difference between superstition and tradition, Mikey. Dat faerie fort was just a ring of auld stones and trees. It wasn't built by faeries or spirits, it was once the home of men, just like yerself, tryin' t' wrestle a livin' off d' land, same as today. But dat's not to say it had no meanin'. In a way it was a monument. It told future generations dey was here once and dat whatever was built, was built on top o' deir bones. Dat's just tradition, but we have to hold onto it or we forget who we are.'

Michael thought for a moment about what the old woman had said. 'Then it wasn't a curse that nearly killed my boy?'

'Listen to me, Michael and more importantly, hear what I say. Dere ain't no curses, except if ya believe you're cursed.' The old woman shook her head. 'Every time a misfortune happens, people try to find some reason to blame demselves. If dere's a curse on d' Irish, it's dat dey're so full of 'emselves, dey t'ink deir every deed has a meanin'.'

'Thank you, Moira.'

'Don't thank me, ya eejit, I'm after tellin' ya how ignorant ya are. Now help me up, I want to go and say an Ave at yer da's grave.

*

The two captains sat facing each other in a quayside tavern in Tramore, on opposite sides of the table, as well as opposite sides of the law.

'Care for a friendly game of chess, Jack?' asked Willoughby. 'We can talk about the privateer who cost you so dearly.'

'I can't tell you much about her, Willoughby. I only saw her bow on, I was too busy trying to show her my arse. She looked about the same size as Prosperity and probably Chesapeake-built. She had a bow chaser and was fitted out for a hunt.'

'Did you recognise her? There can't be many ships out of Baltimore that would take on a French privateer's license.'

'I sail out of Charles Town, sir, but you know those Americans. If the price is right…'

The Englishman registered his disapproval. 'Indeed. They're a motley crew, those Yankees. Every mongrel race in Europe and the dregs of Britain too.'

Jack pulled out the big silver stopwatch that he

carried and checked the time.

'Is there somewhere you have to be, Captain Rackham? We've only just sat down.'

'I have to get to Waterford and send a letter to the owners, explaining the situation.'

'Well,' smiled the Englishman, 'if they see fit to dismiss you, there's always a place for a timid and cautious officer in the Royal Navy.'

If the comment was meant to get a response from Jack, it failed. 'I'll be seeing you, Willoughby.'

'You can count on it, Captain Rackham,' smiled the Lieutenant.

*

'Do you think it's wise to have the boy and his sister here, Ned? It won't be long before they see through the charade.'

'Oy'll let 'em stay a while longer. It gives Alexander somebody his own age t' talk to. Dat boy shipped out so young, he'd started talkin' and actin' like an auld fart. It's only when Oy see d' young folks together dat Oy remember he ain't an adult quite yet.'

'What do you think about him and the girl?'

'I t'ink it's time fer Alexander to shit or get off d' pot. If he's serious about d' lass, den he needs t' talk to her father. If he ain't, den Oy'd best get him out of here before sumpt'in happens. I don't want to give d' girl's grandmother anyt'ing dat'll turn her against us.'

'I saw the note from Jack. What do you think?'

'I don't like d' sound of it. If it was dat easy to make money by runnin' blacks from Africa, sure everybody with a boat would be doin' it. Anyway, I don't want anyt'ing to do wit' dem scalawags on d' Barbary Coast.

Dose feckers would t'ink nutt'n of robbin' ya, stealin' yer ship and sellin' d' crew.'

'Even so,' said Washington, 'there's a lot of money to be made in it.'

'Jayzis, man, yer a black yerself! How can you go along wit' it?'

'I learned business from you, Ned.'

'Well ya learned it too well! Anyway, how's d' plantin' goin'?'

'The first seeds went in yesterday. By the day after tomorrow, the whole crop should be planted. It took forever to get the barrel out of the old church. Mikey had the seeds in their first load and we had to completely empty the church of barrels to get to it.'

'What about water? If we get a dry spell, we'll have to irrigate.'

'The spring the locals call the Holy Well might not have enough flow. I suggest we dig at least two wells while the weather is good, rather than wait until we need the water.'

'Good plan, Abe. Did ya tell Mikey we need him t' go back t' Galway and get dat load o' tobaccy?'

'I did. He said he and Jamie will leave in the morning. The round trip will probably take them at least a week. Does he know you want him to go down to Waterford with the merchandise?'

'Not yet. When he gets back, Oy'll put a few more shillin's in his hand. He'll do it, you wait and see.'

*

'Moira says she can't sleep here in d' village anymore,' Morna told Roisin. 'She says she's goin' to stay at Mick's cottage.'

'Is Mick still up at the big house?'

'As far as Oy know.'

'Then someone will have to take food to Moira. I'd do it but the bar has been so busy lately, now that people finally have some money to spend.'

'Oy'll go up, Mam. She could probably do wit' d' company.'

'Grand so. Tell her I'll get up to see her as soon as Siobhan comes back from Johnstown.'

CHAPTER 26

R ackham was growing tired of waiting for a reply from Ned and his crew was becoming restless. After a few days of spending their money ashore, they were back on board and doing the mundane chores required of them to keep a vessel at the ready, then repeating the chores over and over. Jack decided to take a proactive approach. If you ask a local policeman who the thieves are, he thought, he can tell you in a heartbeat. Ask a shopkeeper who the gyps are and he can do the same. Perhaps they take such a close interest because they wish they'd got the balls to do it themselves, or perhaps it gives them a feeling of moral superiority to look down their noses at villains. Whatever the reason, Rackham decided he should spend a little time at the Customs Office in Waterford because who better than the man in charge of collecting tariffs and taxes to know who the cheats are.

Jack walked into the Customs Office carrying a bottle of cognac from his own private stock. He asked to see the man in charge and was knocked flat when he discovered the chief officer to be no more than twenty-five years old. It was much easier to bribe an older man because he knew his career had already reached its zenith. Younger men were more of a problem. They had goals and aspirations and foresaw their profession someday leading them to a nice, comfortable desk in London. This was going to be difficult and must be done delicately.

'I have a ship in harbour, sir, and I was wondering if you knew of anything that needs transporting to England.'

The young man looked the captain up and down with the air of someone born to privilege. His eyes settled on the bottle in Jack's hand.

'Has the duty been paid on that bottle, Captain?'

'What if it has?' replied Jack.

'Then I have a couple of empty glasses in my desk,' replied the young fellow.

This might not be so difficult after all, thought Rackham, as the officer filled two glasses to the brim. He passed one to Jack, then raised his own.

'His Majesty, King George,' he said, and the two men clinked their glasses together.

The officer told Jack he had some wool which needed to be shipped and, when Jack inquired whether there wasn't perhaps something of higher value, the young man put down his glass and glared at him. That clearly wasn't a good move, thought Jack, but if a direct frontal assault failed, then perhaps I should give thought to laying siege. He began to elaborate, or rather fabricate, his encounter with the fictitious privateer south of the Channel. He left nothing to the landlubber's imagination. The officer's glass was filled several more times during the story and, by the time he came to lock the office up for the evening, the young fellow was well on his way to being three sheets to the wind.

Although Jack Rackham made his living through stealth, speed and deception, he knew that all young men pictured themselves as swashbucklers, so he regaled the inebriated young fellow with anecdotes from the South Seas ... of privateers and pirates, broadsides and cutlasses ... none of which he'd had any personal experience of whatsoever. Finally, he steered his tales towards smuggling, escape and evasion of the King's taxmen. By now, the stuffy young bureaucrat was reduced to a twelve year-old boy, ready to turn in his uniform for a parrot and an eye-patch, but Jack wasn't finished with him quite yet.

Throughout the evening, a not-so-young serving wench had been delivering drinks to the tables and occasionally flirting with the customers. Jack motioned her over and she responded swiftly. By this time, Mr. Smythe had his head on the table. The alcohol had unleashed a broadside and the young fellow was sinking fast.

'Tell me, m' dear, how much do you make a week?'

'I can make a penny on a good week.'

'Jack rolled a shilling across his knuckles like a conjurer.'

'Who do ya want me t' kill?' she laughed.

'It's nothing like that,' Jack smiled. 'All you have to do is take this young man home and show him the time of his life and I'll have another shilling for you tomorrow.'

'You'll have to help me get 'im home so. Where does he live?'

'I don't know. I have a better idea, we'll find you both a room. What's the grandest place in Waterford?'

'Ah now dey might not let me in dere.'

'I can promise you that they will, girl, even if I have to buy the place.'

*

Morna sat with Moira in the darkened room. Light meant very little to the old woman. Her blindness had robbed her of one kind of sight but had blessed her with another … foresight, and that's why she had decided to stay outside the village. It was now as it had always been. When the hag's help was needed, the villagers welcomed her. Once she had performed her duties, her mere presence made them uncomfortable. Gratitude is such a fleeting emotion, she thought. She had spent her life in self-imposed exile, distancing herself from a modern world which was inevitably encroaching on her own world of tradition.

'C'mere t' me, child,' she croaked. 'Let me see yer face.'

Morna moved close to the old woman, who traced the curves of her face with her fingertips. 'Ah yer a pretty lass, dat's for sure.' The old crone stroked her hair. 'What colour is it?'

'It's red, auld mother.'

'…. and yer eyes?'

'Me eyes are green.'

Moira closed her own sightless eyes and created an image in her mind of the woman sitting beside her.

'I t'ought Roisin might come,' she said after a while.

'She's busy at Hogan's.'

'Agh, I suppose dere's money t' be made so dere's no time left to visit an auld friend.'

Morna put up a feeble defense. 'Dere ain't been

239

money in d' village fer a very long time,' she said softly.

'Did she send you in her place so?'

'Yes … well, no. She said somebody ought to bring you a bit o' decent food and Oy said Oy would.'

'Well, you've done yer errand, so why are ya still here?'

'Dere's nob'dy at home sure. Mikey's gone off to Galway and d' kids are at Ned's. Roisin's workin' and Oy'm … well, to be trut'ful, Oy was curious.'

Moira reached out and felt around on the table next to her for the brown-stained dudheen. Then she pulled a pouch out from underneath her apron and she packed the pipe full.

'Would ya light a reed from d' fire, girl, so as I can smoke me pipe? Ya know, folk have got demselves in trouble because o' curiosity.'

The sweet smell of smoke reached Morna's nostrils as it rose around the old woman's head like a halo.

'Oy never smelled tobaccy like dat before,' said Morna.

'Folks was fillin' deir pipes in Ireland long before dey ever brought dat cursed leaf over from d' colonies.'

'Oy never knew dat.'

'Didn't d' auld ones tell ya nutt'n down in Cork?'

'Dere were no auld ones in my village. D' famine….'

'Agh, d' famine. T'ings are gettin' worse dat way. In d' auld days farmers grew more dan one crop so, if one failed, deir families would still have somet'in to eat. Nowadays everybody eats spuds and God help us if anyt'ing happens to d' 'taters. Sure d' whole country'll starve.'

'Oy don't t'ink God would ever let dat happen in Ireland.'

Moira looked at the girl as she would an ignorant

child. 'What happened to d' auld ones in yer village so?'

Morna tried to compose herself. The now-distant memory was still painful, even all these years later.

'When d' crops failed and food grew short in late winter and early spring, d' children began to starve. D' mothers' milk dried up and d' babies went first, den d' little ones. D' auld folk said deir goodbyes, one by one, and went off into d' hills, so nobody would see 'em die.'

'Ireland has always demanded sacrifice from her people, girl. Back in d' days before Saint Patrick, d' pagan priests would sacrifice an important person, den bury 'em in d' bog to be sure of a good harvest. After Christianity came, Ireland didn't lose her thirst fer blood and has always found one way or anudder of extractin' her payment.'

'Do ya t'ink what happ'ned to me son Liam was payment fer d' faerie ring?'

'No, I don't.'

'Mikey says dere's always a reason fer everyt'ing.'

'Your Michael is a modern man. Modern men t'ink dere's an explanation fer everyt'ing, but when you've lived as long as me, and you've seen d' t'ings I've seen, ya know dere's somet'in out dere bigger den all of us.'

'You mean God?'

'Dat's right, girl, God. And if anyone t'inks dey know what God is t'inkin' … well, dat's like a worm saying he knows what you yerself are t'inkin'.'

'Oy'd be t'inkin' of puttin' me foot on 'im.'

'Right again, girl. When a person says dey know d' mind of God, den dey're either a fool or an Englishman and dey can expect d' foot of God t' squash 'em fer bein' so full o' demselves.'

*

By the time Jack arrived at the Customs Office, it was almost midday and the office door was still locked. For a fleeting moment he thought perhaps the Irish girl had stuck the officer in the belly with a knife and robbed him. He immediately ruled it out, not because he had any faith in her morality … he had already established the status of that … but rather because she knew he had a shilling in his pocket with her name on it. He wandered over to the tavern for his first drink of the day. Almost as soon as his backside hit the seat, the Irish lass appeared and sat across the table from him.

Rackham grinned at her. 'So tell me, did you show him the time of his life?' he asked, holding the shilling in his closed fist.

'Not only did I give him d' best night of his life, sir, I gave him d' best mornin' too.'

'Excellent!' said Jack, dropping the shilling into the girl's hand. 'There you are, Mary.'

'How'd ya know me name's Mary?'

'You're Irish, aren't you?'

'I am.'

'Then it was as good a guess as any.'

'Talkin' about names, sir,' said the girl, 'is Smythe a Welsh name?'

'No, I think it's English. Why do you ask?'

'Yer friend behaved like a Welshman in bed.'

Jack was both amused and puzzled. 'Why? Did he break into song?'

'No sir.' Mary grinned and leaned closer. 'He couldn't get enough.'

Jack laughed. 'Ah yes, I hear Scotsmen are the same, they like to get their money's worth.'

Jack finished his drink and strolled back to the government office whistling a tune, his hands in the pockets of his greatcoat. The door was unlocked and he walked in as if he was expected. Smythe shot up out of his chair as the captain entered and bounded around his desk to shake hands with him. He looked none the worse for wear except for his bloodshot eyes.

'You'll never guess what happened to me last night!' the fellow exclaimed. Jack had a very good idea. 'I woke up in the arms of an angel! It was the best....'

Jack interrupted. 'Ah, no details, sir. A gentleman doesn't discuss such things.'

'No, I was just going to say was that it was the best night of my life!'

An excess of alcohol, a virile young man in his prime and a female who was game for anything were the perfect ingredients for a successful recipe, thought the captain.

'Good for you,' he said.

'I'm thinking of taking her back to England to meet my family, Mother would be delighted that I've met such a lovely girl.'

'I'd like to be there to see that,' said Jack, looking down at the table to hide his expression.

'Mary said she found me very charming, with all the things I had to tell her about pirates and smugglers. You know, I'm the first man Mary has ever slept with.' Jack coughed. 'I'm seeing her again tonight,' the young man said, smiling broadly.

Jack coughed even deeper than before. 'Were you perhaps still a little tipsy when you woke up this morning, Mr. Smythe?'

'Maybe just a little, sir. In fact I wish I had a drink

right now. You know it seems to clear my mind.'

Jack pulled out a pint-sized silver flask from a pocket of his coat and placed it on the desk in front of his new acquaintance.

'Here's a gift for you, Mr. Smythe … guaranteed to completely clear the mind and empty the head.'

CHAPTER 27

N ed read the letter he'd received from Charles Town for the third time. The words were still the same. He crumpled up the paper in his hand and threw it into the fireplace. Mr. Washington watched. It was unwise to encroach on the boss when he was busy working himself into a foul mood. Ned looked up at him.

'Shouldn't you be in town,' he said sourly, 'supervisin' d' well-diggin'?'

'The dowser was there yesterday morning and he marked the spots. The men have been digging since then.'

'And how exactly d' ya know dey're diggin'? Ya sit up here like ya was high and mighty, drinkin' me tea and smokin' me tobaccy. Who's t' say dey ain't all sittin' around gettin' drunk?'

'Very well, I'll go and check on them, and it's my tobacco I'm smoking, not yours.'

'Pirates. d' whole feckin' lot of 'em! D' place was

founded by feckin' pirates and dey're still feckin' runnin' it!'

Alexander had heard his father's tirade and had come to find out what all the fuss was about. 'What's happened, Da?'

'What's happened? Oy'll tell ya what's happened, boyo, and it's a good lesson fer you to learn. Before we came over, we had a cargo o' Cuban rum to be delivered. We had money tied up in dat shipment and Oy should o' bin dere to watch it. Turns out d' ship was in d' straits, south o' Spanish Florida, when d' feckin' wreckers led her up onto a reef near Cayo Largo. T'ank God d' ship wasn't ours but we've still lost d' damn rum.'

'What about the insurance, Da?'

'What insurance, boy? Ya can't insure sumpt'in dat don't exist! If ya insure a t'ing, den somebody knows ya have it, and if somebody knows ya have it, den somebody else is goin' to tax it.'

'Wouldn't it have been better just to pay the tax on the rum?'

'Jayzis, sure ya have no head fer business at all! Get yerself off t' Gortalocca wit' Washington and leave me be. Somebody has to do d' t'inkin' around here.'

Alexander knew there was absolutely no point in trying to reason with his father when he was in one of his dark moods. He also knew that, like clouds blowing over the sun, they were only temporary. For the moment, however, it was best to leave him alone.

Liam and Siobhan were still up at the big house and couldn't wait to go home. Liam's hand was bandaged up in a sling and Siobhan was anxious to talk to her mother. She wanted to tell her about all the fine things at the big house, things she'd never had in Gortalocca.

Liam just wanted to be back in familiar surroundings so he could scratch where it itched and fart whenever he felt like it, without a servant hovering nearby.

*

'I must apologise for monopolising the conversation last night, Mr. Smythe. Here, have another drink.'

'Not at all, Captain, my own life makes for a very dull story.'

'Please, call me Jack.'

'My name is Timothy.'

'Do your friends call you Tim?'

'No, they call me Timothy.'

'Well I shall call you Tim. It's more befitting, I'd say, more manly.'

The young man puffed himself up a little. 'Yes, I like it. Tim. Tim Smythe. It sounds much better.'

'Very well, Tim, it's your turn to tell me about yourself. I'm tired of hearing my own voice. Tell me, how did you reach such a high post at such a young age?'

'My father worked for years in His Majesty's Customs Service before he died and he saw to it. He must have made some very wise investments because he left quite a substantial estate to my mother when he passed on. He never would have been able to save such an amount on a few pounds a month.'

'Indeed,' said Jack. 'He must have been a very shrewd businessman, Tim.' Jack knew exactly how old man Smythe had come into his chips. 'Drink up, boyo! There's plenty more where that came from.'

Mary sauntered over to the table and bade a good evening to the captain. 'Helloooo, Timmy,' she cooed.

Jack handed her a penny. 'This is on account,' he said.

Mary smiled flirtatiously, 'On account of what, sir?'

'On account that your services might be needed later. Now would you please give us some privacy?'

Mary sauntered off indignantly. She had been hoping she would be invited to sit with the two men.

'So Tim, tell me your best story about sea rogues.'

'Well I never met a pirate personally, at least not to my knowledge, but there's a fellow who my predecessor had dealings with.' Jack shifted imperceptibly forward in his seat as the young man lowered his voice.

'He's a rough-looking fellow, owns a bar in Ballykinsella. His name is McGee, Barry McGee. There was talk of an accounting discrepancy and when the authorities threatened Sherman … he was Chief of Customs at the time … he sold McGee out to save his own hide.'

'What happened to McGee?'

'They threw him in gaol and he shut his mouth up tighter than a clam's arse. The authorities in England knew he was smuggling but they were never able to find anything they could convict him on. Eventually they had no choice but to turn him loose.'

'What an exciting story, Tim. Thanks, I thoroughly enjoyed it.'

Jack yawned and stretched and looked towards the far corner of the bar, where Mr. Jones had been waiting for a sign from him. He gave him a slight nod, whereupon Jones left his drink in mid-gulp and headed out the door.

'Oh it wasn't a patch on your stories, Jack, but I did tell you that my life is a very boring one.'

Unbeknownst to poor Tim, his life was about to take a dramatic turn.

*

It was Saturday night and Ned, Alexander and Mr. Washington made a grand entrance to the festivities in Gortalocca. Mick had finally procured a pair of matching grey carriage horses and Johnson's old carriage had been brought out from under its dust sheets and polished until it shone. Ned thought their display might provide a touch of spectacle to the party.

Siobhan wasn't at all happy because Roisin had left her in charge of Peg, Robbie's young daughter. Indeed, what sixteen year-old girl would be happy to be relegated to the job of baby-sitter when there were so many people in the village and so much music to be danced to?

Billy McTierney sawed merrily on his fiddle and a few people who'd started to imbibe a little too early were already dancing. There must have been a hundred people or more spilling out of Hogan's onto the street.

Roisin was rushed off her feet but delighted that the money was rolling in. Ned felt self-satisfied, even smug. He'd paid the wages and much of it was coming back to him as it was handed across the bar. Roisin paid a little extra attention to Abraham, making sure his cup was always full. An unspoken truce seemed to have developed between them. Mr. Washington had been accepted by the farm hands too. He had a casual approach to getting them to work. He never scolded or delivered orders harshly and, if someone was doing something wrong, he'd merely say, 'I know an easier way for you to do that.' People had even stopped touching his skin to see if the colour would come off. All was going well in Gortalocca and, on the subject of wells, both had been dug now and the only casualty was that the spring at the Holy well seemed to have less flow than before.

*

Michael and Jamie were over halfway to Waterford when they made their decision to camp just outside Cahir. The hogsheads in the wagon were covered with hay to attract less attention, both from local authorities and from those who might have nefarious intentions. Tomorrow they would reach Carrick-On-Suir and then Waterford by mid-afternoon on the following day. They were making good time and the journey had been uneventful so far.

'Ned said to check in at the sheriff's office in Carrick,' said Michael. 'We have to show them the papers for the shipment we got in Galway.'

'We're just ignorant haulers, right Mikey?'

'That's right, we don't know anything or anybody. All we're doing is delivering a load to Waterford.'

*

Jack Rackham and Tim Smythe left the bar and walked out into the cool night. The captain inhaled the briny air and prepared himself for a performance.

'Did you lock the door of the warehouse when we left, Tim?'

'Oh yes, I always lock it.'

'Are you sure? I don't remember seeing you do it. We were immersed in conversation. Are you absolutely sure?' Plant a seed of doubt, thought Jack, then tend it and water it and soon you'll be able to make the Pope doubt his faith.

Smythe thought for a moment 'I'm absolutely sure I did … didn't I?'

'I don't know, Tim, it would be very embarrassing

for you if someone broke in. It might be wise to just check.'

'You're right, Jack, and I'd probably lose my job over it. It's not far, we'll go and put our minds at rest.'

Jonesey huddled in a circle with four of the crew. 'Now remember what I've told you, lads, nothing too violent. No punching him in the face, we'll just rough him up a bit … a lot of pushing and shouting, that sort of thing. Once he's down, we'll go through his pockets. We're after his keys and his purse. The captain will play the hero and come to the fella's rescue, pretending to fight us off. Is everyone clear?'

One of the crew laughed. 'Jayzis, Jonesey! On his best day and wit' his mammy to help him, d' cap'n couldn't fight me off.'

'Shut yer gob, Jimmy, we're play-acting. I'm just telling you not to get carried away or there'll hell to pay when the cap'n gets back. Now Tom, you said you're good at acting, being as how you went to the theatre back in Charles Town once. Hold the little fecker's face down so he can't see anything. Jimmy, you're the biggest, you get on his back so he can't move. Petey, you go through his pockets and, as soon as you've got his keys and purse, just take off. Now does everyone know their part? Remember, no punching him in the face.'

As the two men rounded the corner, the customs officer spied a figure crouching in the shadows in front of the warehouse door.

'Jack! Look, it's a burglar! The cheeky bastard, let's go and teach him a lesson he'll never forget.'

Jack's pirate tales had filled an impressionable young Smythe with a daring sense of boldness and he ran straight towards the huddled bosun. He didn't get far because Jimmy leapt out from the darkness and grabbed him from behind, piniooning his arms to his sides. Then he picked him off his feet and deposited him on the ground, knocking the wind out of him. The others piled on top, rifling through his pockets and shouting obscenities.

Jonesey and his captain engaged themselves in a mock wrestling contest.

'Unhand my friend, you fiends,' shouted Jack, 'or I will thrash you all to within an inch of your lives!' He grinned in the darkness. 'That's the way thespians talk, Jonesey,' he whispered.

'I wouldn't know, sir,' Jones whispered back, 'I'm Anglican meself.'

'Take that, you scoundrel!' Jack pounded his fist into his open palm for the sound effect and Jonesey got into the spirit.

'Agh! Agh! Oh, sir, I do declare, you are too strong for me! I think you have caused me great harm!'

'Shut up, Jonesy!' Jack hissed. 'You're overacting!'

Petey held up the purse and rattled the keys to indicate that the performance was over, then took off into the darkness followed closely by the others.

Smythe got to his feet, visibly shaken by the experience.

'Good God, Jack, you saved my life! How many of them were there?'

'There had to have been at least eight, possibly more.'

'I'm afraid I wasn't much use to you,' said Tim, his voice trembling. 'I was on the ground the whole time.'

'You did marvelously, my friend. Wasn't it you who kept four of the scoundrels occupied while I tried to tackle the others? How do you feel? Are you hurt?'

Smythe took stock of himself. 'Well I seem to have escaped any injury but the bastards stole my purse.' He checked inside his pockets. 'Oh No! Oh God no, Jack, they've stolen my keys too! This will cost me my job.'

'Now, now, don't upset yourself, my good fellow. The money can be replaced and as for the keys, well, if no one knows they're missing except for you and I … perhaps I can get my ship's carpenter to fabricate a new set for you, then no one will be the wiser.'

'I am twice indebted to you, Captain Rackham, for saving my life and also for saving my career. I doubt I'll ever be able to repay you.'

'Not at all, Tim,' smiled Rackham. 'After all, isn't that what friends are for?'

CHAPTER 28

M r. Washington left the revellers enjoying themselves at Hogan's and he walked across the road to the Holy Well. He looked at the water level and noticed there was mud showing at the margins; the water level had dropped a few inches. He looked eastwards towards the new well which had been dug on the hillside above. In digging it, they'd probably tapped into the spring which had supplied water to the grotto for eons. Even if the new well was filled, it wouldn't matter, the water would just find a new course downhill. It didn't make any difference to him but he suspected the Irish might take this as yet another bad omen. He pulled a pouch from his pocket and filled his pipe. He'd need to return to Hogan's to get a light from the fireplace.

Abraham wasn't the only one who'd noticed the water level dropping. Hidden deep in the shadows of the rag tree, the crone sat silently. Moira had crept into town. It had taken her hours to walk the mile or so from Mick's, where she'd been staying. Caught up in their festivities, the people of Gortalocca had lost sight of something which had once been as important as the earth itself to the village and lands around it. The well had once been this community's life blood. If the well hadn't existed, the first farms would never have been built here. Gortalocca owed its very existence to this little spring which now barely trickled from the rocks. Like the faerie ring, it had received a mortal wound. Moira spoke to the water.

'Well, auld friend, ya gave life to dis village. Season after season passed and ya never froze up in winter and ya never dried up in d' summer droughts. Ya gave 'em everyt'ing dey needed to sustain life and ya asked fer nutt'n in return. I tried to be like you but, sure, I'm only human and I enjoyed d' gratitude I got from folk I helped. You are more pure and holy dan any person could ever hope to be and now dey've destroyed ya. It ain't because dey want to, it's just deir indifference. It'll be d' end of d' rag tree and it'll be d' end of me too. We've done our jobs but now we've overstayed our time and our days are numbered.' The tiny old hag touched the little stream of water and put her fingers to her mouth. Her tears fell and dappled the water's surface. 'I share me tears wit' you, auld friend,' she whispered hoarsely, then tied a little scrap of tattered old lace to the rag tree.

*

'Did you get the wax impressions made of the keys, Jonesey?'

'I did, sir.'

'Give me back the originals then and get back to the ship. Tell the carpenter to make a new set for me.'

'Aye aye, sir.'

Jones was always baffled by the intricacies of what went on in his captain's mind but it usually all made sense in the end, and that was all that mattered.

Jack separated the key ring from the keys and threw it into the bay. He grabbed a handful of sand and rubbed the metal with the abrasive until the keys looked like they'd been newly cast. Some people might have lost sleep over having deceived an innocent such as Tim Smythe. Jack slept like a baby that night.

The next morning, he meandered his way to the warehouse and found Smythe there, worrying and fretting about how he was going to get into the building. Jack decided to have some fun with him. The cat's appetite had been satiated and so he felt like playing with the mouse for a while.

'Can't find a way to get in, eh?' said Jack, managing as much concern as a person such as himself could muster.

'No, and I didn't sleep a wink last night.'

'Have you tried crawling through a window?'

'I thought of that but I still wouldn't be able to open the door without the key, even from the inside.'

'Have you tried picking the lock?'

'I don't know how to do something like that!'

Jack could tell that the young man was about to burst into tears and, as insensitive as he was, he couldn't allow that.

'I can open the door,' he said, grinning and searching his inside coat pocket. 'I misspent my youth.'

Tim stared at Jack in desperate anticipation, waiting for him to pull out some tools of the burglar kind. Instead Jack pulled out a set of keys strung together on a cord. They looked brand new.

'Oh, look what I found,' he said playfully.

'How….? You had them all this time.' Mr. Smythe laughed with relief. 'You sod, Jack, you were just trying to get me wound up.'

'I didn't have to try very hard,' said Rackham, still grinning. 'Here's your new set of keys, Tim. I have to bid you farewell for now, my friend. I need to run an errand so I might not be around for a few days.'

'Thank you, Jack. Thank you for everything. It must have been the luckiest day of my life when I met you.'

'Friends help friends, that's all. The bandits stole your money last night so here are a few shillings to tide you over.'

'I… I can't accept money, sir. It could be construed as a bribe.'

'Now how can a friend bribe another friend? You can give me back the money when you get paid. You'll never be able to court that Irish lass if you don't have any money, now will you?'

It wasn't long before Smythe reluctantly agreed and pocketed the silver coins. Gotcha, thought Jack with satisfaction. A person just needs to know the right bait to use. Jack headed back to the tavern in the hope of finding his bait, which went by the name of Mary.

'Do you want to work here all your life, Mary?'

'I don't t'ink I have any udder choice, sir.'

'We always have choices, Mary. You're a fine looking woman, after all. You underestimate your … er, assets.'

'If yer tryin' t' bed me wit' fancy words, Capt'n, you'll need tuppence too.'

'No my dear, you misunderstand me. Have you ever imagined what life would be like as the wife of a country squire?'

'Ah sure I used t' have notions, a fantasy like, but not since I was twelve years old and lost me virginity to a handsome sailor who said he'd marry me and den took off.'

'That's all in the past, Mary. We're going to make a lady out of you.'

'Dat's a big job, sir.'

'Not so big, Mary. Here are three shillings. Before I give them to you, you have to promise me that you won't use the money to get drunk.'

'D' truth is, sir, I don't really drink much. When it looks like I'm drinkin' wit' d' lads, mine's always well watered-down so I don't get stocious.'

'Alright Mary.' Jack suddenly felt a little sorry for the girl and he gave her a genuinely warm smile. 'Now go and clean yourself up and buy yourself some new clothes. You know that young fellow from the customs office?'

'Timmy? O'course, sir. He told me 'e loved me but I've heard dat a hundert times before.'

'Well Timmy is richer than you think and if the right woman happens to come along, Timmy is ripe for the picking.'

'I always t'ought I'd make a good wife, sir, just nobody ever asked me.'

'I agree with you Mary, I think you'd make a good wife too. I also think it's time for you to begin believing in that fantasy of yours again.'

'Ah I don't know about dat, now. I don't want me heart broken again.'

'I'm sure it won't be, Mary. Here's what you do. You get yourself all prettied up and remember, you belong to only one man and that man's Tim Smythe. Don't let any other man distract you from your goal because, once you're all fixed up, there will be a lot of men who will give you the eye. But you must remember that the only one who matters is Tim. Now do you think you can do that?'

'I don't want t' seem ungrateful, Cap'n, but what exactly's in it fer you?'

'Me? Oh I just like to spread the happiness, Mary.'

*

'I want tenpence a hogshead,' said the sharp-faced old man.

'But sir,' said Michael, 'we already have the paperwork from Galway. We're all paid up.'

'That was Galway. This is Carrick. If you don't pay me the toll, I'll confiscate the whole lot.'

'That's more than we're getting paid to make the haul.'

'Well you should have driven a harder bargain then, shouldn't you. The going rate to pass through my territory is tenpence a hogshead.'

'I'll have to talk to my partner.'

'Talk all you want but you're not leaving this place until I've been paid.'

Mikey walked back to the wagon which they'd parked up outside the sheriff's office in Carrick-On-Suir.

'How much money do you have on you, Clancy?'

'I have nearly two shillin's. I was goin' t' leave it at home but I like t' hear a bit o' money jinglin' in me purse.'

'I have about the same. I'll see if I can make some kind of deal.'

Michael dumped both purses on the administrator's

desk and the hawk-faced old fellow counted out the money.

'And this is all you have?'

Mikey turned his palms up. 'That's it, sir, that's everything.'

'Alright, I believe you. You're in luck because I'm feeling generous so I'll tell you what I'll do. I'll take what you have and you can take eight of the barrels and leave two here. When you come back for them, you can pay me one shilling each for the hogsheads and another for renting the space in my warehouse. That's three shillings in total to come and then you can have the last two back.'

There didn't seem to be much point in arguing. The two men backed the wagon up to the loading ramp and the warehousemen removed two of the barrels under the watchful eye of the boss.

'It's been a pleasure doing business with you, gentlemen. Have a safe journey and, if I don't see you in a week, I'll find a market for the tobacco myself. Good day to you.'

Michael clapped the reins against the horses' backs and got out of town as fast as he could get them to go.

'Ned will piss vinegar when 'e finds out we lost two hogsheads,' ventured Clancy.

'I know that, Jamie, but what else was I supposed to do? I couldn't risk that law man keeping them all and the wagon and horses along with them.'

'What'll we tell Captain Rackham when we get t' Waterford.'

'We'll tell him the truth, Jamie. It's not as if it was our fault, we had to negotiate what we could'

At the very same time, Captain Jack Rackham was involved in some negotiations of his own.

*

In the offices of the Admiralty in London, a wizened clerk scratched his head. He stood at his desk and compared one paper against another. He held both reports up to an oil lamp so he could see them more clearly. It was the duty of the clerk to look for any discrepancies and either reconcile them or bring them to the attention of those higher up. Communications were slow and it was rare for him to see anything newer than several months old. It was just a small thing, something which anyone else might easily overlook, but it bothered him. John Rackham. Hmmm. He was listed as the captain of a Chesapeake schooner named Prosperity, but the report from a sloop of war stated he was in command of a schooner called Camilla, of similar size and proportion to Prosperity, which seemingly had a run-in with a French privateer south of the Channel. If it hadn't been for the peculiar name of the ship and the fact that he remembered hearing about a pirate named Rackham, he might easily have overlooked the facts. A man can't sail two ships at the same time. Of course, there could be some mistake but all the same, it would be prudent to check with the revenue office. Instead of filing the papers, the clerk placed them to one side on his desk.

*

'I t'ink it's best if ya talk to Siobhan's father first, Alexander.'

'Well I spoke to my own father and he said it might be wise to tell you and Roisin first.'

'Our Siobhan is immature fer her age, son. She still

has daft notions about bein' a grand lady. She can read and write and she ain't stupid, but she's Irish and she don't understand how t'ings are in udder countries.'

'Can you keep a secret, Mrs. Hogan?'

'If it's about yer da being in charge and Mr. Flynn being a horse, Oy already know. Dat's anudder t'ing ya need to know about Siobhan. She can't keep a secret to save 'er life.'

Alexander was taken aback. 'Who else knows?'

'Let me t'ink now,' laughed Morna, 'just about everyone in Gortalocca. Sure nobody cares as long as yer da pays good money. He could tell 'em he was d' King o' China and nobody would give a shite.'

'My father says there are certain protocols to be met in an Irish courtship.'

'Oy don't know nutt'n about no pot-o'-coals but if he means traditions, dat's somet'in you'll have to discuss wit' Michael.'

'Do you think I should talk to Roisin?'

'No, let me talk to her first. Your father and my mother-in-law have an odd sort o' relationship and a funny way o' dealin' wit' each udder. Oy don't want it t' spill over into dis.'

'I'm nothing like my father, you know.'

'Dere's no one like your father, Alexander.'

'Da likes playing games and, if he can't find something to play with, then he'll find someone. It makes me a bit ashamed sometimes because all that matters to him is winning. He already has enough money to last ten lifetimes but even that's become a game to him now. He'd risk it all just to get even a small profit.'

'Moira says sometimes people like yer da are too clever by half. Instead of bein' t'ankful fer what dey already have, dey're always tryin' to reach dat little bit further. When Michael gets back from Waterford, yous two can have a talk. Oy'm on your side, mind. Me and yer mam, Alex, we was best friends when we was just girls, back in Cork, and as daft as it might sound now, we always talked about how our children would marry each udder .... and dat's before we even had husbands!'

CHAPTER 29

J ack hired himself a horse and rode down to Ballykinsella in search of Mr. McGee. It didn't require a great deal of research on his part because the one and only building in Ballykinsella township was a spirit grocery with the name 'McGEE's' painted over the door, and a barn nearby. Jack tied the horse to one of two iron rings set into the stone wall of the grocery and opened the door.

'G'way!' came a gruff voice from behind the bar. 'We're closed!'

'That's no way to welcome a paying customer,' responded Jack, jingling his purse.

A short squat fellow stepped out of the shadows and he might just as well have stepped out of a book. He wore a bandana around his grey balding head and he squinted with his right eye. His beard was grizzled and he looked, for all the world, the image of every pirate Jack had ever seen depicted in books.

'Do ya have money?' the shopkeeper asked rudely.

Again Jack rattled his purse. 'Do you have a parrot?'

'I never had no parrot,' growled the codger. 'Dere's somethin' unholy about a bird that can talk.'

'What have you got to drink around here?'

'I've got whiskey and I've got rum, take it or leave it.'

'I'll take the rum. Have you got a name old timer?'

The man slapped a tankard down on the table and slopped some rum into it.

'Are ya an eejit? Me name's written over the door, can't ya read? Gimme a penny for the rum.'

Jack put two pennies on the table. 'I said a penny. Can't ya count either? Jayzis, what kind of an education did ya have?'

'I didn't want to drink by myself, I thought perhaps you'd join me.'

'I'll drink with ya, boyo, but if ya want to hear pirate stories, it'll cost ya another penny.'

'You're an expensive man to drink with. What makes you think I want to hear about pirates?'

'That's the only reason anyone ever comes in here these days. There ain't many of us buccaneers left from the old days.'

'You tell me a pirate story, old man, then I'll tell you one you might not have heard before.'

'I've heard 'em all and you ain't old enough to know anything about pirates, ya young maggot!'

Jack was becoming irritated. 'I'm not an 'eejit' and I'm certainly not a maggot. My name is John Rackham. My friends call me Jack, you can call me Captain Rackham.'

'Rackham, is it? 'Calico' Jack Rackham! Now he was a dandy if ever there was one. Any relation?'

'He was my father.'

'Then your mother was…?'

'Is…… Anne Bonny.'

'… and a more saintly woman there never was!'

'You're a liar, McGee. My mother could still chew us both up, even now, and spit out the mince.'

McGee grinned. 'You have me there boyo. I was just testin' ya. I thought your mam was hung down in Kingston with your father. You must've been the loaf she had in the oven when she got the reprieve.'

'My grandfather used his connections to get her out of gaol. She went back to Charles Town and that's where I was born.'

'So it's no accident that you're here then. What can I do fer ya?'

'It's no accident and we might be able to come to some mutually profitable arrangement.'

'Ya have a ship?'

'Yes. She's anchored a few miles from here in Tramore Bay.'

'The Chesapeake schooner's yours? Now she looks fast.'

'She's fast enough. We load our cargo, we deliver it speedily and we count our money.'

'Have you got a cargo now?'

'In the next couple of days I'll have a few tons of tobacco aboard.'

'Do you have room for a bit more, Captain?'

Rackham smiled. 'You can call me Jack.'

'Let's go and take a closer look at this ship of yours, boyo. It's not that I don't trust you, it's just that I have no evidence to believe you are who you say you are.'

'Fair enough,' replied Jack. 'Then I hope you're ready for a bit of exercise. It's about a mile to the shore and then we have to find a boat and row out to her. I can introduce you to the crew, that should be evidence enough for you.'

'I see ya came by horse, Jack. I have one of me own in that barn over there.'

A hundred feet or so away stood a barn, a single unpretentious structure of lime-washed mud walls with a thatched roof. It was identical to the thousands of others which stood on the hundreds of farms the country over. The only difference was that his one stood alone, with no farmhouse in sight.

'Why don't ya come over with me and help this old man get his horse saddled, then we'll take a ride down to the shore.'

In half an hour or so the two men and their horses were standing at the water's edge. McGee looked Prosperity over from a distance.

'Those raked masts make her look like she's speeding even when she's at anchor,' he mused.

'The new designs are even faster,' said Jack. 'They have a little more beam so they can carry more sail. Some people call them clippers. If the company has a profitable year, the owner says we'll get one of the new fast ones. On the subject of things fast, McGee, what's an old barman like you doing with a fast horse like that?' Jack inclined his head towards the sleek beast under McGee's backside.

It was Barry's turn to play with Jack. 'He's fast enough, I'd say, to get this old pirate out of trouble.'

'You're no more a pirate than I am, Barry McGee, and you never were.'

'How would you know?' snapped the old man.

'Firstly, you're too clever by far to risk your own neck and secondly, you still have your neck. Pirates don't retire.'

'You've got me there, boyo. The thing is, folk are afraid of pirates and it suits me if they're a little afraid of me. I'm a businessman. I run a little customs office of my own on the side, nothing too risky mind, I play things safe these days. That little stint in gaol was enough for me so I keep me head down.'

'Shall we find a boat and go and visit my crew then, McGee.'

'I don't think we need to, Captain. It looks as if your crew is sending a boat for us.'

Jones had been awaiting Rackham's return and, as soon as he'd seen the familiar figure on the shore, he dispatched the jolly boat to pick him up.

*

Michael and Jamie pulled the big dray up to the Customs Office as Ned had directed them. Mikey pulled out a satchel containing papers drawn up by the Scottish customs officer in Galway and he walked inside the dark office. Smythe was wearing his official face and was pragmatic towards the Irishman.

'It says here,' he said, 'that you have ten hogsheads of Virginia tobacco. I'll make a preliminary inspection.'

'We only have eight,' Michael corrected him, innocently. 'We lost the other two.'

'You lost two hogsheads? Isn't a hogshead rather a large item to lose? Did you just misplace them, or did they perhaps fall out of your pocket?'

'No, sir, they were … well, they were sort of stolen.'

'Oh well that explains everything,' said the officer sarcastically. 'You were the victim of a sort of robbery, is that it? Tell me, was the sort of thief dressed in a sort of mask and cape?'

'No, sir, he was dressed in a uniform like yours.'

'You wait here, Mr. ….'

'Hogan, sir, Michael Hogan.'

'You wait here Mr. Hogan while I go and sort this out.'

Smythe disappeared through a doorway into the warehouse.

'I have a bad feeling about this, Clancy,' said Michael quietly. 'I don't think he believes us. Maybe you should get out of here while you can,' he added.

'I ain't leavin', Mikey. What would yer mam say if I arrived back in Gortalocca widdout ya?'

As it turned out, Jamie didn't have a choice in the matter because just then Smythe reappeared, and this time he had two guards with him.

'Show these fellows to their new accommodations, gentlemen.'

'I t'ink we're goin' to gaol, Mikey.'

'That is correct, my good man, but you needn't worry. You won't be there for long. A hogshead of tobacco weighs about half a ton and is worth about eight pounds. We should be able to cover that by selling the two of you into servitude for seven years in the colonies. That's only if the magistrate is feeling generous, mind. For a theft of this magnitude, he might even decide to have you both hanged. It all depends on how believable you make your story and I suggest you start working on it because, so far, it beggars belief.'

Smythe sifted through the papers. The owner of the cargo appeared to be a Mr. Michael Flynn. The shipment was to be delivered into the hands of Captain John Rackham. Tim Smythe smiled. The captain would be pleased that he had caught two crooks trying to cheat him out of his consignment.

*

'The planting is finished, Ned. From now on it's just a matter of tending the crop, weeding and picking off the bugs. The weather here is right for it. There are lots of damp misty days, soft days the Irish call them. That will be ideal to get the roots started.'

'Oy'll leave dat side o' t'ings to you, Mr. Washington, Oy know you're more dan capable. I was t'inkin' of takin' d' coach down t' Waterford.'

'Will you be taking Alexander with you?'

'No, Oy t'ought Oy'd leave him in charge here. D' boy should be gettin' some experience of runnin' t'ings … dat's if ya don't mind, Abe.'

'I don't mind at all, in fact I think it's a good idea. I don't think there will be any problems he can't handle.'

'Oy'll be back in a couple o' weeks or so, maybe less.'

'This business about the Holy Well is bothering me, Ned.'

'Why, fer Christ's sake? It never was much more dan a trickle o' water anyway. It served its purpose supplin' a few houses wit' drinkin' water but we've got an operation to run now and we have to have water.'

'It's probably been there forever…'

'Ah Jayzis, man, you know as well as Oy do, if dere's goin' to be progress, dis auld nonsense can't stand in d' way. Where's Alexander?'

'He and Mick went to Gortalocca earlier. Alex wanted to look at building a bigger oven so that Morna can bake enough bread to feed all the farmers.'

*

'Ya can't build an oven out o' rough stone and mortar, Alexander.'

'We could use bricks.'

'I suppose it's possible, but only if we could get a hold of d' right bricks. Dose common red ones dey use on d' houses in Nenagh would just fall apart in d' heat.'

'How do you think we should go about it, Mick?'

'I know an excellent stone cutter who lives in Coolbawn. He's a nice fella and his wife is a miserable auld cow so I'm sure he'd take d' job just to get away from 'er. He could cut d' stone and dry stack it so as d' oven would be as tight as a brick one, only last twice as long.'

'How long would it take to build?'

'A few days, four at the outside.'

'Very well, we'll get that job underway. The next most urgent job is to get the drying barn built. We'll get it started as soon as Mikey and Clancy get back.'

*

'I don't know why 'e didn't believe us, Mikey. We told 'im d' truth, exactly as it happened.'

'I've no doubt those English Government fellas all stick together, Clancy. Feck it! I'd hate to get hanged for something I didn't do.'

'I'd hate to get hanged, even fer somet'in I did do,' replied Jamie, woefully.

'The worst part is nobody knows where we are. If they ship us off to the colonies, or to Botany Bay, the folks back home won't know anything about it. If they hang us, we'll just get stuck in a hole in the ground somewhere.'

'You mean we'll just disappear and nobody'll ever know what happened us?' lamented Jamie, lapsing into one of his deep depressions. 'How's that possible?'

'This is Ireland, Jamie. People disappear all the time.'

*

'WHAT DO YOU MEAN YOU THREW THEM IN GAOL?'

'Take it easy, Jack, there's no need to get excited. I thought you'd be pleased.'

'Damn it, Tim, those are my men! They're too stupid to steal, you nincompoop!'

'Their story about the sherrif in Carrick didn't make any sense.'

'By God, you have a lot to learn about the customs business, my lad.'

'There's no harm done, we'll just release them.'

'Well you'll have to clean them up because by now I'm sure they've shit themselves. You probably scared them half to death, man. Even if they had stolen it, what in God's name were they going to do with a ton of tobacco?'

'I hadn't thought that far ahead.'

'Well that turd back in Carrick had thought about it, the thieving old bastard. Tomorrow you're coming with me to get the goods back and perhaps you'll learn something in the process. Now let's get those poor sods out of the clink. You owe them a beer.'

'That's another thing, Jack, I spent all the money you gave me. I had no idea women were so expensive.'

'I'll give you more but I might want a favour from you in return.'

'Of course, as long as it isn't dishonest.'

Jack didn't answer, he just handed ten shillings to the officer. Tim was becoming a debtor and Jack had every intention of collecting, sooner rather than later.

CHAPTER 30

'Mick, boyo, get yerself cleaned up and get some food in yer belly. We're takin' a little trip tomorra.'

'I told Alexander I'd go and see a stonecutter I know in Coolbawn.'

'Send someone else. You and me are goin' to Waterford in d' mornin'.'

'Why don't ya just hire a coach? I t'ink I'd be of more use stayin' here and making sure work on d' oven gets started.'

'You mustn't start t'inkin' Mick, dat's my job. It's time d' world met Mr. Michael Flynn.'

'Are you takin' d' big horse, so?'

'No, Mick. D' horse has already done his part, now it's time fer me to do mine. Until Oy say udderwise, Oy am Michael Flynn.'

'You're Michael Flynn?'

'Dat's right, Micko, and Oy'm goin' to make such a ballyhoo from here to Waterford dat everybody will know who Michael Flynn is.'

'But you're Ned Flood.'

'Ned Flood?' Ned smiled craftily. 'Never heard of 'im.'

*

Willoughby had been giving some thought as to whether he should write to the big heads and stuffed shirts in the Admiralty. All the ships had been called to duty, in order to blockade the French ports, and that had left him to single-handedly police the entire southwest coast of England for smuggling activity. He couldn't sail in sight of shore during daylight hours, for fear the outlaws might signal his whereabouts to other smugglers up and down the coast. His only recourse was to stay offshore during the day, then swoop in after dark and try to surprise anyone off-loading illicit cargo. It was ineffective, to say the least. There was several hundred miles of English coastline whose inhabitants were less than welcoming. He even had to send armed marines ashore with his sailors, whenever they went to replenish the water casks, in order to keep the seamen from getting the living daylights beaten out of them by the locals. Willoughby decided against writing. Any request for assistance might be construed by the birdbrains in London as a sign of incompetence on the part of the complainant.

*

'Alright, Micko, first t'ings first. We have to go and visit Mr. Wall, d' solicitor, and make a proper introduction. He's bin doin' business in Mr. Flynn's name and it's about time he met d' fella himself. After dat, we'll go and visit d' sheriff. It's never a bad idea to have d' law on yer side.'

'Won't Sheriff Higgins recognise you?'

'Well if 'e does, den Oy'll have to convince 'im he's mistaken.'

'Dat might take some doin'. Higgins ain't nobody's fool.'

'D' last time Higgins saw me, Oy was a snotty-nosed young deputy, full o' piss and vinegar. Dis time a gentleman will present 'imself.'

An hour later, the two men were leaving the solicitor's office, formal introductions having been completed, and it was time to head to the sheriff's office at Nenagh gaol.

'Dis might be a bit trickier, Mick. You stay in d' carriage, and don't talk to anybody unless ya have to.'

Ned made a grand entrance into the outer office of the High Sheriff of Lower Ormond. The adjutant was suitably impressed by the look of Mr. Flynn and immediately disappeared through a door into the inner office. A few seconds later, Sheriff Higgins appeared and, without looking past Ned's smart apparel, extended his hand to the gentleman before him.

'How do you do, Mr. Flynn?' he said and, for the first time, he looked Ned directly in the face.

'Not too bad at all, Sheriff. Yerself?'

Higgins stood mute for a moment, then a smile crept slowly across his face. 'It's good to see you again. Why don't you come into my office … Mr. Flynn, and have a drink with me?'

'Oy never turn down a drink wit' an auld friend, sir. In fact Oy brought me own fer dat very purpose.' With that he handed the sheriff a bottle of the very best French brandy.

'I don't wish to be disturbed, Chaffee. Cancel all my

appointments for the rest of the day. Mr…. Flynn and I have some catching up to do.'

Higgins still had a grip on Ned's hand and he ushered him inside his office, slamming the door shut behind them.

The sheriff looked long into Ned's face, then beckoned him to take a seat. He produced two glasses, Ned uncorked the bottle and liberally poured out the amber fluid.

'So tell me, what shenanigans are you up to now, you rogue?'

'Well Oy was goin' to try and convince you it wasn't really me, but d' second ya saw me, Oy knew d' jig was up.'

'Who could forget Ned Flood? Remember when old D'Arcy ordered me to teach you how to read? You learned so fast that you scared the living daylights out of me. I reckoned on two, three years at the outside, then the old man would send me packing and give you my job.'

'Ah g'way wit' ya. Anyway, Oy wouldn't of taken it even if he had. Oy wasn't sheriff material. Back den, Oy was happy enough as a deputy, wit' regular meals and a place t' lay me head.'

'Most would have jumped at the chance. It's a good thing for me that you're not an ambitious man.'

'Ah Oy wouldn't say dat now, sir. It's just dat my ambitions took me along a different path.'

'Judging by your attire, I'd say the path you took was a profitable one.'

'Ach, it was never about d' money, sir, it was always about adventure. Money was just somet'in dat happened along d' way.'

'It sounds like you've had quite a few adventures

and I'd like to hear about them. You can start with that escapade you and D'Arcy had down in Cork. I've heard so many versions of it, I've given up trying to work out which one's true and which are fabrications.'

'Dey was probably all bullshite, sir.'

'Well now I can get it from the horse's own mouth but I have to tell you this before you start. I was so damn jealous when D'Arcy chose you to go with him. Back then I was full of my own importance and I thought he should have taken me because I was the more qualified. After I heard what happened I knew that if it was me there, my bollocks would have been just another ornament in that English captain's trophy collection.'

'Ah now dat's not true, sir. At least you'd have used yer head and now dem Prussians would be tellin' deir grandkids about d' wily Irishman dey chased.'

'I know better, Ned. Now just get on with the story and don't spare any details.'

Ned set about filling in the sheriff on the details of the manhunt and the bottle was getting low by the time the tale was told.

'Now tell me about what happened when you and your wife went to the colonies.'

'Jayzis, sir, all dis talkin' about meself is makin' me t'roat parched. Dere's anudder bottle o' dis in me carriage outside.'

'No sooner said than done,' said Higgins, getting up from his seat. 'I'll send my adjutant down to get it.' The sheriff stood looking admiringly at his former subordinate. 'If this story is half as good as the first one, I'll have something to tell my own grandchildren.'

Ned provided Higgins with a full account of his life in the colonies and he captivated the sheriff in rapt attention for most of the afternoon. When he had finally finished the story and the second bottle was empty, Higgins asked him a question which had nagged him all day.

'Tell me, Ned, what's the reason for all this subterfuge and for you using a false identity? If you're up to something dodgy, like perhaps another one of your hairy adventures, then I probably don't want to know any details, at least until after the event.'

Ned grinned. 'If ya don't know anyt'ing, sir, den ya can't say anyt'ing. But Oy promise ya dis, Oy'll be back someday to tell ya how it all turned out … dat's if Oy live dat long o' course.'

*

'I'm delighted to see you two gentlemen again,' said the Carrick sheriff. 'Did you bring my money?'

'We did better than that,' said Michael. 'We brought the owner this time and one of the King's revenue men.

Just then, Rackham and Smythe marched in. 'I want my merchandise immediately,' stated Jack, 'and I want you to pay back these men their eight shillings.'

'I'm sure I don't know what you're talking about,' protested the eagle-nosed sheriff.

'Mr. Smythe,' said Jack, 'I think a formal report is called for on this underhanded embezzler.'

Smythe began an official-sounding interrogation. 'What is your full name, Sheriff?'

'No, wait, I think there's been some sort of misunderstanding.' The man's top lip had sweat on it and his mouth had become dry. 'I got less than four shillings from them sods.'

'Well let's say the other four shillings is a fine,' snapped the Captain, 'for the inconvenience you caused these two gentlemen, not to mention me.'

'That's extortion!' protested the sheriff.

'I think this man is determined to be difficult, Mr. Smythe, there's nothing for it but to report him to higher authorities. If they choose to investigate his accounts, I'm sure the sheriff will be able to give them a plausible explanation for any inconsistencies. If not, then one day he'll be able to give us a first-hand account of the flora and fauna of Botany Bay.'

'Here!' spat the man, throwing a purse at Michael. 'Take the feckin' money.'

'Count your money, Mr. Hogan,' instructed Rackham. 'A man can't be too careful these days.'

Michael dumped the contents of the purse onto the sheriff's desk. 'There are only six shillings here, Captain.'

'Tut, tut, sheriff,' said Jack, 'that's another fine for cheating. Now you owe them four more.'

'I don't have that sort of money!' protested the man.

'That's unfortunate. Mr. Smythe, do you have the power to deputise Mr. Hogan and Mr. Clancy?'

'I do, sir.'

'Good. Do you have the authority to arrest tax cheats?'

'I do, Captain, under the authority granted me by the Crown.'

'Excellent. Mr. Clancy and Mr. Hogan, place this man under arrest.'

The hook-nosed little man held up his hands in surrender. 'Wait! Wait! I have the money here in my desk.' He unlocked a drawer and fumbled around, then produced another purse. He counted out four shillings.

'That's not enough,' said Jack. 'You owe them eight shillings, plus the four shilling fine.'

'This is daylight robbery and I won't give a farthing more!'

'Very well,' said Jack, 'you're obviously a man of conviction. Australia is full of men with convictions. Be sure to give the kangaroos our regards.'

The man pulled two more shillings out of the purse and tossed them on the desk. 'Here! Take it! Now our business is done!'

'Not quite,' said Rackham. 'There's the business of the hogsheads. Get them loaded on the wagon outside.'

The sheriff was relieved to see the wagon leave. What he had thought to be a cunning little business venture had ended in a complete fiasco, leaving him twelve shillings the poorer. He would need to be more discrete in future.

'Bastards!' he shouted after them, having satisfied himself they were out of earshot. 'You're just a bunch of feckin' Irish peasants led by a Yankee pirate!'

Once they were around the next bend in the road, the party pulled to a halt and Rackham laughed. 'I'd say you two Irish peasants should buy us a beer now that you're in the money.'

'We'll buy you more than one before we're home,' replied Michael, delighted with the outcome of the journey.

'I have a little errand for you first, gentlemen. I want you to collect another shipment from Ballykinsella, it's not far, and bring it to Waterford.'

'Isn't Ballykinsella where that old smuggler lives,' enquired Smythe.

'That's right,' replied Rackham devilishly.

'I'll have no part in any illegal activity, sir.'

'It's too late for that I'm afraid, Tim. You've already accepted a bribe and I have the keys to the Custom's House. What do you suppose would happen if those keys were to find themselves on someone's desk in London?'

Smythe felt like he was going to throw up. 'I thought we were friends.'

'We are, Tim, we're as friendly as it's possible for me to be with someone in your position. You wondered how your father became so comfortably-off on a customs agent's salary. Well I'm going to show you.'

Timothy Smythe threw up.

'Relax, man. You'll hardly have to do a thing and, in return, you'll get ten percent of the profits. You might have to stamp a paper or two but mostly you'll just turn a blind eye to whatever happens at night in your warehouse.'

'I can't do that,' the government man whimpered.

'Of course you can, Timmy. It'll be the easiest money you ever made and you can retire back to your family farm in a few years. You'll never have to worry about a thing except keeping your wife happy.'

'I don't have the nerve for it.'

'Well you'd better acquire the nerve, my friend, or you'll be taking a trip to New Holland with your new friend, the sheriff of Carrick.'

The trap had been sprung on the unsuspecting revenue man.

CHAPTER 31

T he first sprouts of tobacco plants had already begun to paint the bare ground with a bright green haze in the fields around the village. The Irish weather was unseasonably warm for the time of year and the seeds had responded with a blush of growth, as if they'd been waiting for the chance to explode. Abraham Washington was assessing the land with Alexander, as the Irish workers tended the plants … weeding and hand-picking the occasional insect attracted by the new bounty.

'This earth is fertile, Alexander. All the years of grazing sheep on it has given the soil what it needs.'

Alexander surveyed the fields. 'How long can the soil last before the tobacco saps the goodness out of it?'

'Tobacco's a particularly greedy crop. After a couple of seasons, the soil will be depleted and there will have to be a cover crop planted or this place will turn into a wasteland. The topsoil is thin. Your father never had any intention of staying here more than a year or two. He's no farmer and this land will be of no interest to him once it becomes valueless.'

'But the land is all these people have.'

'They don't even have that. The company owns the land and can do whatever it wants with it.'

'That doesn't seem right.'

'I'm not sure what's right or wrong anymore, Alexander. I owe your father everything but I don't mind telling you that I get frustrated with him. Sometimes he can't see any further than the end of his nose, sometimes not even that far.'

'But look how successful he's become. He must be doing something right.'

Abraham smiled patiently. 'Your father, my boy, has been blessed with the devil's own luck all his life. He's come to take it for granted, to rely on it even. He can no longer conceive failing at anything he takes on. Right here in Gortalocca, your father is merely playing another one of his games. You see all these people working in the fields? They're just pawns in his game and, when he gets bored with it, he'll up and leave just as suddenly as he came. It's always been that way with him.'

'Perhaps you can talk to him.'

'And say what? I can talk to him until I'm blue in the face and he might even listen to me, but he won't hear me. Why would he? I'm just one of his pawns too after all.'

'No you're not, you're his friend.'

'His friend? Your father doesn't have any need for friends, Alex. I'll grant you he has a certain fondness for me, the way a yeoman has a kinship with the tools of his trade, but I have no illusions about his feelings for me.'

'Da always told me you're his counsellor ... his conscience even.'

The black man chuckled mirthlessly. 'And can you ever remember a time when he's changed his mind following any advice I've given him?'

The young man thought for a moment, then gazed back out at the land around them. 'I'm beginning to grow fond of this country, Abraham, and its people too.'

The black man laughed heartily now and clapped his hand on the young man's shoulder.

'I have a notion there's one particular young lady who's become a firm favourite of yours.'

Alexander shrugged off the man's hand in embarrassment and kicked a clod of earth. He steered the conversation away from himself.

'Look over there, Abe. It's Liam and he has his arm out of the sling.'

Washington went along with the diversion. 'Oh yes, he's talking to the MacGowan girl. He seems to be paying her a lot of attention just lately. He'd better watch his backside. She was raised in a houseful of men, without a mother, and she's every bit as tough as her brothers.'

Almost as if on cue, the diminutive girl of thirteen years delivered a punch to Liam's face which knocked him backwards.

'Hey!' shouted Abraham. 'No fighting!'

The girl cast Washington a withering glance.

'Ya t'ink dat was a fight?' she yelled back. 'I'll show ya a fight!'

'You'd better go and rescue Liam, Alexander, before she hits him again.'

Alex hurried over to the scene of the crime and helped Liam to his feet.

'If I didn't have a bad hand, I could have taken 'er,'

he protested. As Alexander led him away, Liam saw Mr. Washington make his way over to the girl. 'Ya don't t'ink he'll give Josie her marchin' orders do ya, Alex?'

'He'd be within his rights to, but I doubt it, at least not until he's heard her side of the story.'

Abraham had limped over to the girl with the aid of his walking stick and was now standing over her, scowling. 'What did you do that for, girl?'

Josie MacGowan brushed some earth from her dirty linen shift. 'I was tryin' to do me work and yer man comes up and starts talkin' to me. When I told him to feck off and leave me alone, he said he t'ought I was pretty.'

It took all of Washington's willpower to stifle a smile and keep his stern demeanor.

'So let me get this straight, young lady. A boy pays you a compliment and you respond by nearly knocking his teeth out?'

'Ah no, sir, me best punch is me right one. I only hit him wit' me left.'

'What's your name, girl?'

'Me name is Jo, sir, Jo MacGowan.'

'Joe's an unusual name for a girl'

'Me real name's Josephine, but nobody calls me dat. Dey just shorten it to Jo or Josie. Are ya goin' to get rid o' me, sir?'

'I'm thinking about it, but I'm a man who believes in repentance. If you go and apologise to Liam Hogan, I shall give you another chance. Will you do that?'

'I will, sir, but only because I need d' work. I have four brudders and me da at home and we need d' money.'

'Are you the only one working, Josephine?'

'I am, sir. When Mick Sheridan was hirin', he said

women are better workers den men because we don't fight.' Josie blushed when she realised what she'd said.

'Well it seems you're the exception that proves Mr. Sheridan's rule, Josephine. You go over and make your apology, then come back here. While you're doing that, I'll have a think and see whether I might have some work for those brothers of yours. Now, no more fighting. Agreed?'

'Oh yes, sir, t'ank ya, sir. I'll go and apologise after I've finished work.'

'You'll go and do it now, Josie. Go on.'

He watched as the girl ran over to where Liam and Alex stood waiting. It occurred to him that the business of Irish courtship wasn't too far removed from outright combat and he smiled to himself.

Liam's left eye had turned red and begun to puff up and he covered it to hide it from Josie.

'Take yer hand away,' she said, as she approached. 'Let me see.' Liam lowered his hand slowly. 'Jayzis, did I do dat?' Liam nodded. She inspected it for a moment longer. 'Ah sure it'll be a pig's foot in d' mornin',' she said gleefully. 'Anyways, I'm sorry, Liam. I t'ought you was takin' d' piss when ya said ya t'ought I was pretty. If ya was, I forgive ya and if ya wasn't, I t'ank ya. Nobody ever said anyt'ing like dat to me before.'

'I meant it, Josie, in fact I t'ink yer beautiful.'

Alexander took another look at the girl and this time he was able to see beyond the filthy ragged clothes and the unkempt mop of chestnut brown locks. He too could see that under the thatch of matted hair was a pretty girl … nothing to compare with Siobhan, of course, but she certainly had something about her. Josie flushed bright red under the scrutiny of the two boys.

'I have t' get back to work,' she said abruptly and

turned on her heels. She walked back to the field with just the hint of a sway to her gait.

'I think she likes you, Liam,' smiled Alexander.

'Jayzis, I'd hate t' see what she'd do if she hated me!' replied Liam, rubbing his eye. Alexander laughed as he ruffled the boy's hair and gave him a little push.

*

Michael and Jamie dropped off the hogsheads of tobacco at the Customs House, along with the distraught excise man. Then, following Rackham's directions, the three men continued on towards Ballykinsella.

'There are twenty barrels of French brandy that have to be moved tonight, men, so we'd better get a move on.'

It was getting dark when Jack knocked on the door of Barry McGee's bar. It was several moments before the door opened just a crack and McGee's grizzled old face appeared.

'Ye weren't followed were ye?'

'Yes I have the whole bloody English Army behind me,' said Jack sarcastically.

Jones poked his head out of the door. 'I had the boys rig a block and tackle in the barn and we've hoisted the barrels out of the cellar, sir. They're ready to go.'

'Good man, Jonesey. Did you contact the owners of the merchandise, McGee?'

'I'd need to send a message to hell for that.'

'What do you mean?'

'The word is the two Maloney brothers got drowned in that bad storm we had a month or so ago. They were trying to beat the weather and got caught up in it.'

'Did they have families?'

'Davey was a bachelor but Ed, ah Ed, he was a stud. Had seven daughters, none of 'em married yet, all down in Courtmacsherry.'

'In that case, unless there are any objections, here's the split. The boat gets a quarter, I get a quarter and so do you, McGee.'

'I'm Irish, Rackham,' replied McGee, 'not stupid. What about the other quarter?'

'That goes to the Maloney girls.'

'That's bullshit, Rackham! What have they done to deserve a cut?'

'Nothing, but their father deserves his share and, just because he's dead, that doesn't mean we should cheat him out of it.'

'I don't know....'

'When are you ever likely to see a profit of between two to three pounds a barrel again, old man? You can get those pirates from Rush to make the run if you'd prefer, although they'd probably murder you and run the brandy to the Isle of Man for themselves.'

'It just seems stupid to divide the profits too many ways. That's alright though, I trust you.'

'You do, do you? Well I'm glad you trust me because I don't trust you as far as I could throw you.'

Jack had begun to get a little hot under the collar and it showed. Barry McGee was wary of pushing him too far in case the son of a real life pirate might prove to be more than he could handle.

'What needs t' be done?' asked Clancy. He was anxious to get back to Gortalocca.

'We have to load the barrels onto the wagon and get them to the quay at Tramore.'

'It's late, Captain,' said Michael. 'Will we just leave them there?'

'Well I like to think I'm a trusting soul, but I'm not about to leave temptation like that in the path of a bunch of thirsty Irishmen.'

'What about the government fella? He didn't look too good when we dropped him off.'

'Don't you worry about him, Michael, it was just first day nerves.'

'I thought he was going to piss himself with fright.'

Jonesey laughed. 'The captain can have that effect on people, Irish.'

Jack shot a smile at Mr. Jones. 'You go with the two paddies, Jonesey. I'm putting you in charge of the keys. We'll get the liquor out to the ship, then we'll make a quick run to the Isle of Man and see what kind of deal Mr. Rosse has for us.'

'Old Dave Rosse has been dealin' with the Dublin lads fer Irish whiskey. Do you think he's likely to be interested in French liquor?'

'I think he'll be more than interested, Jonesey. I imagine he's had enough of their popskull by now.'

'Will we come back empty, Capt'n? Seems like a wasted trip.'

'No, we won't be empty Jonesey. We'll have a consignment of the Duke's tea. The Dutchmen have a brisk business going with the old boy. Hell, half the tea the English and the Irish have running through their kidneys comes from that island. England might be fighting with France, and indeed everyone else, but the Duke of Athol knows better. He likes to make profit, not war. And, of course, now we're in the enviable position of having a warehouse in Waterford at our disposal to stash our goods in.'

'I don't want to piss on yer party, Capt'n, but have you forgotten about Willoughby?'

'I haven't forgotten about him, but there's little chance of running into the Albatross when Willoughby has such a vast area to patrol.'

'Sorry, sir, it's just that I have a bad feelin' about that fella. And you must admit, this ain't bin the luckiest of trips so far.'

'Don't you worry, Jonesey, our luck is about to change.' The captain flashed a grin at his bosun but Mr. Jones didn't return it.

Jack Rackham had no way of knowing know how prophetic his words were. Their luck was indeed about to change ... from bad to worse.

CHAPTER 32

'D is auld village has changed, Siobhan,' said Moira forlornly as she sat beside the fire in Mick's cottage. 'It's not d' Gortalocca it was years ago.'

Siobhan tossed her red locks from her face and stopped sweeping the floor. 'Alexander says it's called progress. He says if a place don't go forwards, den it goes backwards.'

'But if a village, or a country come to dat, don't keep d' auld foundations dey was built on, dey don't have no bones.'

'P'raps Ireland's got too many bones already,' replied the girl innocently.

The ancient woman cackled. 'Ah ya might be right, child. I'm probably selfish wantin' t'ings to be d' way I'm familiar wit'. When you've seen as many years come and go as I have, ya put greater faith in d' past den ya do in d' future. You're a young woman, pet, and ya have yer whole life stretchin' out in front of ya. As fer me, I've been blessed, or cursed, wit' a life spannin' five generations and I'd rather not see a sixth. I remember dis country when it was covered wit' forest and dere was enough land fer everyone. I heard tales first-hand, when dat divil Cromwell and his armies blew t'rough like a storm and suddenly dere was no land fer anyone …. at least if dey was Irish.'

Siobhan interrupted the old woman. 'You're not selfish, auld mother. You were always dere to help folks in need and ya never asked for nutt'n in return.'

'You're wrong, child, I don't deserve no grace fer me actions. I might not have done dose t'ings fer coin, but I did get somet'in' in return.'

'You're as poor as anyone around here sure. What did you get?'

Moira closed her sightless eyes. She lit her little clay dudheen with a piece of reed she ignited from the turf fire and dabbed the corner of her eye with the back of her hand.

'Ach, I must o' got smoke in me eye.'

'Tell me, Moira, why don't ya t'ink ya deserve any credit?'

'Because, child, I did it to make me feel good about meself. I told meself I did it fer God but I did it fer meself. Dat's pride, Siobhan, and dat's a sin.'

'But ya have a gift, and you've never bin anyt'ing but generous wit' it.'

'See, child? Even what you just said made me feel good. I'm really no better den dat rogue, Ned Flood. He spends his time doin' what gives him pleasure and I've done d' same me whole life.'

The conversation had become entirely too deep for the young woman and she began to weave a new thread.

'Did me da bring a curse on d' family when he burned d' faerie ring?'

'I don't presume t' know what God t'inks, but I can

tell ya what I t'ink. If God knows everyt'ing dat ever was and everyt'ing dere ever will be, den He already knew Michael was goin' t' burn d' faerie fort, even before He created Heaven and Earth. Why would He punish somebody fer somet'ing He already knew would happen? And if He didn't want Mikey to do it, why didn't He just let dat tree fall on him a few days before? I don't t'ink God has any interest in d' likes of faerie rings or holy wells.' The old woman smiled to herself. 'Dem t'ings are only of any interest to daft auld women and wide-eyed children.'

'Are ya sayin' curses don't exist so?'

'Oh dey exist alright, mavourneen, but dey're brought on by human pride and stupidity. Just because ya get away wit' somet'ing by luck once don't mean it'll always work dat way. Ned Flood needs to be very careful. His luck's held out fer so long, he depends on it now. D' further up he rises, d' further he has to fall. Curses don't come from outside. We bring 'em on ourselves, dey come from within us.'

Siobhan hadn't followed everything Moira had said but she looked relieved. 'What do you think about Alexander?' she asked.

'Dat lad ain't nutt'n like his da, t'hank God. Ned is reckless and he always was. Dat's because he's never had anyt'ing but his wits and a pair of fists. Alexander was born a gentleman. He's careful in what he says and what he does, but I do worry whether his father's shenanigans might rub off on him. Next time ya come, pet, bring him wit' ya. I'd like to get a better measure of d' young fella.'

'He was askin' me about d' auld ways and about d' legends, but I couldn't tell him much. P'raps you can tell him, I'd like t' hear too.'

'It'd be grand to have you two young people here together.' chuckled the crone. Siobhan blushed, relieved that the old woman couldn't see the colour rise in her face. Moira sensed it and laughed heartily. 'Your grandad, he blushed like an apple too whenever he was teased.' A hint of melancholy tinged her voice. 'Ever since I've bin back here in Gortalocca, I've thought about Liam every day. Yer da looks just like him. I felt his features and I could o' cried.' Tears began to flow now and the old woman took the pipe from her mouth and covered her eyes with her hands. 'Dere's one difference between 'em, though. Even if anyone tried to influence him, Liam Flynn's decisions were always his own.'

Siobhan detected the old woman's criticism of her father and felt uncomfortable, so she changed the topic of conversation.

'Grandma said she'd come and visit ya dis week.'

'I'd like dat,' replied the old crone. 'She's bin promisin' to come fer a while now but I expect she's bin too busy at Hogan's.'

'Dat's it o' course, she's bin mad busy.' It was a feeble excuse and they both knew it. Business had indeed been brisk at Hogan's but not so much that her grandmother couldn't find time to pay the old woman a visit. The longer she'd left it, the more embarrassed Roisin had become.

'P'raps I'll go into Gortalocca meself tomorra, save 'er the trip.'

*

Mick reined the team to a halt outside Mulcahey's Inn on the waterfront. Ned surveyed the busy harbour and the only ship he could see of any substantial size was an English brig which appeared to be taking on provisions.

'Oy don't see Prosperity at anchor, Mick. I wonder if Jack's already sailed.'

'We didn't pass Mikey and Jamie on d' road,' replied Mick. 'I t'ought dey would already be on deir way back home by now.'

'Well, dey was t' drop d' cargo off at d' customs office so Oy suppose dat's as good a place t' start as any.'

They inquired at the inn for directions to the office of customs, then made their way along the quay to the warehouse. Ned walked in first, followed by the big man. Mr. Smythe was sitting with his elbows on his desk and his face covered by his hands, lost in thought. Ned coughed and startled him half to death.

'Is yer boss here, boyo?'

'I'm the boss here,' snapped Smythe. 'Can I help you?'

'I was wondering if you've seen Captain Rackham.'

The young fellow's face grew pale and, for a moment, Ned thought the lad was going to throw up.

'His ship is anchored in Tramore. If you're here to arrest him, I don't know anything.'

Ned turned to Mick. 'Sounds like he's met Jack,' he said offhandedly.

'What business do you have with Captain Rackham?'

'He has a cargo dat belongs to me.'

'The tobacco?'

'Dat's right.'

'How well do you know this Captain Rackham, sir?' Tim was trying to be coy but he was out of his league.

'Not very well at all, sir,' said Ned. 'Oy'm sorry, Oy ain't even introduced meself. Me name's Flynn, Michael Flynn.'

Smythe held out his hand. 'It's a pleasure to meet you, Mr. Flynn. My name is Timothy Smythe.'

Ned looked Tim Smythe in the eye long enough to make the poor fellow look away.

'Why did ya ask me if Oy knew d' captain?'

'Sir, I fear that the captain might not be as upstanding as you think him to be.'

Ned feigned a look of surprise and indignation. 'Now what makes ya t'ink dat?'

Smythe lowered his voice to not much more than a whisper. 'Last night, I shared a conversation with a certain Lieutenant Willoughby. His is the English brig in the harbour. He said there was something very peculiar about the way Rackham plays chess.'

'Well dat's a daft reason not t' trust a body.'

'I have my own reasons too, Mr. Flynn.'

Ned instinctively shifted his weight onto the balls of his feet as if he was about to engage in a fistfight.

'Did ya discuss yer own reasons wit' d' English fella?'

'I did not. I had no cause to share my suspicions with him.'

Ned knew immediately that Jack had ensnared the young fellow somehow and that, by now, the customs man would sell his own mother to save his hide.

'And what else did dis Willoughby character have t' say?'

'He said something about the ship owner's son and some slave he met down in Baltimore.'

Ned was perplexed and not at all happy that Washington and Alexander had failed to tell him about the British captain.

'What did he say about 'em?'

'He just mentioned that the boy was far too deferential towards the black man and most defensive of him too.'

'So what?' scoffed Ned. 'In Amerrycuh, slaves who take care of children often have more t' do wit' raisin' 'em den deir parents do. What else did he say?'

'Nothing that I remember, sir. Captain Willoughby comes ashore each day for his evening meal. If you'd like to speak to him, I suggest you make his acquaintance at the inn.'

Ned had already made his mind up to do just that. The game he played relied on information.

'Did ya see d' two Irishmen who dropped off d' cargo.'

Smythe pulled a small notebook from a drawer in his desk. 'Here we are,' he said. 'Mr. Hogan and a Mr. Clancy. They were here the day before yesterday at three o'clock in the afternoon.'

The officious little bastard's keeping notes, thought Ned. That wasn't a good sign. It could be that he intended to play both sides and that was a game with which Ned was wholly familiar.

'Oy t'ink dat's them,' he said with a straight face. 'It's hard t' keep track of d' names of all d' fellas Oy hire.'

'They were going on to Ballykinsella afterwards, with Captain Rackham.' He checked his notebook once again.

'Ya keep very accurate records, Mr. Smythe.'

At the perceived compliment, Smythe smiled the smile of the innocent. 'Why thank you, sir. I like to make notes of everything, just in case there are any... discrepancies.'

As the two men left the warehouse, Ned made his own mental notes. That book had to disappear for a start and he was going to have to make sure Smythe was tarred with the same brush as everyone else. He would open a bank account in Cork City, in the name of Timothy Smythe, and he would deposit fifty pounds in it. The next day, he would withdraw it all but for one pound, just to keep it active. Then he would do the same thing in Limerick and Dublin. Timothy Smythe might be a weasel but foxes eat weasels. Ned was a fox.

A few hours later Ned was sitting in the bar with Mick. They were waiting for Willoughby to show up. Mick had already downed a few flagons of ale and Ned was still nursing his first when Lieutenant Willoughby arrived with his sergeant of marines. He scanned the bar for faces, both familiar and foreign, and finally settled on Ned. Flood didn't wait for the officer to introduce himself. He told Mick to go and tend the horses and nodded at the Lieutenant. The Englishman sauntered over and Ned invited him to take the seat vacated by Mick.

'Good evenin', Mr. Willoughby. Will ya allow me t' buy ya a drink?'

The officer was taken aback at being addressed by name.

'I will, sir,' he said formally, 'when I have the privilege of knowing the name of my benefactor.'

'Me name's Michael Flynn, sir, and it'd please me if ya shared supper wit' me.'

The Englishman bowed slightly without taking his eyes off of the Irishman.

'Ah yes, Michael Flynn. I believe you are the owner of the schooner Prosperity. We may have some mutual acquaintances, Mr. Flynn.'

The officer's eyes were still riveted on Ned's and Ned began to feel slightly uneasy. This meeting with Willoughby may not have been such a wise decision after all.

'Prosperity is indeed mine, sir. I believe you already met me son, and Captain Rackham too.'

'Indeed I have. I believe your son came from … Savannah, is it?'

Ned didn't know whether or not he was being tested, and he had no knowledge of what had transpired in Baltimore between Rackham and Willoughby, so he resorted to something he was entirely unfamiliar with … the truth.'

'No, sir. Charles Town.'

'Hmmm. Unless my memory fails me, sir, I assure you that your son said he was from Savannah.' The naval officer shifted his weight forward in his seat and brought his face so close to Ned's that the Irishman could smell the rum on his breath.

Ned decided to do what he did best. 'We have houses in Savannah and Charles Town. The boy was raised by his mother in the Georgia colony. My offices are in Charles Town.'

Willoughby shifted back in his chair. 'Tell me, do you play chess?'

'I don't have time to start a chess game, sir.'

'But you've already started, Mr. Flynn … and I believe I already have you in check.'

CHAPTER 33

C aptain Rackham and Mr. Jones were sitting in the bar at Ballykinsella and Jack was deciding on his next move.

'The tobacco has to be removed from the customs warehouse as soon possible,' he declared.

'I thought it would be safe there until we got back, sir.'

'I thought so too, Jonesey, but if Smythe gets a case of the jitters, he might do something reckless. We need to get it out of there before the idiot's conscience gets the better of him.'

Just then, Ned poked his head inside the door of the tavern.

'Oy'll give ya conscience, ya sod. Oy just shared supper wit' d' captain in charge of dat brig in harbour. Willoughby caught me talkin' bollix and he'd already worked out somet'in was goin' on.'

'Ned, I wasn't expecting you!' said Jack in surprise. 'I thought Alexander and Washington would have filled you in on what happened.'

'Well, they didn't and so Oy sat dere wit' me britches

as good as unbuttoned and me manhood hangin' out.'

'What do you think he knows?'

'He knows we're a couple of slippery eels, fer a start, and he knows where ya have d' boat anchored.'

'I'd already assumed he knew where the ship was but as long as I knew where he was, I didn't think it was a problem.'

'Oh ya didn't? Well put yer piddle stick back in yer trousers and get 'em buttoned up because he says he's uppin' anchor and sailin' on d' mornin' tide.'

'Shit! I thought we had at least another day. I have Jonesey and half the crew here.'

'Load d' men up in d' wagon and get yerselves back to d' boat. You have to be gone by d' time he gets dere.'

'I already had the sails stained with pitch and turpentine. If we can get to the ship within the hour, we should be able to sneak out before dawn. It'll be at least sunrise before Willoughby is on station.'

*

Willoughby was no fool and he was well-versed in deception and games of cat and mouse. He returned to the Albatross and, instead of waiting for the early morning tide, he began to bark orders at his crew.

'Get the longboat over the side. Kedge the ship up to the anchor. We'll tow her out of Waterford as soon as the tide slackens. Put the jollyboat in too, I want every man possible at the oars.'

He gauged the wind, it was just east of due north. If he could get the ship into position, he would have the weather advantage over the Yankee smuggler. Before dawn he would have Captain Rackham in checkmate. He put his hands behind his back and swayed to and fro. He had hoped Jack Rackham would be a worthier opponent but he was turning out to be no better than the others who had challenged him. He smiled and put the tip of his tongue between his teeth. Oh well, he thought, in a few hours I'll seize the schooner and its cargo. The prize money from the Admiralty will look very well in my bank account.

Jack wasn't idle either. 'We can't use Waterford for a while, Michael. You and James will take me and the crew back to Prosperity. We can't leave the merchandise in Waterford; something tells me we can't trust Smythe to keep his mouth shut. The tobacco already has stamped papers from Galway so you can retrieve it tomorrow night. Jonesey, you stay with the paddies. Take the extra set of keys and go to the customs house, make sure it's late at night.'

'Oy'll come wit' ya Mr. Jones. Oy'd like to see what else dat shitebag has in his desk besides his little book. Maybe we'll borry some of his forms and stamp 'em. When it comes time to move the 'baccy out of Oirland, d' paperwork might come in useful.' Ned was still very hot under the collar from his meeting with the English captain.

'Be careful about putting too much pressure on Smythe, Ned,' said Jack, 'or he's in danger of cracking like an egg.'

'Ah sure, who cares. D' divil can take d' little snot-rag.'

*

Tim Smythe was tossing and turning in bed. He hadn't had a decent night's sleep for days. Finally, his conscience got the better of him and he made a decision. The best way to extricate himself from this mess was to approach Captain Willoughby and announce he'd uncovered a band of smugglers who were new to the area. He would claim he'd been merely playing along with them until he'd got enough information to expose their ringleader. Now that he'd met Mr. Flynn, the whole mob could be apprehended. Perfect, he thought. That way, he'd not only be able to wriggle out from under the thumb of that pirate, Rackham, he might receive a commendation, perhaps even a promotion for services to the Crown. Sleep still eluded the crumb-sucking bureaucrat. Now he lay awake imagining his superiors in London congratulating him for displaying such initiative.

*

Less than an hour later, the barrels of brandy were safely stowed aboard Prosperity and the crew was making preparations to sail. At the same time, Willoughby and the Albatross were under full canvas with a favourable wind, past Creadon Head on the west shore of Waterford Harbour. In a couple of hours they should be on station outside Tramore Bay and that would put a stopper in the jug.

'When will ya be ready to sail, Jack?' asked Ned.

'Two hours, maybe a bit more, and we'll be out in open water headed for Castletown on the Isle of Man. We'll stay clear of Waterford on the return and come into Dungarvan. We should be there in a few days with the consignment of Dutch tea.'

'Jonesey, make sure ya watch out fer Michael and Jamie,' said Ned. 'Oy'm goin' down to Cork City. Oy have a bit o' bankin' to do fer our friend Mr. Smythe, damn his hide.'

'Jonesey,' instructed Jack, 'you and the Irishmen move the tobacco back here, then take it to Dungarvan. Put the barrels in the back of the wagon and cover them with hay. Find a friendly farmer who'd be glad of a few shillings to hide the stuff for a couple of days.'

'It might be best if we do it in two loads, sir,' suggested Jones. 'The draught horses are knackered and there's no use in killing them.'

'I trust you to use your judgement, Jonesey. The risky part is getting the stuff out of Waterford so you'd better be sneaky and move the goods late at night. We can get a better price for the tobacco in France than we can in England and the longer this war lasts, the better the price, so we're in no rush to move the tobacco. Be careful.'

'Oy'll get a market fer d' Dutch tea when Oy'm down in Cork City, Jack, so we don't have to waste any more time dan necessary,' said Ned. He looked over at Michael and Jamie and shrugged. 'Sorry lads but yer up to yer ears now. Dere ain't no backin' out Oy'm afraid.'

'Aren't we supposed to be building a drying barn in Gortalocca?' asked Mikey.

'Yer more valuable to me here fer now. If it comes to it, we can always use d' stables at Johnstown fer dryin'.'

That satisfied Michael for the moment but the whole affair was beginning to weigh heavily on Clancy. He elbowed his partner in the ribs and Mikey winced.

'Relax, Jamie. This is the easiest money we'll ever make.'

After Prosperity's crew had been dropped off near the ship, Jones and the two Irishmen headed back towards Ballykinsella to spend the night in McGee's bar. As they left, they could see Ned and Jack engaged in animated conversation and it looked like it was growing into a more of an argument than a discussion. Ned gave Jack a mighty shove. The captain just waved his hand at the Corkman in a gesture of dismissal and disgust.

'What was that was all about, I wonder?' mused Jonesey. 'Them two usually get along like brothers.'

'Brudders sometimes kill each udder,' responded Jamie.

Jones cast him a sour glance. 'I wasn't talking to you, you bog-stomper. I was talking to meself.'

The two men glared at each other for what seemed like an endless few seconds, then ignored each other for the rest of the night.

*

With the wind almost directly astern, the Albatross had Brownstown Head just off her starboard beam by three o'clock in the morning.

'Will we sail into Tramore Bay, Captain?' asked the helmsman.

'No, stay on course. It's too shallow and the tide's still falling.'

Willoughby could see the anchor light of Prosperity's masthead and estimated she was moored about a mile from where the Albatross was now. All he had to do was wait until the sun came up in a few hours, then the prize would be his.

*

'Captain Rackham! There's a sail off the mouth of the harbour!'

Jack had been busy preparing to set sail when the announcement was made.

'Shit! That's Willoughby! His damn brig made good time with that following wind. Douse the lights! We'll go dark! He knows we're here now, all we can do is wait.'

Jack knew how the Englishman's mind worked and tried to get inside his opponents head.

As soon as the lights on Prosperity went out, Willoughby hesitated for only a second. He realised he'd been spotted and waiting wasn't his strong suit.

'Put the longboat over the side. I want twelve oarsmen and all four marines armed. Mount the swivel gun on the bow. We'll make a raid and catch those blighters off guard.'

'Why don't we just wait until sunrise and put a shot across their bow?' ventured a midshipman.

Willoughby looked at the young man in disgust. 'You're an old lady, Parker. You have no sense of adventure whatsoever.'

Rackham had already formulated a plan. 'Raise the main and fores'l, men, but do it quietly. I want no noise. Let the sails luff. Winch us up to the anchor. I want the sharpest eyes forward. If you see anything, shout.'

*

'Put your backs into it, men,' Willoughby whispered urgently. 'Not much longer and then we'll all have our share of prize money in our purses.'

Just then, the moon skidded out from behind a

cloud, just long enough for the men in the longboat to see Prosperity had her sails raised. Willoughby saw it too but his plan was too far along now and the time for turning back had passed. The moon revealed the longboat to the sentinels aboard Prosperity too.

'Cap'n, there's a longboat with a raiding party aboard and it's headed for us. It's a little less than half a mile away, two points off the port bow.'

'Four men on the capstan,' yelled Jack. 'Haul the anchor. Trim the sails. Raise the jib. Helmsman, steer two points to port.'

'We'll run it over!' came a voice from the crew.

'He'll get out of the way,' smiled Captain Rackham, as he went forward to man the swivel gun.

In a matter of minutes, the two vessels were passing twenty yards abeam of each other and well within hailing distance. Each had a swivel gun levelled at the other. Willoughby placed a hand on the barrel of his and lowered it. Jack raised his skywards.

'I thought I had you in check, Captain,' shouted the Englishman. Strangely his voice held no hostility.

'I couldn't let the game end so soon,' replied Jack, 'it's only just started.'

'We both know I'll be the victor, Captain Rackham.'

'Perhaps you will and perhaps you won't, but the winner won't be decided today, sir.'

'You still have to get past the Albatross, Rackham.'

'That's very kind of you to warn me, Willoughby.'

'I'd just like it to be me who finally clips your wings.'

Jack knuckled his forehead in salute to the Englishman. 'Until we meet again then, Lieutenant.'

'It won't be long, Captain Rackham. Don't get yourself killed by some Frenchie in the meantime or you'll spoil the game. Bon voyage.'

As soon as Prosperity had sailed clear of the longboat, there was a boom followed by a splash, twenty yards to starboard.

'Two more points to port!' yelled Rackham. 'The gunner can't see us without a moon. We'll pass the Albatross upwind and gain the weather gauge.'

Several more ineffective canon shots followed at intervals until the schooner was out of range and in the Irish Sea, bound for the Isle of Man.

CHAPTER 34

'I can't say I know much about Ireland's history or her legends,' Alexander told the old woman. 'My father always said the English are the ones with all the power. That's why he made sure I was raised to be a proper English gentleman.'

'A body is what a body is, Alexander,' replied Moira. 'Yer da is Irish and so was yer mother. Ned Flood believes he could turn a fish into a bird if he wanted.'

'All my teachers were English, you see, so I know a lot more about England than I do this country, or even America come to that.'

'Ach, Amerrycuh's still only a baby. Sure you could learn everyt'ing dere is to know about its history in a few minutes. Ireland is ancient, my boy. We had the Brehan laws when Jesus was still shittin' in his nappy.' Moira blessed herself when she realised her blasphemy. 'Dem feckin' English t'ink we're no better than dogs, but dey're d' mongrels. Druids, Celts, Romans, Angles, Saxons, Vikings and Normans. Dem daft feckers have been invaded so many times, I'm surprised dey all talk d' same language. A t'ousand or so years ago, when Ireland was d' seat of all knowledge and England wasn't shite, scholars came to us from all over d' world to get educated.'

'What about the Magna Carta?'

'Who's dat?'

'It's not a who, it's a what. The Magna Carta lays down the rules for the English justice system.'

Moira spat on the ground, just missing Alexander's feet. 'English justice, me arse,' she said bitterly. 'Well deir system seems to be workin' very nicely for 'em, don't it?'

Alex blushed. He realised he'd bought into a fairytale about a justice system which had been written on a piece of parchment, then never fully put into practice.

'Dem English is so full of 'emselves, dey t'ink dey're d' only ones who know what's right, and it don't matter what d' rest o' d' world t'inks.'

'I've heard the same thing said in the colonies.'

'Someday, deir pride will turn around and bite 'em on deir arses.'

Alex was in a state of confusion. By birth he was a Yankee, by education he was an Englishman and by blood he was Irish. Right there, in Mick's cottage, sitting beside the fire with the old woman, was born a conflict of identity within him which he'd carry for the rest of his life.

'I know about America because I lived there and I know about England because I was taught about it. I know next to nothing about Ireland, Moira, and I think you're the one to teach me.' There was a sincerity in the young man's voice which reached into the very heart of the old woman. She knew he wasn't just making conversation.

'Blood always wins t'rough, son. Yer da can't turn a

bird into a fish after all. But if ya really want to find out about Ireland and d' Irish people, ya have to leave dat big house up in Johnstown and live amongst 'em.'

'Well there's enough room for me here in Mick's house. Would it be alright if I stayed here? Then you could teach me every night after work.'

The old crone cackled. 'It's bin a long time since I shared a roof wit' anyone,' she rasped. 'Ya don't snore do ya? I sleep light and I don't want to be kept awake by somebody sawin' wood all night. And don't bother bringin' none o' dat fancy bed finery. A blanket'll do ya. It might be a good idea t' bring a drop of yer da's poteen wit' ya d'ough. Me poor auld t'roat gets dry if I talk too much.'

'I will,' said Alexander excitedly, 'I promise. Shall I go and get my blanket right now and we can start my lessons when I get back?'

'Yes, g'wan, off wit ya … and don't forget d' poteen.'

Once he'd gone, old Moira shook her head and grinned her toothless smile. Times are changing, she thought. While some were forgetting, even denying their Irishness, others were discovering it for the first time and embracing it.

*

Ned, Mick and Barry McGee were already into their third or fourth cup of poteen, and the sun had already begun to paint the eastern sky, when the two Irishmen arrived with Jonesey and the dray.

'Is there anything to eat in this place?' asked Jones, gruffly. He was starving and more than a little miffed that his captain had left him to help the two paddies.

'Look around you, ya daft squid,' answered Barry sarcastically. 'This is a feckin' bar. Round here you drink your supper. Anyway, it's nearly time fer breakfast. You can scratch around the barn with the hens fer eggs if you like.'

'Go and get me eggs,' Jones ordered Clancy.

Jamie was a good six inches taller than Mr. Jones and now he straightened himself up to his full height. The top of his head almost touched the ceiling of the bar.

'Who died and left you in charge?' snarled Jamie uncharacteristically.

'The captain left me in charge.'

'D' cap'n left you to help us, ya runt. Dat makes you d' servant, so why don't you go out dere and bring me some eggs.'

'I'll go and look for the eggs,' said Michael, in an effort to diffuse the situation.

'Shut yer gob, Mikey!' said Clancy. 'Dis is between me and dis English piss squirt.'

Michael's jaw dropped. In all the years he'd known Jamie, he'd never seen him behave this way. Jones squared up to Clancy. He didn't mind being called a piss squirt, he'd been called worse, but he did take exception to being called an Englishman.

'I ain't English, I'm Cornish.'

'What d' feck is a Cornish?'

Ned attempted an intervention. 'It's somebody from Cornwall,' he offered.

'Ach, sure I never heard such bollix,' said Clancy acidly. 'Ya can make a wall out o' stones and ya can make a wall out o' mud. Ya can't make a wall out o' corn!'

'I'm not arguing with you, Irish,' said Jones.

'Fair enough,' said Clancy. 'In dat case, I'll go and see if I can find us some eggs.' He walked out the door and the incident was over as unexpectedly as it had started.

'Mick, will ya go and help Jamie,' said Ned. It was more of an order than a request and the big man complied. When the two large Irishmen had left, the room seemed considerably emptier and Ned began.

'Michael, Oy just wanted ya to know Oy didn't mean fer you and Clancy to get caught up in all o' dis.'

'Don't worry about it, Ned, it's not like you forced us to take part.'

'But Oy did. Ye were starvin' and Oy took advantage. Oy made it sound like easy money but Oy want t' set ya straight. Dis is a dangerous business, Michael. Ya don't just have t' watch out fer d' law, ya have t' keep an eye out fer people who would gladly relieve ya of what ya have too. And make no mistake, dere ain't nobody ya can complain to. Ya can't trust anyone and sometimes ya even have to watch out fer people ya know. If dey t'ink yer handlin' money, dere's every chance dey'll want a share of it, or more.'

'Why are you telling me this, now, Ned?'

'A couple o' reasons, Mikey. Oy don't mind admittin' all dis started as one of me games, a flight o' fancy. Oy t'ought Oy could show ye a way to get yerselves out of money trouble and maybe stick it to d' English aristycrats in d' process. But it ain't about who's English or Oirish anymore, or who's Cat'lic or Protestant. We're outlaws now, d' whole bunch of us, you and Jamie included, and d' only people we can trust is each udder.'

'I don't think I'll tell Clancy that.'

'Probably a wise decision. What Oy'm sayin' is we

can't have any fightin' between us. Ya have t' tell Clancy t' keep his mouth shut and his opinions to 'imself until dis is all over.'

Michael looked at Jonesey. 'I apologise for Jamie, Mr. Jones. I think his blood just boiled over when you ordered him around.'

Jones smiled. 'Oh I'm used to dealing with high-spirited men,' he said, ' but I'll be sure to watch my tone in future and perhaps try not to sound so … English.'

'Alright,' said Ned resolutely, 'dat's settled, now let's get down t' business. Like Oy said, Oy don't trust dat eejit of a customs man in Waterford and Oy want ye to get d' 'baccy out of d' warehouse. Just bring it here and don't go to Dungarvan until Oy get back. Make sure ye use d' backroads.' Ned pulled a map out of his coat pocket and indicated the route he wanted the goods to travel. 'Never use d' same road twice, just in case ye're followed. Be sure to load d' hogsheads after dark and be careful, Jonesey, d' most dangerous part is gettin' it out o' dere. Smythe knows we have to come back fer it and he might have laid a trap fer us.'

'I understand, Ned,' said Jones, 'but the capt'n said we were to take the goods to Dungarvan.'

'Ah sure Jack's always makin' plans den changin' 'em at d' last minute. You have d' keys to d' Customs House. Just get d' stuff out o' dere and Oy'll meet ya back here in t'ree days, Oy'll be back from Cork by den. Don't get too creative, now, I have t' know what's goin' on. When Mick and Clancy get back, we'll have a drink on it.'

*

Jack stood on deck next to the helmsman and looked up at the sky. There were no stars out and, in the east, the darkness was beginning to surrender to day. The moon had started to set over the Irish mainland and was still playing hide and seek amongst the clouds. The ship heaved rhythmically as the seas rolled beneath her. Both men were oblivious of the late spring chill of the morning as each pondered his own thoughts. Stevenson was at the wheel. The lad was barely out of his teens and his wiry hair was pulled back in a braid that was tarred, the custom of seamen.

'I thought we was gonners, Capt'n.'

Jack snapped back into reality at the sound of the young fellow's words. 'We had luck on our side, boyo. A lot of things were in our favour but, if just one of them hadn't been, I would be in irons right now and the rest of you would have been pressed into His Majesty's service.'

'What do ya mean, sir?'

'If the night had been clear and the moon shining, the Englishman would have seen our sails raised and would have just sat and waited until morning. If the wind blew out of the east, we would have been trapped in a lee harbour and would've had to claw our way out. We would have been under the guns for an hour.'

'I couldn't help noticing that you and the English captain spoke to each other like old friends over a card game, sir.'

'Captain Willoughby is a sportsman, Stevenson. Men like him live by a different code to that of most others. He has his own rules for playing the game and, to him, they're more important than any regulations the Admiralty has written in its books.'

'He should have waited until daylight, sir.'

'That might have been the right and proper way to do it, boyo, but shooting fish in a barrel is not his way.'

'You could have raked the longboat with the swivel gun and sent him and some others to perdition.'

Rackham looked sternly at the sailor. 'And that, Mr. Stevenson, is not my way.'

'It's what I would've done, Capt'n.'

'That's because you're a mutton-headed boy. When two men are engaged in what could possibly be the best game of their lives, only a simpleton would spoil the fun by pulling out a gun and shooting the other.'

'You talk like you and him are friends or something, sir.'

'No, not friends Stevenson, but we're not enemies either. We're opponents and our gameboard is the ocean.'

'Beggin' yer pardon, sir, but I'm not clever enough to understand all that shite. I was raised on a farm in Sussex and all I wanted to do was get out of there and find excitement. Now I've got all the excitement I can handle, and all I want to do is make enough money to buy a farm and marry a plump girl who'd keep me warm at night.'

For the first time, Jack noticed how cold it was and he pulled his greatcoat tightly around him.

'Stay sharp, Stevenson. If you see anything unusual, give me a shout.'

With that, Captain Rackham went below to his quarters to get a few hours sleep.

CHAPTER 35

R oisin and Mr. Washington were standing outside Hogan's. They were chatting with Paul Gleeson, who had just delivered a few jugs of poteen to the bar, and the three of them were so engrossed in the business at hand that they barely noticed the dishevelled figure walking towards them.

'I'm back, Mam. I got homesick fer Gortalocca and I missed Peg, so I've come back.'

Roisin span round to face her eldest son. 'Rob….! What….? Where's May, and the boy?'

'Dey're back down d' road a bit. I left 'em pullin' d' cart so I could come on ahead.'

'What happened up north? I thought you were going to make your fortune and come back a rich man,' said Roisin, with an edge to her voice.

'Ah sure dem bastards up dere wouldn't give an outsider a chance. By d' time we got to Letterkenny, almost half me money was gone.'

'I wouldn't be surprised if you ran it through your kidneys and pissed it away.'

'I didn't drink dat much. It cost me a fortune to feed May and d' boy. He's a growin' lad.' Robert looked around him with curiosity. 'Well it certainly looks like t'ings have improved in Gortalocca since I left. Who's dat?' he said, pointing at Abraham who, up until this point, had merely been an interested observer.

Mr. Washington extended his hand to introduce himself. Robert took a step back and didn't look at him. 'I asked ya who he was, Mam,' he repeated petulantly.

Abraham didn't wait for Roisin to answer. 'That's no way to speak to any lady,' he said sternly, 'let alone your own mother.'

'I wasn't talkin' to you, ya…' Robbie didn't get the chance to get his next word out before Washington lunged forward and grabbed him by the throat. Robert responded by slamming the man's forearm with his blackthorn stick, causing the big man to release his hold. Now it was Washington's turn to take a step backwards. As he did so, he shifted his grip on his own walking stick so that he was holding the shaft about halfway down. He struck as fast as a snake, clouting Robbie on the wrist and causing him to drop his bata. The two men glared at each other, the Irishman unarmed now and waiting to receive a blow to the head which never arrived.

'You ever touch me again, darkie, and I'll beat yer brains out.'

'I don't think so,' growled Washington defiantly.

Roisin tried to diffuse the situation. 'Be careful about riling him, Abraham, he knows how to use the bata. It might be better if you turn your back and walk away before this gets out of hand. My son has always been cantankerous when he's tired and hungry.'

'Ned made it clear he wouldn't tolerate any fighting in Gortalocca while the crop's in the field,' replied

Washington, the fog of anger beginning to lift.

'Well I don't take orders from him,' snarled Robert, 'or anyone else for that matter.'

'But I do, Mr. Flynn,' replied the black man, off handedly, and he turned and walked away.

'G'wan!' Robbie shouted after him. 'Go and hide behind Flood's apron, ya coward.'

Abraham swallowed hard as the bitter taste of bile rose in his throat. It wasn't easy to walk away from such an insult but Ned had warned him that, in spite of the geniality the Irish displayed, they also harboured a bitter resentment and fury within them that could explode at the least provocation. Ned had left him in charge and he wasn't going to be the spark that ignited the tinder box. The workers in the fields had heard the commotion and had gathered, laying down their tools in the hope of witnessing a fight.

Paulie Gleeson caught up with Mr. Washington. 'Dat was a mistake, sir, if ya don't mind me sayin',' he told him. 'It's a bad idea to turn yer back on an angry man wit' a stick.'

'I was not about to engage in a fight in front of all those people, certainly not after everything Ned said.'

'Fair enough, boss, but ya just lost all respect from dose very same people.'

Abraham was appalled that so many individuals seemed so anxious to watch someone get his head cracked open, and his bad back was playing him up again too.

'You Irish didn't invent sticks or stick fighting, you know. African people have been killing each other that way since before the time of the prophets. I spent my evenings as a young fellow stick-fighting with my friends. We called it Callenda, you call it Bataireacht, but it doesn't matter. Whatever the name is, it's foolish.'

Just then, Washington's attention was caught by the clatter of sticks clashing together around the margin of the mob. The sound came again, followed by a scream of pain.

'What in God's name is going on?'

'I wondered how long it was goin' to take,' said Gleeson, a fearful expression on his face. 'Ya might not know it, Mr. Washington, but dere's a lot of tension. Dere's feuds and dere's factions and dey've always bin here … it's a way d' men have o' releasin' d' pressure. From d' time Mr. Flood said nobody could fight or drink, it's all bin buildin' up. It's bin like a keg o' gunpowder and when ya let Robbie get away wit' raisin' his stick to ya, ya might just as well have given 'em permission to set light to it.'

'But they've worked peacefully next to each other all this time.'

'Dey worked next to each udder, alright, but on me saintly mother's own grave, God rest her soul,' Gleeson blessed himself, 'dey ain't bin at peace wit' each udder, dey just ain't bin fightin'. Dey didn't dare.'

'Why?'

'Dey all need d' wages, fer a start, and every one of 'em's afraid of Ned Flood. Dey reckon he might be in league wit' d' Divil.'

'They take his money.'

'O' course, and so do I. D' Divil's money's just good as d' Lord's.'

'What are the feuds about?' asked Abraham, rubbing his sore forearm.

Gleeson cackled cynically as if he were talking to a silly ignorant child. 'Ach, sure half of 'em don't know and d' udder half don't care. Sometimes it's one township against anudder, or a parish or a clan. D' Kennedys, fer example. Dey've despised d' Scanlons for longer den anyone can remember, and d' Scanlons hate 'em back. Neider knows why. D' folks in Coolbawn hate d' ones from Carney and both of 'em hate anyone from Borrisokane. My family's had a long-runnin' feud wit' d' McNamara's from Ardcroney.'

'This is all nonsense! I had no idea. What's your feud about?'

'My family's bin in d' whiskey business for t'ree generations. When me da was a boy, d' McNamaras started brewing rotgut. It was just a bit o' craic t' start wit', den it became a business competition and den it got out o' hand and a few people got killed on both sides.'

'Where are the authorities in all of this? Can't they do something about it?'

'Nobody sees nutt'n sure. Dere's never no witnesses.'

'Has no one ever been arrested for it?'

'I remember dey arrested Mike Sheehan once. He stabbed auld Mr. Halloran wit' a pair o' sheep shears after a sheep-shearing competition in Borrisokane.'

'What happened?'

'Halloran had bin champion fer as long as anyone could remember. When he lost to Mike Sheehan one year, Halloran accused him o' cheatin'. Mike told him to take it back and when he wouldn't, Mike stuck 'im in d' leg wit' a pair o' shears. Jayzis, auld Halloran bled like a stuck pig.' Paulie seemed to lose himself in reverie for a moment.

'And ...?' prompted Washington.

'Well, dere must o' bin at least a hundert people dere

321

but nobody saw a t'ing o' course, except fer a Protestant constable who happened to be dere and he arrested Mike. Dey took him before d' courts and d' jury gave him six months hard labour. One of d' fellas on d' jury couldn't stand Halloran and he told poor Mike if he'd have stabbed d' auld bastard in d' heart, he'd have acquitted him.'

'Unbelievable,' said the black man. 'Back in the colonies, he'd most likely have been hanged.'

Gleeson laughed heartily. 'Ah now, dat's uncivilised. It's not like he ate him or anyt'ing, he just stuck him in d' leg wit' a pair o' shears.'

'And what happened to Mr. Sheehan.'

'He's eider wit' God or d' Divil now. After he did his time in gaol, he went to Clare fer anudder shearing contest one day and dey found his body on a crossroads next mornin', wit' his own shears stickin' out of his chest.'

'Was it Halloran?'

'Who knows sure? Maybe he just tripped and fell on 'em.'

'What happened to Mr. Halloran?'

'Dat winter, he was found floatin' face-down in Dromineer Bay. God only knows why he choose t' go swimmin' in December wit' a cord tied around his wrists.' Gleeson gave a wry smile. 'Mike was me cousin.'

'No offense intended, Mr. Gleeson, but you Irish are an impossible race to understand. You welcome strangers with kindness and yet you treat each other savagely.'

'Ah it must be hard fer an outsider to understand, I suppose, but dat's d' way it's always bin. Ya need t' talk to d' auld witch, like young Master Alexander's doin', if ya want to understand better. You should get her to look at dat arm o' yours at d' same time. She might have somet'in fer yer back too.'

While he'd been engrossed in the conversation, Abraham had forgotten about the pain in his back, but realised now that it had become worse. He had thought that, in Ned's absence, he would be perfectly able to handle things but now he realised that he didn't know the Irish at all, and was never likely to. He had thought it was only Ned Flood who was unfathomable but now he'd come to recognise that there was an entire race here which he'd never understand.

He looked down at his arm and at the welt, which was growing more livid by the minute, and he began the walk back to Johnstown. He hoped the workers wouldn't have killed each other by the time Ned returned.

CHAPTER 36

Ned left for Cork early in the morning, leaving Jonesey and the two Irishmen at the bar. They had a challenging night's work ahead of them so it was better for them to rest during the day. Soon after dark, they would hitch the horses to the wagon and make their way to Waterford, where they would retrieve the hogsheads from the Custom's House. With five tons to transport, it was decided that they would make two trips. Unladen, the wagon would take two hours to reach town, but another three for the return trip to their hideout, once it was fully loaded. Clancy slept like a baby but neither Michael nor Jonesey got a wink of sleep. Mikey kept mulling over in his mind all the things that could go wrong and Jonesey, having been put in charge of the operation, was feeling the heavy weight of responsibility.

'I'd feel better if Ned was going with us,' he said to himself, out loud.

Michael assumed he was being addressed and so he responded. 'What happens if the customs fella catches us at it?'

'You don't know nothing. I doubt we'll have any problems in that direction though, not while Smythe is busy chasing that bit of Irish skirt.'

'What bit of skirt?'

'The capt'n got him involved with an Irish lass who works in one of the bars. He made sure she'll be keeping him busy.'

In fact, the Irish lass was not keeping Timothy Smythe busy. He was otherwise engaged, trying to devise a way of extricating himself from the impossible situation he'd found himself in.

'I need the loan of several of your deputies for a few days, sir,' he told the Sheriff of Waterford.

The sheriff coughed and wondered, for a moment, what the customs officer could possibly have in mind. 'That's highly irregular, Smythe,' he said. 'You already have four men at your disposal in the service.'

'I'm aware of that, sir, but I have reason to believe that some illegal activity might be about to transpire and I think that both the local and the Crown services should be involved.'

'What kind of illegal activity?'

'A gang of smugglers, sir.'

The large sheriff ruffled his grey hair with a ham-sized hand and yawned. 'Smugglers are your problem, Mr. Smythe. My job is just to keep the peace around here. There's been smuggling going on in this port ever since it's been a port. Anyway, what would be in it for me?'

'You would most likely receive a commendation, sir, when we catch them.'

'Get out of my office Smythe. A commendation? That's just a piece of paper you can't wipe your arse with.'

'Well there might be some remuneration too.'

'How much?'

'I don't have any figures off-hand, sir, but…..'

Before Smythe could finish his sentence the sheriff stood, walked over and opened the door. 'Get out, you twit, before I box your ears. Come back when you can tell me how much I'll get.'

The low early-morning sun glared into Timothy's eyes as he left the sheriff's office with his tail between his legs, then promptly stepped in a pile of dog muck.

'Shit!' he said out loud. 'How much worse can this day get?'

He was about to find out.

*

'Ya have to understand, Mr. Washington,' said Moira, 'it wasn't always like dis. D' Irish have always bin a fighting people but dey had deir rules. If dere was a feud, or if two families had a disagreement, dey would rather settle t'ings without a war if dey could. One member of each family would face each udder. It was like d' English, wit deir duels.'

'I understand duels, Moira, but this sounds more like outright mayhem.'

Washington was lying on the floor of Mick's house, while Moira poked and prodded at his spine with her boney fingers.

'I found it!' she exclaimed. 'Ya have a bone out o' place in yer back.' She pressed on it and the prostrate black man let out an almighty grunt.

'I think you found it too, old woman, and if you press any harder I might cry.'

Moira shifted on the floor, trying to find a position which would better enable her to press on the displaced vertebra. 'I ain't sure if I'm strong enough to put it back in place. Dis has bin out o' kilter fer a long time.'

'Don't worry about it. I've become so used to the pain over the years, I wouldn't know what it's like to live without it.'

'Now don't you give up so easy. You men make such bad patients.'

A crunching sound came from his back and he let out a deep groan.

'Does it feel any better?'

'I'll tell you if you stop pushing on it. God, I'd rather you'd stuck your finger in my eye.'

'Ah stop bein' such a big baby. Just tell me if it feels any better.'

'If I tell you it does, will you leave it alone?'

'Big baby…'

Washington let out an involuntary yelp which startled the old blind woman.

'Stop! It's better, I swear. Now leave me alone and tell me more about this warrior code.'

'Batareacht, it's called. If groups fought, it was always wit' an equal amount of men. No one would hit a man who had his back turned, or fight two against one. Dey would use bata, or walkin' sticks, and when blood was drawn or a man was taken down, d' fight ended. Dat's how it was done, always wit' honour. T'ings is different nowadays. D' men use loaded bata. Dey drill out d' knob at d' end and fill it wit' molten lead to make d' weapon deadlier. And it ain't enough fer 'em to see a man down dese days. It ain't a sport no more, it's deadly.'

'Why did it change?'

'I've asked meself d' same t'ing, times over. I t'ink it's because d' culture's bin stripped from d' Irish people. Foreigners have tried to undermine all d' t'ings dat made Ireland what she was, and when a folk's culture is t'reatened, dat makes 'em behave like wild animals in a forest.'

The black man thought for a long time before he spoke.

'I've seen it happen before, old woman … in the slave colonies. I've seen people degenerate into savages, peaceful people who'd never had to worry about anything before, other than where to get food to fill their children's bellies.'

He rolled over onto his side, the first time in many years that he'd been able to do so without excruciating pain.

'The pain's nearly gone, Moira. I thought I'd never be free from pain again.'

'Ah dere's all kinds o' pain, Abe Washington. Some's in d' body, like yours, and some's in d' mind, but d' worst pain of all is in d' spirit. I t'ink dat's d' pain of d' Irish right now.'

Abraham paused. He knew there was a lesson being directed at him, and he knew it was something he would remember and ponder over for days to come.

'Perhaps it's the same pain my people in the colonies are suffering with too … the pain of displacement, of having lost a past to guide them. They hold on tightly to despair and bitterness.'

'P'raps. Ah sure I'm just an auld woman who knows more dan she should, and understands little of it.'

The conversation was becoming uncomfortable for

them both and Washington sought a respite from the sombre mood.

'How's Master Alexander doing with his studies?'

'He's a grand young fella, just grand. He's as sharp as his da and he's educated too.' She chucked. 'Sometimes I wonder which one of us is d' teacher and which is d' student.'

Her comment made Abraham puff up with pride. 'It might sound silly to you,' he said, 'but I couldn't be fonder of that boy if he was my own son.'

'Sometimes blood has nothing to do wit' dem kind o' feelin's. D' last time I knew a young fella like young Master Alexander was over forty years ago, and dat was Liam Flynn. He was d' most innocent but, at d' same time, d' wisest person I'd ever met ... until Alexander.'

'I'll tell you something about Alex that I'm sure he won't have told you. He's an accomplished fencer.'

'Ah now dat's a useful trade. It's very important to keep d' livestock from strayin'.'

Washington took a moment to realise the crone's misinterpretation, but he wasn't about to insult the old woman by correcting her.

'It is indeed, yes. Did he ever tell you he's proficient with a rapier too?'

'I know what a fencer is, ya daft sod, it's a sword-fighter. I was coddin' ya.'

'Oh, sorry.'

'It's Irish humour, Mr. Washington. D' ya t'ink we'll ever make an Irishman out of ya?'

'I'd say the colour of my skin limits that possibility.'

'Ah, bein' Irish comes from inside, boyo, from d' heart, not from d' colour of yer skin or where ya was born. Dat young man didn't know anyt'ing about bein' Irish but he's opened up his heart and he's found it inside him. D' t'ing ya have to know about Irish humour is it's often about sayin' d' opposite of we mean. If we insult ya, it's just our way of sayin' we like ya. D' more affection we have fer ya, d' more insultin' we'll be. D' ya understand?'

'No, and I don't think I ever will understand the ways of the Irish.'

The old woman cackled. 'Dere now. Ya just took d' first step to bein' a son of Erin. Sure what sort o' craic would we have if we all understood one anudder?'

*

Smythe called his subordinates together and told them they were to lie low, ready to pounce if the smugglers came back to retrieve their booty.

'How many of the scoundrels are you expecting, sir?' asked one of the younger men.

'I don't know how many there'll be this time. All I know is that there were at least ten or twelve of them who waylaid me.' Timothy Smythe was mustering all the bravado he could. 'There may even have been more, I couldn't tell because I was busy fighting them all off.'

'You fought off twelve smugglers,' said the young man skeptically, looking Smythe up and down, 'and lived to talk about it?'

'I did indeed and I don't mind telling you, I gave a very good account of myself until I was overwhelmed.'

'What do you want us to do?' asked a grizzled veteran of His Majesty's service.

'I want you men to lie in wait outside the warehouse. I'll be waiting inside. When the bastards show up, I'll give the signal, then you leap out and arrest them.'

The officers looked at each other dubiously.

'Don't worry, there'll be nothing to it,' Smythe encouraged, 'a piece of piss.'

Unbeknownst to Tim, the men were already formulating their own plan and it had nothing to do with sitting outside in the dark, with the cold rain penetrating their clothes. As he left, Smythe was convinced that the smugglers would soon be in gaol and that he would surely get a promotion to the Home Office out of it. How wrong he was.

When he'd gone, the four men sat around a table and discussed their commander's orders.

'I didn't sign up to get meself killed, just for half a crown a month,' said the oldest of the lawmen.

'Maybe it'll be a piece of piss, just like old Smythe said,' suggested one of the younger man.

'Old Smythe can shit in his hat and pull it down over his ears if he thinks I'm going to get into a lopsided battle with a crowd of smugglers. I've got a better idea. Why don't we all go and sit in front of the fire at the tavern and drink ourselves senseless?'

It didn't take long for the rest of them to agree that their senior colleague's option was the most attractive. Timothy Smythe would have to execute his plan alone.

It was half nine when Michael, Clancy and Jones pulled the dray up outside the customs warehouse. Jonesey jumped down, produced the keys from his coat pocket and held them aloft. They jingled as he unlocked the door, then he slowly pushed it open. He whispered to his compatriots.

'The coast's clear. Let's get the wagon over to the loading dock and get the tobacco out of here.'

The three men wrestled the first of the big barrels

up onto the bed of the wagon and were doing the same with a second when Timothy Smythe stepped out of the gloom and pointed a large .69 caliber pistol at them.

'I arrest you blaggards in the name of His Majesty, King George.' His voice cracked a little and he looked for all the world like a twelve year-old boy carrying his father's gun. 'Alright men!' he shouted, a little more assertively, 'I have the villains covered and under arrest! You can take them into custody!'

Several silent minutes passed and there was no response. Timothy shifted his weight nervously from one foot to another and shouted again.

'You can come and seize the culprits now!'

Another minute passed and the only sound to be heard was the wind and rain outside. The customs man had become visibly unnerved and Jonesey took advantage of it.

'Your reinforcements appear to have done a bunk on you, ya turnip.'

'Stay right where you are!' ordered Smythe. 'They'll be here at any second,' he maintained, seriously beginning to doubt his own words. 'Don't anyone move or I'll fire!'

'You know as well as I do,' scoffed Jones, 'that if they were coming, they'd be here by now and whichever one of us you shoot, the others will finish you off. Now take that horse gun out of my face or I'll stuff it up yer crap hole.'

Any bravado that Smythe had struggled to muster was rapidly draining away and he felt himself in real danger of panicking and firing the weapon. Jones sensed his growing apprehension and decided it was time to divert his attention.

'Anyway, you can't shoot anyone with that thing.

Look, it ain't even got a flint in it.'

Timothy instinctively held the gun up to the dim light to check his flint and Jonesey grabbed it, blocking the hammer from falling with his thumb. He yanked the firearm out of the young man's hand and gave him a good whack on the side of his head with it.

'Didn't yer daddy ever teach you it's dangerous for little boys to play with guns?' said Jones, levelling the weapon on Smythe.

'Jayzis, ya ain't goin' to shoot him, are ya?' pleaded Jamie. Michael stood dumbstruck.

'Nah, too much noise,' replied the seaman, 'but I should throttle the bastard for scaring the shit out of me.'

'You hit me, you pig!' whined Smythe. 'Don't you know I work for the government? You're in really big trouble now.'

'Shut up, ya tosser, or I'll whack you on the other side of yer head!'

'What will we do with him?' asked Mikey, having finally found his tongue.

'Get some rope and tie him up,' ordered Jonesey. 'I have to re-think the plan.'

Clancy and Michael trussed up the poor man like a pig being taken to market.

'Now what?' asked Michael, when they were done.

'We'll finish loading the hogsheads and we'll take Mr. Smythe here for a nice little ride.'

'Let me go,' pleaded Tim. 'If you let me go, I promise I won't ever say a word about this.'

Jones laughed mirthlessly. 'I don't think so, friend. You're coming with us for insurance and maybe, just maybe, once we've got all the tobacco, and your little book with all our names in it, and a few stamped customs forms, who knows … you might even live to see the morning sun rise.'

CHAPTER 37

Two days had gone by and, in Gortalocca, the farm hands were taking their midday break and had gone to Hogan's for their dinner. Outside, at the crossroads, was Alexander, along with Jimmy Gleeson, Paulie's youngest son of fourteen years, and Siobhan, who almost never left Alex's side now. They were watching as Petey Gleeson and Tommy Casey sparred with bata. Every family practiced their own method of stick fighting and, in this case, each young man's style was different. Tommy fought with two sticks, the so-called 'troidaireacht'. One was a three foot-long walking stick which he held in his right hand. The shorter one was about a foot long and this was held in the left hand and used for defense. Petey used the more common 'bata mor', a three foot-long walking stick made from blackthorn which was held with one hand or two, depending on whether the fighter was on the attack or defending himself.

Alexander was watching the contest with rapt attention and even imagined himself engaged in the mock combat. The lessons he'd learned from his fencing master and then later, with Captain Rackham onboard Prosperity, had taught him to watch out for openings in the opponent's defense, then exploit them mercilessly with expedience.

Siobhan, too, was excited by the game and squeezed Alexander's hand whenever one combatant got the upper hand. Old Paulie Gleeson was shouting instructions to his son, who finally managed to snap his wrist forward and deliver a stinging blow to Casey's right elbow. When Casey dropped his bata Pete moved in, holding the stick over Tommy's head and threatening a death blow.

'I give,' shouted Casey. The two opponents shook hands.

'Now then,' said Paulie to Alexander, 'did ya ever see anyt'ing like dat over in Amerrycuh?'

'Not the same as that,' replied Alexander, 'but I've seen something similar. I noticed some weaknesses in their defense.'

'Did ya now? Well I'm always glad to learn, boyo, p'raps ya can teach us somet'in. Tommy! Give Alexander here yer sticks.'

Tommy Casey wandered across and handed over his two bata. 'G'wan, stick boy,' he said, with more than a hint of distain, 'show us how it should be done, why don't ya?'

Alexander hefted the bata mor and, instead of holding the knob end forward, he held it with the butt end towards him. He flexed his knees slightly and swung it through the air.

'Not dat way round, ya shite bird,' scoffed Casey,

laughing. 'Look, d' eejit's holdin' it backwards.'

'If you shut yer gob and watch fer a minute, Tommy Casey,' Paulie scolded, 'ya might even learn somet'in'.'

Paulie knew, from the way the young Yank was testing the weight and balance of the bata, that he was no stranger to martial arts. 'So what do ya t'ink?' he asked. 'Want t' give it a go?'

'I'd like to try,' replied Alex bashfully.

'Petey, give dis boy a lesson in stick fightin',' Paulie told his son, 'but take it easy on him, mind, until he's learnt d' rules.'

'What are the rules, sir?' asked Alexander.

'Don't kill d' udder fella,' replied Paulie.

Alexander stepped towards his opponent, gave a slight bow and saluted him with the bata. Pete winked at Tommy and returned the courtesy in an exaggerated fashion.

Alex assumed a fencers posture and held his left hand high. Pete faced him square on.

'He don't show ya much to hit, does he?' he shouted to his father.

Paulie ignored his son. 'Commence!'

Pete grasped his bata by the bottom third and circled his opponent, looking for an opening. Alexander turned to face him and feinted a lunge. Pete snapped his wrist forward but the blow fell short, then Alexander lunged, poking the Irishman in the left breast with the end of his stick.

'You're dead,' said Alex.

'Dese is sticks, stupid, not swords,' scoffed Pete, then suddenly rushed at Alexander, who stepped aside and poked him in the ribs for his trouble.

'Ouch! You skinny fecker, I'll brain ya when I catch ya!'

'Petey!' yelled his father. 'Don't lose yer temper! I've told ya time and time again, always keep yer head in a fight.'

Pete rubbed his side and inhaled, gathering himself. He looked for an opening and, seeing none up high, he went for the shins. This was something Alex had been unprepared for. In fencing it was illegal to go for a low touch. He backed up, momentarily losing his balance, and that was the chance Pete had been waiting for. He lunged in and went stick-to-stick, pushing hard with both hands and trying to slide his own stick into Alexander's knuckles. Alex poked him in the ribs again, this time with the short stick.

'You're dead again,' he said.

'Not nearly,' replied Pete. 'How about a Cork kiss?' he said, head-butting Alex in the mouth.

Alexander spat blood and tried to regain the offensive, but he'd already shown his weakness to his opponent. This time the Irishman brandished his stick high and, when Alex went to parry the blow, Pete kicked him a fierce blow to his shins, knocking him to the ground. He stood over his fallen opponent, his bata poised for the final strike, and Alexander held his stick high over his face with both hands to try and deflect what was coming.

'Dat's enough fer one day!' shouted Paulie. 'I'd say ya both have somet'in to learn from one anudder.'

Petey extended a hand to the fallen Alex, helped him up off the ground and clapped him on the back. Tommy Casey came over and offered his hand.

'From now on, stick man,' he said, 'whenever I call you dat, it'll have nutt'n to do wit' ya bein' skinny. How long have ya bin stick fightin'?'

'I haven't,' replied Alexander. 'I studied fencing for

six or seven years, with rapiers, but this was my first stick fight.'

'Well, boyo,' declared Tommy, 'fer what it's worth, you ain't too bad at all.'

Paulie Gleeson came over to inspect Alex's split lip. 'Dat's an interestin' style ya have dere, son,' he said. 'It has a name, ya know, it's called pionsoireacht. It's like sword fightin', but wit' sticks. If ya use a sharp, iron-tipped bata it can be deadly.'

'Sounds like the Scottish Highland sword and dirk technique,' ventured Alexander.

'Jayzis, Da,' exclaimed Petey. 'If he'd had an iron-headed bata, he'd have killed me t'ree times over.'

'You only die once, boyo,' laughed Paulie, but he shuddered as he uttered the words. Petey laughed along with his father. He wasn't to know that it would be his turn to die soon enough, or that Tommy Casey would follow close behind.

*

Ned was in good humour when Mick pulled the carriage to a halt outside the bar in Ballykinsella. He had accomplished everything he'd set out to do. He had implicated that weasel, Smythe, by opening a bank account in his name and he'd also found a market for the tea which Jack would be bringing back to Ireland from the Isle of Man. All in all, it had been a very productive trip. He jumped down from the carriage and entered McGee's.

'WHAT D' FECK'S HE DOIN' HERE?' he bellowed, when he saw Timothy Smythe sitting at the only table in the place, along with Michael, Jamie and Jones.

'He's helpin' us drink d' place dry,' slurred Barry McGee from behind the bar.

'Oy wasn't talkin' to you, shithead, Oy was talkin' to d' person Oy left in charge.'

He glared at Jonesey, who'd drunk so much alcohol in the past two days that, at first, he didn't even recognise Ned.

'Talkin' t' me, friend?' he asked, with a thick tongue.

'Ya blitherin' bollock brain! What in God's name would have happened if he'd escaped?'

'He cootn't escape, boss,' said Jones, grinning. 'Look, see? We got 'is legs tied t' the chair.'

'His hands ain't tied though, are they?'

'Ah now he cootn't drink with 'is hands tied, could 'e?'

'Didn't it occur to ya he might untie himself, ya eejit?'

''E'd never find the door.' Jones burst into peals of laughter.

'Jayzis, Merry and Sent Jawsif! Oy give ya one simple job to do and ya turn it into a feckin' circus! What happens when dey find him gone? Oy'll tell ya, shall I? Dey'll send every lawman in Oirland out to find him.'

All the commotion had roused Mikey and he raised his head from the table, where he'd been catching forty winks between rounds.

'Ned!' he exclaimed jovially. 'Come and have a drink! We've bin waitin' for ya.'

'Looks like ye've bin drinkin' fer me too. What would yer mother say if she saw ya now?'

'She'd say… emm… she'd say… how the feck do I know what she'd say?' He put his head back down on the table.

'She'd be ashamed of ya and so am Oy. Now, Oy'm

goin' to speak very slowly in d' hope somebody here will answer me. What d' feck…. will we do…. when dey find out…. dat little turd…. is missin'?'

'Ahhhh, we thought of that, boss,' grinned Jonesey, trying to tap the side of his nose with his finger, but missing it altogether.

Ned felt his blood boil. Did these idiots have any idea how serious an offense it was to kidnap a public official. 'Is dat right, Mr. Jones? Enlighten me so. What, if anyt'ing, did ye do about it?'

'We got Timmy here to sign a note saying he'd be gone for a few days.'

Ned thought for a moment, then feared he'd spotted a flaw in their plan. 'And did Mr. Smythe write dis note himself, Jones?'

'Nope, Mikey did.'

'What did it say?'

'Dunno.'

'Well wake him up, man! Oy need to know what it said.'

Jonesey poked Michael in the ribs and he woke with a start.

'It wasn't me, Mammy,' he blurted. 'It was Robbie!' His head fell back down onto the table and he began to snore.

Mick walked in, having stabled the horses. 'Whoa!' he exclaimed. 'Looks like we missed a good auld session here, Ned!'

'Oh don't worry, Mick, d' entertainment's only just startin'. Would ya ever go out to d' well and get me a bucket o' water?'

'I t'ink it'll take more dan a bucket.'

'Bring a washtub so. Oy'll get some answers out o' dese sods if Oy have to drown d' lot of 'em.'

A few minutes later, Mick came back in carrying a small water trough. 'I couldn't find a washtub, don't t'ink dere is one. McGee probably just wears his clothes 'til dey fall off him. I brought ya d' horses' water barrel instead.'

'Put it in d' middle of d' floor and fetch Michael Hogan over here.'

Mick did as instructed and dragged Mikey over to where the water trough stood.

'Put his head under and don't take it out 'til Oy say so.'

Mick put his big hand on the back of Michael's head and held it under water. Mikey flailed his arms and struggled, to no avail until finally, after what must have seemed like half an hour to Michael, but was actually only about thirty seconds, Ned gave Mick the nod and the poor man was pulled out, gasping for air and spitting water.

'What did d' note say, Michael?'

'Note?' spluttered Michael. 'What note?'

'Dunk him again, Mick.'

'Wait, wait … gimme a chance to catch me breath.'

'Oy'm waitin'.'

'But I don't know what note you're talking about.'

'D' one Smythe wrote.'

Michael was trying to clear the fog from his brain and Ned was losing patience.

'Dunk him, Mick.'

The big man held Michael by the back of the neck and gave his head a shake. 'Answer him, Mikey, or so help me I'll stick ya back in dat water.'

'Wait, no … yes, I remember. I wrote to say Mr. Smythe would be gone from the office but that he was still conducting official duties, with regard to a smuggling ring he'd got wind of.'

'Who did ya write d' letter to?'

'I addressed it to the sheriff so the civilian authorities wouldn't be involved.'

'Good. Did d' little shit sign it?'

'He did, and I got him to stamp it with his official seal.'

'Ya see, Mikey, dat was easy wasn't it? Ya can go back to sleep now but dere's no more poteen fer you today.'

Michael didn't bother going back to his seat but simply crawled over to the turf fire, curled up and fell sound asleep on the floor.

'Bring Smythe over, Mick. Oy need him to sober up so we can talk business.'

'I have a feelin' dat when he hears what ya have to say, he'll sober up in no time.'

'Untie him, Mick, den Oy want ya to leave. Oy'll give him just one chance to join up wit' us and, if he don't take it, he won't get out of here alive.'

'I'm behind ya all d' way, Ned.'

'T'anks, Mick. Yer a good man and Oy'm sure you'll get to heaven one day. Oy sold me soul years ago. Now it seems like, even when Oy try to do a good t'ing, Oy have to do somet'in bad to get it done. Now go and see to d' horses.'

Mick left grudgingly. Once outside, he didn't stray far from the door, but paced back and forth in the cool misty May rain.

Ned dragged Smythe over to the water trough and, when he tapped the man's face lightly, Tim seemed to come round straight away.

'Wake up, Tim,' Ned told him. 'Ya have to hear what Oy say because yer life depends on it.' Ned dipped the man's head briefly into the water and, when he pulled him up, Smythe's eyes were clear and focused directly on him. 'Did ya hear what I said, boy?'

'I heard you Mr. Flynn. I also heard the others call you Ned. You said your name was Michael.'

'Yer not drunk so?'

'The others drank a lot more than me. I was going to wait until they were all asleep, then I was going to make my escape.'

'It's a good t'ing fer you dat ya didn't. Now Oy want ya to heed what Oy say. Your life is in my hands now and if ya lie, or if ya try to double-cross me, you won't leave dis room alive. Do ya understand?'

'Yes, sir, Mr. Flynn.'

'Good man. Now listen. Oy have a piece of paper from d' Bank in Cork dat ties you directly in wit' dis operation.'

Smythe looked bewildered. 'I don't understand, sir.'

'Oy have in my possession a piece of paper showin' you as bein' on my payroll.'

'But, sir, I don't have a bank account in Cork.'

'Ya do now, Timothy Smythe. Do ya begin to see what a threat Oy can be to your freedom? My solicitor in London will soon have a copy and if anyt'ing happens to me, or to dis operation, Oy'll make sure ya get hung wit' d' same rope dey hang me wit'.'

'You own me.'

'Now yer beginnin' to understand, but try not to t'ink of it like Oy own ya. Try and see it as an indenture. When all dis business is over, Oy'll make sure all d' papers are destroyed and nobody will be any d' wiser.'

Timothy hung his head low. 'I'm a disgrace to my family,' he said resignedly.

'You won't be d' first disgrace in yer family. How else do ya t'ink yer dear auld daddy was able to buy all dat farmland in England on a salary of one or two quid a month?'

'He was a good businessman.'

'Believe whatever ya like but Oy know d' truth and Oy'll see to it dat you carry on d' family business. Now, will we have a drink together?'

'I think I'm going to throw up again, sir.'

'Ah well, suit yerself. Oy'll have yours.'

CHAPTER 38

No one had seen hide nor hair of Jones and the two Irishmen.

'Something must have happened to them,' declared Captain Rackham, 'otherwise Jonesey would have left word at one of the bars on the waterfront in Dungarvan.'

'Maybe they got waylaid on the way here,' ventured the topman, Flanagan.

'That crossed my mind, it's either that or they've got themselves arrested. I can guarantee Jones won't blab but I don't know the Irishmen well enough to be sure they won't spill the beans.'

'I doubt they would, sir, and anyway, the Irishmen don't know nothing.'

'You're probably right, Flanagan, but I have six tons of untaxed Dutch tea in the hold and we can't wait around for Willoughby to get tired of chasing phantoms off the Cornish coast. He's already taken our measure.'

Jack lost himself in thought for a moment. When you find yourself lost, the best thing to do is retrace your steps until you get back to where you made a wrong turn.

'We've been here a day already, I can't risk waiting any longer. Get the ship ready to sail back to Tramore.'

'I'd never question orders, sir, but ain't that where we last ran into the English brig? What if Captain Willoughby decides to check back on Tramore?'

Jack smirked almost imperceptibly at the prospect of meeting his opponent once again, but he had a valuable cargo to protect and business was business.

'That would indeed be the prudent thing for him to do, sailor, but Willoughby's no more predictable than I am and, right now, he's the hound and we're the fox. Get ready to make sail.'

Flanagan knuckled his forehead in acknowledgement of the command and transmitted his captain's orders to the crew.

*

Lieutenant Willoughby was standing on the deck of the Albatross, mindlessly scanning the horizon off the Cornish coast. His voyage, thus far, had not been fruitful and he was bored of chasing and inspecting fishing craft for contraband. His mind was filled with thoughts of Rackham and that damned Chesapeake schooner. His normally methodical thought processes were clouded by how he'd been outguessed, if not outsmarted, by Jack Rackham.

'Bosun!' he barked. 'Set sail for the Isle of Man.'

Willoughby tried to put himself inside the mind of Captain Rackham, analysing the few facts he was in possession of. Prosperity had taken an east-northeast heading when she'd left the Irish coast. If Rackham had sailed from Tramore to the Isle of Man to discharge his cargo, then he was most likely to have filled the ship's hold with illegal goods … maybe tea or silk, or perhaps spices from the Dutch East Indies. If he could get some idea of what cargo Jack was carrying, he'd have a better idea of where Prosperity's next port of call would be. If Rackham had picked up spices or silk, he'd most likely head up the English Channel and offload the contraband close to the London markets. Rich aristocrats didn't give a toss about whether their dinner was seasoned with untaxed spices and they cared even less about whether their wives' dresses were made from illegal silk. Willoughby rubbed his hands together.

'Let the games begin,' he said aloud.

'Did you say something, sir?' asked the helmsman.

Willoughby cast a scowl at the sailor, then he went below to his sparse quarters to look at charts and plan his strategy.

*

'Keep an eye on yer poteen supply, missus,' Gleeson told Roisin. 'Dere's a fair in Borrisokane next week and dey want me to supply d' whiskey. I can only leave ya wit' one keg because d' rest of me stock is goin' dere. It'll be at least a couple o' weeks 'til I can bring ya some more.'

Roisin looked surprised. 'I thought the McNamara's supplied poteen for the fair,' she said.

'Dey did, but last year dey sold 'em rot-gut … made a lot of folk ill.'

'Ah yes, I heard about that. What happened?'

'Dunno, but I wouldn't drink deir shite if it was d' last drop to be had. Dey take shortcuts, and deir still has lead pipes. Maybe dey poisoned d' poor divils, who knows.'

'There's already bad blood between your two families, Paulie. Don't you think it might cause more bother if you supply the whiskey?'

'Don't worry, missus, I already t'ought of dat. I'm sendin' Petey and me youngest to deliver d' brew to d' Mayor's office in Borrisokane tonight. He'll keep an eye on it 'til next week.'

'Well, watch yourselves,' warned Roisin. 'I wouldn't be at all surprised if there's some sort of trouble at the fair.'

'Me neither, missus, but I ain't worried. Pete's bin practisin' sticks wit' Casey fer d' last week. My boy can handle himself alright.'

Ger McNamara had already been notified by Borrisokane's town officials that his services would not be required at the fair, and rage seethed within him when he discovered that the Gleesons would be supplying the poteen. The fair was a major money-maker for his family and they relied heavily upon it. It seemed to McNamara that the Gleesons weren't satisfied with supplying most of the spirits in the vicinity, now they were going to take the very food out of his family's mouths. Ger sent his son Brian to Borrisokane to seek a little professional help with their dilemma.

The country fair was held several times a year. It was a time for farmers to show off their produce, also for them to buy and sell livestock. A considerable amount of money would change hands over the two-day period and whiskey would flow in copious amounts to seal deals. As well as farm goods and foodstuffs, there was entertainment … music, singing and dancing and

various athletic events such as boxing, wrestling and
bataireacht, both amateur and professional. The
amateur stick fighters were farmers or tradesman who
practised the art as a diversion. The professionals,
however, travelled all over the country, making their
living by laying bets and winning purses. Many were
professional in every way, even to the point of teaching
their art. Others, however, were little more than thugs
looking to earn an easy shilling without bothering
themselves with the day-to-day drudgery of the
common man. In a gathering such as a country fair, it
wasn't difficult to find the latter.

A group of men sat in Mulcahey's bar in
Borrisokane, conversing cordially. They were big,
rough-looking individuals who bore the scars of
innumerable battles. These were the warriors who plied
their trade of violence and mayhem at the various fairs
held throughout Ireland. Brian McNamara walked up
to the group and stood silently until one of them, a
man with a broken nose and thick scars over his
eyelids, noticed him.

'Got a problem, laddie?' he growled.

'No, sir ... I mean yes, sir.'

'Well? Which one is it, fish-head?'

'Me da sent me. I'm to hire someone to do a job.'

The man turned back to his cronies. 'Ach, he
probably wants to give us a penny, den expect us to
beat d' ratshit out of some poor farmer.'

'Me da says he'll give half a crown to anybody who
can get rid of some rats fer him.'

'Four-legged rats, is it?'

'No.'

'Get d' feck outta here, shite-breath, and tell yer da
we said he can stick his half a crown up his arse.'

'You speak fer yerself, Larkin,' came a voice from a darkened corner. 'How many rats does he want gettin' rid of?'

'T'ree, maybe four.'

'And what does he want doin' wit' dese rats.'

'He don't care, just wants 'em gone.'

'Do dey have big families? I don't want to spend d' rest of me life lookin' over me shoulder.'

'A few cousins over in Clare, dat's all we know about anyway.'

'It's what ya don't know dat can kill ya, boy.'

A gruff voice came from behind the bar. 'Take yer dirty business outside, Kerr. I can't stand d' smell of ya anymore.'

The man who'd been sitting in the dark corner stood up and, in the weak light of the bar, his face was revealed. A long scar ran from his forehead right down to his chin, tracing its way over his right eye, which remained permanently closed. The scar continued down, crossing the corner of his mouth and puckering the flesh, contorting his face into a permanent sneer. Brian winced at the sight and the fighter shrugged.

'Lost me eye in a stick fight five years ago. Wanna see, laddie?' He cackled and pried open his eyelid with gnarled fingers, revealing a dark cavernous hole that went deep into his skull. It occurred to Brian that the wounds must have been a grotesque sight at the time, to be so ugly this many years later. He felt his supper try to force its way back up his esophagus and he swallowed hard.

The man shrugged again at the boy's reaction and grinned with the left side of his mouth. He'd grown accustomed to people turning aside at the sight of his face.

'Dat's what bataireacht will do to ya, boyo … dat's if yer lucky.' He picked up his bata, which he'd had propped within easy reach beside his chair, and he ushered the lad roughly out of the bar and into the road.

'Is it farmers yer da wants rid of?'

'No, dey're whiskey-makers.'

'Ah now dere's a good trade. I should have gone into dat meself, den I wouldn't be a one-eyed, half-arsed stick fighter now.'

'One of 'em is good wit' a stick.'

'How good?' asked Kerr, squinting his left eye quizzically.

'He's won quite a few local competitions.'

'Was he ever in a real fight, to d' death like?'

'No, nutt'n like dat, just contests.'

The scarred man relaxed. 'Good, he just plays games. I might not be able to see much out of me right eye but I have me own ways of making up fer dat little handicap.' He held the root ball end of his stick out towards Barry, who could see that it had been drilled out and filled with molten lead. 'Loaden bata,' said Kerr, grinning his lopsided grin. 'D' extra weight makes damn sure whatever dis stick hits, breaks, whether it's a man's fingers or his skull. Now, when does yer da want d' job done and when do I get me money?'

*

'Get a move on, Petey, get dem kegs on d' wagon. I want both of ye back here before dawn tomorra. We have to get some mash goin' so we can supply our regular customers.'

'Why don't ya keep Edgie wit' ya, Da? I'm alright

doin' dis job on me own.'

'Yer brother has to earn his keep. Now where d' divil is dat little good-fer-nutt'n?'

'He's at Hogan's, wit' Liam.'

'Liam Hogan might still have one lame paw but dat don't mean Edgie can neglect his work. I'll go and get him.'

'Ah leave him be, Da, he's still a kid.'

'He's nearly fourteen years-old sure. His time fer bein' a child is over, he needs to grow up.'

'He does his share, he puts in a full day's work.'

'None o' your lip. When I was 'is age, I could malt d' barley, and I could cook it and make d' mash as well.'

'I know, Da,' sighed Pete, 'and you could do it all when you was up to yer ears in snow.'

'Dat's enough cheek from you, Peter Gleeson. I don't want to hear anudder word out of ya.'

Paulie Gleeson set off to fetch his youngest son and Petey became sullen. When Pete Gleeson grew silent, he could go for days on end without speaking to whoever had offended him. Paulie Gleeson wasn't to know that those were the last words he and his son would ever exchange.

Young Edgie arrived back from Hogan's ahead of his father and he stood in front of the wagon, frowning.

'What's up, Edge?' asked Pete.

'D' auld man blew up at me in front of everyone, called me all d' names under d' sun.'

'Ah don't you worry about dat, little brother. Remember, sticks and stones may break yer bones, but names can never hurt ya. C'mere to me. We'll go off to Borrisokane together, just d' two of us.'

Edgie's freckled face erupted into a smile and he

flashed Petey a dimpled grin. The taller boy put his arm around his brother's shoulders and the two of them led the donkey and wagon off into the darkness.

CHAPTER 39

'Alright, Mr. Smythe, we've kept ya from yer duties long enough.' Ned pointed his finger menacingly at the customs man as if it was a spear. 'Now remember everyt'ing Oy told ya. Yer on my payroll now so ya work fer Michael Flynn, and as sure as d' sun will come up tomorra mornin', if you try to harm even one of me men, Oy'll cut off yer bollix.' With those words firmly etched on Timothy Smythe's mind, Ned cut him loose from the chair which had held him captive. 'Michael, Clancy, take our new partner back to Waterford, den ye get yerselves off home. Oy'll try to find Jack and get dis business over wit', den Oy'll meet ye back in Gortalocca. Ned pulled Mikey aside. 'Don't give dis weasel any information he can use and don't, under any circumstances, tell him where ye're from. Now, move yer arses.'

Smythe was already seated in the wagon and Jamie sat next to him, holding the reins. Mikey motioned at Clancy to climb down, then whispered in his ear. 'Ned doesn't want us to say anything to Smythe. Be very careful. If he talks to you, just act deaf and dumb.'

'I can do dat,' replied Clancy. 'Can't we trust him?'

'We can't trust anyone anymore, Jamie.'

As soon as the wagon had pulled out of sight of the bar, Smythe found his courage and began jabbering, as young men often do when they perceive imminent danger to have passed.

'Who do you fellows think you are, anyway, threatening one of the King's men? I didn't think that even you and your boss were stupid enough to take on the British government.'

Michael tolerated Smythe's diatribe for a while, then decided to reinforce the fear which Ned had already impressed upon the dubious character.

'Tell me, Smythe,' he said. 'Did you ever hear the story of the phantom priest from Cork?'

'Oh that nonsense has been circulating for years. It's just another tall tale that children tell around the fire at night to give each other nightmares.'

'Is that right?'

'Of course. It's impossible for one unarmed man to take on a dozen professional trackers.'

'You think so, do you Timothy?'

'I know so, and my name's Tim.'

'Well let me tell you a story … Timothy.'

Michael told him the story, throwing in a few gory embellishments and, when he'd nearly finished, Smythe interrupted.

'Even if all you say did happen, it was twenty years ago. The phantom's probably long dead.'

'He's not dead. You met him, back there.'

'Who, Flynn? Even if that fairytale was true, Flynn's neither big enough nor clever enough to have done all you say the phantom did.'

'The story's true alright, bucko, I can vouch for it.

And someone with the devil's own luck, like Ned Flynn, is capable of anything. As for being fierce, he's like a cat.'

Smythe rolled his eyes. 'Cats are hardly fierce,' he snorted.

He's like a cat with a full belly, playing with mice.

'I'm no mouse, sir, I'm a man in the King's employ.'

'You're a mouse to him, Timothy. And if you don't believe me, just try crossing him. You'll find yourself face-down in a bog, like the Jaegers who tried to hunt him down.'

*

Willoughby hadn't yet reached the Isle of Man when the sails of a fishing boat appeared on the horizon, heading in the direction of Ireland.

'I think we have a fish, Captain,' blurted out a bosun's mate.

'Well then, let's reel him in,' replied the commander.

The brig closed in swiftly on the heavily-laden craft and, after an hour of fruitless attempts to escape, the fishing boat hove to.

'Send a boarding party over to carry out an inspection, Bosun,' ordered Willoughby. 'They wouldn't have tried to run if they didn't have something they shouldn't have on board.'

'Aye aye sir.'

Twenty minutes later the inspection party sent a signal to the Albatross, indicating that they'd found contraband.

Willoughby shouted through a speaking horn. 'What have we got?'

'Half a ton of bulk tea, sir. There are three crewmen,

including the skipper.'

'Send him over,' ordered the British officer, 'keep the other two under guard.'

A short while later, a nervous Irish smuggler clambered up a rope ladder onto the deck of the Albatross. He stood facing Willoughby and, had he been wearing any boots, he would have been shaking in them.

'There's no need to be frightened, my good man,' said the Englishman cordially, 'the game's over. Your crew are now pressed into the service of His Majesty's Royal Navy and your cargo has been confiscated by the Crown. Since you are now a member of this crew, I have the option of making your life either an easy one or a living hell. Do you understand?'

The shaken Irishman nodded and mumbled something.

'Speak up man! Your captain is addressing you.'

'I understand,' he said meekly.

'From now on, you will address me as Sir or Captain. Now, what's your name?'

'Dunne. Eddie Dunne, sir.'

'I surmise, Mr. Dunne, from your direction of travel, that you have come from the Isle of Man.'

'No, sir, dat is I never made landfall. I picked up me cargo outside Castletown.'

'Don't split hairs with me, Dunne, or you'll feel a lash across your back! Now, were you on the Isle of Man or not?'

Eddie looked down at his feet. His knew his equivocal Irish ways were no good to him here.

'I was, sir.'

'That's better, and while you were there did you hear word of a Yankee schooner.'

Eddie looked up into the captain's face. He might yet have a chance to curry favour with this new boss.

'I saw her, sir. She has raked masts and she looks fast.'

Willoughby smiled disarmingly and the Irishman returned the grin. 'And would you happen to know what the schooner carried to Castletown and what she might be carrying now?'

'She took on a cargo of Dutch tea, sir, same as us.'

'What did she offload?'

'I t'ink it was French brandy, sir.'

'Not tobacco?'

'Don't t'ink so, sir.'

Willoughby's smile was genuine now. 'Excellent, Mr. Dunne, excellent. Seaman, clap Mr. Dunne in irons. Get the rest of the crew off the vessel, unload the tea and sink the boat.'

'Aye aye, sir!'

I've got you now, Jack Rackham, thought Willoughby. That tobacco's still in the Customs House in Waterford and you'll have to go back and retrieve it. I'll teach you to thumb your nose at me, you Yankee bastard.

'After the boat is scuttled,' he called to his Bosun, 'set a course west, for Waterford.'

Willoughby went below to his cabin for a hot cup of untaxed Dutch tea.

*

The day dawned slowly in Gortalocca, the clouds and rain delaying its arrival. Workers were already toiling in the fields and Paulie Gleeson was becoming more annoyed by the minute. His sons hadn't arrived back from their trip to Borrisokane and, if he found out that rapscallion Petey had stayed on to socialise, he'd put a willow cane to his back. He began soaking sacks of barley to make the malt and wished he'd let Pete deliver the poteen by himself, leaving Edgie behind to help him. An hour passed and his irritation had been replaced by uneasiness. Even if Petey had stopped for a drink or two, he knew there was work to be done and it was out of character for him not to be back by now.

'Mr. Gleeson! Mr. Gleeson!' Liam was running towards the still where Paulie laboured. 'Come quick! For God's sake, come quick!'

'Calm down, boy, calm down. Get a grip of yerself and tell me, what on earth's d' matter?'

'It's Edgie, Mr. Gleeson,' Liam gasped, 'he's in a fierce bad way!'

Gleeson dropped the sack of barley he was carrying. 'What's d' matter wit' him? What's happened?'

'Just come!' panted Liam, his voice breaking. 'Just come, now!' Liam turned and started running back in the direction of Hogan's, where a crowd was gathered in the bar, talking in hushed tones.

Paulie was right behind the boy as Liam burst through through the door.

'Where's Edgie?' he cried. 'My boys … where's Peter?'

Edgie lay on the floor in front of the turf fire. He was swathed in blankets and shivering. His face was as white as death itself, his bottom lip was split open and his eyes were swollen shut. It was clear that he'd taken a savage beating about the head and face.

'Where's Peter?' Gleeson implored. 'Who did dis, Edgie?'

The boy tried to fight the darkness and, just before he succumbed to it, he whispered hoarsely, 'a monster…,' then he slipped into the welcome embrace of unconsciousness.

'We're taking him to Moira,' Roisin said, putting her arms around Paulie. 'Don't worry, Joe Ring's hitching up Clancy's pony. He'll be here any minute.'

'Do ya t'ink d' auld witch can fix him?' Paulie said, a plea rather than a question.

'I'm not sure,' said Roisin, and she pulled back the blankets to reveal the extent of the boy's injuries to his father. Both of his arms were broken. Pinky white bone protruded from them and they were both misshapen. His two hands had been crushed to a pulp and they looked like masses of mincemeat on the end of his arms.

'Oh Jayzis!' wailed Paulie, 'Oh sweet Mother o' God!' Roisin covered Edgie back up with the blanket and pulled Paulie to her.

'We have to find Peter,' he begged, his eyes glazed.

'We have to get Edgie to Moira,' Morna told him. 'Tommy Casey and some of the other boys are backtracking the blood trail Edgie left. Don't worry, Paulie, they'll find him.'

The trail of blood petered out just outside Gortalocca, any older droplets having been washed away by the rain. Tommy and Bob made their way slowly along the Borrisokane road with two other lads, hoping to find some sign of their friend. They moved in and out, one in front of the other on either side of the road, checking hedgerows and ditches. Fury at what had happened to young Edgie hadn't displaced the shock yet and they moved mechanically and methodically, with only one purpose.

'Gently now,' instructed Roisin, 'don't jostle the boy.'

Edgie was lifted carefully and laid on the floor of the cart and Roisin and Gleeson got in the back to ride with him. Roisin wiped the boy's battered face with a damp cloth and fought back tears. She had to be strong, both for Paulie and for his youngest son.

'Will I come wit' ya, Mam?' asked Morna.

'No, the farmers have to be fed,' replied Roisin officiously. 'I'll take care of this.'

Morna returned to the bar where she found Siobhan already cleaning Edgie's blood up off the floor with a rag. The whole time, Robbie Flynn had sat silently in the corner next to the fire, feigning disinterest. He leaned back in his chair now and yawned, as if the morning's events had bored him. He'd never liked the Gleesons, none of them. He liked the whiskey they produced, he just loathed having to pay for it. Alexander stood with Liam, who was inconsolable over what had happened to his friend. There was no point in anyone trying to comfort the lad, he was beyond that.

'I could come to detest this country,' said Alex quietly, 'just as quickly as I came to love it.'

Robbie snorted. 'Dis is d' real Ireland, boyo,' he scoffed, 'not d' luvly emerald green fields and d' little people and all d' music and dancin' yer mam and da told ya about.'

Alexander passed him a sour glance, as did Siobhan and Morna.

'If ya ask me,' grumbled Robbie, 'I t'ink Gleeson had it comin'.'

Siobhan stood up and threw the blood-soaked cleaning cloth at him. Robbie shot up out of his seat and brandished his stick at her, threateningly.

Alexander leapt to the girl's defence. He grabbed a broom and stomped on the end of it, leaving a raw, jagged point.

'Just try it,' snarled Robert and assumed a fighting stance. Then he looked into Alexander's eyes and saw something dangerous there, something he'd never seen before, and it terrified him.

'You're just like d' bastard who spawned ya,' he spat. 'Ya dress up in all yer fine clothes and ya put on yer highfalutin English ways and yer poncey manners, but underneath you're no less bloodthirsty dan a wild beast.' He lowered his bata and walked out the door.

Morna stood agape. She'd never seen Robbie back down before. Siobhan took the stick out of Alex's hand and admonished him, in an effort to break the tension.

'Look at what ya did t' me broom.'

'I'm sorry, I'll get you another one. I would have killed him, you know.'

Morna walked over and put her arm around him. 'Now, now,' she said, 'that's just the grief and anger talking. Take no notice of what Robbie said, you're no beast.'

'I felt like one just then,' he said, and dropped his eyes to the ground in shame.

CHAPTER 40

'Will we go home, Jamie? We've been gone too long and I miss the family, and Gortalocca.'

'Ah dat'd be grand, Mikey. I'll be glad of some peace and quiet. All dis excitement ain't good fer a person wit' my constitution.'

'Well, the wagon's empty except for us, so we can probably be there in three days.'

'What about dat auld sheriff in Carrick? If we go t'rough dere, he might want his money back.'

'We'll go around Carrick. I haven't had this much money in a long time and I'd like it to stay in my pockets.'

'Will Smythe keep his mouth shut, do ya t'ink?'

'Well I wouldn't want to be him if he doesn't.'

'He knows who we are.'

'But he doesn't know where we live, does he, and Ireland's a big country.'

'Even so…'

'Ned has him by the bollocks, Jamie, and I don't think Timothy wants him to squeeze.'

'Ned always seems to know how to get folk to do what he wants.'

'He knows how to twist the thumbscrews alright,' said Michael, with a smile. 'Seems to have the knack.'

*

It was early afternoon when Bob Ring found the first clue as to what had happened. He bent over and touched the ground, then held his fingers to his nose. They were only about two miles from Gortalocca, on the road leading to Carney.

'I t'ink it's blood,' he said, 'but I can't be sure. D' feckin' rain's washed everyt'ing away.'

The young men continued to search for anything that might point to what had happened and, once again, it was Bob who found it. He bent down again and this time he picked something up. He looked at it and rolled it between his fingers, then threw to the ground as if he'd been scalded and wiped his hands off on his shirt.

'Ah Jayzis!' he cried. 'Come over here, lads!' He bent over double, as if he was going to throw up.

'What d' feck is it?' asked Tommy.

'I t'ink it's brains,' said Bob, swallowing hard and trying to lock his throat.

'Lemme see.'

'Look, dere's bits of it all around here.'

Another shout came from a gap in the hedgerow leading to the bog at Lough Claree and Gar Duggan stood pointing at the ground. 'I t'ink I found d' rest of it!'

Tommy tried hard not to retch and he squeezed his eyes shut. Nineteen year-old men don't cry. He steeled himself for whatever it was he was about to see. Gar had picked up a trail now where it looked as if something heavy had been dragged off the road into the bog. Tommy walked over to the gap in the hedgerow and found himself looking down at the brain of a boy who'd been his friend since infancy. He was close to losing his composure but he told himself it couldn't be, that it must be an animal.

Gar was thirty feet or so away. 'Ah, Jayzis Christ Almighty!' he cried, taking off his shirt and throwing it on the ground in front of him. 'Don't come over here, Tommy! You don't want to see dis.' Gar heaved and threw up.

'What is it, Gar?' implored Casey.

Gar closed his eyes to make what he'd seen disappear, then he walked a few paces back as if distance might do the same. 'All dat's left of poor Petey's head is his bottom jaw.'

Tommy didn't want to look but he felt a strange obligation to his dead friend, so he approached slowly to give himself time to prepare himself for the carnage. Pete's right arm was bent at a grotesque angle and, even though he knew his friend had gone to a place beyond pain, he told Gar, 'Fer Christ's sake, man, straighten out his arm.' He turned and made his way back to the road, with Gar Duggan close on his heels.

Tommy's mind was awash with a flood of irrational thoughts. Perhaps, in an attempt to spare old Paulie, they should bury the corpse in the bog. Maybe they should even set fire to it, burn it, tell him they never found it. Tommy knew that wouldn't be right. Even though he'd never even been to Mass, he knew that only the Godless would do such a thing.

'Bob,' he called, 'your brother should have the wagon at Mick's place, dat's where dey took Edgie. Go and fetch it. Bring it back here, and a blanket too so we can cover Petey with it.' Bob took off at a run to cover the mile or so back to Mick's.

The shock had very gradually begun to diminish now. Like sand trickling through an hour glass, the white grains of grief were almost imperceptibly being replaced by the pitch black sand of revenge. Gar spoke first.

'Whoever did dis will pay.'

'We have to try and stay calm,' said Tommy, the fog beginning to clear from his mind. 'D' first t'ing is to bury Petey, den we have to t'ink dis out. We can't just go off half-cocked. We have to be sure who done it.'

'Ah c'mon, Tommy, dis has d' stench of dem bastards from Ardcroney all over it.'

'Now we can't be certain yet. How do we know it wasn't a highwayman after d' poteen and d' donkey.'

'If it was just a t'ief, why would he beat Edgie to within an inch of his life and do dis to poor Pete? It's a message, Tommy. It says don't feck wit' us.'

'Shut yer gob fer a minute, Gar, I'm tryin' to t'ink. Paulie always taught us when we're stick fightin' dat an angry man is d' same as a drunk one in a fight … dose kind only win by luck. Dis is a fight we have to be sure of winnin'.'

They would win, but Tommy wouldn't live to see it.

*

'All I can do is help him wit' d' pain,' said Moira.

'What about his arms,' lamented the boy's father,

'and his poor hands?'

'D' bones are crushed, Paulie. Dere's nutt'n left fer me to put together. His arms ain't d' worst of it. D' poor boy's insides are all busted up. Somebody kicked him in d' guts 'til dey mashed up everyt'ing in dere.'

'Oh God,' breathed Roisin. 'What kind of a man would do that to an innocent boy?'

'Not one man,' said Moira. 'Men ... divils full of hate.'

'What makes you think so?'

'D' poor lad's hands and his arms, dats d' work of a professional. He broke d' boy's hands so that, if he lives, he can't go lookin' to even d' score when he grows up.'

'What about the rest of him?'

'D' rest was a message to Paulie. If d' beast wanted to kill him, he would. Whoever kicked d' boy and beat his face, dat's personal. Whoever it was wanted to do d' most harm dey could to you, Paulie, and what better way dan to take away d' t'ing a father loves most in d' world. Worse dan killin' a man is to kill his children.'

'Is my boy going to die?' asked Gleeson.

'I'm sorry. He'll live fer a few days, p'raps less, only God Almighty knows. D' only mercy is he won't have to live like a cripple.'

'This is slaughter,' lamented Roisin. 'I know men get killed and injured in fights but this is something else, it's butchery.'

'Times are changin', deary. It ain't like d' auld days anymore, and God knows dey was bad enough.'

Joe Ring came in quietly and whispered something in Roisin's ear. She wrinkled her brow.

'Say again, Joey?'

He repeated himself and Roisin paused for a moment, then said she had to go outside and that she'd be back in a few minutes.

'It's Petey, ain't it.' said Gleeson with wretched resignation.

'I think so, Paulie.'

'Everybody I love is dead.'

'Now then, Paulie, Edgie's still here. I'll be back in a little while.'

Abraham Washington was outside and he was deep in conversation with Bob Ring. 'I can't believe it,' he was saying. 'It's barbaric, it just doesn't make any sense.'

'It doesn't have to make sense, Mr. Washington, it's Irish,' replied Bob, as casually as if he'd said the sun would rise in the east tomorrow.

'I need a drink,' said the black man.

'Why don't you go to Hogan's,' suggested Roisin, 'and I'll meet you there later.'

'Thank you, but I'll go back to Johnstown. I'd rather be by myself. I need time to think and to try and make some sense out of this. When you get back, would you tell Alexander I'd like him to come home please?' Abraham walked away, shaking his head. He'd seen more than his fair share of violence in his life, he'd even been on the receiving end of it, but this was beyond the pale.

'Tell me what you found, Bob,' said Roisin.

Bob Ring quickly told her everything. He was anxious to return to the scene and bring Petey's body back to Gortalocca before nightfall. Bob wasn't normally of a superstitious nature but he wanted to be as far away as possible from that accursed bog before darkness fell.

When Roisin went back inside and Paulie asked her about his eldest son, she took the same approach she'd seen both her late husband Liam and Ned Flood take on many occasions. She would say as little as possible and be as vague as she could. Roisin wasn't successful at it, however, and a pall descended on the room. She wished she could run outside and scream out loud to the heavens, but she knew her duty was to her friend and his mortally wounded child. She waited until the last moment to leave, then began the long walk back to Gortalocca, haunted by what she'd seen and heard. She asked herself if it was the savages who made Ireland what it was or whether it was Ireland itself that made her people savage.

*

Rackham finally found Ned. He was ensconced in the bar in Ballykinsella, sharing a few drinks and stories with Jonesey and Barry McGee.

'I thought we were meeting in Dungarvan, Ned,' he said, mildly irritated. 'I wasted the whole day waiting there.' He knew that if Ned changed his plans, there must be a very good reason for it but he was a little cross that it been done without his knowledge.

Ned sensed Jack's annoyance and decided to tease him. 'Yer man here, Jonesey, it's his fault. He kidnapped Smythe in d' process of gettin' d' 'baccy out o' d' warehouse.'

Jack's face flushed red. He glared at Mr. Jones, who looked down at the floor.

'What in God's name were you thinking, man?'

'Ah keep yer britches on, Jack,' laughed Ned. 'Smythe laid a trap and Jonesey turned d' tables on him.' Ned gave Jones a friendly push. 'And under d' circumstances, Oy'd have done d' same t'ing.'

Jack relaxed and exhaled deeply. 'You didn't kill him, did you?'

'Course not,' said Ned. 'We brought him back here and got him drunk fer a few days.' He laughed. 'Relax, Jack, everyt'ing's under control. We found a market fer d' tea, by d' way. How much did ya bring?'

'Six tons. I got a good price for the brandy and I reinvested some of the profit in the Dutch goods.'

The old would-be pirate, Barry, injected himself into the conversation.

'Do I get a cut on d' tea?'

Ned turned in his chair and laughed. 'Always d' businessman, Barry. We used our share of d' profit on d' tea but Oy t'ink we can give ya a cut, bein' as how we've bin usin' yer barn. What d' ya t'ink of five shillin's a ton?'

Barry squinted. 'I t'ink ten would be fairer.'

'We'll say seven shillin's and you'll keep it here fer a few days 'til d' lads from Cork pick it up.'

'Done,' said the old man. 'What does dat make me total take?'

Ned made a quick mental calculation. 'Sixty-two pounds and two shillin's,' he said, 'and ya never had to lift a finger. Pay d' man, Jack.'

Jack counted the money out of a large purse and it was more than Barry had ever seen in his life. He smiled a snaggled-toothed smile. 'If any of ye lads want a bar,' he said, 'ye can have it wit' my blessin'.'

'One more t'ing, Barry. Before ya close down d' bar and drink its contents, will ya get some men to offload d' ship tonight and get d' goods stashed in the barn?'

'I will, o' course. I'll saddle up me horse right now, back in an hour.'

'Well, gents,' said Ned, draining the contents of his

cup, 'our business is concluded and Oy'm headin' back to Tipperary fer a bit of rest and relaxation. Micko, me boy, hitch up d' team.'

CHAPTER 41

R oisin and Siobhan arrived at Mick's cottage early in the morning to find Alexander already there, along with old Moira and Paulie.

'Alexander, I thought I told you last night that Mr. Washington wanted you back up at Johnstown.'

'You did, Roisin, but my place is here.' The boy was growing into a man, Roisin thought. He even seemed to fill out his clothes better, somehow. He was shedding his childhood skin and was rapidly evolving into the man he was to become. His countenance was stern and taciturn beyond his years.

'Shouldn't you two be at the store?' he said.

Both Roisin and Siobhan were taken aback by Alexander's directness. Ordinarily his manner was quiet and circumspect. The older woman looked at him and caught a glimpse of the same ferocity which unnerved Robbie yesterday. If Ned did have the Devil in him, then he'd passed it on to his progeny.

'I've locked up Hogan's,' she told him. 'When they brought back Petey's body, I laid it out in the bar. It's the only place big enough for the wake. Blood's running high already and I thought drinking would only fuel the fire.' Roisin caught herself, wondering why she even felt the need to explain herself to this young pup.

'Good idea, m'um,' responded Alexander, the tone of his voice flat. 'Whatever has to be done will be done in a sober and proper fashion. When the villain or villains are identified, I will take it to the authorities…'

Roisin interrupted him. 'We all know who's responsible,' she blurted. 'Everyone knows it's those bastards from Ardcroney. What do you think the authorities will do about it? There are no witnesses. Anyway, it's already started.'

'The witness is lying here in front of you,' said Alexander coldly, 'and what do you mean it's already started? What's started?'

'Tommy Casey and Bob Ring left a few hours before dawn and they were headed to Ardcroney. They said they would pick off any McNamara who strayed from their place.'

'That's madness! They'll get themselves killed.'

The conversation was forgotten when Edgie began to kick his feet feebly and make garbled noises.

'D' pain potion is startin' to wear off,' said Moira quietly, pouring a thick yellowish liquid into a cup. 'I'll give him a drop more poppy juice.'

Alexander stayed her hand. 'No,' he said authoritatively. 'It makes him sleep, old woman, and I have to see if he can tell us what happened.'

'Dat's cruel,' protested Siobhan. 'D' poor lad must be in terrible pain.'

Alex scowled at her. 'It's the only way,' he told her. 'If we can prevent more bloodshed, then Edgie will have done his last labour before he goes to heaven.'

'I can't see,' the boy whimpered. 'I'm so tired, and it hurts so bad.'

Alexander's air of authority vanished in an instant and was replaced by a tender, almost fatherly demeanor. He placed his hand on the boy's forehead.

'It's alright Edgie, we'll give you something for the pain in a moment. Do you remember anything, lad, anything at all about what happened?'

'I don't wanna t'ink about it,' he pleaded. Tears filled everyone's eyes, except for Alexander's.

'Everything's alright, Edgie. Nothing bad can happen to you anymore. You're safe now.'

'Me arms,' sobbed the young boy, 'd' pain … please … it's so bad. Help me … please.'

Alexander closed his eyes tightly and pressed a thumb and forefinger against the lids in an effort to staunch his tears. His chest felt so heavy that it was difficult to breathe. He swallowed hard so his voice wouldn't crack.

'We'll help you, Edgie, just try to remember what happened on the road.'

Edgie began falteringly, the mental anguish of recall as painful to him as his physical injuries. 'We got to d' Carney road… by d' bog.' The boy's battered face took on a look of dread. 'Dere's a man! He's got a stick… Petey!'

The effort of recollection had taken poor Edgie's mind back to the terrible events of the day before and he was reliving the horror.

'Good lad, you're doing really well. Try to concentrate now, what does the man look like?'

'E's a monster!' Edgie's eyes widened in terror. 'A big… ugly one-eyed monster… Petey!'

'It's alright, son. What's happening now?'

'D' man says… who'll say d'… white o' me….'

Roisin intervened to save the boy's breath. 'Who'll say the white of my eyes are black?' she said, 'It's the standard challenge for stick fighters.'

The boy groaned in agony but he fought on. 'Petey's gettin'… his bata out o' d' wagon… Be careful, Petey! Look out! No! D' man's hittin' him… an' hittin' him! He hit Petey while his back was turned!'

'Edgie,' Alex swallowed hard again, 'who kicked you, son?'

'McNa… please…,' he begged, 'd' pain… somebody, please…'

'Alright, that's enough. Good boy, Edgie, you're a brave man. Moira will give you something to take the pain away.'

Alexander knew the dirty work was done and he turned away. His eyes were wet and he waved his hand at Moira so he wouldn't have to speak, the lump in his throat was the size of a spud. He went outside and Siobhan followed him. Once he'd left the cottage, he allowed his emotions to have free rein and he sat on a tree stump and let the tears flow. Siobhan knelt down quietly beside him.

'I never want to have to do anything like that again,' he choked. He managed to swallow the lump in his throat. 'I'm going to the sheriff. He has one chance to stop this or, so help me God, there'll be a bloodbath like nothing this county's ever seen before. I'll try to keep a lid on it until Da gets back but, one way or another, there will be justice done.'

'It's not your fight, Alex,' Siobhan said gently.

He kissed her softly on the mouth, their first kiss, and she tasted the salt of his tears. 'You're wrong, Siobhan,' he said. Then he leapt up off the tree stump and began to run towards Johnstown. He would get his father's big horse and ride into Nenagh.

*

Tommy and Bob lay hidden at the side of the road between Ardcroney and Borrisokane. They'd known they might have to wait for hours so they'd brought food and something to drink. Stalking prey might be better sport but still-hunting was more effective.

'How long will we wait, Tom?'

'We'll stay 'til after sunset. If none of d' blaggards show up, we'll get back to Gortalocca and come back tomorra, before dawn. Now keep yer gob shut.'

Folk walked by them at intervals, mostly in ones and twos, and occasionally entire families would pass, all making their way towards the Borrisokane fair. When the afternoon sun peeked through the clouds, the sporadic stream of traffic slowed to a trickle. When no one had walked by for over half an hour, Tommy was ready to give it up for the day but, just as they were readying themselves to leave their makeshift hideout, they spotted two people leading a buck goat, a pocan, towards the fair. One was a man and the other was a child of about ten years.

'I'll creep ahead on dis side of d' hedgerow,' Tommy said. 'If dey're McNamaras, you come out from behind and cut 'em off. Take yer shirt off and cover yer face wit' it. Make sure ya don't let d' boy run off. We're goin' to send a message back to dat bastard McNamara.'

It was Brian McNamara and he had his baby brother, Sean, with him. They were taking their father's prize pocan to the fair. The two youths from

Gortalocca waited in silence until Brian passed within a few feet of Bob. Bob leapt over the hedgerow and Brian snapped round abruptly at the commotion, to find himself face-to-face with a masked man.

'Who d' feck are you?' he shouted.

Tommy leapt over the hedgerow in front and the shirt masking his face fell off.

'I know you,' exclaimed McNamara. 'You're Casey, one of Pete Gleeson's cronies.' He'd barely got the words out of his mouth when Tommy struck him a lethal blow to the temple and he dropped as if he'd been poleaxed. Sean tried to dodge past Bob and he almost managed it, but Bob caught him by the heel and tripped him up. Then he jumped on top of him and pinned the boy down. The goat skittered back and forth, unsure as to whether he should keep going in the direction he'd been travelling or back in the direction of his familiar farmyard. There was a rope tied around the animal's neck and Tommy grabbed it. He led the goat to the other side of the hedgerow and pulled out his knife, not the short knife he used to eat with but the double-edged dirk used for battle, and he cut the poor creature's throat.

Bob had his hands full trying to restrain the wildly flailing child and keep a hand over his mouth at the same time. Tommy dragged Brian McNamara's body over the wall so that it couldn't be seen from the road. He cut the rope off the still-kicking goat, brought it over and trussed up the child like a pig being brought to market.

'Take your hand from over his mouth, Bob,' he said, picking up their food sack and throwing it at Ring. 'Here, stuff this in his gob. This young fella and I are going to have a little talk and I don't want him screamin'. Do ya want to live, boy?'

Sean nodded his head furiously, his eyes wide with shock as he looked down at his brother's still corpse.

'You look at me when I'm talkin' to ya, boy. Yer brother's in hell now.' The child began to shiver with fright. 'Now I'm goin' to ask ya a few questions and you're goin' to tell me d' truth, understand?' The boy nodded. 'Do you know who killed Pete and Edgie Gleeson?' The child nodded again, this time with less enthusiasm, and Tommy held the blade a few inches from Sean's face. 'I'm goin' to take d' sack out of yer mouth and if ya scream, I'll cut yer t'roat, just like I did to yer pocan.'

Tommy unstuffed Sean's mouth. 'Ya killed me brother, ya feckin' bastard!' the boy yelled.

Casey stuffed the sack back in. 'Bring him over here, Bob.' Ring dragged the trussed-up child over to the still-quivering animal and Tommy held the boy by the chin over the gaping wound. There were gouts of blood spreading on the ground and the lad tried to turn away, but he couldn't fight the young man's strength. 'See dat, boy? Your t'roat looks just like dat inside … all d' same pipes and tubes and shit.' The boy shook his head wildly. 'Don't believe me? Will we cut it and take a look?'

Sean stopped struggling and fell limp in Bob's arms. 'Aw Jayzis, Tommy, he's pissed all over me!'

Tommy grabbed the boy by his collar and shook him. 'I'm goin' to ask ya one last time, boyo. Who killed Pete and Edgie Gleeson?' The child tried to say something and Tommy pulled the cloth from his mouth.

'Kerr!' he gasped. 'His name's Kerr! He's a big ugly stick fighter wit' a scar down his face and one of his eyes missin'. Me da hired him.'

'And where's dis fella Kerr now?'

'He's gone! He left dis mornin', said he didn't want to wait around in case somebody came after him.'

'Did he say where he was goin'?'

'Said dere was a fair in Kilkenny in a couple o' weeks, said he was goin' dere.'

'Now, wasn't dat easy? What's yer name?'

'Sean. Sean McNamara.'

'Well Sean, I've just got one last question. Who kicked Edgie in d' guts?'

'I don't know, I swear. Da made me stay at home, said I shouldn't watch.'

A cloud of fury temporarily blinded Casey and he was sorely tempted to cut the boy's throat, just to teach Ger McNamara a lesson. He breathed deeply to regain his composure.

'So,' he hissed, 'it's alright fer poor Edgie to see his brother's brains bashed in and fer d' young lad to have his arms crushed, but he didn't t'ink little Seanie should watch? Gag him again, Bob. I'm goin' to show him what he missed.'

Bob shoved the cloth back in Sean's mouth and Tommy pulled out his long knife, holding it towards the boy. Sean's eyes bulged. He was certain his life was over. Instead, Tommy set about cutting off the goat's head and decapitating Brian. After only five horrendous minutes, the job was done.

'Leave the boy. Help me get McNamara's carcass up onto the hedgerow.'

'What are ya goin' to do, Tom?'

'I'm goin' to set d' scene fer a nightmare. Find me a stick and sharpen both ends.'

Brian McNamara's body was left hung up on the

hedgerow as if he'd been crucified, his arms out-stretched and the goat's head pinned onto his neck with the stick, where his own severed head had been.

'What'll we do wit' McNamara's head, Tommy?'

'Paulie will never see his son's face again and we're returnin' d' favour. I'm goin' to bury it in d' bog. You go back home, Bob. I'm goin' to find Kerr and I'll track d' bastard down if I have to go to d' ends o' d' earth.'

'Good huntin', Tommy, and safe home.'

'You too, Bobby.'

Tommy Casey would have been well-advised to follow Alex Flood's example. Tom's hatred and his lust for revenge, combined with his impetuosity, was to lead the boy from the tiny village of Gortalocca on a journey from which he would never return. Those last words he spoke to Bob Ring were the last ones anyone from Gortalocca would hear him speak again.

CHAPTER 42

'What the hell do you mean the tobacco's gone?' demanded Willoughby.

'Someone broke into the warehouse five days ago. They made off with it.'

'I swear to God, Smythe, if you were under my command I'd have you court-martialed! You'd be brought up on charges and stood before the Admiralty.'

'On what charges?'

'Oh I don't know! Stupidity!'

'I'm having another beer. Shall I order you one?'

Willoughby ignored the remark. 'What have you done about it?'

'I filed a report.'

'You filed a report? Is that all?'

'Well no. I went out investigating for three days, but I didn't find a thing.'

'Smythe, you couldn't find your ass with your left

hand!' said Willoughby, exasperated. 'Investigating indeed.'

Tim Smythe had tolerated the Royal Navy officer up to now but his patience was at an end. He decided he'd endured the broadsides for long enough and, with a single shot, he hit Willoughby in the powder magazine.

'So, Lieutenant Willoughby, I assume your presence here means you haven't caught that rascal, Rackham.'

'Don't address me in that manner, you imbecile. I don't have to listen to that from you!'

'I agree, Lieutenant. Why don't you find yourself another table? This one's mine.'

The British officer stood up. He buttoned his coat, straightened his uniform and marched out of the bar, furious at being chastised by someone he considered so inferior to him in every way. Tim Smythe was feeling rather smug. Being in the company of pirates must have had a favourable effect on him. He deliberated briefly on whether he should file a report on Willoughby's insolence. Ah feck it, he thought, I'll just wait here until Mary finishes, then I'll take her home.

*

Jack was standing on the deck of Prosperity alongside Jonesey, who was happy to be back on board. They had a fair south-easterly wind and were south of Cornwall. The ship's cargo was five tons of Virginia tobacco and they had forged papers from Smythe certifying that the tariffs and duties had been paid. Jack Rackham didn't give a monkey's arse now if he was stopped by revenue cutters or the Royal Navy. His papers appeared in order and he was heading for France instead of making a port o' call in England. Isn't life grand, he thought, as he watched the sun grow low in the west. It didn't stay grand for long. Less than fifteen minutes later, he heard a call from the topman.

'Cap'n, we've got a sail a couple of points off the starboard bow. She's closing fast.'

'How far?'

'About eight miles, sir.'

'No problem. Maintain heading.' He called up to the masthead where the lookout was poised. 'Keep your eyes peeled and let me know what colours she's flying.'

'Aye aye, sir,' came the response from above.

Another fifteen minutes passed and again came the topman. 'She's English, sir and … you ain't going to believe this.'

'You'd better enlighten me then, Flannagan.'

'She looks like the same sloop o' war we met off France a while back.'

Oh, shit in a hand-basket, thought Jack. If it is, her Lieutenant-in-Command, whatever the hell his name is, will probably be as mad as a wet bulldog chewing on a hornet.

'Very well, maintain heading. We'll just have to brazen this one out.'

*

The door to the sheriff's office opened and Higgins ushered Alexander in, closing the door behind them. He shook the young man's hand and bade him take a seat.

'So, you're Ned's son. I take it your father has not yet returned from… where was it?'

'Waterford, sir.' Alexander knew that Higgins was testing him and that there was nothing to be gained by starting with an blatant lie.

'Ah yes, that's right, Waterford. As this is the first time you have graced me with a social call, may I assume that your visit pertains to something of an official nature?'

'I must apologise for not calling on you before, sir. It was discourteous of me and I beg your pardon for my bad manners.'

'Apology accepted Alex … may I call you Alex?'

'Of course, sir.'

'Excellent. Now that the formalities have been dispensed with, Alex, let's cut through the dung, shall we? What's the problem? I assume it's a problem you've come about because problems seem to follow your father around like a dog's tail. If this has anything to do with the tobacco you're growing up in Gortalocca, I don't know anything about it. That's between your father and the tax men and I don't like those bastards any more than anyone else does, feckin' bureaucrats.'

'It's not about tobacco, sir, it's about murder. In fact it might be two murders by now, perhaps even more.'

Higgins leaned forward in his chair. He pulled out a piece of paper out from a drawer of his desk and had a pen poised to take notes. His previous mild-mannered countenance had been exchanged for one of complete attention.

'The victims?' he asked sternly.

'Peter Gleeson and his little brother Edgie. Well, Edgie isn't dead yet but he's been badly mutilated and is mortally injured.'

'Aren't those the poteen-maker's kin?'

'Yes, sir, they're Paul Gleeson's sons.'

'I know those boys, and their father. If I remember

rightly, Peter's good with a stick and the youngest son is a nice polite boy.'

'Peter's had his head bashed in, he's dead, and they crushed the boy's hands and arms and kicked him so badly that his insides are crushed.'

'A bad business indeed. Do you know who the perpetrators were?'

'A thug named Kerr, sir, a stick fighter. He carried out the assault but Mr. McNamara from Ardcroney hired him to do it.'

'May I ask how you came by this information?'

'It's you who said we were to cut through the dung, Sheriff. Edgie said so and I heard him.'

'You're right,' said Higgins, standing up. 'I've become so accustomed to acting like a stuffed shirt from sitting behind this desk that I'm starting to sound like the bureaucrats I despise. I'll get my horse. With a deathbed utterance from a victim, I can bring a turnip to court and get it hung.' He took a pair of pistols from a gun locker and tucked them into his belt. He looked at Alex and shrugged. 'Insurance,' he said. 'If they find out you've come here, they might be waiting on the road.'

Alexander lifted the tail of his greatcoat to reveal the pistol he was carrying in his own waistband.

'Your father's son, alright,' the sheriff nodded. 'Let's make haste!'

By the time the two men galloped into Gortalocca, a large crowd had gathered outside the locked door of Hogan's. The murmur of a hundred people talking in hushed tones sounded like a hive of bees. Folk stood in small groups, comparing notes on what they'd heard and gossiping about the day's events. The sheriff forced his horse through the throng of bystanders and dismounted. The crowd parted as he approached the door. Alex dismounted at the crowd's edge and had to push his way through.

'Let him pass!' shouted Higgins and the multitude obeyed mechanically.

The sheriff pounded on the door with his gloved fist and Roisin's voice came from within. 'G'way! I told you, we're not ready yet!'

'This is Sheriff Higgins speaking! Open this door in the name of the law!'

A few moments later, there came the sound of a latch being slid back and the door opened just a crack. Roisin, her eyes red and swollen, poked her head out, briefly scanned the gathering crowd, then ushered Higgins inside. He grabbed Alexander by the shoulder and dragged him in with him. Both Edgie's slight, now-lifeless form, and the covered body of Peter, lay on the floor in front of the fire. The sheriff didn't wait for an invitation. He walked over and pulled back the blanket covering poor Edgie. When he saw the full extent of the child's injuries he winced, as if he could feel the boy's agony himself. He threw the blanket back over the broken little body and shook his head in disgust.

'Contemptible,' he said quietly. He turned to Alex. 'And you said the boy was alive when you came to fetch me?'

'Yes, sir, but barely.'

'Who here, besides Mr. Flood, were witness to the boy's last words?'

Roisin and Siobhan raised their hands and Roisin nodded towards a table where Paulie Gleeson sat, his head resting on his forearms. 'I've been feeding him poteen to try and help numb his grief.'

'Anyone else?'

'Old Moira, but she's still at Mick's place saying her prayers. She's blaming herself because the boy passed away just after she'd given him something for the pain.'

'I'll talk to her later. So we have five witnesses to a deathbed statement. I'll get someone hung for this massacre, that's as long as no one does anything rash.'

'It might be too late for that, Higgie,' said Roisin, in an all too familiar tone.

'I'm not here on a social visit, woman,' snapped the sheriff. 'I'm here in my official capacity this evening so you will address me as Sheriff Higgins.'

'I'm sorry, Sheriff Higgins, it's been a very long day.'

'I know, Roisin, and my long days are just beginning. What did you mean, it's too late?'

'Petey had a lot of friends. You know yourself how hot-headed young men can be.'

'Well let's hope that nothing has been done in retaliation, otherwise there might be hangings on both sides. Do you know who the young fellows were?'

'No, sir,' she lied, 'only rumours.'

Just then, the mob outside raised a cheer and it sounded like a wave crashing against a cliff. Higgins felt goose-bumps rise on his skin and the hair prickle on his arms. Bob Ring had returned like a hero from battle, announcing to all what he and Tommy Casey had done.

'Rumours, is it?' The sheriff glared at Roisin.

Higgins unbolted the door and stood in the doorway. The horde of people were now pressed tightly around Hogan's and, this time, they didn't part when the sheriff appeared. He had to push his way out. Those assembled were working themselves up into a frenzy now, feeding off the news they'd received. Higgins pulled the two pistols from his belt and fired one into the air above their heads. At the sound of a gunshot, the crowd grew silent, momentarily, and gave him some room.

'What's going on out here?' he shouted. No one answered, they just stood and stared dumbly at the lawman. Higgins went back inside Hogan's and bolted the door behind him. 'I'll get to the bottom of this,' he said, 'and I'll do everything I can to staunch the flow of blood but you mark my words, this has all the makings of a faction fight.'

'Faction fight?'

'Yes, Roisin. There was one in Galway a few years ago and in one skirmish, or should I say battle, there were several hundred participants. Thirty men died that day and God only knows how many were killed and maimed in the months that followed. That particular one started over someone buying a lame horse.'

'But that's outlandish! Something like that couldn't happen here.'

'Just listen to the noise that crowd outside are making. That's no longer a collection of individuals you serve here at Hogan's. It's becoming one single-minded beast and the beast is thirsty for blood.' He turned to Alexander. 'I'm going to ask you to do something brave, son. I have to get back to Nenagh in one piece. I have to do whatever it takes to stop this before it turns into an all-out war.'

'I'll talk to the mob, sir. I'm sorry, I didn't mean to get you into the middle of this.'

'You didn't drag me here, Alexander, it's my job. But I do need to get out of here and I don't relish the thought of being ripped apart by an angry pack of wolves, starving for flesh.'

Alex was surprised at how sanguine the sheriff had

become in the face of such a threat to his own safety. The mob was indeed thirsty for blood and it really didn't matter to them whose it was. The fury outside was palpable, even behind the thick stone walls.

'Give me your other pistol please, Sheriff Higgins,' said Alexander. The sheriff complied and Alex opened the door and walked outside, Roisin at his side. When they appeared, the throng grudgingly gave way to them. The gathering had grown significantly, even in the few minutes they'd been inside, as the news had spread. There must be over a hundred and fifty people here, thought Alexander. He tried to speak to them but the commotion they were making drowned out his voice. He fired the pistol and the crowd quietened down.

'My father will be here soon,' he told them, 'and you're all aware of his reputation. If there has to be a war, then you're going to need a general.'

A single voice came out of the crowd. 'We don't need help from any outsiders!' A cheer went up.

'Your sheriff came here voluntarily,' shouted Alexander, 'to help sort this out.'

A murmur rippled through the throng and the solitary voice came again. 'And we don't want his help either!' Once again the crowd voiced their accord.

Roisin recognised the voice; it was her eldest son, Robert. It was typical of him to stay hidden and rouse the rabble. She was mortified.

'You shut your gob, Robbie Flynn!' she screamed. After that, there was no more heckling from him.

'The sheriff and I are going back to Nenagh,' announced Alexander,' and we'll make sure that charges are pressed against those responsible!' The mob became hushed. It was unprecedented for a sheriff to involve himself in an Irish feud. 'The sheriff is just as appalled at the day's events as you are and he has vowed to seek justice.'

Another murmur passed through the crowd and, this time, a different voice rang out. 'English justice fer d' Irish, is it?' It was Bob Ring this time. 'Dat'll be d' day! He can take his justice and stick it up his arse!'

The crowd was still swelling, both in number and in rage, and Alex was tempted to fire the other pistol in his belt.

'If any harm is done to the sheriff,' he yelled, 'the English will send in troops and every man here will be transported! None of you will ever see Ireland or your families again.' Alex's words had caught the mob's attention and he took advantage of the hush that had fallen over the gathering. 'And those will be the lucky ones! If my father comes to hear that any injury has befallen the sheriff, he'll have something much worse in store!'

The knot of humanity slackened around Alex and Roisin and Sheriff Higgins took the opportunity to come out. He made his way through the silent mass of people, escorted by the silver-haired woman and the young man. He mounted his horse at the edge of the crowd and, accompanied by Alexander, he rode back towards Nenagh.

They were nearing Knigh Castle, a mile outside the village, when the sheriff said simply, 'Good work, Alexander.'

Ned and Mick had just passed through Borrisoleigh and, above the din of galloping hooves and carriage wheels, Ned shouted, 'We'll push on t'rough, Mick, we should be back before sunrise. Oy could do wit' a rest and a bit of peace and quiet.'

Mick rolled his eyes and nodded. 'Me too,' he said.

There's a saying which tells us there's no rest for the wicked. Perhaps a similar expression was about to apply itself to the amoral.

CHAPTER 43

'Ease the sails, men. When Whippet comes abeam, let them luff.'

Whippet didn't ease her sails but charged onwards with the south-easterly winds. She passed Prosperity to the port, her guns run out and the tampons off the muzzles. When her bow was just astern of the schooner she came about abruptly, approaching Prosperity on the starboard beam, and eased her sails. The guns were pulled in and lashed down.

Lieutenant Sally stood on deck with a speaking horn. 'Captain Rackham,' he said cordially. 'I'm delighted to see you again.'

'Equally so, Lieutenant,' replied Jack. 'For a moment there, the way you sailed down on us, I thought you were going to rake us with shot.'

'Yes, I apologise for that, sir. I was just checking the name on your stern. As I recall, Captain, the last time we met you were sailing an identical vessel by the name of Camilla.'

'My turn to apologise, Lieutenant,' said Jack, sheepishly.

An odd noise came through the other fellow's bull horn and, for a moment, Jack thought it sounded like someone sawing wood. Then he realised it was laughter, very peculiar laughter at that.

'What are you carrying, Captain Rackham?'

'Five tons of Virginia tobacco.'

'Are your papers in order?'

'They are, sir, signed and stamped.'

'Put a boat over, would you, and bring them here for me to see. Perhaps we can share a glass of French brandy together, that's if you have any.'

'I'll be right over, Lieutenant, and I'll bring a bottle.'

'Bring two!' Again the strange sawing noise came through the speaking horn.

The size of a ship dictates the sort of man who commands it. The heavier ships tend to attract the professional kind, those with well-organised and disciplined natures. The lighter ships however, especially those smaller than frigates, draw a different type of person. Some are merely postmen, bringing dispatches and carrying out reconnaissance, always hoping for a promotion to a larger vessel. Others are hunters. They use the lighter, faster ships to make lightning-fast strikes and raid commercial traffic. Jack had underestimated Lieutenant Sally on his two previous encounters with Whippet. If Sally had been in the Army, instead of the Navy, he would doubtlessly have been in command of a cavalry regiment. Sally and Willoughby were of the same nature. Although he knew that the commander of the Albatross had more experience, and was ten years older, Jack decided that between the two of them, Sally was by far the more dangerous. He possessed the benefits of reckless youth and the advantage of a swifter vessel.

Jack went below and arrived back on deck with the bogus documents, wrapped in an oilcloth, and a couple of bottles of cognac. Jones had already lowered the boat and four crewmen were climbing aboard it.

'You stay here and mind the ship, Jonesey. I'll go and share a glass or two with that braying jackass over there.'

'Careful, Cap'n, donkeys can land you a vicious kick.'

'As long as he keeps laughing, Jonesey, at least he's not shooting.'

Mr. Jones knuckled his forehead and Jack clambered over the rail and into the waiting boat. A matter of minutes later, the jollyboat was being secured to the Whippet and Jack climbed up onto the deck. Lieutenant Sally was waiting for him. He had an enormous buck-toothed grin on his face and his hand was extended in greeting. He was a young fellow, probably in his mid-twenties thought Jack, not very tall but keen-eyed.

'Well, Captain Rackham, we have some business to get out of the way and some pleasure to enjoy.'

Jack gave him the packet containing the papers. 'There's the business, sir.'

'I always say that business should come after pleasure,' said Sally. 'Let's go below. We'll sample some of that brandy you have there and I'll tell you a story.' Jack handed the young fellow the two bottles of liquor and Sally looked at them. 'The illegal stuff always tastes better somehow, don't you think Captain?'

Rackham returned Sally's smile. 'Whatever you say, sir. Call me Jack.'

'Very well, Jack, come with me and I'll tell you about an adventure, and you can call me Sam.'

The two men went below and they had barely reached the captain's quarters when Sally began.

'After you told the Admiral about the French privateer, he dispatched us and the light frigate Achilles to go and find her. We were faster so Whippet got there ahead of the frigate and I decided to go into the harbour without waiting for her to catch up.'

'A daring move,' commented Jack.

'A little reckless perhaps on my part, yes. I'd just got into the harbour, between Tristan Island and the town, when the damned Froggies opened fire on me with a two-pounder. I had the gun crews ready so we silenced their popgun and I thought it was all over. As it turned out, it wasn't. We dropped anchor and I intended to send a shore party to secure your tobacco. We could plainly see the hogsheads on the quay.'

Sally was becoming animated in his excitement and his exuberance was infectious. The young officer lifted a glass of cognac to his lips and Rackham shifted forward in his chair.

'Go on,' he urged.

'Well, there I was getting a boat into the water to get the raiding party ashore, when all of a sudden a shitbucket-load of French mounted infantry turned up. They dismounted and lined up, two men deep, then start firing muskets at us from a quarter of a mile or so away. The musket balls were whizzing all around us and, every once in a while, one would hit the hull with a whack. We were out of range though, so I loaded the canon with the few rounds of chain shot we had and I started firing back. I wish you'd seen it, Jack! We cut the feckers to pieces!'

'I can imagine, Sam!'

'It wasn't over yet! All the shooting got the attention

of a Froggie light artillery outfit who happened to be riding by and they start heading into town. The road coming into Dournanez is really narrow and we had it covered ... we started knocking off the French guns before they were even able to get into town and set up! We were rapidly running out of shot and powder and it was looking like they'd get the better of us.' He stopped and took a big swig out of his brandy glass.

'Bloody hell, Sam, don't stop now!' exclaimed Jack. 'What happened next?'

Sally inhaled deeply and continued. 'Well, I was busy running from gun to gun aiming the shots, and the guns were so hot that, when the gun crew poured buckets of water over them to cool them, steam was coming off. I was just resigning myself to the fact that we were dead ducks, stuck in that harbour, when all of a sudden I heard a roar and the whole bloody town started crumbling right in front of my eyes. Achilles had showed up and hadn't wasted a second. She cut loose with a broadside from her twenty-four pounders, from about a mile out to sea, and started taking the town apart! She fired until only the church steeple was standing, and then she took that down too!'

Jack reached out and shook Sally firmly by the hand. 'Marvellous!' he said. 'What a story, Sam! Congratulations!'

'For my part in it, Captain Brown of the Achilles sent a letter to the Admiralty. He told them I'd showed initiative and daring in the face of overwhelming odds and he put me up for a promotion. What do you think of that, Jack?' He threw his head back and laughed his peculiar laugh and that made Jack laugh too.

'I think it's well-deserved, Sam, and I hope the old men in London appreciate your bravery. Here, let me shake your hand again.' The two men toasted Sam's good fortune then the captain said, 'Much as I hate to spoil the mood, Lieutanant, we should probably talk business.'

Sam brayed like a donkey again and briefly fingered through Rackham's papers. He handed them back, having barely looked at them, and he grew serious for a moment.

'They have your vessel flagged in the Admiralty, Jack. I've been assigned to assist Willoughby in catching you with contraband on board. That's where I'm heading now, to get my orders from him. He's the senior Lieutenant, Jack, he's in charge. I'm just warning you.'

Jack stood and shook the young man's hand. 'Thank you, Sam, and Godspeed.'

Sally smiled his goofy smile. 'Until we meet again, Captain Rackham.'

By the time Jack was back aboard Prosperity it was dark and the lights on the masthead and the stern were lit. He was feeling light-headed from the brandy and was about to go to his quarters when he heard a voice coming through a speaking horn from aboard Whippet.

'Ahoy, Captain Rackham. I hear that Aquitane is nice this time of year. I'm told Arcachon is particularly lovely.' The voice was followed by the now familiar sound of sawing wood.

'Jonesey, stay the course due east. I'm going below to plot a course to Arcachon.'

*

'Get yourself something to eat, Alexander,' said Higgins, in a tone which sounded more like an order than a suggestion. 'I think it's best if you stay the night at Nenagh Castle, I'll have quarters arranged for you. Tomorrow morning I'll take some deputies to Ardcroney and arrest Ger McMahon. You can return to Johnstown then.'

'I really should go back to Gortalocca now, sir. Tensions are at boiling point and I'd like to try and keep a lid on it as best I can.'

'It would be like putting a cork in the spout of a steam kettle, son.'

'I wish my father was here.'

'You're not the only one.'

*

It was half ten and a light misty rain had begun to fall when the coach, driven by Mick, slowed down as it entered Gortalocca. There was still some vestige of the crowd left, milling around outside Hogan's door, but it had the life of a fire. The crowd's emotions, which had burned furiously earlier, were now just smouldering embers and most had returned to their homes, leaving only a few late-comers and a couple of diehards outside the store. Mick reined the horses to a halt.

'What's goin' on here?' demanded Ned.

'A young fella got murdered,' came a response.

'Two of 'em,' came another voice out of the dim light.

Ned thought about Alexander and his blood ran cold. He caught his breath. 'Who?'

'Two o' d' Gleeson boys,' came the reply, 'Peter and Edgie.'

Ned leapt down from the coach and waded through the remaining congregation as if he was pushing reeds aside. He walked up to the door and tried it, then banged on it with the palm of his hand.

'Open dis feckin' door,' he yelled, 'before Oy kick it in!' He began pounding on the door again until he heard the metal-on-metal scratching sound of a latch being slid back. The door opened a crack and he grabbed it, flinging it back and barging in past Roisin, toppling her off balance. He stood in the middle of the room, breathing heavily. 'Where's Alexander?' he demanded. 'Where's me son?'

'It's alright, Ned,' Roisin told him, 'he's safe. He's at Nenagh Castle with Sheriff Higgins, they went a few hours ago.'

Ned breathed a deep sigh of relief. 'Where's Washington?'

'He went back to Johnstown earlier today. We haven't seen him since.'

Ned's face grew red. 'Oy left dat fecker in charge and look what Oy've come back to!'

'It's not his fault, Ned,' protested Morna. 'Dis business is an Oirish t'ing.'

A low knock came, then a whisper from outside the door. 'It's me, it's Mick. Let me in.'

Siobhan slid back the latch and opened the door just enough to let Mick inside. 'I was talkin' to somone out dere,' he said. 'He told me Casey and Bob Ring cut off one of d' McNamara brothers' heads today.'

Ned walked over and uncovered Edgie's body. He looked down at the boy's hands and arms, then quickly threw the cover back over him. 'Holy Mary, Mudder o' God,' he said. 'Who'd do such a terrible t'ing to a little lad?'

Roisin answered his rhetorical question. 'McNamara from Ardcroney. He hired a thug, name of Kerr.'

'Dat explains d' damage to d' boy's arms. D' rat bastard didn't want d' boy huntin' him down if he lived to grow up. Well, he needn't worry about d' boy now,' he said through clenched teeth, 'but Mr. Kerr does have me to look out fer.' There was a venom in Ned's words that sent a chill through the room. He crouched down and uncovered Petey's head, or rather what was left of it. He turned away and tossed the cover back over it. He was breathing heavily like a bellows.

'Jayzis, God Almighty, Oy ain't never seen anyt'ing like dat in me life! Who is dis McNamara?'

'He runs a whiskey still,' replied Siobhan, 'over in Ardcroney.'

'He's a dead man,' replied Ned flatly, 'and Oy'll boil d' bastard alive in his own still and feed him to d' pigs.'

There was total silence in the room for a long minute and Ned took the opportunity to think about his next move. 'It's a good t'ing ya didn't let anybody see dis,' he said. 'We're goin' to need a carpenter. We have to get a couple of caskets built as soon as possible, so we can get dese poor lads in d' ground.'

'Clancy isn't back yet,' said Roisin, 'and the only other carpenter around here is Robbie.'

'Mick, go and fetch Robbie.'

'We ain't d' best of friends, me and him, Ned. What if he tells me no?'

'You're a big strong fella. Bring him over by his neck if ya have to.'

A few minutes later, Robbie was indeed dragged over to Hogan's by the scruff of his neck, like a cat. Mick knocked quietly, was let in, then tossed Robbie unceremoniously to the floor.

'Jayzis, man! Ya almost broke me neck, ya big bully.'

'Don't tempt me,' said Mick, making a motion as if

he was wringing a chicken's neck.

'You want a job, Robbie?' asked Ned.

'Ah now, I wanted to talk to ya about dat very t'ing,' said Robert, rubbing his neck and scowling at Mick.

'Oy want ya to build a coffin fer each of dese poor souls.'

'I had more of a supervisor's job in mind.'

'Do ya want five shillin's or not?'

'I don't have any wood…'

'Dere's empty hogsheads in d' church up dere. Take 'em apart and use d' staves.'

'Right so. I'll get started in d' mornin'.'

'In a pig's arse ya will. If ya want d' five shillin's, you'll have 'em here before first light in d' mornin'.'

'Dat don't give me much time sure.'

Ned pulled a watch from the pocket of his waistcoat and he opened the cover. 'Accordin' to dis be-yootiful silver English clock, dat gives ya at least seven hours.' He snapped the lid shut. 'Now let's get ourselves up to Johnstown, Mick. Oy've got a bone to peck wit' Mr. Washington.'

CHAPTER 44

Abraham Washington was more than a little inebriated. 'I've had enough, Ned,' he slurred. 'I wanna go home…'

'What d' ya mean ya wanna go home? Oy come here to tear a strip off ya and you tell me ya wanna go home?'

'I've had enough of this country. The weather's shite and I don't understand the people.'

'O' course d' wedder's shite, it's Oirland … and as fer d' people, Jayzis, even d' Oirish don't understand each udder.'

'I just wanna go home.'

'Ah sure dat's just d' whiskey talkin'.'

'You're wrong, I've been thinking about it for a while now. I've had enough, Ned, I quit.'

'Ya can't quit! Ya owe me!'

Washington looked Ned square in the eye. 'I owe you nothing, Ned Flynn. Whatever I did owe you, I've paid you back a hundred times over.'

'How about if Oy give ya a bigger piece of d' action?'

'I've already had enough of your action to last me a lifetime. I'm exhausted. Fifteen years of traipsing around after you, trying to make sense of the things you do, it has me worn out. And I don't want your money either, I have all I'll ever need.'

'T'ink about Alexander, Abe, d' boy needs ya.'

'Alexander's no longer a boy, he's grown into a fine young man. He has scruples and that's something neither you nor I have. If you're as clever as I think you are, you'd be well-advised to follow his council from now on.'

'Alright, forget Alex, Oy need ya, Abe!'

Washington cackled a mirthless laugh. 'You?' he said. 'You don't need anyone, you never did. Underneath all your fine clothes, you're still the same orphan who roamed West Cork, living by your wits. God help anyone who got in your way then and God help them now.'

'Just promise me you'll sleep on it, Abe. P'raps when d' mornin' comes, you'll ferget what ya saw today and you'll reconsider.'

'Ned, my dear friend, my only friend, I will go to my grave remembering what I saw today.'

Abraham drained what was left in his glass, stood up a little shakily and, once he was sure he'd got his legs under him, he bid Ned good night and climbed the stairs to his room. Ned heard the bedroom door close and he knew that his life, in that moment, changed as much as it had when Abraham, the half-starved and crippled slave, limped into it all those years before. Abraham Washington had been his one and only voice of reason, his conscience.

The next morning dawned grey and the smell of rain hung in the air, the perfect weather for a burial. Ned got up early and found Washington's two travel bags stacked neatly by the door. He took a brace of pistols and tucked them under his waistband, then put on a greatcoat and buckled a sabre around his waist. Ned was dressing for battle but he didn't have the slightest idea with whom. He looked at the packed bags as he walked out the door in the same way a jilted suitor looks at a picture of their lost love.

Alexander's horse was tied up outside Hogan's. The big chestnut pawed the ground, unnerved by the gathering crowd. Ned pounded on the door with a gloved fist and, when it opened, he barged in. Robbie was hammering the last nails into Edgie's coffin lid.

'You'd better get yerself off to Johnstown,' he told Alex, 'if ya want to say goodbye to Washington.'

Alex looked at him with disbelief. 'You fired him?'

'D' bastard quit on me.'

'I don't understand. You and he are friends. Surely....'

Ned interrupted. 'Oy don't need friends!' he growled. 'Now, what did Higgins have to say?'

'He left for Ardcroney early this morning to arrest Ger McNamara.'

'He should keep his feckin' nose out of Oirish business. Oy was goin' over to deal wit' McNamara after d' boys are buried.'

'Perhaps a public hanging will be satisfaction enough for the mob,' ventured Alexander.

'If he chopped him up into little pieces wit' a dull

spoon, it wouldn't satisfy dis pack of wolves.'

'I'm going to see Abraham.'

As Alexander left Hogan's, Ned snarled, 'Be sure to tell d' traitor safe home'

Alex was glad to be outside. Even the crowd that was already gathering didn't seem as hostile to him as his father was. He mounted his horse and spurred it into a gallop. As he rode past Mick's place, it occurred to him that he hadn't seen Moira at Hogan's. It seemed strange for the old crone not to be at the centre of things at a time like this, dispensing her wisdom in the same way she dispensed her remedies. He would call in and see her after he'd seen Abraham. He had something he wanted to talk to her about anyway.

Mr. Washington was sitting in the grand entrance hall, waiting for one of Johnstown's farm hands to arrive with a wagon and take him to Nenagh. He would take a coach to either Cork or Dublin, travel to England by sea, then on to Charles Town from there.

Alexander burst through the door. 'You can't leave, Abe!'

'I can and I will. I've given it a lot of thought lately, Alexander, and I made up my mind yesterday.'

'But why?'

'I miss Charles Town and the warm breezes. I missed the azaleas blooming this year and, by the time you get to my age, Alex, you'll have found out that sentiment plays a role in many of your decisions.'

'But you'll be bored rigid without anything to do.'

'I've come to a time in my life when I want to be … bored, as you call it. I want to sit by the river bank, go fishing whenever I want, tend a garden and listen to the birds. I asked myself yesterday if I was happy and the answer I gave myself was a resounding no.'

'It's about Edgie and Peter, isn't it.'

'It is and it isn't. I went along with this adventure of your father's, even though I thought it was quite mad, because I'd already decided in my mind that it was to be my last. Thanks to your father, I have almost two thousand pounds in the bank in Charles Town. I can live very comfortably without servants or any of the other trappings that are your father's dream. He thinks that living in luxury and having beautiful things around him will make up for the childhood he never had. As a boy, he roamed those hills in West Cork with a gang of ruffians who didn't know the difference between right and wrong, or good and bad. The only thing that mattered to them was survival and where to get their next meal.'

'Da isn't a bad man.'

'Of course he's not, Alex, but he's not a good man either. Your father's no more a bad person than a wolf is a bad animal. It's instinct, both do what they were reared to do.'

'Da needs you, Abe. You should have seen him this morning. He was chewing nails and spitting out tacks.'

'He'll get over it, he always does.'

'I'm afraid he'll kill someone.'

'A wolf will be a wolf.'

'What about Gortalocca?'

'I've been talking to old Moira about Gortalocca and the village just isn't the same anymore. She says they might just as well change its name. A young man named Liam Flynn, who was wise beyond his years, came here almost fifty years ago. He had a rare wisdom and more than his fair share of common sense and somehow he managed to strike a balance between the old ways and the new. He knew that change was a part of life and he allowed it to happen gradually. When he first arrived, Gortalocca was going through a very rough time but, even so, the village always retained its identity. When your father arrived here, he started throwing fistfuls of money around, like he was feeding pigeons in the park, then he stood back and watched the poor wretches scratch and scramble around for it. It made him feel like their benefactor but, in truth, it was all about asserting his power, about him having his own little kingdom and reigning supreme in it.'

'What about me?'

Abraham looked at Alexander fondly and he smiled. 'Ah, you've saved my best argument for last, my boy. You're what brought me here in the first place and what kept me aboard that cursed ship for all those years. I remember the day you were born. My wife wet-nursed you when your mother, God rest her soul, wasn't able to. I bounced you on my knee when you were a little boy and, when your father was too busy with his many plans and schemes, I did my best to be to you what he couldn't be. Now that I see how you've turned out, even if I do say so myself, I'm proud of both you and me.' Abraham Washington wasn't prone to displays of emotion but he coughed in an effort to clear a lump in his throat. 'Damned Irish weather,' he said. 'I must have caught a chill.'

'What will I do without you, Abraham?' asked Alex despondently.

Washington cleared his throat again. 'If I was you, Alexander Flynn, I would court that beautiful Irish lass of yours, marry her and bring her back to America. Someday, when you have children, you can tell them about how wonderful the old country is. You can sit around the fire with them in the evenings and you can tell them about Ireland's beauty, about her streams and waterfalls, her fields of green and gold that shimmer in the sun, about the friendly people who never met a stranger and their love of music and a drop o' the drink.'

'But that's not the way it is.'

'It could be, boyo. And because that's the way you want it to be, that's the way it will be, in your memories and stories at least. I was born a slave. I choose not to remember the back-breaking labour in blazing sun, or the feel of the lash on my back. I remember warm, sultry Sunday afternoons and a little boy soaking his bare feet in a creek, and I remember hearing the cicadas chirp in the live oaks while I waited for the fish to bite. I remember the mouth-watering smell of my mother's cooking and I remember the old ones describing life in Africa so vividly that I wanted to go and see it for myself.'

'Will you go to Africa, then?'

'No, son. I'd rather have the picture of it in my head, the one the old folks painted many years ago.'

'Will I ever see you again?'

'You'll find me if you want to, Alex. Just look for an overdressed negro sitting on the bank of a stream, his feet in the water underneath a live oak, waiting for a nice fat catfish to bite.'

The old and the young man looked towards the door at the sound of the farm wagon pulling up outside.

'It's goodbye then,' said Alexander, thrusting his hand out and trying very hard not to cry.

Abraham took Alexander's hand and smiled forlornly. 'It's never goodbye, Alex. Wish me safe home, like the Irish do, and we'll shake hands on it.'

The boy shook the black man's hand, then he picked up one of his bags and carried it out to the wagon for him. 'Safe home, Abraham Washington,' he said, his voice cracking.

'Until we meet again, my boy.'

The wagon pulled away and Alex stood in the open doorway of Johnson House, watching until his old friend turned out of the gates and out of sight.

*

Alexander mounted the chestnut horse and rode slowly towards Gortalocca, an empty, hollow sensation in his gut. When he got to Mick's house, he reined the horse and turned towards the cottage. Perhaps Moira could make sense of it all. He rapped quietly on the door and, hearing no response from within, he opened it and announced himself. The ancient crone sat with a sack containing her meager belongings at her feet.

'Are you going somewhere?' the young man asked.

'It's me time,' she answered directly.

Alexander felt sick to his stomach. 'What do you mean it's your time?'

'I've been alive for a very long time, lad, and that's not a blessing, it's a curse. And I lived one day too long,' she added bitterly.

'If you mean Edgie… you did everything you could.'

'I did too much, Alexander. I committed a mortal sin.'

'I don't understand.'

'I could feel d' poor little soul's pain as fierce as if it was me own and I knew me potions couldn't free him from it. D' boy was dyin' and, when I knew I couldn't help ease his pain … I helped him along on his last voyage. I give him a big enough dose of poppy juice to kill him. Dat's a mortal sin in anyone's book.'

'But you did it for the right reasons, Moira.'

'Dat might make it right to you, but it makes no difference to me. I judge meself guilty.'

'Where will you go?'

'Doesn't matter.'

'Won't you even say goodbye to Mick or to Roisin? They've known you all their lives.'

'No, dey'll only try and stop me. I left 'em before but dis time I won't be comin' back. Do an auld woman a favour, will ya? Don't tell 'em I'm gone fer a day or so.'

'Isn't there anything I can do or say to change your mind?'

'Nothing, Alex, and I have one more t'ing to ask. Watch after yer da. He's a strange one. D' only moral code Ned Flynn ever had came from a black man, and I know he's leavin' too.'

The morning's events had taken Alexander completely off-guard and his head swam in confusion. He could think of nothing to say. In one fell swoop, the village had lost both its conscience and its soul.

'I will keep your secret, Moira, to the grave.'

'Be happy, son.'

He walked out of the cottage and, as he closed the door softly behind him, the empty hollow feeling returned.

Alex walked his horse slowly back in the direction of the village. His mind was racing but his thoughts were foggy. Nothing seemed to make sense anymore and he lost all concept of time and distance. He arrived at Gortalocca remembering nothing of how he'd got there. A crowd had gathered outside Hogan's again but this time, instead of cries for vengeance, the mood was sombre, almost reverential. The burial of the Gleeson boys had already taken place and there was a contingent of armed deputies guarding the door. Alexander dismounted and approached the throng. Roisin, Morna and Siobhan stood on the periphery of the gathering as if they had been anticipating his arrival. He casually stroked his horse's neck and asked the women what was happening.

'D' sheriff and yer da are inside,' Morna told him. 'Dey arrested Bob Ring and dey have him in dere.' Alex handed the reins to Siobhan and wound his way through the crowd towards the line of guards. He whispered something to the sergeant and was allowed to pass. He knocked on the door.

CHAPTER 45

A lexander stood in front of the door for a moment to gather himself, then knocked again. A gruff voice, which he knew to be his father's, came from within.

'Who's dere?'

Alexander identified himself, the latch was slid across and the door was opened.

'Sit down, Alexander,' said Sheriff Higgins. 'We have negotiations in progress. We're attempting to prevent a war.'

Three chairs were lined up on one side of a table and Bob Ring sat in a chair facing them.

The sheriff began. 'Mr. Ring, I have a witness who states that you took part in a beating which resulted in the murder of one Brian McNamara, also the subsequent mutilation of his corpse. You are further accused of the illegal detention of his youngest sibling. Do you deny these charges?'

Alex interrupted. 'Wait,' he protested, 'he doesn't understand what the feck you're saying. If this is a trial, then Bob is entitled to counsel.'

'It's not a trial,' said the sheriff, 'it's a hearing. I am

merely ascertaining the facts of the case. However, I agree, Mr. Ring does needs counsel. Bring a chair and sit next to him … and don't say 'feck' at a hearing unless it's relevant.'

'Yes, sir. Sorry, sir. What the sheriff wants to know, Bob, is did you beat up Brian McNamara?'

'I didn't, no.'

'After he was dead, did you have anything to do with the body?'

'I did. I helped Tommy put it up on d' hedgerow.'

'Is that all?'

'No. Tommy asked me to sharpen a stick at both ends and I helped to shove it down his neck.'

'Why the fe… I mean why did you shove a stick down his neck?'

'Well, Tommy chopped off his head … I only had me little eatin' knife and Tommy had a big one … den he chopped off d' goat's head and he wanted to put d' goat's head on McNamara's neck.'

'Jayzis, Merry and Sent Jawsef, Bobby, what d' feck were you boys t'inkin'?' exclaimed Ned.

Sheriff Higgins turned and scowled at Ned for blaspheming and uttering a profanity in the same sentence.

'Tommy said it was a message fer Ger McMahon.'

'And what d' feck message was dat?' demanded Ned.

'Mr. Flood,' insisted the sheriff, 'the same thing goes for you as for your son. Do not use the word feck in this hearing and I'd appreciate it if you'd leave the Holy Family out if it too. This was the Devil's work.' He turned back to the young man opposite him.

'Did you detain … I mean, did you hold the child down?'

'I did, sir, and I even tied d' little fec… fellow up.'

'Very well. That testimony agrees with the witness statement I received from the boy.'

'Tommy should have cut dat feckin' little rat's head off too!' exclaimed Bob.

Higgins slapped his hand down on the table. 'That's enough!' he shouted. 'You feckin' Irish can't seem to have a feckin' conversation without using the feckin' word feck at least a dozen feckin' times!' Everyone stared at the sheriff with astonishment. 'Well that's how it sounds to me!' he said. 'The way I see it is this,' he continued. 'Bob here was an accessory before the fact and after the fact but he is also guilty of false imprisonment, if not kidnapping. Since he didn't remove the boy to a place other than the scene of the crime, then the kidnapping charge is reduced. Bob Ring, I have no grounds to hang you and I will tell the magistrate, when he gets here next week, that any sentence other than a couple of years hard labour, or perhaps deportation, would be excessive.

'De-por-tayshun?' said Bob. 'What's dat?'

'It means they might send you to the Botany Bay colony in Australia,' Alexander told him.

'When can I come home t' Ireland?'

'Never, Bob. If they send you away, you can never come back.'

'Jayzis, dat's harsh just fer tyin' up a little rat bastard.'

'You're getting off easy,' Alex told him. 'The sheriff says he'll speak on your behalf at the trial.'

'Can I go home now?'

'No,' said the sheriff, 'you have to stay in gaol until the trial.'

'What about Tommy?'

'I've signed a warrant for his arrest. When we catch him, he'll be charged with murder and he'll probably hang, due to the particularly heinous manner in which the crime was carried out.'

'What about McNamara?'

'He's already in custody. I have him in the most miserable, dampest cell in Nenagh gaol. He'll hang, I shall make sure of that.'

'And Kerr?'

'It was my intention to sign a warrant for his arrest too but Mr. Flynn has asked, since this is primarily an Irish affair, that I allow him to handle Kerr personally.' With that, Higgins slapped his hand on the table again. 'I call these proceedings to a close!' he announced. 'Mr. Ring, you will accompany me. I will not place shackles on you and would ask that you do not try to escape. It would be such a feckin' shame to have to shoot you.'

'Before ye go,' said Ned, 'can Oy have a few minutes to talk to Bob in private?'

Higgins looked at Ned suspiciously. 'You're not planning an escape are you?'

'Nuttin' like dat, Sheriff.'

'Very well, I'll give you five minutes with the prisoner.'

Ned whispered in Bob's ear and, every once in a while, Bob would turn and look into Ned's eyes, then turn his ear back toward Ned's mouth.

'Do ya understand, Bob?' said Ned, finally. Bob Ring nodded and accompanied Higgins out the door. When they'd gone, Ned told his son, 'Oy wish ya hadn't brought Higgins into dis.'

'I didn't have a choice,' replied Alex. 'The mob outside was becoming hysterical.'

'He t'inks he's put a stop to a war but all he's done is postpone it.'

'I thought the way you left Johnstown this morning, that you were all geared up for war.'

'Ah sure ya know yerself how Oy am, boyo. Oy was pissed off at Washington fer leavin', and us wit' a crop in d' field. Oy was just lookin' fer somebody to take it out on. By d' time Oy got here, me temper had cooled off a bit.'

'Abraham was sorry to go.'

'Ah don't Oy know dat, and to tell ya d' truth, Oy'll miss him more dan Oy let on. Me and him, we've bin partners since before you was born. Oy always told him he owed me but d' truth is Oy owed him more. If d' fella wants to sit and fish, he's earned d' right to do it.'

'What are our plans now, Da?'

Ned smiled. 'Our,' he said, 'Oy like d' sound of dat. A father and his son makin' decisions. Ya sounded like a real solicitor when ya was talkin' to Bob back dere. Maybe ya ought to t'ink about goin' into law. Ned Flood's son, a solicitor … now wouldn't dat be gas?'

'I've already considered it.'

'Well, we can talk about it later, boyo. D' most urgent t'ing now is d' crop. Oy'll get Mikey to take over Washington's job. We'll get a blacksmith shop goin' fer Clancy and, most importantly, we have to take dese peoples' minds off revenge and get 'em back to work.'

As Alexander and his father left Hogan's, the crowd murmured their discontent. They weren't at all happy that one of their own, a man they felt was innocent, had been taken away by the sheriff. Ned put his hands up to quieten the throng.

'Oy want all of yous to go home to yer families. Oy'm declarin' today a holiday. Hogan's bar will open later so ye can drink to d' departed. If any of ye were t'inkin' of goin' after d' McNamaras, well yer too late.

Sheriff Higgins already has d' auld bastard in gaol and, when d' magistrate comes next week, he'll hang him. Bob won't be hung, but he'll have to do some penance fer what he did. If Tommy Casey turns up, Oy want him to turn himself over to me because if d' sheriff catches him first, he'll hang fer sure. Get him to me and Oy'll keep him safe from d' law. Now go home, d' lot of ye, Hogan's will be open at noon.'

The crowd began to disperse, gossiping in small groups as they moved away, and Ned turned to his son.

'Now we have to get Roisin and d' girls here to get d' bar ready.'

As Ned and Alexander made their way over to where the women stood, talking amongst themselves, Robbie sidled up.

'I have somet'ing I wanted t' discuss wit' ya, Ned.'

'Well discuss it den. Oy'm busy.'

Robbie glanced at Alex, disdainfully, then back at Ned. 'In private,' he said.

'Whatever ya have to say, ya can say in front of me son.,' he replied tersely.

'It's… business.'

'We're all ears, bucko.'

'I t'ink ya should put me in charge of Hogan's bar.'

'No,' answered Ned.

Roisin had seen Robbie approach Ned and now she hurried over.

'Dis is private, Mam,' he snapped.

Ned smiled a smile that a crocodile would have been proud of. 'Why don't ya tell yer mother what ya have in mind?'

Robbie spoke to Ned as if his mother wasn't there. 'Mam's gettin' auld,' he said, 'and I t'ink it would be better if a younger person was in charge of Hogan's.'

Roisin gasped and Ned's smile grew wider. 'You heard me d' first time,' he said. 'No.'

'But I have a family to feed,' whined Robbie, 'I need work.'

'Oy agree,' said Ned. 'A man needs work … but you ain't gettin' yer hands on d' bar.' The smile had gone from Ned's face now.

'Well maybe ya can put me in charge of d' farm workers, instead of yer negro.'

'He ain't me negro, he's me partner. Anyway, he's gone back to Amerrycuh and Oy'm givin' his job to Michael.'

Robbie was momentarily struck dumb by the revelation. 'But I'm d' oldest,' he said, once he'd found his tongue, 'and I'm better suited to d' job. I'm a born leader.'

'Born leader, me arse. Ya want a job? Try beggin' yer baby brother fer one.'

'I'd rather die dan beg him fer anyt'ing!' snapped Robert.

Ned narrowed his eyes. 'Dat can be arranged too,' he said, his expression deadpan.

Ned Flynn's words struck terror into the hearts of both Robbie and his mother. It wasn't the words themselves but the tone in which they'd been delivered. Robbie turned and scuttled away to his cottage, slamming the door behind him.

'You wouldn't kill him, would you? I know he's worthless but he's my son.'

Ned put his arm around Roisin's shoulders. 'O' course not, missus, but Oy enjoyed puttin' d' fear of God into d' peacock.'

Roisin breathed a sigh of relief. 'He won't let this go, Ned. He won't confront you but Robbie's a spiteful sod, even if he is my son. Watch yourself.'

'Don't you worry, Roisin. Whatever he tries on wit' me, it'll come back and bite him on d' arse.'

Ned had already begun to formulate a new plan, he was just getting the details straight in his head.

*

Michael and Clancy pulled into Gortalocca. They were banjaxed and road-weary, their horses dirty and exhausted. They'd met a few stragglers from the mob on the road from Nenagh and had been given a brief synopsis of the events of the past few days. The accounts had varied but the gist was clear. Gleeson's sons had been murdered by Ger McNamara and there was a whiff of retribution in the air.

'Take care of the horses will you, Jamie? I'm going to Hogan's to find out exactly what's happened.'

*

Bob Ring was a simple sort of fellow, amiable and easy to get along with. In the hours that Higgins had spent with him, the sheriff had come to regard him the way one would an old hound dog … inoffensive and not too bright. When Higgins brought him to the gaol, he led him to the warmest, driest cell there was but Bob objected, saying he wanted to go in the cell next to McNamara. He said he wanted to ask the old man's forgiveness for conspiring to murder his son. His manner was so sincere that Higgins couldn't refuse, so he was escorted by a guard to his own cell and a clean blanket was thrown in after him. The lock on the door clanked as the guard turned the big key, then returned it to a nail next to the outer door. Bob wasted no time in putting his plan into effect. He sat in a corner with his back against the wall and began trying to tearing the blanket into strips.

'I don't know why you should get special treatment,' growled McNamara, 'D' blanket dey gave me is crawlin' wit' lice. It ain't no better den a rag.'

'Gimme yours so, auld fella. You can have dis clean one.'

'Now why would ya do dat? Are ya an eejit?'

'I don't plan on bein' here long enough to need it. I'm breakin' out.'

'Ya are an eejit.'

'Suit yourself.' Bob went back to pulling at the clean blanket.

'Wait! Alright, I'll swap ya,' Ger eyed Bob suspiciously, 'but we'll make d' trade at d' same time. I wouldn't want ya endin' up wit' 'em both.'

'Fair enough,' said Bob.

Ger had been sitting in a dark corner and now he stood up and came out into the dim light of the cell. Ger McNamara was a peculiar looking fellow. He had rail thin arms and legs which all projected from a fat body. The few remaining teeth he had protruded from his gums like headstones, his skin had a grey pallor and his white hair grew in tufts. Years of drinking his own lead-tainted poteen had left his body a wreck. He was only in his mid-forties but he looked like an ailing old man of seventy.

Bob stood too and held out the blanket. Ger hesitated before offering his, then tried to snatch the blanket out of Ring's hand so he'd have both, but Bob was gripping it tightly. The old man had no other option than to release his own and Bob reciprocated.

McNamara found the driest corner of his cell and wrapped himself in his new cover.

'I was t'inkin' of takin' ya wit' me,' said Bob, 'but I don' know whether I can trust ya now.'

'Ya can trust me alright and anyway, if ya don't take me wit' ya, I'll scream me head off fer d' guards.'

Bob Ring didn't answer. He just went about tearing strips from the rag.

CHAPTER 46

B y the time the bar opened at noon, Ned had already told Michael everything. Although Mikey had been surprised by the murders, he couldn't really say he was shocked. Family feuds were something the Irish were accustomed to hearing about. What did shock him was that the sheriff had mentioned faction fights. This was something new, even in a country whose tales and legends revolved around conflict and warriors. Tipperary was, after all, the ancestral domain of Brain Boru. Michael knew that a faction fight could begin as a disagreement among families or clans but that it could grow like a holocaust to include parishes, townlands and villages. South Tipperary had been plagued by it for years but it hadn't as yet become a problem here on the banks of the Shannon.

'Oy have business in Nenagh,' Ned told Michael, 'but Oy don't want to leave Gortalocca while blood's runnin' high. Oy'm worried dose shites in Ardcroney might be lookin' fer trouble. So Oy'm sendin' Alexander to Nenagh, wit' a letter of instructions fer d' solicitor, and Oy'd like you to go wit' him. Oy want ya to visit Bob Ring in gaol and tell him to keep his shirt on. Tell him to carry on wit' d' plan but tell him Oy might have a way to get 'im out of trouble without him havin' to leave Oirland. Do ya t'ink ya can remember dat?'

'And how the hell do you propose to do that?' asked Mikey.

'If Oy can, Oy'm goin' to buy off d' jury.'

'Jayzis, Ned! Buying off a jury's against the law.'

'Nutt'n's against d' law, Mikey, unless ya get caught.'

'I wouldn't like to be in your shoes if Higgins finds out.'

Ned winked. 'It's yer brother's shoes you wouldn't like t' be in.'

*

Supper plates were removed from Nenagh Castle's gaol cells and all lights, except for the flickering flame from a single candle, were extinguished in the cell block. Bob sat silently, patiently plaiting together the strands he'd torn from the old blanket. When he'd finished, he tested them for strength by slipping a loop around a bar of the prison cell and putting his entire weight on it. The plaits grew tight and, when the cord would stretch no longer, he knew had the tool he needed.

Ger McNamara sat in a corner of his cell, his new blanket draped over his head, watching surreptitiously.

'When will we make our move?' he whispered hoarsely.

'In a couple of hours, when d' guards are asleep.'

McNamara was thinking that this simple-minded fool had no idea the price he'd pay for murdering his son, once they were out of this dungeon. Two hours dragged by endlessly and, when they finally heard the key enter the lock on the outer door, Bob slid his rope underneath him, tossed the lice-ridden blanket over his body and feigned sleep. The guard held a candle up high and looked at each of the prisoners. Satisfied, he turned to leave then suddenly turned back again.

'Ring, wake up! I thought the sheriff gave you a new blanket. What are you doing with that rag?'

'D' auld fella was shiverin' so we traded blankets. Mine was warmer.'

The guard laughed. 'By God, Ring,' he scoffed, 'there's good-natured and there's plain stupid.' He closed the outer door and locked it, still laughing.

'When do we go?' rasped McNamara.

'As soon as I tell ya d' details of me plan.'

The old man climbed to his feet, holding the blanket over his head like a shawl. Bob mumbled something and beckoned him over.

'I can't hear ya,' said McNamara sourly.

Bob repeated the action and the old fellow took the blanket off his head and let it fall around his shoulders.

'What's dat ya say?'

Bob put his finger to his lips and McNamara stepped closer to the bars in order to hear. It was the last step those spindly legs would ever make. Bob slipped the noose over Ger's head and snapped it tight, pulling him against the bars of the cell, then he wrapped the rope around his own hand and pulled as hard as he could. The rope was so tight that the old man never even made a gargling sound. Not a wisp of breath escaped his windpipe. He clawed at the noose with his fingers and then his fingernails, but the cord was already buried in the skin of his neck. The dying man began to flail around and, in response, Bob put his foot against the bars to redouble the pull. In less than a minute the old man was still, but Bob held on tightly for a full five. As Ger McNamara slipped to the floor, Bob hissed through clenched teeth.

'Dat was fer you, Edgie.'

He took the end of the cord and looped it over the cross-brace of the bars. He struggled but finally he managed to lift up the corpse and tie the end of the rope tight, leaving the old man's body suspended, his legs stretched out in front of him and his backside just a few inches off the floor.

'Now don't go anywhere, will ya,' he said and laughed. He grabbed the new blanket for himself. 'Ya don't need dis to keep ya warm now,' he told the cadaver, 'ya have d' flames of hell fer dat.' He wrapped the blanket around himself and slept in a corner, undisturbed, except for a few hungry lice.

The next morning arrived bright and sunny and Higgins pulled his covers tighter around himself, thinking he'd grab an extra forty winks before he got out of bed. He only got twenty.

'Sheriff!' came a voice from outside his bedroom door. 'Sir, you have to come down to the gaol at once!'

'What is it now?'

'One of the prisoners is dead, sir. It looks like he hanged himself.'

'Is it Ring?'

'No, sir, it's McNamara.'

That's a surprise, thought Higgins. If one of them was going to commit suicide, I would have put my money on Bob Ring.

'Give me five minutes.'

In four minutes Higgins was there, still buttoning up

his trousers. He looked at the stiff corpse of McNamara and then at Bob Ring, who was busy shovelling spuds and beans into his mouth with a spoon.

'What's this, Ring?'

Bob didn't bother to swallow but spoke around the food in his mouth. 'Heej dead,' he said.

'I can see that! Now swallow your food, man, and tell me what happened.'

Bob swallowed and looked at the corpse as if he was seeing it for the first time.

'Looks like he tied a rope around his neck and den sat down.' Bob shovelled another spoonful of food into his mouth.

'Take that bloody food away from him!' Higgins ordered a guard. Bob tried to hold onto the rim of the plate but the deputy wrestled it away from him.

'Ain't no need to starve a man to death, Sheriff,' he protested. 'Dat fecker ain't goin' nowhere. He's tied to d' bars.'

'Shut up, Ring, this is serious.'

'You t'ink it's serious? Imagine how serious it is fer dat sod, Higgie.'

'When did it happen? … and don't call me Higgie, except behind my back.'

'Right after d' guard came fer inspection, when dey doused d' candles.'

'Bring the guard responsible down here!' ordered Higgins, becoming more exasperated with Bob Ring by the second.

A few minutes later, the guard appeared in his woollen long johns. Higgins looked him up and down, squeezed his eyes tight and turned his face to the heavens.

'Jeeezus Chrrrrrist! I'm running a feckin' madhouse!'

'Feck never sounds right when an Englishman says it,' observed Bob.

'Somebody give that idiot his food back! If he's stuffing his face, perhaps he'll stop talking.' He addressed the offending guard. 'What time did you inspect the prisoners last night?'

'About half nine, sir, at lights out.'

'Was everything in order?'

'Yes, sir, except that Ring here had the ragged old blanket and McNamara had the new one.'

The sheriff looked and noticed that Bob was sitting on the new blanket. 'How do you explain that, Mr. Ring?'

Bob had finished his beans and now he had half a potato in his mouth. He held his hand up and carried on chewing. Higgins was growing livid.

'Spit that out and answer me!'

Bob spit the half-masticated spud out into his hand. 'He wasn't goin' to need it anymore,' he said, and shoved the potato back in his gob.

'I need a drink,' complained Higgins, totally frustrated with the whole affair, 'and it isn't even eight in the morning yet. I only know one person on God's green earth who can cause this much mayhem. Somebody get my horse. I'm going to see Ned Flood!'

If Higgins needed a drink now, in a couple of hours' time he was going to need a barrelful.

*

Ned was preparing Alexander for his meeting with Mr. Wall. He handed the boy a sheaf of papers in a leather bag and a purse with money in it. He also handed him an envelope addressed to the Customs House in Waterford. Outside Hogan's window, he could see Robbie heading down the road in the same direction the carriage would take.

'If yer brother's goin' to Nenagh, Mikey, give him a lift. No matter what he says, don't let him get ya angry. Just listen to what he says and tell me about it later. Remember now, don't let him get ya mad.'

'If he asks,' said Alexander, 'what reason should I give him why we're going to town?'

'Oh, Oy don't know … tell him yer gettin' me some new lace handkerchiefs. Tell him d' ones Oy have are full o' snot. All d' Oirish t'ink Amerrycuns are rich, he might believe it.'

'And why am I going?' asked Michael.

'Take one of d' meat pies Roisin made last night. Tell him she baked a file in it, so Bob can escape.'

'What if Robbie tells Higgins that?'

Ned laughed heartily. 'Higgie's an Englishman. To d' English, a pie is like a sacrament. You could wrap a dog turd in crust and dey'd give it a name. Are d' horses ready, Mick?'

'Ready and waitin',' replied the big man.

'Right so, boys. Ya both know yer jobs, get goin'.'

The carriage had just passed Knigh Cross when Higgins, accompanied by two deputies, stopped them.

'Where's your father, boy?'

'Hogan's, sir.'

'I should have known,' he said and spurred his horse into a gallop.

'He's chewin' a wasp,' remarked Mick and slapped the reins against the horses' backs. A little further down the road they approached Robert walking in the same direction.

Mick pulled on the reins. 'We're headin' to town,' he told him. 'Do ya want a lift?'

Robbie said nothing and just waved them on.

'It's not like my brother to refuse a free ride.'

'Dat blaggard's up to somethin',' replied Mick, as the horses resumed their long trot towards Nenagh bridge.

*

Higgins barged into Hogan's, leaving the door open. Roisin was busy making preparations for the evening's meal and she scowled at Higgins. 'Were you raised in a barn?'

'Sorry, m'um.' He shut the door quietly and slid the latch across to lock it. 'Ned, there was a death in the gaol last night.'

'Anyone we know?' asked Ned innocently.

'You know damn well it was Ger McNamara.'

Ned picked up a piece of bread from the table and chewed a lump off it. 'Be sure t' pass on me condolences to d' family.'

'I know you were behind this, Flood. Bob Ring's too stupid to think up anything like this himself.'

Ned pushed himself away from the table. 'Bob ain't stupid. He just acts dat way.'

'I'm beginning to think that's the case with all you Irish.'

'Only just worked dat one out, Higgie, and you here nearly nineteen years? Maybe you English act clever but really you're stupid.'

'There's no need for insults.'

'Sorry Higgins, you're right, dat was rude. C'mere!' Ned picked up one of Roisin's pies. 'Have dis as a peace offerin'. Roisin made some luvly meat pies last night and dere's one left. Oy was savin' it fer me lunch but you can have it.'

'It's going to take more than a meat pie to get you out of this, Ned Flood, but I'll take the pie and a cup of tea if you have it.'

'O' course we have tea, Higgie. Don't ya know Oy'm in d' import business?'

'Look, Ned….'

'No, you look. You said you were leavin' it to us to stop a war. Dere are two deaths on each side now, everyt'ing's even. Casey and Kerr will no doubt kill each udder and, if dey don't, whichever one of 'em wins will eider be hung by you or killed by me.'

Higgins had to admit that Ned's logic was irrefutable. 'When are you leaving Ireland?' he asked him.

'It sounds like ya want me gone now, Higgie.'

'I'd just like to know when I can expect things to get back to normal.'

'Oy'll leave as soon as d' tobaccy crop's ready, maybe even sooner. I ain't enjoyin' meself anymore. Oy can't just sit around watchin' plants grow. Dat's fer d' farmers … and fer d' birds.'

Morna placed a cup of tea on the table in front of Higgins, along with a warm meat pie. He took a spoonful and put it in his mouth, then closed his eyes in rapture.

'Ladies,' said Ned, 'Oy'd appreciate a moment of privacy wit' d' sheriff.'

Higgins knew that whatever was about to come was deadly serious and he put down his spoon. When the women had vacated the room, Ned leaned forward over the table and quietly began.

'Higgie,' he began, quietly, 'you've bin sheriff here

431

fer a long time. Oy know you and Oy know yer a good man. Ya treat people fair, just like our auld friend Sheriff D'Arcy before ya. You wanted to stop a war, a faction fight as ya call it, but all we did was delay it. Oirland is like a keg of gunpowder ready to go off, can't ya feel it? Dere's a million people in dis country and dey don't know who dey are anymore, or which world dey belong in.'

'Oh please, if you're going to give me the English versus the Irish sermon again …'

'What's done is done, Higgie. Ya can't un-ring a bell. Oy'm just tellin' ya how it is. Oirish people, dey're frus….Oy can never remember dat word, dey're confused and angry and if dey can't take it out on d' English, den dey'll take it out on each udder.'

'My job is to keep the peace, Flood, and I take it as seriously as D'Arcy did. What can I do?'

'One man can't stop a plague, Higgie. It'll be over when dere's bin enough killin'.'

In an accidental stroke of insight, Ned Flood had observed a sociological phenomena that would not be written about for another hundred and fifty years. Anomie is when a cataclysmic change in the economic fortunes of a society causes feelings of alienation and hopelessness in that society's individuals. If political or structural limitations are applied which limit people's ability to achieve goals legitimately, they will turn to a more violent approach. The rate of suicide in Ireland today gives some indication that anomie still exists in a fashion, when violence is turned in on the individuals themselves.

CHAPTER 47

A lexander sat watching Mr. Wall thumb through the pages which Ned had prepared for him. Finally, the solicitor looked up over the top of his reading glasses at the young man seated before him.

'Are you aware of what this is, Alexander?'

'Yes, sir, those are my father's wishes, written in his own hand.'

'They read almost like a last will and testament.'

Alex smiled, 'Hardly that, sir, although they might possibly herald the demise of Mr. Michael Flynn and his recent … endeavours.'

'Let me get this clear. Your father wants the ownership of Hogan's to be passed to Roisin Flynn, with the stipulation that she is not to have her son, Robert Flynn, in her employ.' Wall smiled a faint smile. 'It also states that, if she wishes, she may sell the said property for a fair market value, as long as it's not to the said Robert Flynn.' His smile widened slightly.

'Yes, sir.'

'It further states that ownership of the Gortalocca cottage which was built by Roisin Flynn's husband, Liam, shall also be transferred to her name for

433

perpetuity and that, on her death, it shall pass to whoever is the oldest Flynn heir at the time, again with the stipulation that it is not to be Robert. Your father has a distinct crossed hair when it comes to Robbie, doesn't he, Alexander?' he said, sticking his tongue between his teeth.

'Indeed he does, sir, and if you read on you'll find out just how crossed it is.'

'I can hardly wait,' said Wall, flipping over another page. 'It states here that he wants the land which is currently under cultivation to be signed over to those who work on it, and there are … let me see, fifty-three said workers, each of whom is to receive two acres from the Michael Flynn holdings. Is that correct?'

'Yes sir. Keep reading.'

Mr. Wall dove back into the papers and chuckled, then he banged on the table top and burst into peals of laughter. He took off his glasses. 'Remind me never to get on the wrong side of your father,' he said, wiping his eyes.

Alexander knew exactly was in the notes and he couldn't stifle his own laugh. Even though he wasn't amused by what his father had written, the normally taciturn solicitor's laughter was contagious. Wall read the page a second time and laughed heartily again, banging on the table like a gleeful child. Finally he composed himself.

'Let me be clear,' he said. 'It states here that the above-mentioned land is currently being leased by one Robert Flynn, and that the crops thereon are the sole property of the lessor.'

'That is correct, sir.'

'I see only one flaw in your father's scheme, Alexander. There will need to be three papers signed by

Robert … one for my records, one for the courthouse in Nenagh and one to be kept on central file in Dublin. Robert isn't the brightest of individuals but I don't think even he is foolish enough to sign a blank piece of paper.'

'Do you have a copy of his signature on file, sir?'

'I do but I will have no part in forgery.'

'Would you show me the signature, sir? And did I hear you say you needed to visit the privy?'

'Indeed, thank you for reminding me. I shall be back in ten minutes. You'll be sure to lock the front door, won't you my good man.'

Mr. Wall left the room and Alexander looked at Robbie's signature. He attempted to replicate it several times, to no avail, then he had an idea. He placed the original under the blank sheet, then put them both against a window pane. The sunlight was strong enough for him to trace Robert's signature onto the blank page. He repeated the process on the other two pages and, when Wall returned, he looked at Alexander's work.

'Ah,' he said. 'I see Mr. Flynn must have come in and signed these in my absence. I'm indeed sorry to have missed him, however that's very fortuitous.'

'My father wants to know how long it will take to get the papers registered.'

'I can get them to Nenagh courthouse this afternoon but it will take at least a week to get the papers to Dublin by post.'

'That's too long.'

'I could hire a courier and have them in Dublin in two days, but that will cost an additional one pound sterling.'

'Excellent, sir, use the courier.'

'Very well. Now, young man, we come to the

unpleasant subject of my fees.' Wall made a few scratchings on a piece of paper. 'Including the courier's fee, that comes to a total of … oh, let's round it off … six pounds.'

Alexander counted out the money and handed it over to the solicitor who counted it again, then smiled.

'No honour among thieves, eh boy?'

The implication irritated Alex. 'In fact that is a corruption of Shakespeare, sir,' he said. 'The actual quote is from Henry the Fourth, Part 1, where Falstaff says, 'A plague upon it when thieves cannot be true to one another'.'

'I stand corrected, young sir. I see I shall have to study the Bard more closely.'

Alexander shook the solicitor's hand. He wanted to get out of that office as quickly as possible, the whole business having left him feeling rather slimy. As he was leaving, Wall asked, 'Is it your father's intention to turn Robbie in?'

'No sir, Robert will do that himself.'

Alex walked outside and filled his lungs with the fresh air.

Michael stood outside the gates of Nenagh Castle. He had been denied entry although the meat pie was allowed in. Bob Ring would never see it, of course, the guards would see to that. It seemed that some sort of incident had occurred the night before and Ger McNamara was sharing breakfast with Satan this morning. Sheriff Higgins had left instructions that Bob Ring was to have no visitors until he'd returned from Gortalocca so there was nothing left to do but wait for Mick and Alexander to return in the carriage. Mikey could hear snippets of gossip passing from one mouth to another, as people left the castle. The running theme seemed to be that the phantom of West Cork had returned and had somehow convinced McNamara to hang himself. Michael knew that Ned could do many things but even he couldn't be in two places at once and Mikey himself, along with several other people, had dinner with him last night.

In due course the carriage pulled up and Michael climbed on board. He sat in the seat facing Alexander and noticed that the young man's countenance was more sombre than was usual for him.

'What's troubling you, Alex?' he asked.

'There's something I have to discuss with you, sir. It's with regard to Siobhan.'

Michael felt his skin tingle. He'd heard that Alexander and Siobhan had been keeping company and he vowed that if this boy had in any way violated his daughter, he would throw him out of the coach and onto his head.

'Go on,' he said, his guard now up.

'I want to marry your daughter, sir,' Alexander blurted, 'and I think she wants to marry me.'

Mikey's guard was still up and he narrowed his eyes. 'She's not…'

'With child?' Alex answered the unspoken question. 'No, sir, of course not. We haven't… emm…'

Michael breathed a sigh of relief. 'That's a very big decision for a young man to make,' he said.

'I realise that, sir.'

'What does your da think of your plans? I assume you've told him.'

'He's very much in favour, sir. He says an Irish woman would make a much better wife for me than an English or an American one.'

'Well, this is a surprise. Siobhan is the apple of my eye, as you know, and I'm very proud of her but …'

'But, sir?'

'Well, you do know that Siobhan can be very hot-headed, don't you? There's a lot of her grandmother in her, also she's more ambitious than the average country girl. Siobhan wants more from life than most and she's determined to get it.'

'I know, sir. Da says that's a good thing because sometimes I'm too easily contented with things.'

'Now that we've brought your da into this conversation, it's normal for a son to follow in his father's footsteps. I have to say I'm not comfortable with my daughter being married into a family whose men live from one adventure to another. I wouldn't want Siobhan to become a young widow.'

'No one could travel in my father's footsteps, sir. His shoes are too big and his strides are too long. My plan is to enroll into university and become a solicitor.'

'Ah, like Mr. Wall.'

'No sir, not like Mr. Wall. He's nothing but a toady and a lickspittle.'

'Do you intend taking Siobhan to Amerryca?'

'I do, sir. It's a new land and there are opportunities there which don't exist anywhere else, except perhaps the Australia Colony.'

'Alright so, son, I give you my blessing.'

Mick had been sitting quietly in the driver's seat, up front, and now he belly laughed and turned to his passengers.

'I'm glad ye t'rew d' elephant out,' he said. 'D' horses were gettin' tired.' He thrust out his arm and shook Alexander's hand, then winked at Michael. 'Yer fam'ly just grew a bit, Mikey.'

A grin split Michael's face. 'Now, if I can just get Liam married off,' he said, 'p'raps Morna and me can finally get a bit of peace and quiet, not to mention privacy.'

Mick laughed again. 'Ah so dat's it, is it, ya auld dog? T'inkin' about makin' some more little Hogans, are ye?'

The rest of the trip was spent in light conversation until they crested the little rise which led into Gortalocca. Once again, people had gathered at the crossroads outside Hogan's.

'Now what?' said Mick. Michael didn't like the look of a group of men who were talking animatedly amongst themselves. Mick engaged the brake on the carriage and tied the reins to the lever arm, then he dismounted and used his bulk to clear a path for his passengers.

Again, the door of Hogan's was locked but Siobhan had seen them arrive from a window and, wordlessly, she let the men in, then slid the iron latch back in place behind them.

'What's happened?' asked Michael.

'Dem eejits outside want to know what happened to Casey,' replied Ned. 'Nobody's seen him and dey're lookin' fer an excuse to go across to Ardcroney. Oy'd say dey have mayhem on deir minds.'

'I thought you'd be able to keep a lid on it for a few weeks, at least until emotions had quietened down.'

'So did Oy, especially if Oy kept d' bar closed, but Paulie Gleeson's bin feedin' dem fellas a diet of poteen and it's gettin' hard to tamp down d' fire in deir bellies.'

'I'll talk to him,' ventured Michael.

'Don't bother, bucko, Oy already did. D' auld goat said if Oy troyed to close him down, he'd start a riot. Oy can't even t'reaten him because he don't care whether he lives or dies anymore.'

'I'll get Clancy to try and talk reason with him. They're good friends.'

'Oy had Clancy wit' me sure. Auld Gleeson brought up some shite about his older brother gettin' killed by Sheriff D'Arcy when a gang of roughnecks tried to kill Liam Flynn. It was forty-odd years ago, if ya don't mind. Typical feckin' Oirish. When ya want 'em to remember somet'in, dey forget, and when ya hope dey've forgotten somet'in, dey drag it up and t'row it back in yer face years later.'

'What are you going to do?'

'If Tommy don't show up in d' next couple of days, Oy suppose Oy'll have to go and find him.'

*

Kerr's trail wasn't a hard one for Tommy to follow. Someone with only one eye and his face badly scarred was always going to find it hard to be inconspicuous. Tommy discovered that Kerr had been drinking at a bar in Cloughjordan where he had bragged about a stick fight he'd been in recently, and how he'd bested a man half his age. Most of the patrons who'd heard it told Tommy they'd taken the tale with a pinch of salt … a man who was blind on one side would be at a serious disadvantage, after all … but that it had made for a good tale and, the way Kerr told it at least, it was a heroic battle. A good story is a good story, whether it's fact or fiction, especially when the listeners are in their cups.

When he'd left, Kerr had told them he was heading towards Templemore, by way of Moneygall. Tommy went to Templemore but couldn't find anyone who'd seen the blaggard. He saw a road which led, more or less, towards Kilkenny and Casey decided this would be Kerr's most likely route. As he trudged along, Tommy day-dreamed, as young men are prone to do. He thought about what he'd do to the one-eyed man when he caught up with him. Perhaps he'd put the other eye out or maybe he'd crush all his limbs, the same way the bastard did to poor little Edgie. When he got back to Gortalocca, he'd get a hero's welcome and all the men would buy him drinks, just to hear him tell the story.

Ahead of him, at a fork in the road, he saw a two-storey farmhouse, the ground floor having been converted into a bar. As he approached, he caught the putrid sour smell of swine. He jingled his purse. He had his wages from Ned, almost three shillings, and he decided that if he bought a beer the landlord might more readily give him information. The hand-painted sign over the door read 'COX'S'. The smell of pig grew stronger and he wrinkled his nose.

Paint was peeling from the yellow front door and, when he tried to open it, he found it was stuck. He pushed harder and it opened. A bell above the door announced his arrival and a man appeared from the back, wiping his hands on his trousers.

'What can I do for you?' he said cordially He reeked of pig.

'I'd like a beer.'

'Dat'll be tuppence … in advance.' He watched as Tommy took out his purse and craned his neck to see the contents.

Tommy put the two pennies on the bar and the man scooped them up. He poured a flagon of ale.

'Tell me,' said Tommy. 'Have ya seen a one-eyed fella in d' last couple o' days? He has a scar runnin' right down his face.'

The barman smiled disarmingly. 'Indeed I have. Ya must mean Kerr, Ciaran Kerr. D' ya have business wit him?'

'Ya could say dat,' said Casey. 'He killed me best friend.' Tommy had given away too much information.

'He's out d' back sure, sleepin' off a bellyful o' beer in me barn.'

Tommy was elated. Not only had he found his quarry but he could even creep up on the piece of shite while he was sound asleep. 'I'll give ya a shillin' if ya show me where,' he said.

'Jayzis, ya have a whole shillin' in dat purse o' yours?'

'I have almost t'ree,' boasted Tommy.

'Come wit' me, I'll show ya.'

The proprietor led him to a low door at the back of the bar and, when Tommy bent to go through it, the man slipped a two-pound cudgel out from under the bar and struck him a blow, just below the nape of his neck, Tommy went down. As he lay senseless and moaning, he received a second blow to the top of his head and he became still and silent. Blood pooled around his crushed skull. The owner had slaughtered Tommy Casey in the same way he would kill a pig and now he yelled out the back door.

'Cousin! Come and help me drag this piece of meat to the barn!'

CHAPTER 48

'Captain Rackham, we have a sail dead astern,' announced Jonesey.

'What do you make of her?'

'Can't tell, sir, she's too far away.'

'Take a new heading, Jonesey, take us four points north.'

The captain looked at his watch; it was a little past four in the afternoon. He unrolled his charts. They were forty miles south-west of Cornwall, on a westerly heading, and there was plenty of sea room between Prosperity and the English coast. With the south-east breeze, the ship was pointing into the wind as far as she could without tacking. All he could do was wait. It was probably nothing more than a fishing vessel, he thought, no reason to get jumpy. Sails were a common sight on the sea lanes.

An hour later Jack was on deck with his brass telescope trained on the horizon astern.

'She's a few points north of dead astern now, sir,' remarked his second.

'I can see that, Jonesey. No need for alarm just yet. Resume our westerly course.'

A quarter of an hour later, the distant sail was dead astern again and Jack was becoming slightly apprehensive.

'It'll be sunset in two hours,' he said. 'I don't want any lights showing, Jonesey. As soon as it gets dark, we'll tack the ship south-west and get some room between us.'

'Aye aye, sir.'

He went below to think. That braying jackass, Sally, he thought. He gave me a kindly suggestion about where to go in France to get rid of the tobacco, and now I have a hold full of untaxed French brandy. Willoughby's probably waiting near the Isle of Man for us to show up, then he'll pounce when we're off-loading. Don't get paranoid, he told himself. Neither Sally nor Willoughby can guess what's in another man's mind. He decided he'd head to Fastnet as soon as he shook the tail, then up to Galway to sell the brandy on the Irish market, or get customs papers forged for it and bring it back to England. In the meantime, he needed a drink and a few hours of shut-eye.

Four hours later, Jonesey came below with another announcement and Jack woke with a start.

'Sir, we've been heading south-west for a few hours now and that same ship is off our port beam. She's running under full lights.'

'I'll come on deck,' said Jack, grumpily.

Sure enough, the same ship was due south of Prosperity, a little closer now and lit up like a Saturday night in Charles Town.

'The fecker's not worried about being seen, that's for sure,' muttered Rackham, half to himself.

'But how the devil can he see us in the dark, sir?' said Jones. 'Is he guessing where we are?'

Jack looked astern and saw that their wake was phosphorescent with the glow of plankton. It was as though they were leaving a trail of breadcrumbs behind them.

'He's not guessing, Jonesey, he can see us,' he said, pointing to the glowing stern wake. 'That buck-toothed bastard's herding us like a sheepdog and there's not a damn thing we can do about it.'

'Maybe we should think about jettisoning the cargo while it's still dark, sir,' suggested Jones tentatively.

The same thought had occurred to Jack but that would be tantamount to conceding the game.

'Unthinkable, Mr. Jones.'

*

It was the predawn hours and Ned couldn't sleep. He went downstairs to his study and stoked up the embers of the fire in the grate, then he lit an oil lamp and unrolled a map of Ireland. When he was young, he'd done things spontaneously, and he'd always got through with a combination of sheer luck and his own innate cunning. Now he needed to employ the ways that Robert D'Arcy, the old sheriff of Lower Ormond, had taught him. Preparation and planning were essential if he was to succeed in this operation. He circled the town of Ardcroney on the map, that's where Tommy would have taken up Kerr's trail. Then he drew a circle around Kilkenny, since that was Kerr's suspected destination. Perhaps, he thought, it would be advisable for him to head straight for Kilkenny, then retrace his way back to Ardcroney in the hope of crossing paths with Casey and Kerr from the other direction. He calculated that, with a coach and well-rested horses, he and Mick could be in Kilkenny in a little over a day. It wasn't a game this time, however, and he wasn't about to engage either man in a stick fight. In this case, winner takes all. His gaze wandered up to an old fowling piece which hung over the fireplace. He took it down and inspected the shotgun. Old man Johnson must have been a keen sportsman in his day, he mused. He cocked the weapon and inspected the flint. Perhaps he'd take the piece down to Gortalocca when the sun rose and have Michael or Clancy cut off the barrel to a handier length. If it had to be used, it wasn't going to be for shooting geese or ducks at long range. Ned was no marksman and he knew it. A wise man knows his limitations.

Alexander was now back at the big house at Johnstown now with his father, there having been no reason for him to stay on at Mick's after Moira left. He was having trouble sleeping on his soft feather bed and he went downstairs. He saw the light coming from his father's study and went in.

'Put d' kettle on d' fire,' said Ned to his son. 'We're up before d' servants.'

Alexander shook the copper kettle to see if there was enough water in it for a few cups of tea, then he hung it on the fireplace and threw another piece of turf on the smouldering embers. A few strokes of the bellows was all it took to get flames lapping around the bottom of the pot.

'When you go looking for Tommy and Kerr, Da, I want to go with you.'

'Dat ain't happenin'.'

'I thought you wanted us to do things together, as father and son.'

'Not dis, Alexander. Dis is a dirty business and t'ings

446

might get ugly.' As if to illustrate the danger, he picked up the fowling piece and aimed it at the fire. 'Did ya ever see a man get his head blown off wit' one of dese t'ings, boyo?'

'No, but I've seen a man's face smashed to a pulp with a bata, and a little boy's arms crushed with one.'

'Yes, and Oy'm sorry ya had to see dat. Meself and Mick leave fer Kilkenny tomorra.'

'Then you won't reconsider?'

'No, dis discussion is over. You get yerself to Gortalocca and make yer weddin' plans wit' d' pretty Hogan girl and we'll have an almighty celebration when Oy get back.' Ned studied his son's face for a moment in the glow of the fire. 'Oy can hear dem little wheels turnin' in yer head, boy. You're not to follow us, do ya hear?'

'I won't follow you, Da, I promise.'

Alex wasn't lying. He had no intention of following his father. He would try to pick up Tommy's trail from this direction. He put a few spoons of tea into a pot and poured in boiling water.

*

Robbie arrived in Limerick City late in the evening. His intention was to go straight to the administrative office of the Chief Tax Collector as soon as they opened in the morning. He would report the nefarious goings-on in Gortalocca. He would inform him about the illegal crop of tobacco and about how the sheriff and Nenagh's senior solicitor were in on it, along with a man named Ned Flood, who also happened to be the legendary phantom priest of West Cork. Robert looked forward to seeing the tax man's face.

As it turned out, Robbie was only able to get as far as the chief's subordinate, who had been unsure as to whether he should throw this Tipperary idiot out on his ear or contact the local authorities to report a madman in his office.

The assistant chose the former option and Robert strolled down to the riverfront sulkily. Perhaps he should write down the information he had in the form of a letter and send it to the chief himself. He decided it was harder to ignore information when it came by way of post, since bureaucrats in other government offices might have received the same report. He went looking for a dry goods store to find paper, a pen and ink. He would write his letter, post it, then head back to Gortalocca and act the innocent. He wasn't to know that his letter would get stuffed at the bottom of a large pile of official correspondence and that no one would even read it for weeks.

*

Jonesey stood in the captain's quarters. 'We lost sight of her, Cap'n.'

'You did what? How in God's name can you lose a ship, man?'

'She fell off us just before dawn and we think she's at the back of us again. We can't tell for certain because she's got the sun behind her.'

'Jonesey, I think it might be a good idea to take the barrels out of the hold and lash them topsides. We can dump them if we have to.'

'With all that weight on deck, sir, we'll sail like a turtle.'

'If you have a better plan, Mr. Jones, I'd like to hear

it. I don't mind admitting that this fellow has me unnerved.'

It was the first time Jones had ever heard the captain say something of that nature and his confidence began to wane. 'What's the brandy worth, sir?'

'About a hundred and eighty pounds. Why?'

'What's the ship worth?'

'I don't know … probably twenty times that.'

'It's something to keep in mind, Cap'n.'

'Leave me, Jones, I need time to think. Tell me when you spot her again.'

The captain spread his charts out on the table in front of him and studied them. They were a day and a half from Fastnet Rock at their current pace and they'd be slower once the cargo was on deck. That meant that if Sally continued to play his game of cat and mouse with them, they'd be close to the shoals of Clear Island in the dark tomorrow night. If Sally was afraid to risk his ship, they could shake him off by using the strait between Clear and Sherkin Islands. It wasn't the best plan he'd ever had but it was the only one he could think of, short of jettisoning the contraband.

*

Ned and Mick sat in Hogan's with the map spread out in front of them. Mick pretended to know what he was looking at but, in truth, the map might just have well have been written in hieroglyphics. In any case, he knew the way to Kilkenny better than he knew the way to Waterford. He yawned and stretched his big body. He'd already heard Ned go over the plan one time too many.

'Is it too early for a beer?' he said.

Siobhan walked in. 'Where's Alexander?' she asked.

Ned replied without looking up from the map. 'He's at home, sulkin'. Dat's what he does when he don't get his own way. Get used to it, girl.'

'Why's he sulkin'?' asked the pretty young woman.

Ned looked at her now. 'Because he wanted to come wit' me,' he said, 'and Oy told him he's to stay here.'

'I'm glad,' said Siobhan, relieved. 'It might be too dangerous fer him.'

'Dat's why Oy did it, but dat's not what Oy told him. Oy said he has to stay to help plan a weddin'.'

The girl face coloured scarlet and Ned laughed.

'The blushing's a Flynn thing,' said Roisin.

Clancy arrived, cradling the sawn-off fowling piece, and he handed it to Ned. Ned shouldered the weapon and aimed it upward, swinging it from side to side. The thirty-eight inch barrels had been cut in half, making the gun handier to use at close quarters.

'Remember d' long knife ya made fer Sheriff D'Arcy all dem years ago, Jamie?' Jamie nodded. 'Well Oy still have it, it's back home in Amerrycuh.'

Clancy grinned. 'I made it from d' tip of a sabre he'd asked me to cut down in size.'

'Oy know, bucko, he told me. What you don't know is dat t'ing saved me life down in Cork, when d' Prussians was after me. Dat means Oy owe ya me life, James Clancy.'

'Ah g'way,' said Clancy, modestly. 'I'm just glad yer alive.'

'Dat's somet'in we have in common!' exclaimed Ned, smiling. 'Now, Oy'm goin' to make ya a business proposition, Mr. Clancy, to show me gratitude.' Jamie looked puzzled. 'You come to Amerrycuh wit' me and

Oy'll set ya up in d' finest blacksmith shop in Charles Town. Dere's no strings, it's just me own way of sayin' t'anks.'

'You can't take Clancy!' protested Roisin.

'Why not, missus? Oy'm makin' d' same offer to Michael and d' same to yerself too.'

'You're a cheeky bastard, Ned Flood,' she snapped.

'Oy've bin called worse, woman. But while Oy'm gone lookin' fer Casey, Oy want yous all to t'ink about me offer.'

CHAPTER 49

T he day passed quickly in Gortalocca. Ned gave Michael instructions to have a proper blacksmith shop built on the site of the old one. He suggested that, this time, a roof of slate from the quarry near Portroe should be used to prevent a repeat of Gortalocca's disaster.

'A village needs a blacksmith shop,' Ned told him.

Mikey pointed out that only about half the workers had showed up over the last few days to work the fields.

'Oy give 'em an inch and dey take a mile,' he said sourly. 'Get d' names of d' ones workin' and make sure d' udders don't get paid.'

Back at Johnstown, Alex was busy trying on various articles of clothing, choosing those most comfortable and functional. He decided that the English greatcoat was too cumbersome so he would wear the shorter American-style, indigo-dyed jacket which draped only to his fingertips. He put on the saffron-coloured Irish shirt which he'd been told was called a leine. Cinched at the waist, it was loose and comfortable. He paired it with tight, white English riding breeches and knee-high black boots and looked at himself in a full-length mirror. Who am I, he asked himself, and what the hell am I?

He divided up his money, five shillings in a purse that he'd carry on his person and another fifteen that he'd keep in a sack with an extra leine. It crossed his mind that he would be vulnerable to any bandit who might waylay him on the road and so he decided he needed weaponry. An unarmed man is a man without options.

He wandered into his father's quarters. There was a handsome cased pair of duelling pistols on the nightstand next to his father's bed. Alex smiled. His old man wouldn't be able to hit a damned thing with those, he'd be better off grabbing them by the barrel and using them as clubs. He chose a plain, ugly sixty-nine calibre horse pistol. He would put it in a scabbard on the left side of his saddle, where he could draw it easily and threaten any would-be robber. He buckled a sheathed rapier over his short coat, so that it hung on his left side. All the lessons that Ned had insisted he take had made him feel comfortable with a blade in his hand. His previous swordplay had been just that. Now that he knew he might have to engage a man in mortal combat, it made the hair prickle on the back of his neck. He wasn't sure if he had the mettle his father had.

Alexander stood before a mirror and drew the blade. It made a hissing sound, like a snake, as it came out of the scabbard. He turned sideways and assumed a fencer's position. He remembered what Paulie Gleeson had said when he'd sparred with Petey. Trodaireacht, sword and dagger, he needed a short weapon for his left hand. He knew what he wanted and went back to his own room. He rummaged through his belongings and found it, the ten inch double-sided blade which the frontiersmen in America called a 'toothpick'. Those fellows used it for everything a long rifle couldn't do, from skinning a deer, to eating, to using it in combat with the red men or each other. He held it in a stabbing fashion, remembering something an old mountain man had told him years ago … that it was too easy for a knife to be knocked out of your grasp if you held it like a pointer. You must hold it so that, when your hands are up, you can use the tip to block a man's punch, or use the edge to hook his wrist. Alex again stood in front of the mirror and sparred with his reflection, Pionsoireacht, thrust with the tip and withdraw. He was familiar with the style, at least in theory.

Back in Gortalocca, Ned was trying to teach Mick the basics of firearms, with little success. He handed the big man a pistol he'd been carrying for the last few days. Mick looked at it like a monkey looking at a pocket watch and handed it back.

'Dere's nutt'n to it Mick. Ya just pull d' hammer back, point it at whatever ya want to hit, and pull d' trigger. C'mere, Oy'll show ya.'

A small gathering of locals had stood to watch the display. Ned cocked the hammer and fired at a tree stump about ten feet away. He missed.

Mick looked at him suspiciously. 'Are you sure ya killed all dem Prussians in Cork?'

'Here, Oy'll show ya again,' said Ned, recharging the pistol. 'Oy'm a bit out of practice.' Roisin stifled a snigger.

He took careful aim and pulled the trigger. The hammer snapped and nothing happened.

'Ah feck!' he said, somewhat embarrassed now. 'Oy forgot to prime d' pan.'

A buzz went through the crowd and Ned ignored it. He placed a small amount of black powder in the priming pan and moved a step closer. He pointed the weapon at the stump and fired. This time, when the smoke cleared, a splinter off the edge of the log was the only evidence of a glancing strike.

'Oy hate dese feckin' t'ings!' he exclaimed, realising his credibility was rapidly ebbing away. He passed the pistol to Mick and motioned for Michael to hand him the shotgun. He cocked both hammers and touched off both triggers at once. The gun roared a double boom and kicked so hard that he almost dropped it. The air filled with a pale grey smoke and, as the cloud cleared, it was plain to see that the log had almost been reduced to fragments by the goose shot.

'Now,' said Ned triumphantly. 'Dat's how Oy killed dem blaggards in Cork.'

'Was dey wooden soldiers?' came a gibe from the crowd.

'Who said dat?' exclaimed Ned. No one owned up. 'Oy didn't need guns to kill dem Jaegers,' he said. 'Oy used me head.'

He turned his back to the onlookers to reload his pistol and the same voice piped up. 'So ya beat 'em to death wit' yer noggin?' The crowd tittered.

Ned ignored the retort and continued to fill the pistol with goose-shot, just as he'd done in Cork almost a generation ago. This time he remembered to prime the gun. He pointed it at the log and splinters flew in all directions. He turned and scowled at the mob.

'Anybody got anyt'ing to say now?'

A hush fell over the crowd.

*

Jack Rackham was having an equally discouraging day. He stood on the fantail of his schooner for what seemed like endless hours and stared at the horizon. The wind had freshened and Prosperity heeled uncomfortably with the extra weight of the barrels on her deck. The white speck which was their pursuer was still dead astern. Why doesn't the bugger just close with us and get it over with, he asked himself. What's he doing? What the hell is he thinking?

Jonesey broke the captain's concentration. 'Any change in his position, Cap'n?'

'No!' snapped Rackham. 'Don't you think I'd have mentioned it?'

'Looks like some weather ahead of us, sir. Should I pipe the men on deck to shorten sail?'

'Not yet, Mr. Jones.' Jack turned his attention astern, then wrenched his focus away from the hunter and peered forward. 'Head straight for that squall under full sail. Maybe we can lose him in the weather.' Even Jack doubted his own words. That sod Sally was a bulldog in the guise of a donkey.

In less than half an hour, Prosperity was entering the curtain of rain. The ship was still under full sail and Jonesey was having the devil of a time keeping the ship on an even keel.

'Cap'n, we have to either shorten sail or get rid of some of the cargo on deck.'

'Pipe the men on deck then and shorten sail,' said Jack absent-mindedly. He had lost sight of Sally's craft in the weather. That meant the pursuer couldn't see him either. 'As soon as we have the canvas shortened, we'll jibe and head due north.'

'It'll be nasty, Cap'n, what with all our weight topsides.'

'I have complete confidence in your abilities, Mr. Jones. Now get the available crew on the weather side. We'll need all the weight we can to windward.'

A short time later, Prosperity was running under reefed sails. The jib was down and Rackham kept the mizzen up.

'Prepare to jibe,' he shouted. The men rushed to the starboard rail and grabbed anything they could to steady themselves. 'Jibe ho!' he yelled. Jonesey fought the wheel and brought her about. For a sickening few moments the ship stood still. The booms swung around with a bang and the rattle of running rigging, when the wind filled her sails from the opposite side. Jonesey was engaged in a wrestling match with the wind, the sea on one side and the ship in between. For a few seconds, the vessel was in grave danger of capsizing as Prosperity leapt forward, but Jones fought and brought her under control.

'Nice work, Mr. Jones,' said the captain as he exhaled the breath he'd been holding.

'I think I've shit meself, sir,' replied Jones.

'Keep this heading. That fecker can't have guessed what we've done.'

*

Willoughby sat in his favourite watering hole in Baltimore. He stood up, finished the last drop of his claret, straightened out his uniform and walked outside. He inhaled a great gulp of the sea air and looked skyward.

'You're in check, Jack,' he said aloud. 'The game's

almost over.' He walked to the wharf where his longboat awaited and he felt very pleased with himself as he climbed aboard, finding it hard to hide the smile on his face. The oarsmen pushed off and began the rhythmic cadence that would soon bring them to the Albatross.

It had been Sally's plan but, since Willoughby was in command, he would receive full credit for it. He would take the Albatross out and wait, anchored in the shadow of Sherkin Island, while Whippet drove his quarry to him. Sally had described it to him as a grouse hunt, where the beaters drove the game towards the concealed hunters. The biggest problem he faced now was how to minimise Sally's contribution and maximise his own. He was aware that, although Sally might look silly and sound ridiculous, his appearance belied the mind he possessed.

Sally had a plan of his own and he didn't like Willoughby one bit.

*

After three hours of battling the storm, Rackham gave new orders.

'Come about, Mr. Jones, and take her on a heading due west. We're going to thread the needle between Clear and Sherkin in the dark.'

'That's difficult enough in the light of day, Cap'n, and it's a wild night.'

'I checked the barometer, Jonesey, and it's rising fast. With a little luck we may get ourselves out of this storm with enough lead time on Sally to get us through.'

'What if he heads us off and is waiting for us on the other side, sir?'

It would be another hundred years until light bulbs were invented but, if they'd had them in the eighteenth century, one of them would have lit up over Jack's head now.

'That's it, Jonesey! You're a bloody genius!'

Jones looked baffled. He'd been called a lot of names in his life but genius wasn't one of them.

'What did I say?' he muttered.

'The reason Whippet hasn't come up and sailed us down is that she was never supposed to. Willoughby wants the credit for capturing me and he doesn't want to share it with his junior.'

'How does that change our situation, sir?'

Jack thought for a moment. 'When we get out of this storm,' he said, 'and if we still have a couple of hours' daylight, then we can stash the brandy in one of South Cork's bays.'

'What happens if we haven't shook Whippet off our tail by then?'

'Then it's checkmate, Mr. Jones.'

CHAPTER 50

Alexander's preparations were complete, so he saddled the chestnut and headed for Gortalocca. He had no intention of telling anyone his plan but he wanted to see Siobhan before he left. He passed Mick's house and he thought about old Moira. He'd made a promise not to tell anyone about their last conversation but, if he was ever asked, perhaps he would just make allusion to it. He was going to be asked. In fact he was about to undergo an interrogation.

When he opened the door and walked into Hogan's, Mick was the first to address him. This was a rarity in itself, since he was a man of few words.

'You were stayin' up at my place,' he said. 'I've just bin down to see Moira. Her stuff's gone and dere's no sign of her. When did you see her last?'

Alexander did his best to feign ignorance. 'I've been staying at the big house the last couple of nights.'

'Dat's not an answer, Alexander,' said Ned. 'When was d' last time you saw d' auld woman?'

'A few days ago, the day after Edgie died.'

Roisin joined in the cross-examination now. 'What did she say to you?'

'She swore me to secrecy,' replied Alex enigmatically. There's a funny thing about secrets and oaths. We hold our own to be sacred but we rarely have a problem betraying other people's.

'What secret, Alexander?' asked Roisin, growing uneasy.

'If I told you, then it wouldn't be a secret anymore and I would have betrayed the old lady's trust.'

'Did she say where she was going?'

'She said she was going away?'

'Where?'

'She just said, away.'

'Did she say when she'll be back?'

'Never.'

A sensation of shock permeated the room. 'We have to find her!' gasped Siobhan.

'She said no one was to go looking for her. She said she's lived long enough and she's tired.'

Siobhan understood exactly what she'd meant by that. Old Moira had told her about the old ones who just upped and left in times of hardship, so that the younger ones could live. She began to sob softly.

Roisin wasn't satisfied. 'We have to organise a search party,' she said. 'God only knows what could happen to a frail old lady!'

'You won't find her,' said Alex, looking Roisin squarely in the eyes, 'and even if you did, would you hold her against her wishes? Would you want to keep her captive just to satisfy your own consciences?'

'Don't be impertinent, Alexander!' snapped Roisin.

'Impertinent? When was the last time anyone ever visited Moira just to spend some time with her? Who was the last person to bother with her at all unless they needed her help? I can tell you because she told me.'

'Is that right?' said Roisin indignantly.

'That's right. She told me it was a young man called Liam Flynn. She told me he's been dead a long time now and she said I reminded her of him. After what she told me about him, I'm proud of that.'

'You?' Roisin spat. 'You're nothing like Liam.'

'No, Mam, Moira was right,' said Michael. 'Alexander's more like da than even I am.'

Roisin's eyes stung. She didn't want this argument to be over but she knew it was. 'Well, I don't think so.' She turned and walked outside where no one would see her cry.

'Now look what ya've done,' said Ned. 'Ya've upset d' un-upsettable. Yer lucky she didn't clout ya on d' way out.'

'I didn't mean to distress her,' said Alex in an apologetic tone.

'Here's a lesson fer ya, boy. When it comes t' women, sometimes a little soft soap is better den d' unvarnished truth.'

'You'll never lie to me, will ya Alex?' cooed Siobhan.

Alex looked into her eyes. 'Of course not,' he said. Thank God she hadn't asked if he'd always tell her the truth. He wasn't about to tell Siobhan or anyone else that he would be leaving on his quest tomorrow, a few hours after Mick and his father left on theirs.

As if the day wasn't going badly enough, Robbie Flynn returned from his sojourn to Limerick. However, instead of his usual pompous, arrogant self, his trip had seemed to improve his mood considerably and he appeared good-humoured, sociable even. It was so out of character that even Roisin noticed and everyone was thinking the same thing. What's he up to? Ned already knew and he also knew that his own time in Ireland was rapidly drawing to a close. After a while, Ned asked Robbie if he'd like a job. Robert was delighted at first but, when Ned invited him outside to discuss it, he hesitated. He was afraid that the all-knowing, all-powerful Ned Flood might have got wind of the reason for his trip to Limerick. Finally, he consented.

Once they were outside Ned spoke to Robbie in hushed tones, as one conspirator might to another. They walked to the old churchyard.

'Here's what Oy'd like ya to do fer me, Robbie. Oy want ya to go down to Nenagh and hang around d' courthouse. When ya find out who d' jury in Bob Ring's trial is, Oy want ya to make a note o' deir names and bring d' list back to me. Oy'll give ya five shillin's in advance and one more fer each name. Now, do ya t'ink ya can handle dat?'

Ned knew he could get the names from Wall for nothing but he was weaving a tangled web around Robbie, the likes of which even God himself would be hard-pressed to undo. Robbie agreed whole-heartedly. Being paid for just hanging around was, after all, his dream job. Ned told Robbie it wouldn't be a good idea to go back inside Hogan's tonight because, if Mikey found out what an easy job he'd been given, he'd be jealous. Robert went straight home and Ned was satisfied. For one evening, at least, he wouldn't have to look at Robert Flynn's stupid face.

Ned returned to the bar alone. 'You didn't hurt my boy, did you?' asked Roisin immediately.

'He was still alive when he left me, missus.'

'Did you give him a job?'

'Oy did.'

'It can't have had anything to do with hard work,' said Michael. 'Was it to do with drinking?'

'Or talkin'?' added Mick.

'Not at all,' replied Ned. 'Oy gave him a job just standin' around.'

'Ah well he'll be good at that sure,' said Roisin.

'Every man has his place,' smiled Ned, 'and Oy t'ink Oy've finally worked out where Robert's should be.'

What he didn't say was that he'd worked out Australia would be an excellent place for Robbie and that his passage there should be courtesy of the Crown.

*

Speaking of the Crown, Jack was having his own problems with the Royal Navy. Prosperity had sailed clear of the squall. There was a glorious sunset, as often happens after a storm, and Jack had decided that, since Whippet was nowhere in sight, he would just claw his way south past Fastnet Rock and show the Royal Navy his arse. He wasn't to know that he was about to get it spanked by Lieutenant Sally.

'Cap'n, come on deck and look at this.'

'What is it now, Jonesey?'

'It's Whippet, sir. She's only about four miles away.'

'You have to be joking.'

'No sir, sorry sir. She's right off our port beam and she's pacing us, about four miles away.'

'Very well. Keep her headed west, Mr. Jones. We might as well keep going and see where this leads.'

'Why hasn't she signalled us to heave to, Cap'n?'

'Because Sally is enjoying the chase, Jones, and he doesn't want it to end.'

Rackham went on deck and looked over the port

rail. Whippet had closed to within three miles now and she signalled for Prosperity to heave to.

'The game's over, Jonesey. It's checkmate. Order the men to comply.'

'Should we cut the barrels loose, sir?'

'It's too late for that now,' said the captain, his tone one of resignation. 'He has us in plain sight.'

'He's signalling permission to come aboard, sir.' Jones handed the telescope to Jack and Rackham looked through it at his adversary, now only a mile away.

'Signal permission granted,' he said. 'No doubt he wants to come aboard to gloat over his victory. He deserves it I suppose. He's won fair and square.'

Captain Jack Rackham went below to put on his best uniform. A surrender is a formal occasion and protocol must be met. Within half an hour he was on deck again and the boat from Whippet was bounced against the hull.

'Permission to come aboard, Captain Rackham,' shouted Sally.

'Permission granted,' replied Jack.

Sally climbed the rope ladder to the deck of Prosperity and looked at the barrels tied to the gunwales. Jack followed his gaze.

'Let's go below, Captain Rackham. I have something I wish to speak with you about.'

Jack glanced at the Whippet, just a hundred yards away now, and he noticed that her guns weren't run out. He looked back at Sally and saw that infuriating buck-toothed grin across his face.

'Shall we?'

As they were going below, Sally remarked, 'Jolly good chase, wasn't it?' Jack didn't answer. When they entered the cramped captain's quarters, Sally asked, 'What day is it Captain?'

'It's the thirty-first of May,' said Jack, 'but you know damn well what day it is, Lieutenant.'

Sally brayed his donkey laugh. 'I do indeed, Jack, and as of midnight tonight I am no longer in the employ of the Admiralty.'

'You resigned?' exclaimed Jack. 'But your promotion …'

'While you were in France drinking wine and eating cheese, I received a dispatch saying that my application for promotion had been denied, courtesy of that bastard Willoughby. He didn't want me to be his superior in this endeavour. He wanted to arrest you personally. My response was to tender my resignation forthwith and it is effective as of midnight tonight.'

'Does Willoughby know?'

'I doubt it.'

'But you're still in the Royal Navy as of this moment.'

'A mere formality. If I could have got off my ship when I received the dispatch, I would have walked home.'

'Why did you keep up the chase?'

'Because I was enjoying myself, of course. I was imaging you shitting ballast stones whenever I kept popping up.' He brayed again.

'What will you do now that you've caught me? By the way, how did you guess I was going to sail north in that storm?'

'I'll answer your second question first, Captain Rackham. Pure serendipity, call it the Devil's own luck, if you will. Whippet started to take on water and I feared she'd founder, so I went to storms'ls and ran

466

with the wind and seas. When I got out of the rain curtain, there you were, sitting pretty.' He laughed like a forester cutting a log but, strangely, it didn't grate on Jack's nerves this time. 'As to the first question, I see you have ten barrels of France's finest invention. You will cut four barrels loose. Let's call it the spoils of war.'

'And Willoughby?'

'Willoughby? Who's Willoughby? Now, let's drink to our game, Jack. Jolly good sport, wouldn't you say?' Sally smiled like a piano keyboard. 'Don't concern yourself with him. He'll be sitting in the dark, anticipating victory, and I am going to sail around in circles until midnight, then I'm entering Baltimore harbour and I'm going to have a drink of my French brandy. You, Captain Rackham, can go wherever the hell you please.'

Just one more thing, Sally, how will you be recording this in the ship's log?'

'I lost you in the storm. My ship's rigging failed and the brandy was simply flotsam which we recovered off the Irish coast.'

Jack raised his glass. 'You're just enough of a scoundrel to be interesting, Lieutenant.'

'I'll drink to that and, as the Irish say, safe home, Captain Rackham.' He laughed his peculiar laugh and this time, Jack joined in.

CHAPTER 51

I n Johnstown, a light misty rain was falling in the gloom of the early morning. Ned was already up. He was packing a few of his belongings and Alexander was watching him with a measure of apprehension, akin to that of walking through a graveyard at night. The young man was anxious for his father to leave but, at the same time, a feeling of dread hung in the air around him.

'Me and Mick should be in Urlingford by dis evenin', boyo, and tomorra by midday we'll be in Kilkenny. If we don't find d' bastard dere, we'll just work our way back here. We shouldn't be gone longer den four, maybe five days at d' outside.'

Alexander didn't speak, he just watched his father in silence. 'It's all in d' preparation, Alex, always remember dat.'

Mick had been feeding the horses and hitching them up to the carriage and now he poked his head inside the front door. 'D' horses are waitin', Ned,' he yelled.

Ned picked up the shotgun and the horse pistol that he'd used the day before, along with a flask of black powder and a small sack of lead shot. He put the pistol in his belt under his greatcoat.

'Carry me bag downstairs will ya, Alex.'

'What are you going to use the pistol for, Da? You know you can't hit a damn thing with it.'

'Oy have it loaded wit' goose-shot. Wit' dat many little balls comin' out d' end, Oy have to hit somet'in. If not, Oy'll use it as a club. Anyway, it ain't fer me, Mick can keep it in d' carriage by his feet. If any rascals try to bother us, he can shake it at 'em and scare 'em away.'

Alexander carried his father's carpet bag down the stairs and, when he got to the door, Mick took it from him as if it was as light as a feather and stashed it in the boot of the carriage. Ned had followed Alexander down the stairs cradling the shortened shotgun in his arms like a baby. He stopped at the door and checked his purse. He had four pounds in sterling and some shillings. Just because he was going on a short trip didn't mean he had to rough it. He tousled the young man's hair as if he was a child.

'Don't worry, boyo, and keep an eye out fer Casey. If he turns up, hide him in d' barn.'

Alexander nodded. He couldn't shake the uneasy feeling. Ned climbed up into the carriage and waved to his son. Alexander returned the wave and stood in the open door, watching as the horses carried the two men into the morning mist and out of sight.

He returned to his room and took stock of his provisions. He had the sack under his bed, except for the spare horse pistol which he'd left in his father's room, so he went and retrieved it. He decided he would try it out in the barn. He unscrewed the ramrod. The little worm on the end not only held it in place but, if screwed into the soft lead ball, could be used to pull it. He unloaded the hog leg and poured the powder into a pile on the bedside stand. He searched for the powder

flask in the little drawer of the table but discovered that
Ned had taken it with him. Shit! He at least had to
make sure the flint would strike a spark. He scraped the
priming powder from the pan onto the table. He
cocked the gun and pulled the trigger. The hammer fell
and struck a healthy spark which ignited the residual
powder in the pan. It gave a dim flash and a soft puff
of smoke, which hung in the air. The pistol worked
well enough but he wouldn't be able to get the practice
shot he wanted.

Carefully, he swept the pile of powder onto a piece
of paper, rolled the paper into a funnel and poured it
down the bore of the four-pound weapon. He tapped
the paper to make sure every last bit was in the gun.
Thank goodness his father had left the patches and lead
balls for it. He placed the patch over the muzzle and
pushed the ball as far as he could by hand, then
rammed the lead home until it seated against the
powder. Then he swept the priming powder onto the
paper and, as carefully as he could, he placed it in the
pan. At best, he thought, he'd have one shot, that's if
the gun fired at all. He protected it from the weather by
wrapping the pistol in an oil cloth. It would have to be
the weapon of last resort instead of the first, as he'd
initially thought.

Ned had left the map on a table in the drawing
room and now Alexander unrolled it. His father had
traced the route he'd take to Kilkenny and back. I'll
start from here, he thought. I'll take the road to Carney
and continue on through Ardcroney. I'll gallop through
that nest of assassins and then I'll go to Cloughjordan;
perhaps I'll get word about Tommy there. That should
be a start.

Ned and Mick had already passed through Nenagh

and now they were trotting the horses along the Thurles Road.

'Dis is d' road Liam Flynn came in on, Ned, Michael's da, when he first came t' Gortalocca. Dat was more den forty years ago now.' Ned nodded and fell sleep to the rhythmic bouncing of the carriage springs.

Alexander brought his gear down to the barn. 'Well, Mr. Flynn,' he said, patting the horse on the neck, 'we're going on an adventure, you and I.' The beast pricked his ears at the sound of the young man's voice. Alex put a halter over the creature's nose, brushed the animal down and picked his hooves clean. 'I don't want you going lame on me, big fella,' he said. The horse was saddled, a bit placed in his mouth and now Alexander slid the bridle over his ears. The horse stamped on the ground impatiently. 'Yes, yes, I want to hit the road too, my friend.' Alex stroked the animal's neck then tied the sack containing his spare shirt and pistol to the saddle. He tried to mount with the rapier strapped around him and hesitated.

'Tell me when I'm wrong, Mr. Flynn,' he said gently. The boy took his foot out of the stirrup and buckled the rapier on the left side of the saddle. 'We're ready now, let's get out on the road.' He had no sooner rested his backside in the saddle when he remembered the map. His father might not need it because he had Mick, he thought, but he didn't want to risk getting himself lost. He tied the horse's reins and went back to the big house, returned presently with the map, then folded it and put it in his sack.

For a brief moment Alexander considered visiting his betrothed in Gortalocca but dismissed the thought immediately. His route was on the same fateful road

Petey and Edgie had travelled just a few days before. He galloped the horse at first and, when he came to the bog by Claree Lake, he slowed to a trot. This is where they killed Peter, he thought, and continued at the slower pace. He didn't want to use up his mount so early in their search for the errant Casey.

In Gortalocca, Siobhan began to get a little apprehensive when Alexander didn't appear and she expressed her concern to her father. Michael was already in deep discussion with Clancy and a few builders he'd employed. They were talking about the construction of the blacksmith works.

'Ah the lad's probably sleeping late, macushla,' he replied.

'Not Alexander. When dere's a job to do, he's always early, and his da told him to come and help me plan d' weddin'.'

Mikey was tempted to tease her and suggest that perhaps Alexander had got cold feet, but the look on his daughter's face made him think twice.

'If he's still not here by the time I'm finished, I'll go up to Johnstown,' he said. 'How's that?' Siobhan was satisfied for now but she still couldn't quite shake off the feeling of unease.

Alexander had reached Ardcroney and he spurred the horse into a gallop until they were well out of the village. It seemed eerily quiet to him. Soon he arrived at Cloughjordan. He asked a small gathering of people if they'd seen either Tommy or Kerr and got no response, except for a few suspicious glances at his rapier. They probably think I'm a highwayman, he thought, with amusement. A little further on, a group of men stood talking and they grew silent as he approached. Again he made his enquiry and received the same stony silence.

'I have tuppence for anyone who can give me information,' he stated.

One man separated himself from the group and said that he'd heard Kerr had been seen in Moneygall a few days ago, but that he didn't know any Casey. Alex tossed him the coins and began to ride.

'Not dat way,' the man shouted and he pointed south. Alex corrected himself and headed in the direction indicated.

It took over an hour to reach the ramshackle village of Moneygall, It was little more than a collection of derelict hovels and the only thing which distinguished it from any other village was the presence of a cobbler's shop. Alexander dismounted in front of a bar and entered. A young woman in a shabby dress looked at him curiously. Strangers were a rare sight. He asked her if she'd seen Tommy and he described him.

'I have,' she replied. It seemed she'd seen him a few days ago. 'He was lookin' fer an ugly feller, name of Kerr,' she said. 'I hope fer his sake he don't find him. Kerr's a nasty piece of work.' She told Alexander that he'd been heading for Templemore. Alex unfolded his map and checked the direction. The easiest way would be to go east, to the crossroad, then south. It was about fifteen miles, perhaps a little less, and that would take almost three hours. He thanked the girl, gave her a few pennies and set off again.

It was late afternoon when he approached Templemore. It was quite a contrast to the other villages and towns he'd passed through in that the main street was remarkably wide and had several two-storey stone houses along it. It was a market town, although on a much smaller scale than Nenagh, and people bustled around the numerous stalls which sold produce and meat, as well as prepared food. The small town even smelled prosperous. Alexander asked a few passers-by about Tommy and Kerr but they seemed unable, or unwilling, to provide him with any information. He grew discouraged and decided to find somewhere to get a bite to eat and spend the night.

Ned and Mick had already passed through Thurles, with its imposing castle, and were approaching Twomileborris at the same time Alex reached Templemore. Unbeknownst to each other, they were less than fifteen miles apart. In about an hour or so the carriage would carry its occupants to their first night's destination, Urlingford. Ned was bored with the travelling and was looking forward to getting out and stretching his legs. He'd already known that Mick provided no company whatsoever on a journey like this. The big man was lost in another world, his brain completely shut off from everything except the road in front of him.

Alexander found a place to stable his horse just east of the busy town centre, in a coaching inn. After he'd tended to the animal, he brought his belongings with him into the bar. He'd received no helpful response whatsoever from his enquiries about Tommy or Kerr's whereabouts and now he spread his map out on a table and ordered something to eat and a beer. While he was studying the chart, an old man who'd been sitting at the bar became curious about the strangely-attired young fellow and he came over. He stood silently while Alex examined the map, deciding on his next move.

'Are ya lost?' the old fellow began.

Alexander looked up into the man's pale rheumy eyes. 'No, sir,' he replied. 'I'm looking for someone.'

The old boy cackled. 'I reckon ya won't find him on dat piece of paper. Who ya lookin' fer? Dere ain't much gets past dese auld eyes.'

'I'm looking for a friend of mine named Tommy Casey. He's about twenty years old with a shock of curly blonde hair. He's tracking a murderer named Kerr.'

The old man looked startled, glanced furtively around the room, then sat down at the table opposite Alexander.

'Keep yer voice down, boyo. Dere's dose who'd kill ya just fer d' blade yer carryin'.'

Alex motioned for the barman to bring another beer for the old fellow. This was the first time anyone had shown any interest at all since Moneygall. The barman slopped some beer on the map and Alexander looked at him sourly and wiped it off with his hand.

'I know who yer lookin' fer,' said the old man in hushed tones when they were alone again. 'I didn't know his name was Tommy but I can tell ya he come t'rough here a few days ago askin' about dat scar-faced bastard, just like you are.'

Alex leaned closer until he could smell the beer on the man's breath.

'Go home, son,' the old man whispered, glancing around the room. 'Ya seem like a nice boy. Give up dis shite, no good'll come of it.'

'I can't go home without Tommy, or at least without finding out what's happened to him.'

'He's probably feedin' d' pigs,' said the old man quietly, 'or worse.' His face grew pale and he told Alexander a story that made the young man push his food away.

Mick and Ned made themselves comfortable in an Urlingford hotel and they went to the dining-room to eat and gather whatever information they could. They received none and so they ate their meal occupied in inane chatter. Before they retired to their room a couple of hours later, Ned went to the desk. Desk clerks knew everything and were usually willing to share their local knowledge for a penny. Ned asked the clerk about Kerr and the man put his fingers to his lips.

'There's rumours,' he hissed, looking around him.

Ned wrinkled his forehead. 'What kind of rumours?'

'It's just talk but, well, Kerr has a cousin named Cox who has a bar about ten miles from here. Kerr spends a lot of time there with him and the talk is that, sometimes, travellers go in there and they never come out.'

'Oy've heard about places like dat,' said Ned.

'Oh no, sir, I doubt you've ever heard about anything like this. About eight years ago, you'll remember we had the big freeze, lasted two years. I'm sure you know that the famine spread all over Ireland and people starved by their thousands. People were lying frozen stiff on the roads. The whole population looked like skeletons, that is except for the landlords … and Cox.'

'Ya mean….?'

'It's just talk mind, sir.'

Ned tossed a few coins on the desk and walked up to his room, his imagination filling in the details he hadn't got from the clerk.

CHAPTER 52

M ichael walked up to the big house in Johnstown that afternoon. Alexander hadn't shown up at all and he wanted to know why. When he got to the door and knocked, a woman servant answered. She told him that Alexander had taken off on his horse a few hours after his father left. She said she believed he'd been heading in the direction of Carney. That in itself was odd but, when she told him he'd had a sabre strapped to his saddle, Mikey grew apprehensive. He wondered if perhaps the boy's intention was to go to Ardcroney to wreak some kind of revenge. He reminded himself that Alexander was normally level-headed and that would be out of character but still…. What was he to tell Siobhan and the others? It also crossed Mikey's mind that, as Alex has been the last one to speak to Moira, he might have gone in search of the old lady. That's it. That's the story he'd tell them.

Alexander woke early from a fitful sleep, haunted by what the old man had told him the evening before. He didn't want to bat around a hornets' nest but perhaps it wouldn't do any harm for him to simply ride past and reconnoiter Cox's bar. Then, if his father had no luck, he could pass on the information.

Ned, on the other hand, wanted nothing more than to bat the hornets' nest. Mick had told him that Cox's was within an hour of where they were and so, when Ned and Mick went down for breakfast, they discussed the matter. A soldier should take whatever time he can to eat. One never knew when the next chance to eat would be. If what the desk clerk had said was correct, they had all the time in the world to go there and see for themselves.

Alexander saddled his horse and tied the sack containing the horse pistol to the right side of it. He buckled the rapier onto the left side, where he could draw it quickly if an armed retreat was necessary. He had fifteen miles to travel until he reached the fork in the road where the farmhouse and bar were. He inhaled deeply to steady his nerves and he climbed up into the saddle. He had no intention of tangling with a paid killer single-handedly and told himself that he would just check the place out from a distance. He trotted his mount onto the muddy road. The previous day's drizzle had stopped during the night and it was promising to be a glorious day. It was a straight shot from here to where he was heading and a beautiful warm sun fell on his face.

After breakfast, Mick went out to harness the team. Ned went upstairs to his room and re-primed the fowling piece and the pistol. He was in no great hurry. It was almost eight when Mick came up to the room. He had grown impatient waiting in the carriage.

'When are we leavin'?' he asked.

'Yer in a God Almighty rush ain't ya, Micko? Ya don't even know what's out dere waitin' fer us.'

'I just want to get it over and done wit'.'

'Ya can't just go rushin' headlong into t'ings, friend.' Ned smiled as he said the words, trying to instil confidence into the burly man, but his smile was not a merry one. 'We'll get dere when we get dere. Probably nutt'n will come of it anyway.' He handed Mick the pistol and told him to put it under his shirt. Mick tucked the gun into the cord that held up his britches. 'Not dat way, ya eejit,' corrected Ned. 'Put it in so as ya can get it out in a hurry.' Ned tucked the pistol in front of Mick's big belly, on his left side, so he'd be able to reach across and pull it out without having to get undressed. 'Put yer shirt over d' top of it so nobody can see. If ya need it, just pull up yer shirt wit' yer left hand and pull d' gun wit' yer right. Don't ferget to cock d' hammer back, or all you'll have is a club.' Ned wished he'd rehearsed the action but it was too late now. 'Alright, big man, let's hit d' road.'

Mick went over Ned's instructions in his mind … over and over.

Alexander was just past the sparse village of Templetouhy, another one of the depressed and depressing Irish villages he'd grown accustomed to seeing. It was just a small cluster of mud cottages on the side of the road, most of them uninhabited and roofless. There were only about five more miles to go now and he'd begun to get a slight case of the nerves. He hadn't eaten any breakfast and his stomach grumbled its complaint. I'll just ride past the bar, he thought. I'll just ride past, take a long look and keep going. Alex wasn't looking for trouble and he began to doubt the wisdom of this journey.

'Dat must be it,' said Mick, nervously, 'up ahead dere.'

Ned craned his neck to see and, sure enough, there was a two-storey farmhouse at the turn of the road and it had a barn at the back. In between the two was a pigpen. In a few more moments the unmistakable smell of swine reached his nose.

'Only d' feckin' Oirish would have a pigpen right at d' back of d' house,' he remarked. 'Let me do all d' talkin', Mick. Just keep yer gun handy. If dat fecker Kerr is inside, just pass d' pistol to me and Oy'll shoot him dead on d' spot.'

Their carriage ground to a halt outside the yellow door of Cox's bar and Ned got out, while Mick set the brake and tied the reins to the lever. Ned waited for the big man to catch him up before he tried the door. At first it resisted and then it swung open suddenly as it came unstuck. The bell over the door announced them and it took a second or two for their eyes to adjust to the dim light inside. No one was there and, for a moment, they thought their trip might have been wasted. Just then, the back door squeaked and the proprietor entered. The aroma of pig wafted in even stronger than before. Ned grimaced but Mr. Cox seemed oblivious to the stink.

'Can I help yous two gentlemen?' he asked cordially.

'A couple of beers to wash d' road out of our mouths would be appreciated,' Ned replied, equally amiably.

'Comin' right up.' The man held two almost-clean mugs under the tap of a keg which stood behind the bar. 'Nice travellin' weather today,' he said. 'D' sun's shinin' fer a change. Are ye off to d' fair in Kilkenny?'

Ned knew Cox was testing them because their coach was parked outside the open door and it was facing towards Templemore, in the opposite direction to Kilkenny.

'No,' said Ned. 'Oy've got some business up in Nenagh.' With that, he made an exaggerated motion of pulling out his purse, letting the coins jingle. He reached inside and tossed a shilling on the bar. 'Is dat enough?' he asked Cox innocently.

Cox could barely pry his eyes away from the purse. 'I t'ank ya, sir. If dere's anyt'ing else I can do fer ye, just give me a shout. I'll be out d' back doin' me jobs.' The proprietor hurried out the same back door he'd come in through.

As soon as Cox was gone, Mick asked why Ned had shown his purse to the stranger.

'Bait, my friend,' he answered. 'Oy'll be back in a few seconds wit' d' scatter gun. Get yer pistol ready Mick, Oy t'ink dere's goin' to be a shite storm!'

Alexander was only about a quarter of a mile away when he spotted the carriage outside the bar. It looked familiar to him but all carriages looked similar from a distance. He trotted on and a few seconds later he saw a man who looked distinctly like his father come out of the door and retrieve something from the boot. A flash went through his mind. It was his father and he was carrying that cut-off fowling piece back into the building. Alex spurred the horse into a lope and then spurred it again into a flat-out gallop. Holding the reins with one hand, he fumbled with his right hand in the bag containing the horse pistol until finally he held the oilcloth-wrapped gun and let the sack fall to the ground.

Cox came back in, just as carefree as before, and he slipped behind the bar. Ned stood about five feet away from him, his hand underneath his greatcoat, concealing the coach gun. Mick stood sideways, just a few feet from Cox, with his shirt-tail in his left hand. A few seconds later the hinges on the back door squeaked.

The loudest sound in the entire world is that of a shotgun going off in a small room. The second loudest is the noise a shotgun's hammers make when they click into the cocked position. Ned cocked the fowling piece and the sound caught Cox's attention, galvanising him into action. He pulled a cudgel from under the bar and, before Mick could draw the pistol from his belt, the barman swung the club down. Mick managed to turn his head just enough to avoid getting his skull crushed but the blow hit him square on the shoulder. The pistol skittered out of his grasp and into the corner.

'I got d' big one,' yelled Cox. He leapt over the bar and was poised to clout Mick a lethal strike when Ned turned and blasted him into perdition with both barrels of the coach gun. The villain landed on his head, his body folded up on top of him, but he'd already given Kerr the cue he was waiting for.

The big chestnut skidded to a halt outside the bar just as the double blast of the fowling piece met Alexander's ears. He grabbed the rapier as he leapt from the horse. The sound of scuffling and furniture being overturned came from inside and he knew a fight was in progress. He barged in through the door and saw his father trying to fend off Kerr's bata swings with the empty shotgun. He tossed a stool in the way but the manic assassin kept on coming. When Kerr saw the new threat at the door he stopped for a moment. Alexander took the opportunity to toss the oilcloth-wrapped pistol to Ned, who was by now on the floor on his back. He had tripped over Mick who lay prone on the ground, dazed. Kerr turned and faced the new threat and Ned managed to extricate the pistol from the rag. Kerr looked back and forth from the boy with the blade to the man with the pistol and was frozen for a split second. Ned cocked the gun and fired. The pistol sputtered. There wasn't enough priming powder in it. He threw the gun at Kerr who now thought he had the upper hand.

The one-eyed fellow now turned his full attention to Alexander. He tapped the loaded bata against his left palm in an effort to intimidate him. In the meantime, Ned was trying to untangle himself from Mick so he could get to the pistol the big man had dropped.

'Yer goin' to die, boyo,' snarled Kerr, to further gain psychological advantage. Alexander sighed. He didn't reply but instead feinted a thrust toward Kerr's good eye. Kerr switched the hold on his bata to a defensive two-handed grip. Alex again feinted to the eye and, when Kerr raised his bata to block, Alexander lunged and stuck him right below the sternum, burying the tip about five inches into the man's liver.

'You're dead,' he said.

One of the complications involved in fighting with a rapier or a foil is that even a lethal wound takes time to kill and, often, both combatants die as a result.

'It doesn't even hurt, snot-rag,' growled Kerr in response. He put a hand against the wound and looked at the black blood.

Alexander remembered the low attack that Gleeson had told him about. He stepped back a half step and again feinted a lunge, this time at Kerr's bollocks. There's a peculiar response which males have when their manhood is threatened. A man will sacrifice any other part of his body in order to protect his family jewels. Kerr brought the stick low and Alex went over the top of it and straight into his heart. Kerr's eyes widened now as he realised he was indeed a dead man and the next thing he did, if not unthinkable, was surely not anticipated. Instead of trying to pull away, he moved in, the rapier still stuck through his heart, and he went nose-to-nose with Alexander.

Ned had now managed to get his hands on the gun but he couldn't fire the weapon for fear of hitting his son. He was impotent. Kerr tried to bring up his stick, two-handed, to break Alexander's jaw but he couldn't get it past the basket hilt of the sword.

Alex felt his adversary begin to weaken, then he remembered the knife in his belt. Their faces were so close together now that the one-eyed man couldn't see what was happening elsewhere. He was about to spill his guts, literally. He slumped to the floor taking Alex down with him. Alexander loosened his hold on his weapons and stood back in shock. Ned pushed him out of the way and fired the shot-laden pistol into the already dying man's head. The young man turned away.

Alexander was saturated with blood and not a drop of it was his own. He went outside and started to strip off his clothes. Ned was soon at his side.

'Are ya hurt, son?'

'He never touched me,' said Alex quietly. 'Go and see to Mick, Da, I'm alright.'

A few seconds later Ned came back out with Mick.

The big fellow had his good arm around Ned's neck to support himself.

'Yer goin' to have to go on a diet, Micko, if we're goin' to make a habit of dis,' groaned Ned.

Alexander was still stripping off his bloody garments when the two older men approached. He looked stricken with the thought of what he'd done and Mick tried to be light-hearted.

'I t'ink yer finally puttin' some weight on dem bones of yours, boyo.'

Alexander tried to smile but he couldn't manage it. 'Are you alright, Mick?'

'I t'ink d' bastard busted somet'in in me shoulder.'

Ned scolded Alex now. 'What's d' feckin' idea of givin' me an unloaded gun in a fight?'

'Well,' Alexander retorted, 'if some greedy old fecker hadn't taken all the feckin' powder in the first place…!'

'I t'ink yer boy is growin' up, Ned,' grinned Mick.

'Oy don't know about dat, Micko. Dere he stands as naked as d' day he was born and he'll probably sulk all d' way home.'

Ned went back to get the sack containing his son's spare clothes and, while Alexander was getting himself dressed, he set fire to the building. The three men watched as it became engulfed in flames.

CHAPTER 53

T he three men travelled the road back to Gortalocca together. They were in no great hurry. Alexander initially rode in the carriage with the other two, the chestnut horse tied to the back, but he grew weary of Ned and Mick telling and retelling the story of the fight. He hadn't minded the first few times but by the time the tale had reached its twentieth or perhaps fiftieth version, he'd had enough. After they'd stopped for lunch, he mounted the big horse and rode apart from the older men.

'I t'ink d' boy feels guilty,' said Mick.

'Oy remember d' first time Oy killed a man. It was two, in fact. Dey was bandits and Oy was on d' road to Killarney. Oy was wit' auld Robert D'Arcy. Oy remember me gob felt like it was filled wit' wool. It was a long time ago but Oy ain't forgot.'

'I never killed a soul in me whole life. I wanted to once but I never did.'

'How's yer shoulder, Micko?'

'It ain't great and dat fecker must have hit me ear when he clubbed me, because me feckin' ear hurts worse den me shoulder.'

'It'll all feel worse tomorra, Micko.'

'Ah t'anks, Ned, just what I wanted to hear.'

It was long after dark when the trio reached Nenagh. For Alexander, the day had seemed longer than any other day of his life. Ned told his son that if he wanted to carry on to Gortalocca it would be alright, but that he and Mick would spend the night in Nenagh because he wanted to speak to the sheriff. Alex's mood lightened considerably at the prospect of seeing Siobhan and it had a positive effect on his demeanor. Ned and Mick headed for Nenagh Castle and Alexander took the road to Gortalocca.

The first thing Sheriff Higgins asked the moment he saw Ned was what the hell had Robbie Flynn been up to, standing around the courthouse for the last couple of days. Ned denied any knowledge of it which, of course, Higgins had expected. He asked if they'd found Kerr and Ned related the story in a way to rival even his own legendary exploits in Cork.

'Ah the fruit doesn't fall far from the vine,' said Higgins.

Ned shook his head. He knew that his son would take his own path in life and, besides, he wouldn't want Alexander to follow in his footsteps.

'D' only t'ing me and Alex have in common, Higgie, is dat boy has d' Divil's own luck too.'

Alexander hurried to the village that had become like home to him now but, at the same time, alien. A light was still on inside Hogan's and he didn't want to wait another moment before he saw his beloved Siobhan. He tied the horse hurriedly and entered. Siobhan didn't waste any time in throwing her arms around him and she kissed him on the mouth. Michael interrupted the reunion before Alexander had the chance to speak.

'I need to talk to you, boyo … outside!' Alex complied meekly.

Once they were outside, Mikey spoke in hushed tones. 'Where the hell have you been?'

'I went to find Tommy Casey.'

'I told them that you went to find Moira. Did you find Casey?'

'I think so,' said Alex. The mixture of sadness and regret in his tone spoke volumes.

'I'm sorry, Alexander,' replied Mike. 'I suppose your father is handling Kerr?'

'Da's in Nenagh with Mick. Kerr's dead.'

'I knew the phantom priest would do it!' said Mikey, with a note of triumph.

'Yes … he did it,' answered Alex.

The two men went back inside and the women folk hovered around their knight errant. Even Roisin had warmed towards the young man when she'd heard he'd gone to look for Moira. Siobhan told him all about the wedding plans they'd made and Alex half-listened. He was just happy to see her face. Less than a day ago he wasn't sure if he'd ever gaze into her eyes again. Those assembled couldn't help but notice his melancholy but they attributed it to his failure to find the old woman. Roisin told him about how her husband, Liam, and a young Jamie Clancy had also searched for Moira once for days without finding any trace of her. Suddenly Alex grew very tired. Two days on the road, coupled with his own mental anguish, had taken their toll on the lad. He excused himself, went out to the waiting horse and rode back to Johnstown.

Ned and Mick arrived back in Gortalocca the

following morning and, before Michael had a chance to tell them about the deception, they related the story of Alexander and Kerr. They made it sound like a battle royale when, in truth, it probably hadn't lasted more than a minute. Siobhan's emotions were conflicted. On one hand she was angry at the deception, whether it be directed towards her father who'd told the lie or at Alexander for perpetrating it. On the other hand, when she saw the awe on people's faces as they heard about Alex's exploits, she felt proud. The story spread, as Irish stories do, and those who heard it were as incredulous about the tall, thin young man as they had been about the phantom priest when they'd first met Ned. They both looked so ordinary and everyone knows that heroes are giants.

Alexander didn't come to Gortalocca that morning and Ned and Mick rode up to the big house to find out what had become of the lad. They found him sitting in front of the fire, so lost in his own thoughts that he was unaware of their arrival.

'What's troublin' ya, son?' asked Ned. 'Ya did what ya had to do to save me and Mick.'

'I'm not sorry about what I did, Da. It was the way I did it.'

'I don't understand.'

'When you tell the tale, you make it sound like I acted in the same way you did down in Cork. But you were thinking all the time, planning and scheming, and it wasn't like that with me. I lost my mind the second I walked through that door. I vaguely remember Kerr saying something but I couldn't hear him. He might just as well have been one of those straw-filled practice dummies I fenced with. I don't remember anything and I didn't feel anything … no fear, no anger, nothing until his guts spilled out over the floor. It was like someone else did it and I just watched.'

Ned put his arm around his son's shoulders. 'It's hard to kill a man, even if he needs killin',' he said soothingly.

'But Da, that's my point. It wasn't hard, it was the easiest thing I've ever done.'

'Get yerself washed, Alex, and dressed. Ya can't sit around here all day. Dere's a pretty red-haired girl in Gortalocca and she's worried sick about ya.'

Word of Alexander's triumph had spread like a wild fire and Hogan's bar was full to overflowing with locals wanting to hear the story. Even Sheriff Higgins was there. When Alexander walked in there was a hush, followed by a cheer. He was a local hero, even if he was a 'blow-in'. He managed to push his way through the crowd, shrugging off the slaps on the back and the congratulations. He bellied up to the bar and Siobhan glared at him for a moment, then softened.

'Let's get out of here,' he said above the din of the mob.

Siobhan looked at her grandmother and Roisin nodded, then smiled at Alex. The young couple went out the back door and Alexander was glad to be outside. The stale smell of beer and tobacco smoke inside had been nauseating. He breathed deeply.

'I told ya, Alexander,' the girl said, her eyes brimming with tears, 'ya mustn't ever lie to me. Whatever would I have done if you'd bin killed?'

'I'm sorry, love. I did what I thought was right but I should have told you.'

'Promise me you'll never do anyt'ing so stupid again.'

'You have my word on it.'

She threw her arms around him and, again, she kissed him on the mouth. This time, she let their lips mingle for a moment or two but the romantic scene didn't last long. Higgins appeared, accompanied by Ned and Michael.

The sheriff coughed. 'Pardon the interruption,' he said, bowing slightly. 'I was just speaking with the bride and groom's fathers about the upcoming nuptials and I'd like to offer my congratulations and best wishes. Michael has informed me that, in the absence of a Papist priest, he would be happy to perform the ceremony. I find that highly irregular, if not vulgar. As High Sheriff of Lower Ormond, there is very little around here that I'm not aware of and I happen to know of a Franciscan priest who performs clandestine services in my district. Indeed I have spoken to him on several occasions. If it meets with your approval, I shall … ahem … request his presence at the upcoming event. Furthermore, since the celebration might provide an opportunity for provocateurs to attempt some disruption to the blessed event, I will post my entire contingent of deputies discretely around the perimeter of Gortalocca and no one will be allowed to carry their … ahem … walking sticks into the village.'

Siobhan was elated, she was going to have a 'real' wedding.

'Is it alright if an Irish girl hugs an Englishman?' she grinned.

Higgins smiled. 'If the girl didn't, I would feel slighted.'

Siobhan wrapped her arms around the sheriff's waist and delivered the promised hug, squeezing him until he said, 'That's enough young woman. A man of my years can't stand too much affection.'

Alexander extended his hand and Higgins took it. 'Hmmm,' he said, 'I thought you'd be much bigger.' He turned and winked at Ned.

Unnoticed by anyone, a little scrap of tattered Irish lace had dislodged itself from the withering rag tree and now it fluttered by in the breeze.

EPILOGUE

G ortalocca's tobacco crop was never harvested
... perhaps it was never meant to be.

The letter Robbie Flynn had posted to Limerick's
Chief Tax Collector finally came to the attention of a
petty bureaucrat and the matter was investigated. The
crop was subsequently plowed under and, when the
paperwork was examined, Robert Flynn's name figured
prominently. He was convicted of an array of criminal
offences, including the illegal production of a
prohibited crop and the illicit smuggling of the seeds
which must surely have led to it. He was also accused,
but not convicted, of jury tampering in the case of Bob
Ring, who was acquitted of all charges. Robert and his
family were transported to the Botany Bay colony in
Australia. After he'd done his seven years hard labour,
plying his trade as a cabinet-maker, Robbie opened a
shop in the settlement of Melbourne. His son took part
in the great Australian gold rush and was modestly
successful. His daughter, Peg, emigrated back to
Ireland as soon as she was of age and settled into the
family home in Gortalocca, a lifelong spinster.

Mick's shoulder never healed properly and Roisin gave him a job tending Hogan's bar. She always maintained that it was out of pity but, in truth, it was a kindness on her part. Roisin had a soft spot for the big man. The two of them were like an old married couple, with Mick bearing the brunt of Roisin's hot-headed, but ultimately harmless, temper. They worked together long into their dotage until Mick passed away. Roisin lived long enough to bounce her great-grandchildren on her knee and tell them great adventure stories. She finally sold the bar and store to the O'Kennedy's from Knigh.

Mikey and Jamie worked together, as they always had, in Gortalocca's new blacksmith shop. Clancy had decided that Amerrycuh was too far from home for a man of his constitution and so he'd declined Ned's offer. Jamie died of the croup ten years later, a year after his wife Kate passed on. Michael carried on the business with his son Liam whose hand, although weakened, never proved to be a handicap. Liam married Josie MacGowen and she proved to be a real handful. Roisin seemed almost saintly in comparison. Michael and Morna enjoyed many more years together before Mikey's heart failed him, just as his father's had. Liam continued his work at the blacksmith shop until, finally, he sold it to the same family who now ran the village store and bar, the O'Kennedy's from Knigh. Liam and Josie bought a farm down in Grange, South Tipperary, near where his grandfather and namesake was born and raised.

Siobhan and Alexander went to America. Alex worked hard to earn a University degree and he became a practicing solicitor. He also took an active role in

American Independence. He became an advisor to the firebrand himself, Patrick Henry, who once said, 'Give me liberty or give me death.' After the birth of the new United States of America, Alexander served in the House of Representatives for a term, then in the State assembly of South Carolina. He never let it be known that he was Catholic, although rumours persisted every election day. Alex and Siobhan had four children. One of them, Edmund 'Ned' Flood, returned to Ireland during the rebellion in 1798. He is laid to rest there.

Jack Rackham continued his smuggling exploits on his own side of the Atlantic. During the War of Independence he took out a privateer's license and crossed back again. He was to become the scourge of English commercial vessels in the Channel and in the Irish Sea. He found safe harbour in France until he was finally captured by none other than his old adversary, Captain Willoughby. Jack died of typhus on a prison ship in Southampton, along with his friend, Mr. Jones.

What happened to Ned Flood? Well, Ned grew bored with the smuggling business and turned the operation over to his corpulent wife and his overbearing mother-in-law in Charles Town. He had always harboured the notion that a successful Irishman should possess good horses and own a bar. He already had the horses. Ned moved down to Savannah, in the Georgia colony, because he'd heard the place was teeming with Irishmen. He bought a piece of land near the waterfront and built an Irish Pub on it. Not just any pub, mind you, a real feckin' Irish bar, full of character. The walls were two feet thick, made of limestone which was quarried nearby and whitewashed. The roof was thatched with reeds, harvested from upstream in the Savannah River. He could well afford a mahogany bar but, instead, opted for one made of Irish oak which he imported from County Wicklow. The fireplace was a grand wood-burning affair and, when the cold fronts of winter raged through, it offered a homely feel to the place.

An Irish bar, of course, needs Irish music to set the atmosphere. Ned sent for crippled Billy McTierney, who arrived with his blind sister, Lizzy, six months later. Ned set the girl up in her own shop, making lace for the wealthy ladies of Savannah. Lizzy's lace collars and cuffs became legendary and she and her brother lived very comfortably together, Billy leading the sessions in Flood's bar and winning more than his share of arm-wrestling contests.

The moment Ned stepped behind the bar, he knew he'd found his true calling. For a fellow like Ned Flood, it was perfect. He had a captive audience, after all. Below the gold-leafed sign outside which read 'NED'S' was a smaller handwritten one which read, 'NO FIGHTIN!' and, in smaller letters, underneath, 'widdout the express consent of d management'.

There was only one minor incident which was to mar Ned's new life. One day, Abraham Washington grew tired of fishing and tending his garden, and he decided to visit Ned for a while. It was the talk of Savannah that a negro was drinking alongside white people. Ned didn't give a damn, of course, but a local deputy took exception to it and made his feelings known. Ned paid the sheriff a visit and, as a result, the misguided deputy was out looking for a new job. It seems that Sheriff Bernard Higgins had finally got a bellyful of dealing with the bureaucrats above him. He was also at his wits end, trying to keep some sort of order in a now chaotic Tipperary, so he'd tendered his resignation and returned to England. A few years later, he wrote a letter to Ned. The next thing anyone knew, he had been appointed the Sheriff of Savannah.

Ned never returned to Ireland. He didn't need to, he'd brought it with him. Some people are just born with the Devil's own luck.

Made in the USA
Middletown, DE
14 February 2021

33757757R00298